HERE
and
NOW

Santa Montefiore

HERE
and
NOW

**SIMON &
SCHUSTER**

London · New York · Sydney · Toronto · New Delhi

First published in Great Britain by Simon & Schuster UK Ltd, 2020

Copyright © Santa Montefiore, 2020

The right of Santa Montefiore to be identified as
author of this work has been asserted in accordance with
the Copyright, Designs and Patents Act, 1988.

3 5 7 9 10 8 6 4 2

Simon & Schuster UK Ltd
1st Floor
222 Gray's Inn Road
London WC1X 8HB

Simon & Schuster Australia, Sydney
Simon & Schuster India, New Delhi

www.simonandschuster.co.uk
www.simonandschuster.com.au
www.simonandschuster.co.in

A CIP catalogue record for this book
is available from the British Library

Hardback ISBN: 978-1-4711-6966-3
Trade Paperback ISBN: 978-1-4711-6967-0
eBook ISBN: 978-1-4711-6968-7

Typeset in Bembo by M Rules
Printed and bound by CPI Group (UK) Ltd, Croydon, CR0 4YY

MIX
Paper from
responsible sources
FSC® C020471

For Lily and Sasha

Chapter 1

It was snowing. Fat, fluffy flakes, as large as cotton balls, tumbled from the sky, while dawn struggled valiantly to herald the day through the canopy of dense cloud. Marigold stood by the kitchen window with her cup of tea. A stout figure in a baby-pink dressing gown and matching fluffy slippers, she watched with delight as the landscape was slowly revealed to her in all its glorious softness. Little by little the garden emerged out of the night: the yew hedge, the borders and the shrubs, the trees with their gnarled and twisted branches, all hunched and still, sleeping deeply beneath a luxurious quilt. It was hard to imagine life there in the frozen soil. Almost impossible to picture the viburnum and syringa flowering in the spring. Impossible to think of spring at all in this dead of winter.

At the bottom of the garden, beside her husband Dennis's shed, the apple tree was materializing through the falling snow. With its thick trunk and knobbly branches it resembled a mythical creature caught in suspended animation by an ancient spell, or simply petrified by the cold, for it really was very cold. Marigold's eyes caught sight of the feeder hanging forlornly from one of the branches. It was still attracting the odd intrepid bird which fluttered around it in the hope of finding an overlooked seed. Marigold had filled it the day before but now it was empty. Her heart went out to the hungry birds who survived the winter on account of her feeder. As soon as she'd finished her tea, she would put on her boots and go out to refill it.

She sensed she was being watched and turned to see Dennis standing in the doorway, gazing at her with a tender look. He was dressed for church in a dark blue suit and tie, his grey hair parted at the side and brushed smooth, his beard clipped. He was handsome to Marigold, who still saw him through the eyes of the twenty-year-old girl she had been when they'd met over forty years before. She lifted her chin and smiled back at him playfully. 'What are *you* looking at?' she asked.

'You,' he replied, denim eyes twinkling.

She shook her head and turned her attention back to the garden. 'It's snowing,' she said.

He joined her at the window and they both stared out with equal pleasure. 'Beautiful,' he sighed. 'Really beautiful.' He put his arm around her waist, drawing her close, and planted a kiss on her temple. 'You remember the first time I held your hand, Goldie? It was snowing then, wasn't it?'

Marigold laughed. 'You remind me of that every time it snows, Dennis.'

His smile was bashful. 'I like to remember it. A beautiful woman, a beautiful night, falling snow and her hand in mine. It was warm, your hand. You didn't take it away. I knew I was in with a chance then. You let me hold it. That was a big deal in those days.'

'What an old romantic you are!' She tilted her head, knowing he would kiss her again.

'You love your old romantic,' he whispered into her hair.

'I do,' she replied. 'You're a rare breed. They don't make them like you anymore.' She patted his chest. 'Now go and sit down and I'll bring over your tea.'

'They don't make them like *you* anymore, either,' said Dennis, moving towards the kitchen table where Mac the black-and-white cat sat awaiting him on his chair. 'I knew I'd caught someone special when I held your hand.'

Their daughter Suze shuffled sleepily into the room in floral pyjamas, a long grey cardigan and bed socks. Her blonde hair was unbrushed and falling over her eyes in a thick fringe, her attention on her smartphone. 'Morning, sweetheart,' said Marigold cheerfully. 'Have you seen the snow?'

Suze did not look up. She had seen the snow. What of it? She sat down in her usual chair beside her father and mumbled a barely audible 'Good morning'. Dennis caught Marigold's eye and a silent communication passed between them. Marigold took down two mugs. She'd make Dennis his tea and Suze her coffee, just as she did every morning. She enjoyed the routine. It made her feel needed and Marigold loved feeling needed. Then she remembered they were no longer just three and took down another mug.

'Oh dear, have you seen outside? Snow! The whole country will grind to a standstill,' said Nan gloomily, wandering into the kitchen. Marigold's mother searched hard for the negative in everything and was only truly happy when she found it. 'Do you remember the winter of '63?' She sucked air through her lips. 'We were stuck indoors for a week! Your dad had to dig us out with a spade. It did his back in, that did. He came out of the war without a scratch but did his back in digging us out with a spade.' She pulled her dressing gown tighter across her body and shivered. 'I'll never forget the cold. Oooh, it was Siberian.'

'Have you ever been to Siberia, Nan?' asked Suze in a disinterested tone, without taking her eyes off her phone.

Her grandmother ignored her. 'We didn't have the luxury of

central heating like you do, Suze,' she said. 'It was bitter. There was ice on the inside of the windows and we had to run across the garden to use the toilet. We didn't have an indoor toilet back then. You don't know how lucky you are, you people.'

Marigold glanced out of the window. The sight of snow had lifted her spirits. The country might grind to a standstill, she thought happily, but it would look like a winter wonderland.

'Lovely,' said Nan as a cup of tea was duly placed in front of her. At eighty-six her curly hair had turned white, her body was frail and her face as creased as crêpe paper, but her mind was as sharp and focused as it always had been. The years had taken much, but they had not taken that. Marigold gave Nan the crossword from the newspaper, then went to the sideboard to put two slices of bread in the toaster. Nan had moved in with Marigold and Dennis only the week before after months of gentle persuasion and encouragement. She had been reluctant to leave the home she had lived in through-out her marriage and where she had raised her two children, Patrick and Marigold, even though she was only moving a few minutes up the road. She had insisted that she was perfectly capable of looking after herself and complained that she felt as if she was being shuffled into Heaven's waiting room when she wasn't in the least ready to go. However, in spite of her grumbling, she had sold the house for a tidy sum and moved in with her daughter, making herself comfortable in her new room. She had demanded that Dennis replace the pictures on the wall with her own and Dennis had obliged in his good-natured way while Marigold had helped unpack her things and arrange them to her satisfaction. In fact, mother and daughter had rapidly slipped into an easy routine. Nan discovered that she rather enjoyed having someone at her beck and call after all and Marigold relished having another person to look after, because she enjoyed being useful. She ran the village shop and the post office, as she had done for over thirty years. She also sat on various committees, for the village hall and the local church and the odd charity, because she liked to keep busy. At sixty-six Marigold had no intention of slowing down. Having Nan at home gave her a warm feeling of being needed.

'Well, I adore snow,' she said, cracking eggs into a pan.

Nan studied the crossword through her spectacles. 'The whole country will grind to a standstill, mark my words,' she repeated, shaking her head. 'I remember the winter of '63. Livestock died, people froze to death, nothing worked. It was death and destruction everywhere.'

'Well, I remember the winter of 2010 and we all managed,' said Suze, still gazing into her phone.

'What are you doing on that thing anyway?' asked Nan, peering at it from across the table. 'You haven't taken your eyes off it all morning.'

'It's my job,' Suze mumbled, raking the fringe off her face with a manicured hand.

'She's an "influencer",' Marigold interrupted, giving Suze a nod, although Suze didn't see it. Nor did she see the proud though slightly baffled look on her mother's face.

'What's an "influencer"?' Nan asked.

'It means everyone wants to be me,' Suze informed her dully and without irony.

'She writes about fashion and food and, well, lifestyle, don't you, love?' Marigold added. 'A bit of everything and she posts it all on her Instagram account. You should see it, the photographs are lovely.'

'Do you make any money doing a bit of everything?' Nan asked, sounding unconvinced that being an 'influencer' was a worthwhile form of employment.

'She's going to make lots.' Dennis answered for his daughter because making money was a sore subject. Suze had turned twenty-five in the summer, but had no plans to move out and get a place of her own, or get what they considered a 'proper' job. Why would she want to leave home when her mother made it so comfortable, when her parents paid for everything? The little she earned as a freelance journalist went on clothes and make-up, fuelling her social media platforms, but neither parent was prepared to confront her about it. Suze had a temper, aggravated by a deep frustration at the slow progress of her ambitions. While her older sister Daisy had gone to university and now lived a sophisticated life in Milan with her Italian boyfriend, spending weekends in Paris and Rome and working in a world-famous museum, *she* was stuck in the small village where she had grown up, living at home and dreaming of fame and fortune that never materialized.

'I make money writing for newspapers and magazines, things like that. I'm building a profile, gathering a following. It takes time.' Suze sighed, lamenting the fact that old people didn't understand social media.

'You modern people!' said Dennis with a grin, hoping to appease his daughter. 'Baffles us oldies.'

'I've got nearly thirty thousand followers on Instagram,' she said, brightening a little.

'Have you, dear?' said Marigold, not knowing quite what that meant but assuming it was a lot. Suze had set her mother up with an Instagram account so that she could keep in touch with her daughters. And it did keep her in touch, although she didn't post things herself. She didn't much like the mobile telephone. She'd rather talk to someone's face.

Dennis opened the newspaper and sipped his tea. Marigold was making him his Sunday Special: two fried eggs, crispy bacon, a sausage, a piece of wholemeal toast and a spoonful of baked beans, just the way he liked it. As she put it in front of him he smiled up at her, his eyes sparkling with affection. Dennis and Marigold still looked at each other in that gentle, tender way that people do whose love has grown deeper with the years.

'Suze, do you fancy anything?' Marigold asked. Suze didn't answer. The curtain of blonde hair formed an impenetrable barrier. 'I'll go and feed my birds then,' she said.

'They're not *your* birds, Mum,' said Suze from behind her hair. 'Why do you always call them *your* birds? They're just birds.'

'Because she feeds them, just like she feeds you,' said Dennis, chewing on the sausage, and the rest of the sentence *and while she feeds you and looks after you, you can show her some gratitude and kindness* was left unspoken. 'This is very good, Goldie. Delicious!'

'They'll die anyway in this cold,' said Nan, thinking about the birds and seeing, in her mind's eye, dead ones all over the garden.

'Oh, you'd be surprised how resilient they are, Mum.'

Nan shook her head. 'Well, if you go out like that, you'll catch your death of cold and you won't make it to spring either.'

'I'll only be gone for a minute.' Marigold slipped her bare feet into boots, picked up the bag of birdseed which was on the shelf by the back door and went out into the garden. She ignored her mother shouting at her to put on a coat. She was well over sixty, she didn't need her mother telling her what to do. She hoped she wouldn't regret having suggested she move in.

Marigold sighed with real pleasure as she put the first footprints in the snow. Everything was white and soft and silent. She wondered at the magical hush that came over the world when it snowed. It was a different kind of hush to any other. As if someone had cast a spell and stopped everything, suspending the world in a state of enchantment. She trudged through the stillness and lifted the feeder off the tree. Carefully, she filled it up with seed and then put it back, hooking it over a twig. She noticed the resident robin on the roof of Dennis's shed. It was watching her with beady black eyes and hopping about, leaving clawprints in the snow. 'You're hungry, aren't you?' she said, smiling at the plucky little bird who often came close when she was on her knees in the border, planting or weeding. In the spring the garden was full of birds, but it was late November and the wise ones had left for warmer climes. Only this robin remained, with its fluffy red breast, along with various blackbirds and thrushes, and the pesky pigeons and seagulls of course, because the village was a couple of miles inland from the sea. 'Don't listen to Nan. You're not going to die,' she added. 'As long as I feed you, you'll see out the winter and soon it will be spring again.'

Marigold walked away and the robin flew onto the feeder. It warmed her heart to see it eating. Soon others would join in. It was amazing how quickly word got around – a bit like the village grapevine, she thought with amusement. As she pulled open the back door, her mind turned to church. She'd have to go upstairs and change. She'd clear the breakfast away once she was dressed. Dennis liked to get there a little early to chat to people. She did not like to keep him waiting. He worked hard during the week, toiling in his shed, making exquisite things out of wood as his father had done before him; it was nice for him to have a rest on a Sunday and spend time with his friends. For Marigold and Dennis church wasn't just about God, it was a social event too, with tea and biscuits afterwards in the church hall. They always looked forward to that.

In the old days Dennis would go to the pub every evening, play darts, drink a couple of pints of bitter and catch up with friends that way. Now he preferred to stay at home and indulge in his hobby of making figurines, which he created himself with his big but steady hands, and displayed on shelves he'd put up all around the house. There were knights of old, soldiers from the Great War and fantasy characters he fished out of his imagination. His latest project was a church – well, it had started as a church but was fast becoming a cathedral and Marigold thought it might very well develop into an entire village with all the people to go in it. It kept him quiet for hours while he carefully cut the plastic and moulded the putty and painted with the flair of a natural artist. It reminded her of the doll's house he had made for the girls when they were little. That was a labour of love, complete with furniture, oak floorboards, fireplaces and wallpaper. A beautifully crafted miniature more exquisite than anything one could buy in a toy shop.

Suze was on her phone talking to her boyfriend Batty when Marigold went upstairs to get ready. The difference in her daughter's tone was remarkable. It was as if she were two people. One sulky and silent, the other animated and chatty. Atticus Buckley, known as Batty, and Suze had been going out for three years. Marigold wondered whether they'd ever get married. People seemed in no rush to marry these days. When she and Dennis had met, they'd walked down the aisle in less than six months. Batty was a good boy, she thought, despite his silly nickname. His parents were both teachers and he still lived with them, in their large house in town. Marigold wondered why he didn't move out and rent a place of his own; after all, his garden-design business seemed to be doing well from what Suze told them. *Young people*, she thought with a shake of the head. Perhaps they were on to something, she mused. After all, why spend hard-earned cash on rent when they could live with their parents for free?

Just as Marigold was about to go downstairs to clear away breakfast, the telephone by the bed rang. She frowned, wondering with a spike of irritation who would bother them on a Sunday morning. She picked it up.

'Mum?'

Her irritation evaporated at the distressed sound of her elder daughter's voice. 'Daisy, are you all right, dear?'

'I'm coming home.'

Marigold realized she did not mean just for Christmas. Her heart stopped. 'What's happened?'

'It's over.' Daisy's voice sounded strained, as if she was trying very hard not to cry. 'I'm leaving as soon as I can get a flight.' There was a moment's silence as Marigold sat down on the edge of the bed and tried to digest what her daughter was telling her. Marigold liked Luca. She liked him a lot. He was eleven years older than Daisy, which had concerned Marigold at the beginning, but then his charm had won her over, and the tender way he had looked at her daughter. He was a photographer, which was romantic. Marigold liked creative people, after all, she'd married one herself, and Luca had the colourful, passionate character of an artist. She had thought that their relationship would last. She had never doubted it. Six years was a long time and she'd taken it for granted that they'd eventually marry and start a family. 'I just want to be at home, Mum,' said Daisy. 'With you and Dad.'

'We can talk about it over a cup of tea,' said Marigold in a reassuring voice. 'There's nothing like a cup of tea to make everything feel better.'

Sensing her mother's assumption that the split would be a

temporary one, Daisy added firmly, 'It's over for good, Mum. I won't be coming back. Luca and I want different things.' Her disappointment was palpable. 'We just want different things,' she repeated quietly.

When Marigold hung up she remained on the bed, worrying. Daisy was thirty-two. Time was running out. She had met Luca when she had gone to work in Italy after reading Italian and art history at university, then moved in with him shortly after. Marigold wondered what kind of 'different things' Daisy referred to; one of them was likely to be marriage. What else could it be? Had she wasted six years of her life hoping he would be The One? As modern as young women were these days, Marigold still believed that a woman's nesting instincts were very strong. Would Daisy have time to find someone else before it was too late?

Unable to cope with the uncomfortable feeling those thoughts induced, she searched for something positive, for a silver lining to the black cloud. With a sudden burst of happiness she found it: Daisy was coming home.

She hurried downstairs to find Dennis. He was in the kitchen working on his miniature church. Nan had gone to her room to get ready for the Sunday service, Suze was in the sitting room, still on the phone to Batty – she had given up going to church years ago. 'That was Daisy,' Marigold told him breathlessly. 'She's coming home.'

Dennis put down his paintbrush and took off his glasses.

'She and Luca have split up. She says they want different things.'

'Oh.' He looked baffled. 'And it took them six years to find that out, did it?'

Marigold began to clear the table. She was so used to clearing up after her family that she did it without thinking, and without annoyance that no one ever helped her. 'It'll be nice to have her home again,' she said.

Dennis arched an eyebrow. 'I know one person, who's not a million miles from here, who's going to be none too happy about this!'

'Well, Nan is in Daisy's old room so Suze will have to let Daisy share with her. She's got twin beds, after all.'

'But Suze is used to having all that space, isn't she?' He grinned. 'Perhaps it'll encourage her to get a proper job and a place of her own.'

'Children don't move out these days. I read about it. I can't remember where. They live with their parents for ever, I think, because they can't afford to get on the property ladder.'

'You can't get on the property ladder if you don't get a job.' Dennis sighed and shook his head. 'You spoil her,' he added. 'We both do.'

'She'll get a proper job one day and move out and then we'll miss her.' Marigold put the frying pan into the sink and sighed. 'Lovely that Daisy's coming home.'

'I'd keep it to yourself, if you don't want your Sunday ruined,' said Dennis, getting up and moving the miniature church onto the side table.

Marigold chuckled. 'Yes, I agree. Mum will say it was never going to last and Suze will have a meltdown. Let's keep it to ourselves for the moment.'

Wrapped in coats and hats, Dennis, Marigold and Nan made their way through the snow to the church, which was a five-minute walk up the lane. Nan held on to Dennis as if her life depended on it, while Marigold walked on his other side with her hands in her coat pockets. They passed the primary school that Daisy and Suze had attended, and the village hall where they had been Brownies. But some things had changed: the village had once boasted a small petrol station where Reg Tucker, in his ubiquitous blue boiler suit and cap, had filled the cars himself, invoicing the locals with a monthly bill, but that had been converted in the 1990s into a posh house with a thatched roof, which was covered in snow. Reg had died years ago, buried in the churchyard, which now came into view beyond the fork where the lane divided. A blackbird sang from the top of the war memorial, built in the triangle of grass in front of the gate. At its foot a wreath of crimson poppies seemed to seep into the blanket of white like the blood of the fallen.

Nan complained all the way. 'It only looks pretty for the first few hours, then it turns to brown slush and people slip and slide all over the place. I'll probably slip and break my neck. It would be just my luck, wouldn't it, to slip in the snow and break my neck? They should have known it was coming and put salt down. But no, it'll turn to ice overnight and I'll slip on it and break my neck tomorrow.'

Marigold didn't try to change her mother's mind. She was used to Nan's complaints and they fell off her like rain off a tin roof. Instead, she enjoyed the sight of the village, swathed in snow. 'Pretty, isn't it, Dennis,' she said, linking her arm in her husband's free one.

'Very pretty,' Dennis agreed, taking pleasure from being outside in the crisp morning air, on his way to seeing his friends. 'Isn't this grand, girls?' he exclaimed jovially. 'The three of us walking in the snow together.'

'Speak for yourself, Dennis,' grumbled Nan. 'You'd better hold on to me tightly or I'll slip.'

'I thought you were going to slip and break your neck *tomorrow*,' said Dennis with a grin.

Nan didn't hear him. She was already distracted by people filing through the gate and onto the path that led up to the church doors. 'They've cleared the path, I see,' she said, squinting. 'But they haven't done a very good job of it. You'd better hold on to me all the way into the church, Dennis,' she said. 'We should have stayed at home instead of coming out in this dreadful weather.'

Dennis did as he was told and escorted his mother-in-law up the path, greeting friends as he went. 'Isn't it lovely!' they all gushed, for commenting on the weather is the British people's favourite topic of conversation.

'I've had to get my snow boots out of the cupboard,' said one.

'We had to clear the front drive with a spade,' said another.

Nan gave a disapproving sniff. 'My husband, God rest his soul, did his back in digging us out with a spade,' she said. 'I'd be very careful if I were you.'

The church smelt pleasantly of wax and flowers. Nan let go of Dennis's arm. She didn't like talking to cheerful people and went on ahead to find a seat. Dutifully, Marigold followed.

Like his father before him, Dennis was the local carpenter. There was barely a house in the village where he hadn't worked. A dresser here, a table there, a set of bookshelves or kitchen cabinets, a Wendy house for the children or a garden shed for Grandad. He knew everyone and loved shooting the breeze. He was considered by many to be a local treasure, an honorary member of the family, for as much time was spent chatting as putting up the pieces he made, and often, once on site, he'd replace the odd doorknob that had come off or re-grout the bathroom for no extra charge. He was like that, Dennis; a good man.

However, his trade had taken its toll on his body. He had bad knees and chronic back pain from carrying heavy things, and his left thumb bore the scars from the sharp tools he used, but he never complained. Dennis had always considered himself lucky that he was able to do what he loved. The duty on his health was a small price to pay.

Marigold was proud of her husband. He was a master of his trade. 'Just give him a piece of wood and he'll be as happy as a beaver,' she'd say when someone else put in a request, and it was true, Dennis was never more content than when he was working in his shed, listening to Planet Rock on the radio while Mac the cat observed him silently from the windowsill.

But nothing satisfied Dennis more than making Marigold's Christmas present.

Every year he made her a jigsaw puzzle. It was no surprise, she knew what she'd be getting, but not what it would look like. There was always a surprise in that. He'd choose a theme first and then find pictures which he'd stick onto a six millimetre sheet of plywood before cutting it with a scroll saw. It was a fiddly job, but Dennis was good at fiddly things. Last year's had been flowers, Marigold loved flowers. The year before had been birds. This year he had chosen an old-fashioned scene of an ice rink with grown-ups and children skating in the falling snow. He'd found the picture in the charity shop and thought she'd like it. As he sat in the pew his mind turned to her puzzle and his excitement warmed him on the inside like the baked potato his mother used to put in his coat pocket when he walked to school in the wintertime. Marigold had always loved jigsaw puzzles and Dennis was very good at making them. Every year he tried to make it a little more complicated or a little bigger, to give her a greater challenge. This year he knew he had outdone all the others. It was made up of over a hundred small pieces and would take her a long time to put together because he hadn't taken a photograph of the original picture for her to copy. He glanced at her, sitting beside him with her cheeks rosy from the walk and her hazel eyes sparkling from the pleasure it had given her. He took her hand and squeezed it. She squeezed it back and smiled. Nan noticed, tutted and shook her head. They were much too old for that, she thought sourly.

After the service the congregants gathered in the hall for tea and biscuits. This was the bit Marigold and Dennis liked the best. Nan liked it the least. She had lived in the village all her married life and had suffered the socializing her husband had enjoyed, but after she had been widowed she'd always taken herself home as soon as the vicar had said the Blessing. Now she had no choice but to mingle because she was dependent on Marigold and Dennis, and she needed Dennis's arm to help her back to the house.

Marigold and Dennis were talking to their neighbours, John and Susan Glenn, when Marigold felt a light tapping on her shoulder. She turned to see the round, eager face of Eileen Utley, who was in her nineties and still played the organ at every Sunday service without making a single mistake. She was holding Marigold's handbag. 'You left this in the pew,' she said.

Marigold looked at the handbag and frowned. Then she looked at her right arm, expecting the bag to be hooked over it, as usual. To her astonishment, it wasn't. 'How strange,' she said to Eileen. 'I must have been thinking about something else.' *Daisy coming home, perhaps?* 'Thank you.'

She sighed. 'I've been getting a bit forgetful lately. This isn't the first time I've left something behind. But look at you, Eileen. As sharp as a tack. Nothing forgetful about you!'

'I'm ninety-two!' said Eileen proudly. 'I've still got all my marbles. The secret is crosswords and Sudoku. They keep your mind working. It's like a muscle, you see. You have to exercise it.'

'Mum does the crossword every day.'

'And look at her.' They both turned their eyes to Nan, who was holding a cup of tea and complaining to the vicar about the lack of salt on the road. He was listening with the patience God had given him for these very moments. 'She's still got all her marbles too, hasn't she?'

'Oh, she has.'

'How is it, having her at home?'

'I think she's happier living with us. Dad's been gone over fifteen years now and it's lonely on your own. She doesn't like animals, so she was never going to have a dog or a cat for company. She tolerates Mac and he gives her a wide berth. He only has eyes for Dennis anyway. It seemed logical as we had Daisy's old room with no one in it. And it's the least I can do. After all, she looked after me for eighteen years, didn't she?'

'You're a good girl, Marigold,' said Eileen, patting her on the arm. 'I'll see you tomorrow,' she added, because Eileen popped into the village shop at nine every morning, not because she really needed anything, but because she didn't have anything else to do.

Marigold hooked her handbag over her arm and wondered how she hadn't noticed it was missing. She hadn't, until recently, been the sort of person who left things behind. *I suppose I am getting old*, she thought, a little dispirited. Her mind searched for something positive. Then she found it: *Daisy's coming home* . . .

Chapter 2

The next day Daisy telephoned at dawn to tell them that she had managed to get a flight out of Milan late that morning and would be home by nightfall, sending Suze into a spin. 'She's not sharing my bedroom!' she declared, only to be told by her mother that she'd have to because there were no spare rooms in the house now that Nan had come to live with them. 'It's not fair!' Suze had cried, tossing her mane and flashing her blue eyes. 'Where am I going to put all my clothes? Can't she sleep on the sofa? I mean, it's temporary, isn't it? She'll be back with Luca by the end of the week. It's ridiculous me having to move all my stuff, just because she decides to come home. It's perfectly comfortable on the sofa. Can't she sleep there!' She had stormed up the stairs and slammed her bedroom door.

Marigold had gone out to feed the birds. It had stopped snowing during the night and now the sky was flat and white, the snow flat and white below it, waiting for the sun to rise and turn it into diamonds. Marigold unhooked the feeder from the tree and looked for the robin to appear, which it did, on the roof of Dennis's shed. 'Suze has always been selfish,' she told it as she carefully poured the seed. 'I suppose I'm to blame. I've worked hard all my life, as has Dennis, so that we can provide for our children and give them an easier time than we had. But in so doing we've made it too easy for her.' The robin's little head jerked from side to side as if it was trying to understand her. 'Life is complicated for us humans. I think it's easier being a bird.' She hooked the feeder back on the branch. 'At least Daisy is coming back. I can't help being excited about that, although I'm sad she's broken up with Luca. I've hated her living abroad. I can only admit that to you. I've hated her living so far from home.'

When Marigold returned to the kitchen Nan was sitting in her usual place at the kitchen table. 'Daisy's going to set the cat among the pigeons,' she predicted, pursing her lips. 'This house is too small for all of us.'

'It's too small for Suze. It's fine for the rest of us,' Marigold corrected her.

'Are you going to let her live with you for ever? She's twenty-five years old. Time to move out and make her own way in life, I would have thought. When I was her age—'

'You were married with two teenage children, well, almost,' Marigold interrupted. 'It's different nowadays. Life is harder.'

'Life has always been hard and it always will be. Life is what you make of it, that's what your father always said and he knew a thing or two about that.'

'I must open the shop,' said Marigold, edging towards the door.

'Suze should help you out in there, instead of doing all that silly stuff she does on her telephone. It would do her good to do some proper work.'

'I don't need an extra pair of hands,' said Marigold. 'I have Tasha.'

'Tasha.' Nan sniffed. 'I don't call that an extra pair of hands. I call that a headache.'

'She works hard.'

'When she's here.'

'She's here most of the time.'

'Most is not the word I would use, but then you're a people-pleaser, Marigold, you always have been. Well, off you go then. I'll hold the fort in here, cheer Suze up with a few tales of the deprivation I suffered as a child.'

Marigold laughed. 'Oh, she'll love you for that.'

Nan smiled back. 'The young don't know how lucky they are.' Then when Marigold was halfway out the door, she called after her, 'Be a dear and bring me some digestive biscuits when you have a moment, the chocolate ones. I like to dip them in my tea.'

Marigold had owned the village shop for over thirty years. It had been convenient for her when the children were little because the house was separated from the shop by a small, cobbled courtyard, so it was easy to dash back and forth. The buildings were pretty white cottages with small windows and grey slate roofs, and the gardens at the back, although not very large, gave onto rolling fields. Fields that belonged to the wealthy landowner Sir Owen Sherwood, so there was no danger of them being developed to expand the village. There was always talk of the need for more houses, but that land prevented them from being built there, in Dennis and Marigold's view. The farm was so big, with woodland and fields, that the whole eastern side of the village was protected from developers, while the western side was protected by the sea. It was an idyllic place to live. The only complaint, if Marigold had one, which she didn't like to admit to because it went against her nature to moan, was that the big supermarket, built in the 1980s a few miles outside the village, had stolen much of her business. Still, she took care to stock essential items as well as gifts, and the post office, of course, was useful to the locals. She made a decent living. So did Dennis. They were comfortable and happy.

Tasha was already in the shop when Marigold appeared. A single mother with two children under ten and the unfortunate disposition of being a little delicate, Tasha was not someone who could be relied upon. Her children were often sick, too, or she needed to stay home for an electrician or a delivery, or she was overtired and run-down and required the odd day at home to rest. Marigold was indulgent. She didn't like confrontation and she didn't like hard feelings. And she reasoned that, although Tasha wasn't very dependable, she was a nice, smiley presence to have around the shop, and that counted for a lot. The customers liked her because she was polite and charming, and when she was there, she did the job well. The devil you know is better than the devil you don't, Marigold figured.

'Good morning.' Tasha's cheerful voice lifted Marigold's spirits.

'You're here,' said Marigold, pleasantly surprised.

'Well, I was wondering if I could leave a little early today. Milly's in a play and I promised I'd help with the make-up.'

Marigold could hardly deny her that. 'Of course you can. What play is it?' And Tasha told her about it as she began a stocktake of the shelves. 'Did you remember to order baked beans, Marigold?' she asked. 'We're totally out of them and they're very popular.'

'Baked beans? Are you sure?'

'Yes, I asked you last week. Remember?'

Marigold didn't remember. She couldn't even recall having had the conversation. 'How odd. I'll do it right away.'

At nine Eileen Utley came in. She bought some milk, then spent the next hour chatting to the locals, who filed in one after the other to buy a newspaper, a pint of milk or to post a parcel. Eileen enjoyed watching the bustle of village life. It made her feel part of the place, rather than on the periphery, which was what staying at home with the telly did.

The shop was quite busy when Lady Sherwood came in. Elegant in a loden coat and matching green hat, she smiled at Marigold. Although the two women were of similar age, Lady Sherwood looked a decade younger. Her skin was smooth, her make-up carefully applied and her shoulder-length blonde hair had no sign of grey. It was obvious to Marigold that she had it dyed, but it appeared natural nonetheless. Marigold wondered whether her effortless glamour was due to her being Canadian. She imagined women from that part of the world were naturally glamorous, like film stars. Marigold had never crossed the Atlantic and Lady Sherwood's Canadian accent gave her a thrilling sense of the exotic.

'Good morning, Marigold,' said Lady Sherwood agreeably. However, as friendly as her manner was she still succeeded in maintaining a certain distance, due to their very different stations in life, she the wife of a squire and Marigold the wife of a carpenter. Though, as Nan liked to point out, 'There was once a simple carpenter . . .'

'Good morning, Lady Sherwood,' said Marigold from behind the counter. 'What can I get you?'

'Are you making Christmas puddings again this year?'

'Yes, I am. Would you like one?'

'Yes, I'd like two, please. My son's coming over from Toronto and we're going to be a lot of people. They went down very well last year.'

'Oh good. I'm happy to hear that.' Marigold pictured the

Sherwoods' grand dining room filled with elegant people eating her Christmas puddings and felt a rush of pride.

'And I'd like a couple of books of first-class stamps while I'm here. Thank you.'

Marigold gave her the stamps and carefully wrote the Christmas pudding order in her red notebook. She noticed Lady Sherwood's fine leather gloves and the gracious way she moved her hands and thought her the most stylish woman she'd ever met. When Lady Sherwood departed, leaving a lingering smell of expensive perfume, Eileen leaned on the counter and lowered her voice. 'As you know, I'm not one to gossip, but I've heard that father and son don't get along at all,' she said. 'That's why the lad went to live in Canada.'

Marigold put the red book beneath the counter. 'Oh dear, that's sad. There's nothing as important as family,' she said, her heart warming once more at the thought of seeing Daisy. She'd be on her way to the airport, she suspected.

'I don't know what will happen to the estate when Sir Owen pops off,' Eileen continued. 'I gather Taran makes a lot of money in Canada.'

'If Sir Owen lives as long as you, Eileen, Taran won't inherit for another fifty years!'

'He's the only child. It will be his duty to come back and run the estate. Sir Owen's a man who understands the countryside, like his father, Hector, did. Now *he* was a good and decent person and let my father live in one of his cottages rent free when he lost his job and took months to find a new one. I don't think Taran is like them. I think he's one of those banking people who only think about making money.'

'How do you come to that conclusion, Eileen?'

'Sylvia's not a gossip, but she lets the odd thing slip out,' said Eileen, referring to the Sherwoods' housekeeper, a good-natured, slow-moving fifty-year-old who had worked for the family for over a decade. 'When Sir Owen pops off there'll be trouble.' And she licked her bottom lip at the thought of such excitement.

Marigold tried to get on with serving people while Eileen shared the village gossip. She had something to say about everyone who came into the shop. John Porter was squabbling with his neighbour Pete Dickens over a magnolia tree which had grown too big, and Mary Hanson's St Bernard had killed Dolly Nesbit's cat, causing Dolly to drop into a dead faint in the middle of the green. 'She's still in bed recovering,' said Eileen. 'Mary has offered to find her a new cat but Dolly says her Precious is irreplaceable. If you ask me that dog should be put down. No one should have a dog the size of a horse running loose about the village.' Jean Miller, who had recently been widowed, was struggling to cope with living on her own. 'Poor dear. I can tell her that you get used to it after a while and there's always the TV for company. I love *Bake Off*, especially, and *Strictly Come Dancing*, but there are all sorts of things to watch these days. That nice Cedric Weatherby, you know, the one who's just moved into Gloria's old house, made her a cake and took it round. It had enough brandy in it to put her out for a week!' Then there was the Commodore, who lived in a much-admired Georgian house with his wife Phyllida, and had resorted to shooting moles from his bedroom window. 'He tried gassing them with a pipe attached to his car exhaust but that backfired and he nearly gassed himself,' said Eileen gleefully. 'He says they're a plague, putting mud hills all over his lawn, but since reading Beatrix Potter as a child I've always been rather partial to the furry little friends.'

At midday Nan wandered in, complaining of the cold. 'It's Siberian!' she said as she hurried through the door, bringing snow in on her shoes. 'Ah, lovely and warm in here.' She waited for Marigold to finish serving and then reminded her about the digestive biscuits.

'Oh, I'm sorry, Mum. I forgot. Eileen's been distracting me,' she said.

'Our Daisy's coming home today,' said Nan with a smile. 'Suze is none too happy about it. They're going to have to share a room.'

'She's home a bit early for Christmas, isn't she?' said Eileen.

Before Marigold could make something up, Nan had told the biggest gossip in the village about Daisy and Luca's split.

'I'm sure they'll kiss and make up,' said Marigold, struggling to do some damage control.

But Nan shook her head. 'I think over means over, Marigold,' she said. 'You don't break up after six years and then get back together. Mark my words, it's done.'

Suze came into the shop in the early afternoon with a bag of parcels to post. In order to keep buying clothes and make-up she had to sell things she no longer wanted. She had a site online for selling second-hand things and was making a small business out of it, although not one that would ever be in profit. She was still furious about her sister coming home and hadn't moved anything out of her bedroom to accommodate her. 'Like I said, she can sleep on the sofa,' she repeated. Marigold was relieved that Eileen had eventually gone home so she didn't pick up on the impending feud.

'It's between you and Daisy. I'm not getting involved,' said Marigold. 'Although I think a little kindness would not go amiss, considering.'

'Who chucked who?' asked Suze.

'I don't know. She didn't say. She just said they want different things.'

Suze grinned. 'Luca doesn't want to get married and Daisy does.' Then she added provocatively, 'Marriage is so old-fashioned.'

'I'm glad your grandmother isn't around to hear that,' said Marigold.

'Oh, I'll happily tell her to her face. Times are different now.' With that, she flicked her hair and skipped out of the shop, leaving her mother to weigh and pay the postage for all her packages.

Tasha had left. The place was quiet. Marigold looked outside. Night came early now. She sat on the stool behind the counter and took a deep breath. She felt tired. It must be the weather, she thought, those dark mornings and dark evenings sap one's energy. The sun hadn't come out at all today, so although the snow remained there were no diamonds to sparkle and glitter. The roads were icy. She thought of her mother declaring that she'd slip and break her neck today and hoped she had done the sensible thing and spent most of the day indoors.

When she locked up at closing time she saw Suze's parcels still waiting to be posted. She frowned and stared at them as if seeing them for the first time. She was sure she had sent them off. But no, there they were, and they hadn't even been stamped. Marigold felt a strange prickling sensation creep across her skin. It took a while for her to recognize what it was, but when she did, the realization that she was afraid made the prickling sensation even more intense. She felt fear, deep and cold and unmistakable: something was wrong. She'd left her handbag in church the day before and now she had forgotten to post Suze's parcels. Marigold was not a vague person. Quite the opposite. She was someone who could be relied upon to organize things efficiently. Her entire life she had defined herself by her sharp and lucid memory. Manning the shop and the post office, with all the demands that that entailed, required her mind to be quick and her powers of recollection razor-sharp. They hadn't, until now, let her down.

Marigold stepped out into the dark and locked the door behind her. Then she walked carefully across the icy courtyard towards the house, feeling strangely unsteady. The lights inside were golden and she could see her mother and Suze through the window, sitting at the kitchen table. The packet of digestive biscuits was open beside her mother. Her spirits sank as she remembered she had forgotten those too. *I really am losing my marbles*, she thought to herself despondently. She resolved to exercise her mind as Eileen had suggested.

When she went through the back door, Nan was halfway through a story and Suze was hovering in the doorway, trying to escape. Marigold glanced out of the window. The lights in Dennis's shed were still on, blazing through the darkness. He'd been in there all day. She knew he was making her Christmas present and wondered what the picture would be. The thought of it made her smile and she began to feel brighter. She was tired and, as much as she didn't want to admit it, she was getting older. It was perfectly normal to forget things at her age. She'd just have to make more of an effort to remember.

At seven the front door burst open and Daisy fell into the hallway, all tousled brown hair and big puffy coat, dragging a large suitcase behind her. Marigold dropped the wooden spoon she was using to stir the sauce and rushed to embrace her.

'Darling, what a surprise! You should have called. Dad would have picked you up at the station.'

'I got a cab,' said Daisy.

'You look exhausted!' Marigold exclaimed, maternal instincts kicking in fiercely at the sight of her daughter's waxen face. 'Come in out of the cold at once.'

Dennis, who had just shut up his shed, smiled broadly. 'Let me take that,' he said, relieving Daisy of her suitcase. 'What have you got in here? The Crown jewels?'

'My life,' Daisy replied, smiling weakly. She wrapped her arms around her father and began to cry.

'You're home now, pet,' he said, patting her back. 'Where you belong.'

'We'll look after you, love,' rejoined her mother, taking in her daughter's unkempt hair and the purple shadows beneath her eyes that were bloodshot and full of pain. She longed to run her a hot bath and give her a good meal to restore her back to health.

Suze appeared at the bottom of the stairs with a sheepish look. 'Hi,' she said, without making a move to approach her. 'Sorry about Luca.'

'Thanks,' Daisy replied, but her attention was diverted by Nan, making her way down the hall towards her.

'You're too good for him,' she said, hugging her granddaughter. 'Italian men can't be trusted. We need to find you a nice Englishman.'

Daisy laughed in spite of her heavy heart. 'I don't think I want anyone right now, Nan.'

'Of course you don't,' said Dennis.

'What you need is a nice cup of tea,' said Marigold.

'You'll be back together by the end of the week,' said Suze, fervently hoping that they would.

Daisy lifted her chin. 'I don't want him back,' she replied crisply. 'It's over. I'm home.' She looked at her mother and smiled wanly. 'Now, where's that tea?'

Chapter 3

'I have a plan,' Daisy said. She was sitting at the kitchen table beside her father and Nan, and opposite Suze, who looked at her from under her long fringe, trying unsuccessfully to feign interest. Her sister, with her sensible nature, independent life and talent, had always made her feel unworthy.

Marigold was at the stove. How typical of Daisy to have it all worked out, she thought proudly. She had always been organized and self-sufficient. 'What is it?' she asked.

'I've saved enough money to do what I've always wanted to do,' she said, a shy smile creeping onto her face.

'What's that then, dear?' said Marigold.

'I'm going to draw and paint. I mean, not as a hobby – I've been doing that for years – but as a profession.'

'About time too,' said Dennis happily. He'd always wanted Daisy to be an artist. It's what she was good at. What she was born to do. In his opinion she'd been wasted working in a museum instead of allowing her creativity to blossom.

'Yes,' she said, taking a deep breath, as if nervous of the risks. 'I'm going to give it a go.'

Nan pursed her lips. 'I doubt if painting will make you much money,' she said.

'I don't think Hockney would agree with you, Nan,' said Daisy.

'Or Peter Doig and Damien Hirst,' Dennis added with a smile.

'Who's Peter Doig?' asked Suze, screwing up her nose.

'But think of the thousands of painters out there who no one's ever heard of,' Nan continued. 'Penniless, living off the kindness of family.' She gave Marigold a meaningful look. Marigold pretended she hadn't seen it. She knew her mother would have a lot to say if she and Dennis ended up having to support *both* daughters.

'We all have to start somewhere, Nan,' said Daisy. 'I'll never know if I don't try.'

'What are you going to paint?' asked Suze, anxious now because her sister really did sound as if she had no intention of returning to Milan.

'Animals,' said Daisy. 'I'm going to paint animal portraits. I'm good at those. Then, when I get my confidence, I'll do people as well.'

'That's a great idea,' enthused Marigold.

'Thanks, Mum.'

'Have you quit your job then?' Suze asked.

'Yes.'

'And they just let you go? Just like that?'

'They did.'

Suze raised her eyebrows. 'Won't the place fall apart without you?'

Daisy laughed. 'I was working in a museum, Suze, not running the country!'

Suze's shoulders slumped. 'So you really are here for good?'

'Yes. I'm not going back.'

'We're happy about that, aren't we, Goldie?' said Dennis cheerfully.

'Very,' Marigold agreed, feeling her heart swelling with happiness, leaving no room in her chest for concern and doubt. She untied her apron and held up a wooden spoon. 'Dinner is ready,' she announced. 'And I think we should open a bottle of wine, don't you, Dennis? To celebrate Daisy's homecoming.'

'I'll raise a glass to that!' said Dennis, getting up.

'And I'll lower a glass to Luca,' said Nan, pulling a face. 'I never liked him in the first place.'

After dinner Dennis hauled Daisy's suitcase upstairs and put it in Suze's room, silently and decisively declaring an end of the discussion. Suze had to bite her tongue and accept that her sister was moving back in, for *now*. There was always a chance that Daisy and Luca would reconcile their differences, or that Daisy would find her new living quarters claustrophobic and look for somewhere to rent. Suze certainly did not envisage sharing her room for long. The fact that Daisy did not even attempt to unpack her clothes gave her hope. She watched her burrow about for her pyjamas and did not offer to clear a few shelves. She barely had enough space for herself.

Later, when the two girls went to bed and turned out the light, Suze's heart mollified at the sound of Daisy softly crying into her pillow. Selfish by nature did not mean Suze was unfeeling. 'I'll move my things tomorrow so you have some space,' she whispered, knowing she'd regret saying that in the morning.

'I'm sorry. You didn't expect to have to share your room, did you?'

'That's okay. We'll make do for a while. It's not for ever, is it?' she said hopefully.

'How's it going with Batty?'

'Good. Very good. What happened with Luca?'

'He doesn't want to get married and—' Daisy took a ragged breath. 'He doesn't want children.'

'Oh.' Suze hadn't expected that. 'You really do want different things.'

'Yes.'

'I know just the animal for you to paint,' she said brightly. 'A dog. He's massive, as big as a horse, and he's just killed a cat so he's got a mean and hungry look, which will make it more fun for you.'

'Did he really kill a cat?'

'Dolly Nesbit's cat, to be precise.'

'Oh, that's bad. What was it called? Precious? She must be heartbroken.'

'She fainted. Actually, she might die.'

'Oh, Suze! You can't say that.'

'Well, she's old, isn't she, and old people can't take shocks like that.' Suze giggled. 'She looked half dead before. Now I'd say she's pushing three quarters dead.'

Daisy laughed with her. 'You are funny.'

'I know.' Suze sighed heavily. 'I should be a comedian.'

'I wouldn't go that far.'

'Anything would be better than what I do,' she added. 'Mum and Dad and Nan think I should get a proper job.'

'I don't think they'd consider a comedian a proper job.'

'Still better than what I do.'

'You should write a book. You always wrote stories when you were little. You're good with words, and you're talented. You just lack belief in yourself.'

Suze chuckled. 'I wouldn't know what to write about.'

'Draw from your experience. Isn't that what writers do?'

'I don't have much experience, Daisy. Unlike you, I have

spent all my life in a small village by the sea and nothing very exciting has ever happened to me.'

'So, write about what interests you then.'

'The sort of things that interest me would not make a good book. Fashion and make-up are better suited to magazines – and my Instagram account.'

'How's that going, by the way?'

'Slowly.'

'Is it going to make you any money?'

'It will in the end. If I get enough of a following, companies will pay me to post things.'

'How many followers do you need for that to happen?'

'A few hundred thousand.'

'And you've got how many?'

'Nearly thirty thousand.'

There was a short pause as Daisy tried to think of some-thing encouraging to say. 'Okay, so you've got a way to go, but you'll get there.'

'I'm working on it. Sometimes I believe I can conquer the world, most of the time I doubt I can conquer anything.'

Daisy chuckled. 'Aren't we a pair!'

'Yes, we are,' said Suze, surprised how much being a pair warmed her. 'Night, Daisy.'

'Night, Suze.'

And they fell asleep to the familiar sound of the other's quiet breathing.

The following day the sky cleared and the sun shone brightly on the snow. Marigold was behind the counter of the shop when Mary Hanson came in to buy beer for the builders painting her house. She had tied Bernie, her St Bernard, to a post and the dog had lain down on the snow, making the most of the cold before it melted. He panted heavily, exhaling clouds of hot breath. Eileen was leaning on the counter and Tasha was in the back, unpacking the delivery of baked beans. Marigold hoped Eileen wouldn't mention Dolly's cat.

'Good morning, Mary,' said Marigold.

'Good morning. And isn't it lovely? Sunny at last.'

'Makes a nice change, doesn't it?' said Marigold.

'It certainly does.'

'Um, Mary, I was wondering whether I could ask you a favour.'

'Sure, Marigold. What can I do for you?' Mary raised her eyebrows expectantly, hoping it wouldn't be an imposition. She really had to be getting back to the painters.

'My daughter has just come back from working in Italy and she'd like to try her hand at painting. She's very good. She's always been good, she's just never had the confidence. She was wondering whether you'd allow her to paint a portrait of your dog.'

Mary's face lit up. 'Bernie? She'd like to paint Bernie? Well, of course she can. He'd love to be painted.'

'Oh, good. I'll tell her. She's nipped out but she'll be back later.'

'I'll give you my mobile number and you can ask her to call me.'

Marigold gave her a piece of paper and a pen and Mary proceeded to write it down. 'He's a handsome devil, my Bernie,' she said, 'and he just adores people.' She then went to the back of the shop in search of beer.

'We can't say the same about cats,' said Eileen under her breath.

A moment later Mary returned with twelve cans of beer.

'I'll expect Daisy's call,' she said, taking her wallet out of her handbag. 'And I'll tell Bernie the good news so he can get excited. He's never been painted before.'

'If it's good enough she might display him in the village hall,' said Marigold. 'She's hoping to make a career of it, you see.'

'What a good idea. A great place to advertise. The English are potty about their dogs.' Mary smiled mischievously. 'I'd rather have Bernie painted than my children, but don't tell Brian!'

Marigold laughed. 'I won't.'

When the door closed behind her Eileen shook her head. 'And I won't tell Dolly. To have her cat's killer immortalized in paint might just tip her over the edge.'

Daisy walked up the path that snaked along the clifftops. She hadn't walked there in ages. In spite of coming home a couple of times a year, for Christmas and usually once in the summer, she never found the time for walks. She remembered skipping up this path as a little girl, her mother's voice calling her back snatched by the wind that blew in gusts off the sea. It hadn't changed. It was exactly as it always had been. But *she* had changed. She yearned for her childhood now. Life had been simpler then. Fewer worries, or so it seemed. Six years in Italy, which had been good, now felt like lost years, wasted years, years invested with no return. She worried that her heart would never mend. It felt like grief, this leaden feeling in her chest. She was mourning the death of a relationship, yet her love lived on and had nowhere to go.

The truth was that Luca had never lied to her about not wanting marriage or children. It had been *she* who had foolishly believed she could change him. She had believed he would love her enough to give her what she wanted, that if she hung in there he would eventually back down. There came a moment when she realized he never would. That was last week.

Luca hadn't betrayed her; *she* had betrayed *him*. After all, they had so much in common. She was bohemian, like him. An independent free spirit, like him. They both loved art and music and culture. Neither was particularly materialistic. They'd lived simply but well, relishing Italy's sensual bounty: the food, the sunshine, the art and architecture and, most of all, the beautiful countryside. He had believed they'd wanted the same things, while all along she had secretly wanted more. It wasn't *he* who had moved the goalposts, it was *she*. If she had gambled six years of her life and lost, she had only herself to blame.

Now she was home she had to start again. A new career and a new life – it felt more like the picking up of the old one. She didn't want to live at home, like Suze. She didn't really want to live in this small village either. She was used to living abroad, in a cosmopolitan city. Used to living independently, but she had no choice. She didn't have the money to buy a place of her own and she didn't want to waste what she had on renting when she could live at home rent-free. And she needed to watch her pennies if she was going to give painting a go. She wouldn't get clients for a while and when she did, she wouldn't be able to charge much, being a novice. Nan was right, she wasn't going to make much money, but did that matter if she was happy? Surely it was more important to do what one loved than to slog away doing something unin-spiring just to earn more money? If she could establish herself as an artist and make a living out of it, then she could decide where she wanted to put down her roots. The trouble was she had made a life for herself in Milan; nowhere else felt like home, not even here.

Although the sun was out her walk was bracing. Snow still clung to the hills and the air was cold and crisp. The wind that raced up the cliff face bore sharp teeth. Seagulls wheeled beneath an icy blue sky and on the sea small boats bobbed up and down while fishermen put out their nets. It was all so very pretty and Daisy sighed with pleasure as her sorrow slowly lifted a little. It was lovely to be back, only sad that her homecoming was accompanied by heartbreak. She knew she'd miss Italy and all her friends there, but she had to learn to live in England again. Try to make some new friends. It was a daunting thought, starting over. She wondered whether she'd ever fall in love again. She put her hands in her pockets and walked in the direction of her village. She had to discover who she was here, without Italy and Luca to define her, and she had to come to love that person before she could even contemplate giving her heart away again. Right now she couldn't contemplate loving anyone else but Luca, ever.

When she got home she went to find her mother in the shop. Marigold was serving the Commodore, whom Daisy had known since she was a girl. Commodore Wilfrid Braithwaite, as he was really called, had been a friend of her grandfather's. When he saw her his small eyes lit up and his wrinkled face creased further as he smiled, revealing a crooked set of teeth. 'Well, what a sight for sore eyes,' he exclaimed. 'You back for Christmas already, Daisy?'

Daisy returned his smile. In a three-piece tweed suit, complete with a tie and trilby hat, the Commodore looked quite the country gentleman. 'I'm back for good, actually,' she said.

He drew his feathery white eyebrows into a frown. 'Oh dear, have you left your Italian fellow behind?'

'Yes, I have,' she replied.

'I'm sorry to hear that.'

'It's nice to be home, though,' she said, sensing an awkward pause brewing.

'I don't suppose it snows much in Italy.'

'Actually, I was in Milan where it snows more than here.'

'So it does.' He paid for the chocolate digestive biscuits. Marigold stared at them and frowned. She'd seen them on a table recently, but she couldn't remember where. 'I like dipping these in my tea,' said the Commodore. *So does someone else*, thought Marigold, but she couldn't for the life of her remember who.

The Commodore left the shop and Marigold went to the magazine stand to look for a book of Sudoku puzzles. She really needed to exercise her brain. Tasha took over the till. 'Nice to have you back,' she said to Daisy. 'Only sorry it's, well, you know.' She smiled anxiously, not knowing how to put her sympathy into words. 'Mary Hanson was in a while ago and left her number with your mum. She says you can paint her dog.'

'Really? That's great. He's the big one, isn't he?'

'Yes, he's a St Bernard. You know, those Swiss dogs with barrels of brandy around their necks, except Bernie doesn't wear one of those. Well, he'd be a bit more popular if he did.' Tasha crinkled her nose.

Marigold appeared with the book of Sudoku puzzles. 'This is to exercise my brain,' she said with a smile. 'I'm becoming so forgetful these days.'

'We could all do with exercising our brains,' said Tasha with a grin.

'I hope it works,' said Marigold. 'I'm not ready to go gaga yet!'

They laughed. 'Tasha says you have Mary Hanson's number for me,' Daisy said.

'Oh yes, so I do.' Marigold put her hands in her pockets. She frowned. 'Goodness, where did I put it?' She realized as a cold feeling slithered over her skin that she couldn't remember anything about the piece of paper. She knew Mary had written her number on something, but she had no recollection of having been given it. 'I don't think she gave it to me,' she said, certain now that she hadn't.

'It's here,' said Tasha, picking it up off the counter. 'Easy to miss. It was partially hidden underneath your red book.'

'Of course it was. I remember now.' Marigold watched Tasha give the note to Daisy. 'You'd better start doing your Sudoku,' said Daisy.

'Yes, I will,' said Marigold, hiding behind a smile the anxiety that was shrinking her heart. She suddenly felt rather unwell. 'I think I need some tea,' she said. 'Tasha, man the shop for a minute, will you? Yes, a cup of tea is just what I need.' And she hurried across the courtyard to the kitchen, her face taut with worry.

After closing the shop at the end of the day Marigold rushed off to attend a committee meeting for the Christmas fair, which was due to take place in the church hall at the beginning of December. The meeting was hosted by the vicar's wife, Julia Cobbold, in the Old Vicarage, an austere flintstone mansion lacking both warmth and charm, but impressive in size and history because it had been built in the time of Henry VIII and boasted a priest hole which had allowed persecuted men of the cloth to escape via a secret stair and an underground tunnel. Julia was very proud of her house but Marigold knew to take a shawl because the place was always cold, even with the great fires burning.

She walked up the road. The ice had melted and the tarmac glistened with slush, but it was no longer dangerous. Nan hadn't slipped and broken her neck, which was a blessing, but now she was claiming that black ice would take her instead, because unlike snow it was impossible to see. It had been a long day and Marigold really wanted to put her feet up. But she'd never missed a meeting and, apart from feeling weary, there was no reason why she should.

As she made her way up the Cobbolds' drive she heard the screech of an owl close by. She stopped, cocking her ear to ascertain from where it came. Then she spotted it. Although it was dark, the moon was bright and she could see, in the crook of a tree, the unmistakable white face of a barn owl. She stood still and watched. A moment later two more appeared. Three owlets peered out with their big, curious eyes, as they waited for their mother to return to feed them. Marigold was enchanted. For a long while she was lost there, beneath the tree, and the joy of finding herself the lucky spectator of such a heart-warming scene gave her a surge of energy so that when she arrived, finally, at the front door of the Old Vicarage, she was feeling herself again. Positive, lively and ready to take on whatever challenge was thrown her way.

'Ah, Marigold,' said Julia when she opened the door and saw Marigold standing there with her nose red from the cold. Julia looked typically chic in a pair of olive-green slacks and matching sweater. Marigold noticed the gold buckles on her court shoes, which matched her gold earrings and the chain necklace hanging over her bosom, giving her a sophisticated air. Marigold couldn't help but think how much easier it was to look polished when one was tall and slim like Julia. 'The last to arrive,' Julia added, a touch impatiently.

'Sorry I'm late. I couldn't help but stop and watch those dear little barn owls.'

'Barn owls?' Julia frowned. 'Are they back again?'

'Haven't you seen them?' Marigold couldn't imagine having a family of owls on her property and not knowing about it.

'They were here last year. How nice. Come on in. We need to get this meeting underway as I have a dinner at eight and I need to get ready.'

Marigold followed Julia into the drawing room, which was large and square with a fire burning unenthusiastically beneath a mantelpiece displaying a row of stiff white invitations embellished with flouncy gold writing. Floral-patterned sofas and armchairs were assembled around a coffee table, laden with big glossy books on art, and on these uncomfortable pieces of furniture perched the four other members of the committee, being careful not to disturb the pointy, diamond-shaped cushions which were arranged behind them in tidy rows.

Marigold smiled at the women, all of whom she knew well. Among them was Beryl Bailey, her dearest friend. Beryl was a large woman with spiky auburn hair and a surprisingly young face for a woman approaching seventy. She wore a patterned dress that reached mid-calf, exposing the rings of wool at her thick ankles where her tights had gathered. She wore a pair of sturdy lace-up shoes, which were the only shoes she could wear on account of her bunions, and a walking stick rested against the arm of the sofa as a reminder of a recent hip replacement. 'Come and sit beside me,' Beryl said to Marigold, patting the cushion with a pudgy hand.

'I'm a little late.'

'That's not like you.'

'I haven't been myself recently,' Marigold confessed in a quiet voice.

Beryl frowned. 'Is everything all right?'

'I'm just becoming so forgetful.' She lifted a notebook out of her bag and tapped it. 'I have to write everything down now, you know.'

'Oh, I'm terrible!' said Beryl, lowering her voice. 'I forget people's names all the time! I open the fridge and then forget what I was looking for. I leave everything behind. You know what it is, Marigold?'

Marigold swallowed and looked at her friend apprehensively. 'What?'

'Getting older.'

Marigold felt a wave of relief. 'Really? Is that all it is?' She laughed to cover her anxiety. 'I thought I was getting dementia.'

'Nonsense!' said Beryl. 'If that were the case we'd all be getting it. Just write everything down. It's normal. I'm afraid that's one of the downsides of growing old. That's what we have to look forward to: forgetfulness, sagging skin, fading eyesight and aching joints.'

'And the upside?'

'Family,' said Beryl, and Marigold smiled. 'Children, grandchildren and friends. That's what makes life worth living.'

And Marigold knew she was right. She would try not to worry about it anymore.

Chapter 4

Daisy was eyeball to eyeball with Bernie. His nose was an inch from hers, as were his glistening chops and sharp white teeth. She hoped he didn't decide to take a bite. She was holding his enormous paws for he had jumped up the minute he was introduced and was now standing on his hind legs, as tall as she was, staring at her with shiny brown eyes, the colour of chestnuts.

'He likes you,' said Mary.

'I'm glad to hear it,' Daisy replied, thinking how it might have been had he *not* liked her.

'He only does that with people he likes. You don't mind, do you? You're not wearing anything smart, at least.'

Daisy was, in fact, wearing something *she* considered smart, but Mary obviously didn't rate her indigo jeans and cashmere sweater. She was only visiting, to get to know her subject and to take a few preliminary photographs, but Mary probably assumed she was in her working clothes. 'I bet he eats a lot,' Daisy said, letting go of the dog's paws.

'Not as much as you'd think. He eats the same amount as a Labrador. But he loves his food, so I tend to spoil him. You know, the odd piece of bacon or sausage. Whatever I've got left over.' She gazed into his big face and smiled at him lovingly.

Daisy took out her phone and began to take photographs. 'He's a beautiful animal,' she said, watching Mary's face flower into a radiant smile. 'I don't think I've ever seen such a beauty.'

'He can be quite scary, you know.'

Daisy decided not to tell Mary that she *did* know exactly how scary Bernie could be. 'Not Bernie, surely. He's as good as gold,' she said instead.

'He doesn't like delivery men in bright yellow jackets or small, yappy dogs,' Mary explained. Daisy bit her tongue as the word 'cat' teetered on the end of it. 'He loves rabbits and pheasants, and occasionally catches them around Sir Owen's woods. I'm sure he'd get into terrible trouble if the game-keeper found out. You know, they're very funny about their birds. They raise them just to shoot them, but when they're eaten by a dog like Bernie they get ever so cross. Seems a bit illogical to me.'

'He doesn't strike me as a shooting dog.'

'Oh, he'd love to be out there with the guns. All those eager spaniels, putting up the birds. He'd like to be one of them. But he's not trained. He won't come when he's called. He's got a mind of his own and there's no arguing with a dog his size. You just have to let him get on with it. Once, I tried to restrain him and he ended up dragging me a hundred yards across the field. I learned my lesson: Bernie rules. It's as simple as that.'

Daisy was excited about her new profession, although a little nervous. It had been a while since she'd done a portrait. Might she have forgotten how to do it? Would her picture be any good? At least Mary wasn't paying, but still, she'd be very disappointed if it didn't look anything like Bernie.

That afternoon she borrowed her mother's car and drove into town to buy supplies. Her mother had told her there was a good art shop on the high street where she could get paint and paper, but when she got there she couldn't find it. She walked up and down a few times, dwelling occasionally on the happy memories certain parts of the street inspired, until she finally resorted to asking someone. 'Oh, that shop hasn't been here for twenty years,' said the passer-by. 'I know the one you mean. It used to sell proper stuff for artists. I'd order online if I were you. There's nothing of that quality here now.'

Daisy was baffled. Her mother was a regular in this town. She must know every inch of the place. It wasn't very big. How had she not noticed that the art shop had closed down *twenty years ago.* But then she didn't paint, Daisy reasoned, so why would she notice it had gone? She'd probably bought some supplies for her when she was a little girl and painting was her passion, and then not noticed when it disappeared. She would tell her when she got home and they would have a laugh about it.

Later she found her mother in the shop, chatting to Eileen. Eileen was leaning on the counter, talking about the Commodore. 'He's going to flood the ground with water when it freezes, so that the mole holes block up with ice. It seems a little cruel to me, but I don't want to speak ill of anyone. I mean, those moles don't know what a nuisance they are, do they? I bet there's a perfectly humane way of trapping them. He should look it up on the internet. You can get everything on Amazon these days, you know.'

Marigold turned to Daisy. 'Hello, dear. What are you up to?'

Daisy was on the point of telling her about the art shop when something stopped her. A strange feeling in the middle of her chest where her intuition was. She noticed her mother looked tired. Perhaps now wasn't the time. After all, if she was getting forgetful, teasing her about it might not be very kind.

She decided to let it go. 'Nothing,' she replied breezily. 'Just popping in to say hello.'

The reason for the strange feeling was confirmed when, later that evening, her mother sat at the kitchen table with her book of Sudoku. 'This is very taxing,' she said to Nan, who was good at Sudoku. 'I can feel my brain aching.'

'It's doing it good,' said Nan. 'Though nothing stops the ageing process. That's just life and the only thing we can do is accept it.'

Daisy sat down. 'Mum, are you seriously worried?'

'No,' Marigold replied a little too quickly. 'Not at all. I'm just getting on a bit as Nan says.'

'Good, because you don't need to worry. You're all there.' She smiled reassuringly. 'And sixty-six is not old, by the way.'

'Wait until you're eighty-six. That's old. I've one foot in the grave and the other on a bar of soap,' said Nan. 'One false move and it's curtains.'

Suze sat in the café in town. It was quiet and warm and she had a large soya milk latte beside her, which made her job more enjoyable. She'd read an interview with an author once who had said that the key to writing a book was to make your work space as pleasant as possible; that way, you'll always want to get back to it. Suze eyed the flapjacks on the counter and knew that one of those would most definitely enhance the appeal of hers, but do nothing positive for her figure, so she restrained herself. It was too unrestful at home to write there, now that Nan and Daisy had come to live with them. Before Nan had moved in Suze had had the kitchen to herself. It had provided the perfect ambience for her writing. Now she had to share it, and Nan was a real chatterbox. That was the trouble with old people, she thought, they didn't know how to edit their stories. They went on and on and on. Unimportant details, long boring meanderings. It made her really twitchy. As much as she would have preferred to be sitting in her own home right now, she was happy she didn't have to endure Nan's reminiscences about her youth, or her unsubtle hints that Suze should be doing something better with her time. And she disapproved of the hours she spent on the telephone to Batty (she disapproved of his name too), so it was better that she sat here in this café, where she could talk to Batty for as long as she liked.

She'd acquired eleven more followers on Instagram that morning. The post she'd put up the evening before, showing off the five little diamanté hoops she'd put in her ear, had clearly been a winner. She'd got five thousand likes and lots of comments. She'd make sure the shop where she'd bought them saw it, because they gave her a discount. Now she was writing an article for *Red Magazine* about how the hoop ear-ring was a classic that never died. Dress it up, dress it down, it was always chic. Easy article. She could do it off the top of her head, with a few references to celebrities, which she could quickly find online.

Suze enjoyed her job, even though it was shallow and unchallenging. But what was wrong with that if it made her happy? She loved fashion and beautiful things and writing about them was simple. There was very little effort required, which suited her, because she was intrinsically lazy. She liked the comfortable feeling of doing something familiar and knowing she was doing it well. She would have liked to have been a model, but although her face was pretty and photogenic, she hadn't had the figure for it. She was short and pear-shaped like her mother. She knew she had great hair and big almond-shaped eyes, the colour of topaz, with long black lashes, and she knew she had sex appeal and charisma too. Men fancied her and since her schooldays girls had always copied her. All the ingredients for a successful influencer, she figured. She just needed more followers. Like, *many* more; a few hundred thousand. But Rome wasn't built in a day and she'd only decided to do this eighteen months ago. The thing with social media was that you had to post all the time and the pictures had to be curated to make people want what you had. The truth was that none of them would want to live in a small cottage in an insignificant village in the middle of nowhere with Dennis and Marigold and Nan – and now Daisy too. But that was the *good* thing about social media, you only showed people what you wanted them to see.

She allowed her gaze to stray out of the window where it lingered, lost in the half-distance, somnolent and unfocused. It was in that moment of nothingness that Daisy's suggestion about writing a book popped into her mind. Suze rather fancied herself as a novelist. She could even see her imaginary book in the shop window. Yet before her fantasy carried her away, she reminded herself that she couldn't think of a single thing to write about. Not a thing. She sighed and turned her eyes back to the computer screen where her article about hoop earrings was nearly finished. No point dreaming about being a famous novelist when she didn't even have an idea.

The following Saturday Marigold drove into town with Suze and Daisy to do some Christmas shopping. It was drizzling. A thick layer of cloud hung low over the wet rooftops and chimney stacks and bedraggled seagulls squawked crossly as they bickered over the odd crusts they found in the bins. The place was busy. It seemed everyone had decided to do their shopping today. The pavements were glistening and full of rushing feet. Marigold thought the lights looked pretty, shining like gumdrops in all the shop windows. She smiled as she remembered the sweets she'd enjoyed as a child. She hadn't thought of gumdrops in sixty years!

They decided to split and regroup at midday, by the car, as they wanted to buy presents for each other. Marigold wandered up the street, past the town hall and the Bear Hotel, and browsed in the shop windows. Eventually, she bought a sweater for Nan and a scarf for Dennis. She enjoyed the festive feel of the town. There was a giant Christmas tree in the square, a gift from some town in France, but Marigold couldn't remember why. It was decorated with big colourful balls and tinsel. Marigold loved tinsel. She loved things that glittered. Santa Claus sat in a special red-and-white-striped tent and there was a queue of children and their parents waiting to visit him. Someone had dressed up a pair of donkeys to look like reindeer and attached them to a sleigh. How little things had changed over the years, she thought. She'd taken the girls here when they were small. Marigold stood there a while, smiling. This town was full of memories, and all of them golden. Not one bad one, she realized. Indeed, every corner inspired a recollection and she basked in the warm glow they gave her. Life was good. She'd been lucky.

It was nearly midday when Marigold noticed the clock on the church tower. How fast the morning had gone. She still needed to get a present for Tasha. Something small but thoughtful. She looked at her watch, hoping the one on the church was wrong, but they were in sync. She'd have to come back another time. She hurried off towards the car park; except she couldn't remember where it was.

She stopped and looked around. She tried to shift her mind into focus, but it was like trying to make out a form in thick fog. Nothing came. Nothing. A cold fear edged over her skin. She couldn't recall the car park. She couldn't even picture it. It was as if it had vanished – or as if it had never been there. The more she tried to conjure it out of her mind, the further it sank into oblivion. She stood there, in the middle of the pavement, as people hurried past her with their shopping bags and their sharp, purposeful expressions, and felt dreadfully alone.

'Mum?' Marigold blinked and Daisy's anxious face shifted into view. 'Mum, are you all right? You've gone very white.'

The relief at seeing her daughter gave her a jolt and she was yanked out of her stupor. Registering Daisy's worried face, she forced a smile. 'I'm fine. I've just taken a turn. Must be low blood sugar or something.'

Daisy examined her mother with concern. Marigold looked smaller, suddenly, and frail. Perhaps she *was* getting older, Daisy thought with a sense of regret, for she'd been abroad for so long she hadn't noticed. 'Come, let me take your bags. I won't look inside, I promise.' She linked her arm through her mother's and they started off down the street. They walked slowly, as if Marigold needed time to find her feet again. Daisy noticed that Marigold's hand was clenched into a tight fist. There was something about it that made Daisy feel uneasy.

As quickly as it had gone, the image of the car park returned. Marigold was overcome with relief. She knew exactly where it was. She saw it clearly, as she always had. She couldn't imagine how it could have vanished like that.

'Did you get everything, dear?' she asked, feeling brighter.

'Everything except something for Suze.'

'Oh, I got her a make–up bag full of lovely things. It comes in a box, as a set. I hope she'll like it.'

Daisy laughed. 'You know she will. She loves make-up.'

'I didn't get anything for Tasha, so I have to come back.'

'I'll come with you,' said Daisy, and Marigold almost cried with relief. What if it happened again? What if the car park vanished and *didn't* return? What then?

Marigold made an appointment to see the doctor. She had to wait a couple of weeks because there was a long waiting list with all the coughs and colds going round. She didn't tell her family because she didn't want to worry them – although not all of them would worry. Nan would say she was being ridiculous, that she shouldn't waste the doctor's time just because she was getting forgetful. Old people just *were* forgetful, she'd say, and then list all the times *she'd* forgotten things. Dennis would worry, not because of her forgetfulness, but because *she* was worried. That's the way he was. He hated seeing her upset and he'd insist on coming with her, which she didn't want. She wanted to see the doctor alone, so that if it was nothing, she wouldn't feel like a fool.

When the day arrived, she sat in the surgery waiting room, flicking through magazines, but not really reading any of them. The doctor was busy and appointments ran on, which meant that by the time Marigold's turn came she'd waited over an hour.

'I'm sorry to have kept you waiting,' said the doctor, who was very young, Marigold thought. She hadn't met him before. It had been years since she had seen a doctor. Up until now she had enjoyed very good health. 'I'm Dr Farah. What can I do for you?'

Marigold felt the colour warm her cheeks. She already felt foolish. The poor man was so busy and here she was coming to see him about such a silly thing. She took a breath. 'I was in town a couple of weeks ago and had a frightening moment where I forgot where I was.' The doctor tilted his head, listening carefully. 'I couldn't remember where I'd parked the car. I couldn't remember where the car park was. I couldn't visualize it. Yet I've lived here all my life.'

'Did you suffer any other symptoms?' he asked. 'Sickness, dizziness, shortness of breath, pain in your body?'

Marigold shook her head. 'No, it was just in my mind. A total blank.'

'How long did it last?'

'A few seconds, I suspect, but it felt much longer.'

He smiled. He had a kind smile, Marigold thought, and felt reassured. 'Horrible moments always feel longer, don't they. How old are you, Marigold?' He looked down at his records, but she answered him anyway.

'Sixty-six,' she said. 'I've become very forgetful too. Silly things, like forgetting where I've put things.'

Dr Farah took her blood pressure and asked questions about her history and her parents' histories. Then he sat back in his chair and took off his glasses, looking at her sympathetically with his dark brown eyes. 'I suspect you are simply getting older, Marigold,' he said.

Marigold hadn't realized how tense she had been until her shoulders dropped with relief. 'Is that all it is, do you think?'

'Absolutely. I'm afraid everything slows down as you age. Everyone ages at different speeds. Some are very lucky and remain lucid and others get a little foggy. But it's nothing to worry about. Do you take exercise?'

'Not really,' she confessed.

'I suggest you start. A brisk walk in the country air will do you a lot of good. Drink lots of water. Keep your mind active.'

'I've started doing Sudoku,' she told him proudly.

'That's good, Marigold. Very good.' He stood up, indicating that the appointment was over. 'If it gets worse and you have another frightening episode, please come back and see me. In the meantime, I hope you have a lovely Christmas.'

'I will now,' she said happily and walked out of his office with a spring in her step.

'Hey, Suze, are you asleep?'

'Well, if I was, I'm not now.'

'I need to tell you something.'

'That clearly can't wait until morning.'

'You know when we went into town to do our Christmas shopping?'

'What about it?'

'Mum took a funny turn.'

'She did?'

'Yes, I didn't tell you because I didn't want to worry you, but I have to tell someone.'

'Well, you're worrying me now, so thanks for that.'

Daisy could make out Suze's face through the darkness and saw that she was smiling. 'Look, I'm sure it's nothing, but it's been bothering me. She's been getting very forgetful.'

'She's old, Daisy!'

'She's not old. She's not even seventy and Nan is nearly ninety and has all her marbles.'

'Nan does nothing but sit around drinking tea, doing crossword puzzles and playing bridge with the few people she can tolerate. Mum's tired. She works hard. She takes on too much. She needs a rest.'

'When was the last time she had a holiday?'

'I can't remember. A long time ago, I think. If you're going to suggest we send her to the Caribbean, you'll have to pay for her yourself because I don't have any money.'

'And I don't have much,' said Daisy. 'But we could suggest she and Dad go away for a weekend somewhere. A country house hotel. Somewhere quiet, so she can have a rest.'

'It's not a bad idea.'

'I have enough for that.'

'Great, that's their Christmas present sorted.'

'I thought you said you'd done your Christmas shopping.'

Suze grinned, her teeth white in the blackness. 'I have now! Thanks, Daisy.'

Chapter 5

As Christmas approached, the snow melted, leaving the ground waterlogged and slippery, but Marigold still got up an hour earlier than usual to walk along the clifftops. She believed it was in her power to hold back the corrosive effects of time if she did as the doctor suggested. Exercise and Sudoku were going to be her weapons against memory loss. Her weapons against time; the only weapons she had.

It was always dark and cold when she set off up the path and she was always alone. By the time she had reached the top of the hill she was short of breath and hot, and the sun was a glowing coal rising slowly out of the eastern horizon. If she had known how magical that time of the morning was, up there by herself, she would have come sooner. The air was crisp and clean, the weedy smell of the ocean ripe and uplifting, the sound of seabirds waking to a new day enchanting. It was as if she had sneaked backstage and was witnessing the world preparing for the daily show. There was a stillness in spite of the motion of the waves and the gulls in flight, of the wind blowing off the water and the rising sun; a deep, eternal stillness that, in those moments of contemplation, Marigold felt inside herself. She took deep breaths. She filled her lungs and she felt her chest expand with gratitude for her life, for that is what beauty did to Marigold, it made her feel grateful.

She walked briskly along the path where she had walked so many times over the years. She wistfully recalled those times as the dawn broke and turned the sea pink and the light caught the edges of the clouds and turned them pink also, like candyfloss. And the candyfloss reminded her of the summer fair where her parents had taken her and her younger brother Patrick, as a treat. How sweet it had been on her tongue. Marigold relived the delight of those happy childhood outings, taking the time to dwell on each one because she had the time up there on the cliff path, as much as she wanted.

She relished this hour alone, without anyone making demands on her. She loved looking after her family, and yet she treasured the sense of freedom that being alone in nature gave her. She listened to the wind and the cries of seabirds, the roaring of the ocean and her own deep breaths, and it was as if she was being refilled, for when she returned home she was buoyant and bursting with energy and enthusiasm. She had even forgotten about her forgetfulness.

A week before Christmas she was in the shop listening to Eileen sharing the village gossip, when a ruggedly handsome man walked in. Marigold knew she'd seen him before, but she couldn't place him. Eileen stopped mid-sentence and stared. The young man walked up to the counter and smiled. It was the kind of smile that could launch a thousand ships, Marigold thought, even though she did not like the fashion for long hair and unshaven faces.

Eileen smiled up at him with all the charm she could muster. She barely reached his waist. 'Taran Sherwood,' she said. 'Haven't you grown up. I remember you when you were a boy,' she said. 'I'm Eileen Utley. And this is Marigold.'

Then Marigold remembered him as well. She also remembered what an obnoxious little boy he had been. 'Home for Christmas?' she asked.

'Yes, it's been a year since I was last home,' Taran replied and the slight intonation in his voice suggested a glamorous life across the Atlantic. He looked at her with eyes as green as aventurine and she was embarrassed that a woman like her could find a man of his age attractive.

'Your parents must be happy to see you,' said Eileen and her gaze intensified, searching for any sign of discord.

'I think so,' he replied.

Marigold sensed he did not want to be scrutinized. 'What can I do for you?' she asked.

'I've come to pick up the Christmas puddings for my mother.'

Marigold searched for any memory of a Christmas pudding but found nothing. Just a blank. A great big cavernous blank.

The door opened, the little bell tinkled, and their attention was diverted to Daisy in a scarlet coat and purple bobble hat, coming in with a happy smile on her face. She noticed Taran at once, but she was used to good-looking men, having lived in Italy, and simply acknowledged him with a breezy 'Hello'.

Taran turned back to Marigold. Daisy sensed her mother's anxiety. Her smile faltered. 'Mum, can I help?' she asked.

'I'm just trying to recall a pair of Christmas puddings that were ordered,' she said, beginning to search through papers beneath the counter with a trembling hand.

'You wrote it in your red book,' said Eileen helpfully.

'Did I?' said Marigold. She felt the ground spinning away from her and heard, in the distance, the sound of fingers drumming impatiently on the counter.

'I know all about them,' said Daisy, taking off her coat and hat and joining her mother. 'Leave it with me. Mum's had so many orders she's a little inundated. I'll get them to you this afternoon. How many were there?'

'Two,' said Taran, seeming eager to get going.

'And what's your address?'

'He's Sir Owen's son, Taran,' said Eileen, prompting her with a nod.

Daisy stopped writing and looked at him. 'How funny,' she said. 'We were at school together. I'm Daisy Fane.'

Taran did not remember Daisy. She could tell by the way he narrowed his eyes, searching for her in his past like her mother was searching for the Christmas pudding order in hers. 'Were we in the same year?' he asked.

'We were in the same class,' she replied. 'But it was a long time ago. I know where you live. I'll bring the puddings up later today.'

'Thanks,' he said. 'Mum is counting on them.'

'Of course she is,' said Daisy with a smile. 'They're the best.'

He left the shop and Marigold sank onto the stool.

'You wrote it in your notebook,' persisted Eileen. 'I saw you.'

Daisy found the red book and the order. 'It doesn't matter, Mum. We all forget things,' she said.

Marigold's eyes shone. 'What are we going to do? I can't make two Christmas puddings by five o'clock! It takes weeks to make a really good one.'

'I'll buy them and pass them off as our own,' said Daisy.

'I have a better idea,' said Eileen. 'Cedric Weatherby has made a whole batch. I'm sure he'll sell you two, if you ask him nicely.'

'I'll go now,' said Daisy, putting on her hat and coat again.

'Thank you,' said Marigold in a small voice.

'Taran's very handsome,' said Eileen with a mischievous grin. 'What do you think, Daisy?'

'Not my type,' Daisy replied briskly, leaving the shop.

'Then what is her type?' Eileen asked Marigold in surprise.

'I don't know,' said Marigold with a sigh. 'I don't think she's looking for anyone right now. She's still nursing a broken heart.'

Eileen grinned. 'If you ask me, Taran Sherwood could mend a heart broken to smithereens!' She sighed then shook her head dolefully. 'I don't think he and his father get on at all,' she continued. 'I've heard they have a difficult relationship. They're very different, you see. Sir Owen is a man for all seasons, a man who loves nature. Taran is a materialistic man. You can tell.' She inhaled through her nose. 'Still, he's a handsome devil, isn't he?'

Daisy knocked on Cedric Weatherby's front door, which was painted purple and adorned with an extravagant fir wreath. She heard a rustling and then an unbolting. The door opened a little and Cedric's face peeped through the crack. 'Hello, Mr Weatherby, my name is Daisy Fane, I'm Marigold and Dennis's daughter.'

Cedric's face relaxed and he opened the door wide. 'Ah, Marigold's daughter. The one who lives in Italy? How lovely. Do come in.' Daisy stepped into the hall and immediately noticed a fluffy honey-coloured cat staring at her from halfway up the stairs. She turned her attention to Cedric who was tall and a little stooped with a thick thatch of blond hair and a matching moustache. He wore a green-and-white shirt over a substantial paunch. He smelt strongly of lemon cologne to mask the smell of cigarettes, she thought, and cat. The house smelt *very* strongly of cat.

'What's your cat called?' Daisy asked.

'I have five ladies,' said Cedric proudly. 'This one is a Ragdoll called Jade. Her sister is Sapphire. Then I have three Siamese cats called Topaz, Ruby and Angel.'

'Angel? Doesn't that spoil the theme?'

Cedric's lips pursed in mock disgust. 'Angel does not deserve to be named after a jewel. I'm hoping that by calling her Angel she will grow into her name. Right now she should be called Queenie. But we can't have two of those living in the same house.' He laughed and Daisy laughed with him. 'And I don't want any competition.'

'I think Jade has a regal look.'

'They all do, darling. You know what they say? That dogs have owners and cats have staff. It's spot on, that is. I'm the servant, running around after five very demanding ladies. Anyway, what can I do for you, Daisy?'

'I have a peculiar request. Mum forgot to make two Christmas puddings for Lady Sherwood. She's very upset. She thinks she's losing her mind . . .'

'We all are, darling. As soon as you pass sixty, it starts to go. I forget things all the time. I'm terrible with names. I just call everyone darling and that avoids the problem altogether.'

'Well, Mum's a bit sensitive about it. So Eileen told me to come and ask you whether you had any I could buy from you. Apparently you make very good ones.'

Cedric put his hands on his hips. 'I don't hide my light under a bushel and I don't let other people praise my talents when I can shout about them myself. Yes, I am a gifted baker and I'll happily give you a couple.'

'You don't have to give them to me, because Lady Sherwood will pay for them.'

'Very well. Lady Sherwood can afford me. Come.'

Daisy followed him into the kitchen. It looked out over a wintry garden. Daisy was amused to see that Cedric fed birds too, just like her mother. His feeders hung on long metal sticks with hooks, like old-fashioned shepherd's lanterns, which were stuck into the grass. Little birds fluttered around them, busily scattering seeds onto the ground.

The kitchen was immaculately tidy and painted a bright blue with white marble worktops. A vase of red tulips placed in the middle of the round table looked a little incongruous there, seeing as it was December. The room smelt of freshly baked bread and cinnamon. 'I've been baking currant buns,' said Cedric, pointing to twelve buns cooling on the sideboard. 'Would you like one?'

'I always think of currant buns as an Easter treat.'

'Nothing is seasonal in my house, darling, except of course the Christmas puds. I have tulips in winter and holly in summer. I like what I like and I won't be dictated to by convention.'

'In that case, I'd love one, thank you.'

He lifted a bun off the cooling tray and popped it onto a plate. It was still warm. Daisy took a bite. The sweet, buttery taste melted on her tongue. 'Oh, this is delicious!' she gushed. 'You really are a wonderful baker!'

'Bless your heart,' said Cedric, putting his hand on his chest. 'You've made my day.'

Daisy laughed. 'If your Christmas puddings are as good as this, Lady Sherwood will be in heaven.'

'Oh, they are. They're my speciality. They take months of careful nurturing – and doses of brandy, every few days for weeks.' He disappeared into a store room and returned a moment later with two puddings, wrapped in newspaper.

'How many have you made?' Daisy asked, wishing she hadn't eaten her bun so quickly because now it was gone.

'Eight,' said Cedric.

'What are you going to do with the rest?'

'Give them to my friends. I've already given one to poor Dolly, who's very sad about her cat, and Jean who's on her own, poor love.'

'Yes, I heard about the cat.'

'Devastated, that's what she is, devastated.'

'I'm sure Mary is too,' said Daisy.

'Not as devastated as she should be. That dog is a menace.'

'He's very sweet, actually. I'm about to paint him.'

Cedric raised his eyebrows. 'You paint animals, do you?'

'Yes, I haven't done portraiture in years, so Bernie is being a guinea pig for me, as it were.'

'Well, if you discover you have talent, you can come and paint my ladies, and I'll give you all the currant buns you could wish for.'

Daisy smiled at the thought of a commission. 'I'd love that, Mr Weatherby.'

'Don't Mr Weatherby me! I'm Cedric.'

'Okay, Cedric. Thank you for the puddings, and the bun. We really owe you one.'

'You owe me nothing, darling.' He grinned. 'Daisy. You see, sometimes I do remember a name. Yours is very pretty, as are you. I hope some lovely young man is making you happy.'

Daisy blushed. 'A lovely man did make me happy, but sadly no longer.'

'The brute!' exclaimed Cedric dramatically. 'Stupid man! Anyone would be lucky to have you. You have a pretty smile. Now you tell your mother not to worry about forgetting things. She's not alone. I'd say half the village is more forgetful than she is.'

'I'll tell her. She'll be relieved to hear it.'

Cedric escorted her to the door. By now all the cats had gathered there in the hall. They watched her suspiciously, as cats do. 'And don't forget I'm at the top of the list when you turn out to be Cassius Marcellus Coolidge,' he said. 'I have five beautiful ladies ready to give you their best angles.'

When Daisy returned home triumphantly with the Christmas puddings she found her mother in the shop, serving customers with a smile and a little chat as she always did, yet the sparkle had gone out of her eyes. As soon as there was a lull, Daisy asked her if she was all right. 'I still don't know how I managed to forget,' said Marigold. 'It's so unlike me.'

'Mum, it's just a couple of Christmas puddings,' said Daisy.

'I wish it was, but it's more than that. I'm forgetting things every day. I feel like I'm navigating my way through a fog.'

'A fog? What kind of fog?'

'I don't know. Some days it's thick, other days it clears and I think I'm back to being myself again. Today, I feel quite well. But yesterday, I just wanted to go to bed and hide.' She looked at her daughter anxiously. 'Don't tell your father, will you? I don't want to worry him.'

'I won't tell anyone. Anyway, Cedric says he forgets things all the time.'

'I know, everyone says that. Perhaps I'm just not very good at coping with it.'

'He's given us two Christmas puddings and I'll drive them up this afternoon. No harm done. Lady Sherwood will be delighted. I'm sure his are just as good as yours.'

'You don't have to take them up for me. I can do it after I close.'

'No, I want you to put your feet up.' Daisy looked around. 'Where's Tasha?'

Marigold sighed. Tasha was trying her patience. 'She had to take her daughter to the doctor.'

'Okay, you have a break and I'll look after the shop. And by the way, Mary has chosen the pose for the picture from the photographs I took of Bernie and I think I know him well enough now to get started.'

'That's wonderful, dear,' said Marigold.

'I'm going to set my easel up in the sitting room, by the window. I need light and lots of it.'

'I'm sorry we don't have a room for you.'

'It's okay. I can work there. Perhaps one day, when I'm rich and famous, I'll rent a studio.'

'When you're rich and famous you'll be able to *buy* a studio.'

Daisy laughed. 'In the meantime it's either the sitting room or the bathroom.'

'Then I suggest you use the sitting room. Suze won't be so accommodating if you make her move all her stuff out of the bathroom as well as the bedroom.'

Later that afternoon Daisy drove up to Lady Sherwood's with the Christmas puddings. It was already dark and a thick mist was moving inland, rolling up the beaches and settling onto the fields. She thought of the fog in her mother's mind and wondered whether she should see a doctor.

The entrance to the Sherwoods' farm was an unimposing brown post-and-rail fence with an electric gate. Daisy rolled down her window and pressed the button on the intercom. A long while later, just when she was about to give up and turn the car round, a man's voice answered irritably. She gave her name and the gate duly opened, allowing her to motor onto a gravelled driveway and park in front of the big white house.

Sir Owen and Lady Sherwood were not ostentatious people. Sir Owen had been given his knighthood for his charity work but he wore it lightly. He was a community-minded man, involving himself in causes that mattered to the local people. He had tried very hard to prevent the supermarket from being built nearby, concerned that it would stifle small, independent shops like Marigold's, and fought off developers who wanted to build houses on his land. Sir Owen was a man who did not crave more wealth than he had. A more materialistic man would have happily sold out for the substantial money he was offered, but Sir Owen lived modestly, albeit well, and was content with what he had.

The house and farm, however, were impressive. Hector Sherwood, Sir Owen's father, had bought them just after the Second World War for five hundred pounds. With three thousand acres, which included woodland, there was plenty of land for Hector and his five daughters to ride on. Owen had not been very interested in horses, so when his father passed the farm on to him after his daughters had been successfully married off, the horses were sold and Taran was brought up walking the dogs rather than riding out with them. Owen hoped his son would love the countryside like he did, but Taran wanted to be an architect, not a farmer, and set his sights on Canada, where his mother was from. Owen could not understand why he wanted to live so far from home. What was wrong with being an architect in England? But Taran went to a Canadian university and ended up working for a prestigious firm in Toronto. Owen worried about leaving the farm to his son and considered changing his will and leaving it to his eldest nephew instead. It mattered very much to him that his home should remain in his family. It seemed not to matter to Taran at all.

Daisy got out of the car and went to the front door. Before she had time to ring the bell, it opened and Taran appeared, looking down at her with an air of impatience. 'I've got the puddings,' she said with a smile, attempting to lift his mood.

'Thanks,' said Taran, taking them. A couple of spaniels and a black Labrador rushed past his legs and began barking at the car. 'Bloody dogs!' he exclaimed. 'They're driving me nuts! They want to go for a walk, but it's too foggy. I can barely see beyond my own nose.' He frowned at Daisy. 'And you were okay driving up here?'

'I just drove slowly,' she said, watching the dogs sniffing her wheels and cocking their legs on the tyres. 'And I'll drive slowly back again.' She smiled in a breezy way that aroused Taran's curiosity. There was something about it that told him she wasn't very interested in him.

'I wouldn't drive back if I were you,' he said. 'Not right now, anyway. The fog is really thickening and that lane is precarious, even when it's clear.'

'Really, I'm fine. I've driven in Italy for years, this is nothing.' She made for the car.

Taran watched her go. 'You know, I *do* remember you from school,' he said, then chuckled. 'Didn't you have pigtails?'

Daisy turned round. 'I'm sure I didn't have pigtails.'

'Or plaits. They could have been plaits.'

She laughed. 'I think I'd prefer you didn't remember me at all!'

He shrugged. 'Sorry. It came to me later.' He whistled for the dogs. They chose not to hear him and trotted off into the garden, disappearing into the fog. 'Why don't you wait a little. Come in and have a coffee. I'd never forgive myself if you had an accident in the lane on account of Mother's Christmas puddings.' He flashed his megawatt smile.

Daisy laughed in that carefree way of hers, as if she hadn't noticed it. 'I hope you enjoy them,' she said, climbing into the car. Then she rolled down the window and waved. 'Happy Christmas.'

Taran watched her drive away. He had been alone in the house all day, wishing he was in Toronto. It would have been nice to have had the company of someone his age. Christmas promised to be grim with his father's enormous family, and he was counting the days until he could leave. Daisy would have been a welcome respite. He was a little put out that she hadn't taken up his offer. He made a fine cup of coffee.

He didn't remember her at school at all. He'd looked up his old class photograph in his parents' album and spotted her immediately in the front row. Round-faced, smiley, plaits or pigtails. They'd been in the same class until he'd left at eight to go to boarding school. However, *she* had remembered *him*, he thought, cheering up.

He whistled for the dogs and, when they finally appeared, he went back inside. He couldn't understand why she had declined his cup of coffee.

Chapter 6

Marigold kept the little notebook in her pocket and wrote everything down, even things she thought she would never forget, like where she'd hidden the Christmas presents. She noted every special order taken in the shop, Tasha's requests for time off, Nan's requests for biscuits, Dennis's mid-morning cup of coffee, which she liked to bring him when he was working in his shed, and all the little demands Suze made without realizing she was being demanding. Daisy demanded nothing, but Marigold wrote down a mid-morning cup of coffee for her too, which she took into the sitting room, because she didn't want her to feel overlooked. Her notebook was her lifeline in the fog that all too often drifted into her mind; the lifeline that no one knew she needed.

It felt good to be in control, to feel confident that she could hide her growing forgetfulness from her family with this very simple method. Every time she went to the loo she looked in her notebook, reassured that everything she needed to remember was in there. She hung a big calendar on the fridge in the kitchen and wrote things on that too: *Suze out for dinner with Batty. Batty dinner here. Take cottage pie out of freezer.* The good thing about living next door to the shop was that if she forgot to buy something, like cream to go with the apple tart, she could just nip next door and help herself. Her main concern was concealing her fears from her family. She did not want to worry them.

Marigold's family were very busy. Daisy was working hard at her easel in the sitting room. Marigold had seen the preliminary sketch of Bernie in charcoal and it was impressive. She'd always known her daughter had talent and it gave her pleasure to see her doing not only something she was good at but also something she loved. She sensed it was helping to heal her broken heart. Daisy didn't talk about Luca and she put on a good show when she was with people, but Marigold knew her well enough to know that beneath it all she was hurting and being creative helped soothe that hurt. In times of sorrow Dennis would withdraw into his shed, seeking solace in creativity, just as Daisy was doing now. Although Dennis was comforted by rock music and Daisy by the likes of Hans Zimmer, two very different styles but both equally therapeutic for the heart.

Dennis was still busy making Marigold's Christmas present. He was clearly pleased with it because he came in at the end of the day with a big smile on his face. He kissed her affectionately on the forehead, as he always did, but in the run-up to Christmas he held her a little longer and that meant a lot to Marigold. Perhaps he sensed her anxiety, or perhaps they were just appreciating each other more. She didn't know. Anyhow, she looked forward to her jigsaw. This year it mattered more, because it was going to exercise her brain.

Suze worked away in the café, writing pieces on fashion for magazines and local newspapers, and spent hours in town taking photographs for her Instagram account @Suze_ontrend. Batty seemed to have enough spare time in the day to talk to her endlessly on the phone, then when they met in the evenings, they still found something to talk about.

Nan didn't think that Daisy should stand so long at her easel. She said it would give her varicose veins when she was older. She thought Suze should do something more interesting than photographing the rings on her fingers or her cup of coffee for her social media accounts. She thought Dennis worked too hard and would likely suffer a heart attack if he didn't slow down. She said Tasha was lazy and without a work ethic and Eileen was a gossip, even though 'the old bat' started sentences with 'I'm not one to speak ill of people'. Even her son Patrick, who lived in Australia with his family, came in for criticism because he never flew to England, not even for Christmas, and this one could very well be her last. Nan sat in the kitchen, dipping chocolate biscuits into her tea and finding fault with everything. She found no fault with Marigold, however. She didn't realize how hard her daughter was working on hiding her forgetfulness and her fear, and making such a success of it.

At last Christmas arrived. The rain turned to snow and the puddles turned to ice and Nan said she wouldn't go to church unless Dennis drove her right up to the gate, because she really would slip and break her neck this time. So Dennis did as he was told and drove both Nan and Marigold while Suze and Daisy were happy to walk.

The lights of the church blazed through the falling snow as Daisy and Suze approached the church doors. They could hear Eileen's organ-playing floating out and smell the familiar scent of candle wax and Christmas. Daisy had always loved Christmas because it was the same every year. Marigold gave them both a stocking, just as she had done all through their childhood, leaving it on the end of the bed, where it lay heavy and full of promise. They had breakfast together in the kitchen, which Marigold had festooned with tinsel and shiny baubles, and opened their stockings with gasps of delight. They had all decorated the tree this year, with the same decorations they used every year, pulling them out of the box that was kept in the attic and reminiscing over where they had come from. Nan had said the baubles looked a little tired and wasn't it time they bought some new ones, but Suze and Daisy had insisted on everything staying the same and so stay the same it did.

Suze loved Christmas because of the presents. She loved presents more than anything. The big present-giving event was always after Christmas lunch, which Marigold cooked beautifully. She was very good at Christmas lunch. The turkey was always succulent, the roast potatoes crispy, the bread sauce and gravy delicious and the Christmas pudding juicy and full of five pence coins, which as children they had been eager to find. Nan said the coins should be bigger because it was easy to choke on a small five pence coin, but again, the girls had insisted that nothing change. Christmas was all about tradition and their family traditions were the most important of all.

The girls entered the church. It was crowded with not only the locals but also their families and friends who had come for Christmas. Candles flickered, the gold plates and candlesticks on the altar gleamed, the Christmas tree glittered with all the sparkly decorations the primary school children had made and the displays of holly, red berries and fir, which were arranged in each window, sparkled with battery-operated tea lights. Outside, the snow continued to fall. Inside, the atmosphere was festive and excited, because there is something very magical about a white Christmas.

Dennis was in the aisle, talking to Sir Owen. Daisy and Suze slipped past them, greeting Sir Owen politely and wishing him a Happy Christmas. Suze made it into the pew but Daisy was detained by a hand on her shoulder. She turned to see Taran, in a heavy coat and cashmere scarf, his hair swept off his forehead, his face darkened by stubble. 'Hi,' he said and smiled. 'I take it you got home okay the other day.'

'I did, thank you. Luckily no one was coming the other way.'

'Mother stayed with friends until it had lifted. She was there until eight.'

'I'm glad to hear it. I wouldn't want to have crashed into *her* on my way down the lane. That would have been embarrassing.'

His laugh was deep and croaky, like his voice, and she noticed how green his eyes were. 'Mind you, the snow is worse. It would have been more sensible to have skied here.'

'Yes, but you can't ski back up again.'

'That's true, but you always enjoy the downhill more if the uphill has been a challenge. It makes it more precious.'

Daisy was about to say that she wouldn't know, because she didn't ski, but she noticed people sitting down and a silence falling over the pews and realized it was time to join her family. She sensed Taran was a little regretful to end the conversation and was flattered. She remembered him being quite pleased with himself as a boy and assumed he still was. Handsome men, in her experience, had a sense of entitlement. If she ever managed to get over Luca she would avoid falling in love with a handsome man.

The carols brought tears to Marigold's eyes. Dennis took her hand. His was rough and calloused, the hand of a carpenter. Hers felt comfortable there, in that warm, familiar place. Marigold was relieved that he was here to look after her. More than any other year the carols made her nostalgic for the past, for the time before fear had slipped in and cast a shadow over her present. Before anxiety had cast an even greater shadow over her future. She felt more appreciative of her family than ever. More appreciative of life. Of today, Christmas, and the many blessings God had given her. She wanted to hold on to it, this precious day.

She looked around at the familiar faces of people she had known for years. There was her friend Beryl, who caught her eye and smiled. Eileen at the organ. Recently widowed Jean Miller, who gave Marigold a little wave. She noticed Cedric Weatherby, who noticed her too and winked. She smiled with gratitude for the Christmas puddings he had given her and he smiled back, dapper in a yellow bow tie and orange waistcoat. She saw their neighbours, John and Susan Glenn, and poor Dolly Nesbit. And so many other friends besides. Marigold was grateful for all of them on this Christmas Day, which somehow didn't feel like any of the others. It felt different, as if she were watching it play out from a distance. Only Dennis's hand gave her a sense of being fully present. A hand anchoring her to the moment as the fog in her mind grew thicker.

After the service they went into the hall for Christmas drinks. Marigold usually let Dennis wander off on his own to talk to people, but today she stuck beside him. She patted her handbag, thankful that she hadn't left it in the pew. She wasn't that bad, she reassured herself. Surely she was just being paranoid.

Mary Hanson weaved through the crowd to talk to her, holding a plastic cup of mulled wine. She wore a knitted hat, which was meant to look like a plum pudding, and a wide smile. 'Ah, there you are, Marigold. Goodness, doesn't Daisy draw well. She's shown me her early sketch and it's caught my darling Bernie to perfection. She's so clever.'

'That's nice to hear. She's been working very hard,' said Marigold. 'There's barely enough room in the house for all of us, but she manages to find a little space of her own somehow.'

A man appeared and stood next to Mary. 'Happy Christmas,' he said to Marigold.

Marigold put out her hand and smiled. 'Happy Christmas.'

The man looked at her hand, then at Mary, and they both laughed. 'That's very formal of you, Marigold,' he said. Marigold felt the ground spin away from her. The way he said her name indicated that he knew her, but she couldn't for the life of her recall who he was.

'Silly of me,' she mumbled. 'Habit, I suppose. My mind is on the turkey.'

'Of course,' the man agreed. 'Mary put ours in at eight this morning.'

'It must be a very big one,' said Marigold.

'It's enormous,' said Mary. 'But we have Brian's sister and her family coming for lunch.'

Ah, Marigold thought. *Brian. Of course. Brian is Mary's husband.* How could she have forgotten that? She felt her face flush with embarrassment that she had put out her hand as if she had never met him before. Then came the cold, prickly sensation, creeping across her skin. The icy damp fear. The dizziness. The sense of helplessness. 'Excuse me,' she said. 'I think I need to sit down.'

Dennis sensed his wife wilting beside him and took her hand. 'Are you all right, Goldie?'

'I feel a little light-headed.'

'Not too much mulled wine?'

'I haven't had any.'

'Come, let me find you a chair and I'll get you some. You're probably just hungry.' He led her to a chair at the edge of the room. She sank into it with a moan. Then he left her a moment to fetch her a drink.

'Are you all right, Marigold?' It was Beryl. She pulled up a chair and sat down, resting her walking stick against the wall. 'There, that's better. My legs are aching after standing for all those carols. Some of them are much too long, don't you think? People of our age don't want to be on our feet for hours.'

'I agree,' said Marigold, who didn't really mind the standing.

'I've got a house full of people, but I left Martin in charge. As you know, he doesn't like church.'

'Very convenient having Martin at home to look after the lunch.'

'Not that he can be trusted. He's hopeless in the kitchen. But with my hip I can't do it all.' Beryl carried on, telling Marigold about her son who had promised to help and her grandchildren, who she hoped would not make a mess of the house. All the while Beryl chatted Marigold tried to steady her pounding heart. All her joy at the magic of Christmas had died, leaving nothing but an aching terror. How could she have forgotten who Brian was? Brian, whom she had known for twenty years.

'Here you are, Goldie,' said Dennis, handing her a cup of mulled wine. Marigold took a large gulp and waited impatiently for it to reach her stomach and calm her nerves. She took another. Dennis looked down at her with a concerned expression. 'Stay here a minute. I'll be back.'

'I know how you feel,' said Beryl.

'You do?' said Marigold, surprised. Did anyone know how she felt?

'Christmas is tiring. To think of all this fuss just for a couple of days.'

Dennis waded through the room in search of Daisy and Suze. He found Daisy talking to Taran. 'Hello, Taran,' he said. 'Might I have a word with Daisy?'

The light in Taran's eyes dimmed with disappointment. 'Of course, no problem.' He moved away reluctantly.

'Daisy, I need you and Suze to help Mum at lunch today,' said Dennis. 'I don't think she's feeling very well.'

'I don't think she's felt well for a while,' Daisy replied. 'She needs a rest, Dad. She works too hard.'

'You're right, she does. I wonder whether she'd agree to have someone else help her in the shop.'

'You'd have to be very careful how you worded that. She's very proud. She thinks she can do it all. But she's not getting any younger.'

'And Tasha is very unreliable.'

Suze appeared. 'Shall we go home? I'm bored.'

'Yes, time to go home. I'll go and get your mother,' said Dennis.

'Where's the Grinch?' said Suze with a grin.

Daisy laughed and pointed. 'Over there.' Nan was deep in conversation with a group of people neither of them knew.

'Being her usual chirpy self, I see, wishing everyone a miserable Christmas. She'd find fault with an angel,' said Suze. 'Too good. Too holy. Not enough of a sense of humour.'

'Shall *you* extricate her, or shall I?' Daisy asked.

Suze lowered her voice. 'I think there's someone who wants to talk to you.'

Daisy raised her eyes and saw that Taran was hovering nearby. She found it curious that he should want to speak to her, but then there were very few people their age in the hall. Suze left to go and rescue the poor visitors before Nan had ruined their Christmas cheer and Daisy hesitated a moment, unsure whether to follow her, or wait for Taran. She decided to do neither and made to leave. She'd meet her parents, Suze and Nan by the door.

'Hey, Daisy.' It was Taran.

'I've got to go,' she said.

'Sure. Listen. Have a good Christmas.'

'You too.'

'I'm sure we will. Those Christmas puddings look delicious.'

'Don't choke on the coins.' He frowned. 'My grandmother always worries that we'll choke on the five pence coins,' Daisy explained. 'Mum always puts them in the mixture.'

'I see. I'll make sure everyone knows.'

She turned to go.

'Hey, Daisy, can I have your number? You know, to keep in touch. I know it's been, what, over twenty years since school, but it would be nice to see a friend when I come home. I'm usually stuck with the parents and *bored*!' He pulled a face.

Daisy laughed. 'Give me your phone and I'll put it in for you.'

He handed it to her. She typed in her name and number and handed it back. 'Let me know that no one's choked on a five pence piece, won't you?'

He held up his phone. 'Gotcha.'

She smiled and threaded her way through the throng to the door, where Suze was waiting for her. 'Dad has driven Mum and Nan home.'

'Was Mum all right?'

Suze looked surprised. 'Yes. Why, was something wrong?'

'No, nothing. I think she's just tired.'

'Well, she's going to love our Christmas present, isn't she?'

Daisy sighed. '*Our* Christmas present, which *I'm* paying for.'

'I don't have any money,' Suze protested. 'I'm as poor as a church mouse.'

'Who manages to buy new clothes all the time.'

'Because I sell my old ones. It's my job.'

'Sure it is. Come on. Let's hurry home. Dad wants us to help Mum with the lunch.'

'Oooh lunch,' gushed Suze. 'Then presents. I do love presents.'

Marigold was surprised when Daisy and Suze began to buzz around the kitchen being helpful. Suze laid the table while Daisy cooked the vegetables. Dennis made sure everyone had a glass of wine while Nan sat by the fire in the sitting room, doing the crossword. 'Agree silently, three letters,' she shouted into the kitchen.

'Nod,' Marigold shouted back, without hesitation.

'Oh, I knew that,' mumbled Nan to herself.

Marigold felt good for having known the answer and so quickly too. On the wave of feeling good, she decided that she could enjoy Christmas with her family, as she always did. Now wasn't the time to be self-indulgent. She wasn't sick, she told herself firmly, she was just getting older, like the doctor said.

Thanks to her little notebook she hadn't forgotten anything. The turkey was just as delicious as it always was, the Christmas pudding, which she had bought at the local farm shop (because not only had she forgotten to make two for Lady Sherwood, she had also forgotten to make one for herself), was very good in spite of not containing any coins and Nan was relieved because, as she told them for the hundredth time, someone could choke and die on one of those pieces! It was an enormous relief to Marigold that she hadn't forgotten anything important. She could dismiss the fog in her head as tiredness because, besides the momentary lapse in memory in the church hall, today had gone exceedingly well.

After lunch Patrick called from Australia. He spoke at length to Nan. When she put down the phone she had the beatific expression of a congregant who has just taken holy communion. 'What a good boy he is calling his mother on Christmas Day,' she said. 'The months go by without a squeak and then he calls on Christmas Day.' She beamed a radiant smile. 'They toasted us over lunch, you know. They all raised their glasses. Isn't that nice? So like Patrick to be so thoughtful.' Marigold caught Dennis's eye. Patrick was anything but thoughtful. He had always had the charm of the devil. It amazed Marigold that in one phone call all the hurt he had inflicted on his mother during a year of no contact was swiftly forgotten, and like the Prodigal Son he was forgiven and even applauded.

They went into the sitting room to open the presents. The tree sparkled with multicoloured fairy lights and tinsel, and beneath it the gifts were arranged around the base with ribbon and wrapping like a magical scene on a Christmas card. Marigold settled into the sofa beside her mother, glass of wine in hand, yellow paper hat from the cracker she'd pulled on her head, and allowed a dizzy happiness to spread through her. *This could not be more perfect*, she thought, running her gaze over the flushed faces of her two daughters, husband and mother. 'I'm so pleased you've come home,' she said to Daisy. 'I mean, to stay, not just for Christmas. We're a family again, aren't we?'

'We are, Mum,' said Daisy. 'I'm happy I'm home too. I'm grateful that you and Dad are here to catch me when I fall.'

Dennis patted Daisy on the shoulder and went to sit in the armchair. 'We always will be,' he said.

'Shall we open the presents now?' asked Suze, heading for the tree. 'Daisy, this is from me to you.' She handed Daisy a small package.

'Thanks, Suze.' Daisy pulled open the paper to find a pair of earrings. 'Oh, they're so pretty. Thank you!' She smiled at her sister. 'You have such great taste, Suze.'

'Wait!' Suze exclaimed as Daisy got up to find a present for Nan. 'I need to photograph you with the earrings.'

'Oh, really! Do we have to do that now?' said Daisy, mildly irritated that Suze had to post a minute-by-minute account of her day on social media.

'We really do,' said Suze.

Nan was pleased with her sweater from Marigold, Suze with her make-up. Dennis had bought Daisy a box of Sakura Cray-Pas oil pastels. 'Oh, Dad, they're perfect!' she enthused in delight, running her fingers over the tidy row of twenty-four drawing sticks.

'Only the best for our artist,' he replied. 'They're top quality pastels, they are.' For Suze he had made a wooden desk tidy with a special slot to hold her iPad.

'You think of everything, Dad,' she exclaimed happily, then returned to the tree to find more gifts.

Dennis got up and poured more wine. Nan had already had too much. 'Well, Dennis. Where's your gift to Marigold?' she said, slurring her words. 'We're all waiting, aren't we, Marigold?'

Dennis beamed and went to the tree. He pulled out a box wrapped in red-and-gold paper and tied with a gold bow. 'Here you are, Goldie,' he said, handing it to her with a broad smile.

'Oh Dennis. You never disappoint, do you?' said Marigold happily.

'I think you'll like this one.'

'I'm sure I will.' She carefully untied the bow and unwrapped the paper so that she could recycle them next year, and lifted out a wooden box. 'There's no picture,' she said, running her fingertips over the lid.

'Over a hundred pieces, Goldie, and no picture.'

Marigold grinned. 'A big challenge then!'

'The biggest you've ever had.'

She lifted the lid. 'Aren't the pieces small,' she murmured, picking one up and looking at it closely. 'It must have taken you weeks. It's wonderful, Dennis. Thank you.'

Dennis bent down and kissed her on the forehead. 'Happy Christmas, Goldie.'

Suze held out an envelope. 'And this is from me and Daisy.'

'What's this then?' asked Dennis, looking from one daughter to the other.

'Open it,' said Suze, wriggling with excitement. 'You're going to love it!'

Marigold frowned at Daisy. 'What have you two been plotting?'

'You open it, Goldie,' said Dennis.

Marigold peeled open the envelope and pulled out the letter. Both she and Dennis read it together. 'A weekend away in Cornwall?' said Marigold in surprise.

'Just the two of us?' said Dennis. He put his big hand on Marigold's shoulder. 'Just the two of us, eh? Like a honeymoon.'

'Who will man the shop?' asked Marigold anxiously.

'Daisy will,' said Suze. 'We've got it all planned. You just have to pick your weekend. We've found a gorgeous hotel by the sea. Spring will be the nicest time. May, perhaps? We thought you'd like a rest, Mum.'

Marigold's eyes filled with tears. 'Oh, you really are both so very sweet.'

Daisy got up to embrace her. 'We love you, Mum.' She held on to her for an extended moment, sensing her mother's fragility.

'Yeah, we do,' Suze agreed. 'We love you both. You too, Dad.'

There was a pause as the four of them waited for the inevitable dry remark from Nan. But none came. They turned to her in surprise. The old lady had fallen asleep on the sofa, clad in her new sweater.

'I hope she's not dead,' said Suze with a grin.

'Oh, Suze! You're dreadful!' gasped Daisy.

Marigold was laughing. Big tears rolling down her cheeks. 'This has been the best Christmas ever,' she said. 'We're all together and it's a white Christmas as well. I couldn't ask for more, could I? I really couldn't.' And she put down her wine glass and leant her head back against the cushions. 'I think I'll just close my eyes for a moment,' she said. 'I'll start the puzzle tomorrow. It'll exercise my brain. Stop me forgetting things. Thank you, Dennis. Thank you, girls. The best Christmas ever.' And she went to sleep.

Chapter 7

Daisy missed Luca so much that sometimes the ache in her heart was intolerable. She thought of him every morning on waking and every evening on going to bed. She missed his shaggy head on the pillow next to hers and the sound of him breathing deeply as he slept. She missed his chaos, the way he never tidied up after himself, the way he left books and magazines and papers all over the furniture so there was barely any space to sit down. She even missed the smell of his cigarettes, which he had never even tried to give up in spite of her endless nagging. She thought of him over the Christmas period and wondered whether he was missing her too. Whether he was even thinking of her. Regretting perhaps that he had asked her, 'Isn't my love enough for you?' Regretting perhaps that he had not understood that his love couldn't possibly be enough for a woman who yearned for a child. Motherhood was not an outlandish demand and yet he had accused her of being selfish. The truth was they were both selfish and neither was willing to back down. Luca had never wanted to get married, either. He had made that perfectly clear when they had first met. His own parents had divorced and his childhood had been very unhappy. He did not want that for himself and he did not want to bring a child into the world. He didn't want to be committed in that way. Marriage and children, he had told her, would pin him down and make him less, not more. Daisy was angry with herself for not having faced sooner what she had known deep down inside for a long time. Why had she wasted years hoping that they would, in the end, settle down and have a family like everyone else? Why had her romantic heart overruled her head, which knew very well how things really were?

And her romantic heart yearned for him still with every injured fibre of it. Instead of focusing on the arguments, of which there were many for Luca was a headstrong, passionate character who believed that he was always in the right and, by virtue of his sex, should have the final say, she recalled the laughter. The running jokes, the affectionate teasing, the fun. She chose to overlook his possessiveness – the way he grew angry if she innocently flirted with other men – even though *he* flirted with every woman who caught his eye. She recalled only the love.

The idea of loving again was terrifying. She wasn't sure she'd ever feel for another man the way she felt for Luca. She wasn't sure she had it in her to love like that again. She'd spent all her energy on him and he'd left her feeling bruised and bleeding and spent. Her body was numb too. She couldn't imagine making love to somebody else. Being held by another man's arms, kissed by another man's lips; she just couldn't envisage 'another man' at all. Had she made a mistake in leaving Luca? Would she end up an old spinster with no one to love her? Might she never have children and wish she'd found enough fulfilment in loving Luca alone? She didn't know the answers, but she knew she had to try to move on.

The day after Christmas Taran texted to tell her that no one had choked on the coins in the Christmas pudding – because

there hadn't been any. There had, however, been a little plastic
Santa Claus and five plastic elves, in each pudding, which he
had thought hilarious. Daisy gasped with embarrassment, but
she couldn't help laughing too. She decided not to tell her
mother, because she'd be horrified. Lady Sherwood might
not have found it as amusing as her son. Plastic Santa Clauses
and elves were incredibly tacky. There followed a little banter,
witty texts going back and forth, and then Taran invited her
for a drink in the pub. She declined, however, claiming that
she was busy with her family. The texts stopped after that.
Daisy sensed he was offended, but she didn't feel bad; it was
better to be honest and not mislead him.

After New Year she threw herself into her work. She tied
her unruly hair into a high ponytail, rolled up the sleeves of
one of her father's old shirts and put on the playlist she had
made especially. She decided to try the pastels her father had
given her for Christmas. She hadn't used that medium in a
long time, but no sooner had she begun to draw than she
discovered how smooth and easy they were to apply. It wasn't
long before she realized, to her intense satisfaction, that she
had succeeded in capturing Bernie's spirit. It shone through
the eyes. There was life in them that couldn't be found in photographs. Something beyond what the camera could capture.
He stared out at her, as if he were really looking at her, and
seeing her, and when she moved, his tender gaze followed her.
She had pinned the photographs to the top of the easel, but
he lived more vividly in her memory, not just in the way he
looked but in his nature. She had got to know the very essence
of him, and it was this which she had transferred onto the grey
paper most beautifully. She stood back and admired her work.
She had done it, she had *really* done it. She had brought Bernie
to life in pastels. After the eyes, the rest was easy and swift.

Mary was thrilled. 'My goodness, you can draw, can't you?' she exclaimed when Daisy invited her round to see it. She was astonished that Daisy was so talented, and delighted that she had got a beautiful portrait of her beloved dog, for free.

Dennis and Marigold were impressed as well. 'I always knew you were an artist,' said Dennis, eyes gleaming with pride.

'I'm so pleased you're giving it a go,' said Marigold. 'The important thing is to spend your life doing something you love, that's what Grandad would say.'

Nan pursed her lips. 'It's all very well doing something you love,' she said. 'But you can't live off air, Daisy. Few are lucky enough to do something they love *and* bring home the bacon. Grandad would have been happy anywhere, that's just the way he was. He made the best of everything. A wonderful attitude to have. Take a leaf out of his book and you'll discover that doing a proper job isn't the end of the world.'

Daisy took the picture to the framer's in town because she didn't want the wrong frame to cheapen it. She chose an expensive one, but it was worth it. The portrait looked stunning. Other people would see it and perhaps commission her to draw their animals. She wondered how much she should charge. Being an amateur, she knew she couldn't ask for more than a few hundred pounds at the most.

Mary was so happy with the picture that she allowed Daisy to hang it in the village hall so that everyone could admire it. Daisy knew one person who would *not* be admiring it! However, she hadn't anticipated it being seen by Lady Sherwood. As chairwoman of the Parish Council, Lady Sherwood chaired a monthly meeting there, and it was during the January meeting, while everyone helped themselves to tea and coffee, that she spotted it hanging on the wall above the piano.

'What a lovely painting,' she said, getting up with her teacup and saucer to take a closer look.

'It's Mary Hanson's dog, Bernie,' Julia Cobbold told her, keen to be helpful. 'And it's oil pastels, I believe, not paint.'

'It's very good. Who did it?'

'Daisy Fane.'

'Marigold's daughter?'

'Yes, that's the one. She's been living in Italy, but now she's back. A love affair that turned sour, I believe. I imagine she must be very sad. She's a wonderful artist, isn't she?'

'Yes, what a surprise. She really is awfully good.' Lady Sherwood thought a while, her eyebrows knitted, a look of concentration on her face. 'I wonder whether she'd draw my dogs,' she said at last.

'I'm sure she would,' Julia replied, thinking that, if Daisy Fane was good enough for Lady Sherwood, *she* might commission her to draw her terrier.

Marigold was in the sitting room at the long table which was set up especially for her jigsaw puzzles. It was too big for the cramped room now that Daisy had put her easel in front of the other window, and Nan was sure to complain that there was nowhere to go for some peace, except her bedroom, but there simply wasn't another corner of the house large enough to accommodate a jigsaw puzzle of one hundred pieces.

It was a Sunday morning and unusually quiet. Marigold had been for her morning walk and Dennis had taken Nan to church. Suze was spending the weekend with Batty at his parents' house and Daisy had been invited up to the Sherwoods' farm to meet their dogs, whom Lady Sherwood wanted Daisy to draw. It was a crisp winter day. The sky was as pale as watercolour and the sun low, shining through the latticework of branches silhouetted prettily against it. Marigold was momentarily distracted by the birds who settled into her garden to feed. Blackbirds and thrushes mostly, and the cheerful little robin who wasn't at all intimidated by the bigger birds. She smiled as she watched them, knowing that she could spend all day here at the window, absorbed in their coming and going, and not notice the passing of time.

After a while she turned her attention to the jigsaw. She was good at puzzles and the thought of the challenge ahead gave her a frisson of pleasure. She began by drawing out the straight-sided pieces. This took some time. She had to put on her glasses to really study the colours and pictures and try to match them. She concentrated hard, aware that she was exercising her brain. Certain that, with every piece she connected to another, she was somehow reinforcing the connections there, staving off its corrosion, defying time. She felt triumphant as little by little the outside edge of the picture took shape. The top was sky, the bottom snow. It was surely a winter scene. Dennis knew how much snow enthralled her, and she was delighted now by the thought of her husband taking such trouble with her present.

It wasn't long before she felt thirsty. She went into the kitchen and boiled the kettle. It was cold outside, which made a cup of tea all the more rewarding. The first sip was always the best. She closed her eyes a moment and savoured it. Then she sat at the table, put on her specs and began to read the newspapers.

Dennis and Nan brought in a gust of chilly wind as they opened the front door and stepped into the hall. It raced down the corridor and into the kitchen where Marigold was reading the papers, making her shiver. 'It's bitter out there,' said Nan, bustling into the kitchen. 'I'm not going out again today. I don't want to catch a cold, not at my age. It soon turns to pneumonia, you know. My dear friend Teddy Hope died of pneumonia simply because he insisted on popping to the corner shop in cold weather to buy cigarettes.'

'It might have had something to do with the cigarettes, Nan,' said Dennis.

Marigold looked up from the papers.

'How's that puzzle going?' Dennis asked.

She frowned. *The puzzle!* She'd totally forgotten she'd been doing it. She pictured herself coming in from the sitting room to make tea and then sitting down at the table to read the newspapers. 'I've started,' she said, masking her concern with a smile. 'It's a winter scene,' she added, just to reassure herself that she remembered. 'I got distracted by the papers.' Easy to do. Everyone got distracted, didn't they? It didn't mean anything.

Daisy followed Lady Sherwood into the house. Lady Sherwood was wearing a pair of muted green moleskin trousers and a Fair Isle sweater with the white collar of her shirt sticking up stiffly at her neck. She looked very together, exuding an air of serenity, as if she was never hassled or rushed but glided through life at an even pace. The dogs scampered around Daisy's legs, tails wagging with the excitement of having a visitor, and Lady Sherwood spoke to them in a calm and patient voice, which they ignored. 'Now let's not make a fuss. Daisy's not the first visitor who's come to the house, is she? So let's be polite and not let ourselves down, shall we?'

'They're beautiful dogs,' said Daisy.

'They are, aren't they,' Lady Sherwood agreed. 'Though

Mordy is a terror, running off to the village at every opportunity. He's the Labrador. Very randy, I'm afraid.'

Daisy laughed. She didn't think elegant women like Lady
Sherwood made remarks like that.

The drawing room was big and square with tall windows
and sumptuous heavy curtains that framed them from the ceiling to the floor. There were paintings on faded silk walls and
the fabric on the sofas and chairs was faded too, from the sunshine that flooded into the room, no doubt, and age. It looked
like a room that hadn't been decorated all at once, but layered
over the years with knick-knacks, photographs in frames,
coffee table books and Persian rugs. There was a baby grand
piano in the corner, its top cluttered with family photographs,
and a tasselled lamp that glowed warmly. Lady Sherwood was
clearly a woman of good taste, but also frugality, it seemed, for
there was nothing precious or contrived about the room and
everything looked a little shabby. A fire glowed hospitably in
the grate. Lady Sherwood offered Daisy a chair.

'Thank you for coming to see me,' she said, sitting on the
sofa opposite. The dogs settled down around her, the Labrador
making himself comfortable on the stool in the middle of
the room as if it had been put there especially for him. 'I was
very impressed with the drawing you did of Mary's dog. You
captured him beautifully,' she said. 'I'd love you to draw mine.
All three of them. Can you do that, do you think?'

Daisy noticed that Lady Sherwood had the same green eyes
as her son. They were a rare shade of bluey-green and very
expressive. 'I'd love to draw them in pastels,' she said. 'As I
did with Bernie.'

'Ah, pastels, was it? Very effective.'

'Thank you. I like to work with pastels. I start with charcoal
and then move on to coloured chalks.'

'Well, whatever it is you do, you do it extremely well. How do we proceed?'

'I take photographs of the dogs and spend time with them, so I can get to know them. I need to get a good sense of their personalities. They're all so individual and I want their characters to shine out of the paper.'

Lady Sherwood smiled then, a wide and girlish smile. 'Oh, that's wonderful. They really are very individual. Mordy is mischievous, although he's now eleven years old, Archie is a little shy, and Bendico, who's Archie's brother, is very strong and determined and a bit overenthusiastic. I'd love you to get to know them. I know they'd love that too.' She patted one of the spaniels at her feet. 'Won't you, Archie? You'll love to get to know Daisy. They'll do anything for attention,' she added with a grin.

Daisy noticed how Lady Sherwood became softer and less formidable as she talked about her dogs, so she decided to ask her more questions. Lady Sherwood got up and took a big album down from a glass-fronted bookcase. 'You must see them as puppies,' she enthused. 'They were incredibly sweet. Come and sit beside me, then we can look at them together.'

Daisy did as she was told and Lady Sherwood laid the album across their knees and proceeded to make her way through it, page by page. There were lots of photographs of dogs, and of a younger Taran too. 'You know my son, don't you?' said Lady Sherwood.

'Not really. We were at school together when we were little, but I only met him properly this Christmas.'

'He lives in Toronto now. You see, I'm from there so it's logical that he should feel a connection with the place. I still have family there and he's close to his cousins. I think he finds England very dull.' She gave a little shake of the head. 'He hasn't really given it a chance. That's the trouble. Still, as long as he's happy, I suppose. There! Isn't that a delicious photograph of Mordy?' She lingered on it for a long time. 'What a sweet puppy he was!' she said quietly and Daisy wondered whether the dogs had filled Taran's place somehow.

They were just finishing the second album when Sir Owen walked in. His face was ruddy as if he spent most of his time outdoors, or drinking port, and his stomach was a little round beneath his orange sweater. 'Ah, Daisy,' he said, smiling genially.

Lady Sherwood lifted the book off her knee so that Daisy could stand up and shake his hand. 'Is Celia boring you with photographs of the dogs?'

Lady Sherwood smiled indulgently.

'Not boring me, Sir Owen,' said Daisy. 'They're lovely photographs. And they're lovely dogs. I'm looking forward to drawing them.'

He swept his eyes around the room. 'We'll have to find somewhere suitable to hang it.'

'Won't it be splendid to have a portrait of the dogs,' said Lady Sherwood.

Sir Owen made a face. 'She never wanted to have Taran painted, or me, but the dogs. Well, that's another matter.'

'Taran would never have sat still and besides, he never did anything we wanted him to. And you don't have the time or the patience, Owen.'

'I haven't painted people for a long time,' said Daisy.

'Just as well,' said Sir Owen. 'I'm not certain I'd want a portrait of my son following me around the room with his eyes full of rebuke! Can I get you something to drink?'

'No, thank you. I think I'd better be getting home. Mum will be cooking lunch and I'd like to help her.'

Lady Sherwood looked at her and her face softened. 'You *are* good,' she said in a voice full of wonder.

'I'm not sure I do enough, actually. I've just come home from six years in Italy and all I've done is take over the sitting room with my easel.'

'You need a studio,' said Sir Owen.

'One day, when I've saved enough money, perhaps I'll rent somewhere.'

'Speaking of money,' said Lady Sherwood. 'I haven't asked you how much you charge.'

Daisy had dreaded this question. She hated talking about money. It was awkward and she really wasn't able to quantify her value. 'Well, for three dogs, I'd ask for five hundred.'

'Grand?' said Lady Sherwood, going a little red.

'No, pounds,' Daisy corrected her.

Lady Sherwood looked surprised. Daisy wasn't sure if she'd asked for too much. She held her breath. Lady Sherwood looked at her husband. Sir Owen hesitated a second. Then he smiled and gave a nod.

'Done. And if you need a studio we'd be very happy to lend you the barn.'

'Yes, very happy,' Lady Sherwood agreed. 'I'll show it to you when you come and play with the dogs.'

'May I come tomorrow?'

'Of course. I'll be here and if I'm not, my housekeeper will look after you. She's called Sylvia.'

'You have a beautiful home,' said Daisy, patting the dogs who got up as they made to leave the room.

'Thank you,' said Lady Sherwood, pleased. 'It's a bit of a mismatch, but it seems to work.'

'Do you play the piano?' Daisy asked as she walked past it.

'I used to. I don't now. It's been too long. Taran did when

he was young. He was quite good, but I don't think he's played in years, either.'

'Waste of a good piano,' grumbled Sir Owen. 'It takes up a lot of room there, doing nothing.'

'I think it looks pretty,' said Daisy.

'You don't play, do you?' he asked hopefully.

'Sadly not.'

'Then it will continue to be a useless but pretty ornament.'

The dogs followed Daisy into the driveway. Sir Owen and Lady Sherwood stood on the doorstep and waved her off, calling back the dogs as they revved up to follow her. Daisy glanced at them in the rear-view mirror and thought how nice they were and how welcome they had made her feel. She hadn't expected that. She hoped she hadn't asked for too much money.

'Five hundred pounds?' Sir Owen exclaimed to his wife.

'I know, ridiculous,' she agreed.

'She'll charge five times that much when she realizes how good she is.'

'I suppose she will. Isn't it lucky then that we've discovered her before she becomes famous.'

Sir Owen laughed. 'Very lucky.' He walked back into the house and closed the door behind them. 'It was the least we could do to offer her the barn.'

'No point *that* being pretty but useless as well,' said Lady Sherwood.

'Quite, and Taran didn't want it.'

'Sadly not, after all the trouble I took to decorate it. It'll be nice to have someone making use of it. Beautiful big room, lots of light, perfect for an artist, and she can get to know the dogs as she draws.' She wandered into the kitchen to prepare lunch. 'Nice girl. She really liked the dogs. And *they* liked *her*. I'm very excited about this, darling.'

Sir Owen poured himself a large glass of red wine and sat down at the kitchen table. Lady Sherwood took some smoked salmon and new potatoes out of the fridge. 'I have a good feeling about her,' she added. 'I don't know why, but she's a breath of fresh air and that's just what this house needs.' Sir Owen wasn't listening. He was reading the Sunday papers. Lady Sherwood envisaged Daisy in the barn, drawing, and herself popping in to check on her and chat, because Daisy was quite chatty. The thought warmed her. She'd been lonely in this big old house on her own while Owen was out on the farm, or more typically playing racquet sports with his friends. A lovely presence in the barn was just what she needed.

Chapter 8

The following morning Marigold crossed the courtyard to the shop. She went inside via the back door as she did every morning and turned on the lights. Rows of neatly arranged shelves lit up like a ship. She stood there a moment in the glare of electric light, uncertain of what to do next. She knew there was something she was meant to be doing, besides opening up for the day. She went to unlock the front door and tried to remember what it was. She strained her brain but nothing came. Just a blank. She was getting used to these blanks now and was gradually learning how to deal with them. The trick was to breathe, remain calm and wait for the fog to lift, which it always did, eventually.

She was distracted by an impatient rapping on the window. She blinked and focused and Eileen's red face came into view, wrapped in a woolly hat and scarf. Her breath was misting in the cold and she was rubbing her mittens together to keep warm. Marigold unlocked the door and opened it.

'Ooooh, it's cold out here this morning,' said Eileen, eagerly shuffling into the warmth.

Marigold had already been for her walk along the clifftops and had almost been knocked off them by the gale. 'Very windy too. I think it might snow again,' she said hopefully.

'Wouldn't that be lovely,' said Eileen. 'I love it when the village turns white.'

'Why don't you go and make yourself some tea in my kitchen,' Marigold suggested. 'Suze is in there, writing, but you won't disturb her.'

'That's a good idea,' said Eileen. 'Would you like one?'

'I'm fine for the moment, thank you.' Eileen left through the back door and Marigold looked at her watch and wondered where Tasha was. Her attention was diverted by the little bell alerting her to another customer. It was the Commodore, in his three-piece tweed suit and trilby hat. The only indication that it was cold outside was the scarf around his neck and the heavy boots on his feet.

'Good morning to you, Marigold,' he said crisply. 'Fine day, isn't it?'

'Very fine,' said Marigold.

'I caught a mole last night,' he announced triumphantly.

'How did you catch it?' she asked.

'Ah, that's a very good question. First, I tried freezing them to death, but that didn't work. They'd wised up to me, you see. Very cunning they are, these moles. Then I tried smoking them out and gassing them, but without success. I even tried Dettol and, as a last resort, shooting them from my bedroom window. But Phyllida told me off because my eyesight isn't very good, you see, and she thought I'd shoot the dog by mistake.' He leaned on the counter. 'So I bought a trap. One of those traps you put down mole tunnels. Can't think why I didn't buy one before. I suppose I thought I could do it myself. I've always been a bit of a do-it-yourself man. It's my training you see, in the Navy. Why get someone to do something for you if you can do it yourself.'

'You bought a trap and captured a mole?' Marigold scrunched up her nose. 'Was it dead?'

'As dead as a dodo,' he replied, pleased. He went on to explain how such traps worked.

Shortly Eileen came back with her cup of tea.

'The Commodore caught a mole, Eileen,' said Marigold. 'He killed it.'

'Shame,' said Eileen. 'It's not fair to kill a creature just because it's inconvenient for you. Moles were in your garden long before you were, I suspect.'

'Well, not those ones,' said Marigold.

'Their ancestors, then. I think you should try and find a humane way to trap them.'

'Why don't you ask Dennis,' Marigold suggested. 'He could make you something out of wood. I'm sure he could. Dennis can make anything.'

The Commodore scratched his chin thoughtfully. 'That's not a bad idea, ladies,' he said. 'My grandchildren would be very happy with that. They get awfully upset at the thought of me killing them.'

'I'd keep quiet about your small success, then,' said Eileen.

'Now what did I come in for?' The Commodore swept his eyes around the room. 'Phyllida gave me specific instructions, but you've distracted me.'

Marigold was heartened that the Commodore was forgetful too.

'Ah, now I recall. She wanted dishwasher salt and Dijon mustard.'

'Let me get those for you,' Marigold suggested, coming round from behind the counter. 'I can't think where Tasha is. Really, she's very late this morning.' She looked at her watch and sighed, thinking that if Tasha was going to be late she should at least have the decency to tell her.

The little bell sounded and Carole Porter entered. 'Good

morning,' she said, smiling at Eileen and the Commodore. Being a brisk and efficient woman in her early forties, she didn't linger but strode down the aisle to find what she needed.

'Her husband John is still feuding with Pete Dickens over the size of his magnolia tree. It's getting rather nasty,' said Eileen in a low voice. 'I wouldn't put it past him to sneak into Pete's garden in the middle of the night and poison it.'

'Gracious, that bad, eh?' exclaimed the Commodore.

'John and Carole are very precious about their garden and they say the shadow of the tree is preventing plants from growing.' Eileen grinned mischievously. 'I think you should put your moles in there, when Dennis builds you a trap to catch them alive. That would give them something proper to worry about.'

The Commodore chuckled a little uneasily. This kind of subversive behaviour was not what he was used to and he wasn't sure he could condone it. 'I'll let them out in the open countryside,' he said as Carole marched to the counter and placed her basket on top of it expectantly. She looked around for Marigold.

'Sorry to keep you waiting, Carole,' said Marigold, returning with the dishwasher salt and mustard for the Commodore. 'I don't know where Tasha is this morning. Really, I'm sorely tried.'

Once the Commodore and Carole Porter had left the shop, she shook her head at Eileen and sighed despairingly.

'What you need is someone you can rely on,' said Eileen as the door opened and Cedric Weatherby and Dolly Nesbit came in together, arms linked. Dolly looked pale and fragile, but Cedric was as perky as a parakeet in a purple jacket and orange trousers.

'Hello, Cedric. Hello, Dolly,' said Marigold, giving Dolly a sympathetic smile. 'Are you all right?'

'We're coping, aren't we, Dolly,' said Cedric, squeezing her hand.

'I'm okay,' said Dolly in a voice so small Marigold barely heard her. 'It's very quiet in the house without her.'

'I bet it is,' Eileen rejoined. 'Time is a great healer, though,' she added unhelpfully.

'We're still waiting,' said Cedric. 'No sign of any healing yet.' They went down the aisle together at a slow and stately pace.

Marigold looked at her watch again. 'Where's Tasha? This is most unusual.'

Eileen frowned. 'Are you sure she didn't ask for the morning off?'

'No, she didn't. I'd know about it if she had.'

'Why don't you check that red book of yours. You've become very forgetful lately, Marigold.'

A patch of fog cleared in Marigold's mind and she remembered that she hadn't yet looked in her red book. 'How strange. I always look in that book first thing in the morning, before opening the shop.'

She bent down and took it out from under the counter. When she saw *Tasha morning off, dentist,* in big letters, she blanched. She had absolutely no recollection of writing that down, none whatsoever. Nor did she remember Tasha asking her for time off. When she closed the book she noticed her hand was shaking. The cold damp fear, now a familiar foe, crawled across her skin. 'I think I'll have a cup of tea now,' she said to Eileen. 'Would you mind fetching me one?'

Daisy and Lady Sherwood stood in the barn, which was adjacent to the main house and built out of an old, weathered grain store of blackened wood. It had enormous windows, high ceilings and an oak floor, which was heated. Lady Sherwood had decorated it beautifully but simply. There were large, comfy sofas, armchairs one could fall asleep in and colourful rugs on the floor. It smelt of new wood and new furnishings. Clearly it had never been lived in.

'I hoped that Taran would use this as a weekend or holiday home. I never thought he'd go and work in Toronto. It was going to be the perfect house for him and his family, close enough to us for company, but not too close.' She sighed. 'As it turns out he won't be looking after us in our old age, or keeping us company either.'

'It's a great room, Lady Sherwood.'

She smiled and Daisy saw Taran in her expression. 'Do you like it? Will it work for you, do you think?'

'It's perfect. Lots of light, that's the most important thing. You're very generous, Lady Sherwood. Are you sure I can't pay you rent?'

'No, it will be very nice to have someone in here, making use of it. Perhaps when your career takes off and you start making money, we can negotiate. But for now, you must enjoy it.'

Lady Sherwood showed Daisy around, pleased that she liked it. There were two downstairs bedrooms and bathrooms, a spacious kitchen and laundry room, and a master suite upstairs in the mezzanine with the most heavenly view of the countryside. It was the perfect home, Daisy thought, wishing she had the money to rent something like this so that she didn't have to live with her family, as if she were a child again.

When Daisy returned home she was full of enthusiasm, packing her easel and artist's bag into the back of the car in her eagerness to get started. Suze was at the kitchen table, talking on the phone, twirling a lock of hair around her fingers. Nan had returned from bridge and was in her usual place, dipping a biscuit into her tea, listening to Suze's conversation with interest.

'What's it like up there then?' Nan asked Daisy, just as she was on the point of leaving.

'It's really lovely,' Daisy replied, hovering in the doorway, keen to get away.

'I know what it's like to have a son who chooses to live on the other side of the world.' Nan shook her head and drew her lips into a thin line. 'They don't realize how much they hurt us.'

'At least you have Mum, Nan,' said Daisy. 'Lady Sherwood doesn't have any other children.'

'But sons are special, dear,' Nan confided tactlessly and Daisy realized then how much her grandmother took Marigold for granted.

'I think Mum is special, looking after us all the way she does.' *Looking after* you *the way she does.*

'Oh, don't get me wrong, she's a good girl, make no mistake. But Patrick can light up a room, if he chooses to. When he said he was going to Australia, he broke my heart. Your grandfather accepted it. He was always accepting. Philosophical is the word. What Suze would call "going with the flow". Your grandfather said *that* was the key to happiness. I'm sure he's right, although I can think of other keys to happiness besides going with the flow. But Patrick really can light up a room. *My* room is a bit gloomy without him, but I mustn't complain. You'll think me very ungrateful. Ungrateful is not in my nature. Your grandfather also used to say that our children come through us but do not belong to us. He used to read *The Prophet*, you know, that wise book people always read at weddings and funerals. A bit clichéd, but still, the words are timeless.' Daisy didn't want to be rude, but she really had to go. 'Did I ever tell you about the time Patrick . . .'

Suze hung up. Sensing her grandmother was launching into a long-winded story, she decided to cut her off before she started. 'Nan, what's Mum made for lunch?'

'I don't know, pet. She didn't say.'

Suze got up and opened the fridge. Usually there was something in there, like a quiche or a pizza, but today there was nothing. She closed the door and caught sight of the list. It distinctly said *Take cottage pie out of the freezer for lunch.* 'God! Mum is getting so forgetful!' she complained in exasperation. 'I'm going to tell her.'

Daisy stopped her. 'Don't, Suze.'

'Someone's got to say something. She's got worse since Christmas.'

'It's not her fault.'

'She needs to get a grip. She's not even seventy yet. She has no excuse!'

Nan nodded in agreement. 'If she's going to write lists, she should at least look at them.'

'You have legs. Go and get a pizza from the shop,' said Daisy crossly. 'And don't upset her.'

Suze put her hands on her hips. 'You'd be frustrated too if you lived here all the time.'

'No, I wouldn't,' said Daisy firmly. 'I'd like to think I'd be a little more compassionate.'

'We'll see about that in the summer. When Mum repeats herself for the umpteenth time.'

Daisy looked concerned. 'You've noticed that too?'

'We've *all* noticed,' said Nan solemnly. 'But we're trying to be compassionate.'

'Has Dad said anything?'

'I'm not sure he's noticed,' said Suze. 'Anyway, they're going to go away in the spring for that weekend we gave them for Christmas. That'll help, I'm sure. She's just very tired, and getting older, of course.'

'I'm nearly ninety and I never forget anything,' said Nan.

'Everyone's different,' said Daisy.

'Marigold takes after her father. Patrick takes after me,' said Nan. She shook her head again. 'Patrick can light up a room. My room's very dull these days.' Suze and Daisy caught eyes. Marigold wasn't the only one who was repetitive.

Daisy was checking the sitting room for anything she might have forgotten to put in the car when her eyes were drawn to her mother's jigsaw puzzle on the table in front of the window. She wandered over to have a closer look at how she was getting on. Perhaps she'd be able to tell what the picture was going to be. She was surprised to see that she had not done very much. Marigold usually finished Dennis's puzzles in a few days, but this one was clearly posing more of a challenge. Perhaps it was because her father hadn't included a photograph for her to copy. Or perhaps she'd just been busy. She'd completed the outside border, but that was about it. Daisy stared at it for a long while, trying to make sense of the uneasy feeling in her gut. There was something about that forlorn puzzle that disturbed her, but she couldn't put her finger on what it was. She decided she'd talk to her father about it. She wanted him to put her mind at rest and tell her there was nothing to worry about.

In his shed at the bottom of the garden, Dennis was working on a drinks cabinet for Carole Porter, while Mac the cat watched him from a bed of wood shavings on the floor.

A drinks cabinet was just the sort of job Dennis relished. Something that started from scratch and required careful design and craftsmanship. It was going to be painted scarlet and light up like the *Queen Mary* with mirrors at the back and glass shelves to hold the bottles. He had been round to look at photographs of bars that Carole had seen online, and to measure up, and she had told him about John's feud with Pete Dickens, their neighbour, about the magnolia tree. She'd even taken him into the garden to have a look at it. The branches did not extend over the wall, but it was so big that it did cut out the light, there was no doubt about that. But Dennis had not wanted to get involved. He was a peaceful man who liked a peaceful life.

Dennis liked working alone. He liked to listen to the radio and concentrate on his assignment. He stood at the workbench, which was made up of a smooth wooden board placed on top of some old kitchen cabinets. In front of him was the toolbox he had made as an apprentice almost fifty years ago. Every apprentice made one, at least they had in his day. Inside, he kept his hand tools – a hammer knife, measuring tape, chisels, coping saw, screwdrivers – and it accompanied him on every job. He stretched his back, groaning as the ache in his muscles eased a little, then reached for the box of paracetamol which he kept near his workbench.

He was busy cutting a piece of oak with a handsaw when the telephone rang. It was the Commodore calling to tell him about his mole problem and the trap he wanted Dennis to design. Dennis loved a challenge like that. It made him think and he liked to use his brain as well as his hands. He agreed to look at the Commodore's garden and the existing mole trap, which had killed the poor creature in the night, and make some preliminary drawings. He knew Marigold would approve of a trap that caught the animal alive, rather than killed it. He liked to please Marigold.

There was a knock on the door and Daisy walked in. 'Sorry to disturb you, Dad.'

Dennis smiled at his daughter. 'You're not disturbing me. You all packed up then?'

'Yes, I'm excited. It's a great room.'

'I'd have offered you my workshop but it gets very dusty in here.'

'That's okay. The Sherwoods' barn is perfect, and quiet.'

He arched an eyebrow. 'No Nan and Suze to distract you.'

'Exactly.' She hesitated, not knowing how to approach the subject of her mother's increasing forgetfulness without alarming him. 'Dad, is Mum all right? She's a bit vague at the moment.'

Dennis's smile faltered. 'She's been vague for a while now, Daisy. We're all getting on.'

'But Nan's not vague.'

'She's just repetitive. Age affects each of us in different ways.'

'I suppose Mum's got a lot on her plate with Nan living at home now, and me.'

Dennis put down the saw. 'She's looking after all of us, and the shop and post office as well. Tasha isn't very reliable. Mum really needs someone to share the load, but she won't hear of it. She's insistent that nothing change. She doesn't want to admit that she's slowing down. She takes herself on that walk every morning as if her life depends on it. Then there are those committee meetings she attends.' He scratched his head. 'But she won't listen to me.'

'Then she won't listen to me either,' said Daisy. She decided not to mention the unfinished puzzle. It seemed trivial now and was perhaps creating drama where there was none. 'As long as you're not worried.'

'I'm not worried and you shouldn't be either. You've been away for so long it's hard for you to have some perspective.' He grinned. 'The Commodore wants me to design him a mole trap that catches them alive. It's going to be an interesting project.'

'Where will he put them once he's caught them?'

'I don't know. I'll leave that to him.'

Daisy nodded. 'He'll know what to do. He was in the Navy,' she said, imitating his voice. They both laughed. 'Amazing what the Navy prepares one for.'

Daisy drove up to the Sherwoods' farm feeling calmer. Her father was right. Having lived abroad for so long it was hard for her to have any perspective. Perhaps her mother had been growing increasingly forgetful for years. How would she know, not having been around long enough to witness it?

She parked the car outside the barn and unpacked her equipment. When her easel was set up, in front of the enormous windows, she felt a surge of pleasure. She knew she would draw beautifully in this room.

Lady Sherwood brought the dogs over and Daisy started taking photographs. There was tea and coffee in the kitchen and milk in the fridge – Lady Sherwood had thought of everything. The sun came out and flooded the room with light. The view of the farm was beautiful, even in winter when the trees were bare and the ground dull green in colour and sodden. She knew she'd have to start walking soon as her parents might need the car. She didn't want to waste precious funds on a new one, even a second-hand one. It wasn't too far, if Sir Owen let her cut across the fields. But right now she was satisfied, and, she noticed, thinking a little less about Luca.

Chapter 9

As winter thawed and spring ushered in longer days and warmer winds, nature awakened from her long sleep. Daffodils opened their pretty yellow trumpets, forget-me-nots spread over the grass in puddles of blue and the woods began to bud with new life. Daisy began to walk to work, and, as spring gained momentum, those daily walks became more pleasurable. Sir Owen allowed her to use the farm tracks, which cut the journey by half, and she no longer needed to wear a hat and scarf, but a light denim jacket. The sun was higher in the sky and warm upon her face. The twittering of birds in the hedgerows was a heartening affirmation that winter was over at last.

It wasn't long before she completed Lady Sherwood's drawing. It had taken more time than she had intended because she had had to draw three dogs rather than one. They had agreed on the composition from the photographs Daisy had taken, deciding on Mordy and Archie lying on the stool in the middle of the drawing room while Bendico watched them from the floor. It had worked very well and Daisy was pleased to have caught them like that without having had to arrange them artificially. Sir Owen and Lady Sherwood were astonished with the final result. Lady Sherwood had followed the whole process, wandering into the barn every now and then for a chat and a sneaky peek at the picture. But she had refrained from looking at it in the last days, in order not to ruin the big reveal. Sir Owen had exclaimed, 'Good Lord!' when he saw it for the first time, his ruddy face deepening to purple as he gazed into the oddly living eyes of his pets. 'What a talented young lady you are.'

Lady Sherwood had clapped her hands with pleasure and praised Daisy for capturing her pets so beautifully. 'How different it is from a photograph!' she had exclaimed and Daisy had been delighted, because that was exactly what she had wanted her to say.

They decided to hang it above the fireplace in their hall, which was an unexpected honour for Daisy. She was pleased she had spent so much on the frame, because it looked wonderful up there on the wall and everyone who came in would see it. Lady Sherwood had paid her cash and told her that, in future, she really should charge a little more. Especially now that she had a couple of works under her belt. Daisy decided she would, but not too much; she didn't want to put anyone off at a time when she needed to attract clients.

Now she was working on Carole Porter's Pekineses, all three of them, which was quite a challenge as they were skittish and very attached to their mistress. They couldn't have been less interested in her.

Dennis completed the mole trap. He had tried a couple of designs that hadn't worked, and evidence that the mole had been there and got away had infuriated the impatient Commodore. However, after a little tinkering, the trap was successful and the Commodore captured his first mole. His excitement was such that one could have been mistaken for thinking he had been awarded the Victoria Cross. He burst into the shop with the tiny mole in the trap.

'What have you got in there?' Eileen asked, peering at the box. 'Is it dead?'

'It's a mole and it's alive,' said the Commodore gleefully.

Marigold, who loved animals, immediately grew anxious at the thought of the poor creature imprisoned in a box. 'You must let it go at once!' she exclaimed.

'Would you like to see it?' he asked.

'Will it bite?' said Eileen.

'No, you must take it out right away and put it somewhere safe,' said Marigold firmly.

The door opened and Dolly appeared with Cedric. 'Good morning, everyone,' she said. Spring had put some colour in her cheeks.

'What have you got there, Commodore?' asked Cedric.

'A mole,' said the Commodore, eyes gleaming. 'Caught it this morning in the trap Dennis made me. Would you like to see it? It's not dead. It's very much alive. I'm about to put it somewhere safe.'

'Not in *my* garden, I hope,' said Cedric, thinking of his immaculate lawn.

'Nor mine,' said Dolly.

'Where are you going to put it?' asked Eileen.

The Commodore opened the lid and they all peered in, except Marigold, who did not want to see a trapped animal, vermin or otherwise. 'I'm going to let him out in the countryside,' said the Commodore.

'Oh, he's adorable,' gushed Dolly, letting go of Cedric's arm. 'May I hold him?'

'He bites,' said Eileen. 'You don't know what diseases he might have.'

Dolly reached in with her finger and stroked the mole's back. 'They're much smaller than one thinks,' she said quietly. She sighed heavily.

'Let's go and find the cocoa powder,' Cedric suggested, drawing her away.

The little bell tinkled again and in came Mary Hanson. The Commodore shut the box, glancing anxiously at Mary's feet. Fortunately, she had not brought her dog. Dolly looked at Mary. Mary caught her eye and turned away. Cedric sniffed loudly, lifted his chin and ushered Dolly down the aisle. Eileen watched them closely, then murmured to Marigold under her breath, 'Knives at dawn.'

'Will you tell Dennis of my success,' the Commodore said to Marigold.

'I will,' said Marigold. 'He'll be very pleased. Now off you go and put him somewhere safe, where he can dig away to his heart's content without having to worry about being caught in a trap.' She turned to Mary. 'Good morning, Mary,' she said, aware that Dolly and Cedric were loitering at the other end of the shop on purpose. 'What can I get you?'

'Don't worry,' said Mary, blushing. 'I'll come back later.'

'Don't let them chase you out of the shop,' said Eileen in a sympathetic voice. 'You have to stand up to bullies, Mary.'

Mary sighed. 'I just wanted some teabags,' she said. 'I've run out.'

'You stay here and I'll get them for you,' said Marigold.

She got to the end of the aisle and began searching. But she couldn't remember what it was that Mary wanted. She knew it was somewhere here, because this is where she had walked immediately after Mary had told her what she wanted. She tried to focus. If she'd had cogs in her brain she would have heard them turning, or rather grinding, with the effort. She was used to these lapses of memory now. Blanks where nothing remained, like black holes in her mind. She stared into the black hole and felt the familiar fear creeping across her skin, the dizziness in her head and the strange feeling of detachment, as if she were miles away, watching herself failing from a distance. She took a deep breath. She could feel Dolly and Cedric's eyes upon her as they lingered near the sugar. Marigold knew she needed to hurry, because Dolly and Cedric couldn't leave while Mary was at the till, and Mary couldn't leave until Marigold had got her what she wanted. What was it? But nothing came into her mind.

She ran her eyes over the shelves, hoping that something would jog her memory. She felt very hot and wondered whether it was time to turn off the heating. After all, it was March and the weather was mild. Her gaze fell upon the boxes of Tetley teabags. She wished she could go home and have a cuppa right now. Just the sight of them there, on the shelf, restored her a little. Then the black hole disappeared, quite suddenly, and she remembered. *Tea!* She picked up the box with a trembling hand and walked unsteadily back to the counter. Mary and Eileen were busy chatting and Mary didn't raise an eyebrow when Marigold put the teabags through the till. It felt like she'd been lost there in the aisle for a long time, but no one else seemed to have noticed.

Mary paid for the teabags and left the shop. Tasha returned from her tea break with a smile. Dolly and Cedric bought the cocoa powder and departed. Marigold looked at her watch. It was time to take Dennis his tea.

She found him in his shed, working on a bookcase for the vicar's study. 'Hello, Goldie,' he said when he saw her coming. 'You're a love.'

She put the mug down on his workbench. 'The Commodore caught a mole,' she told him, pleased that she remembered without writing it in her little book.

'Did he now? Alive?'

'Alive and well, I think.'

'That's good. I'm glad the trap worked. Where's he going to put it?'

'I can't remember, but hopefully somewhere safe.' He watched her leave then went back to work.

Marigold walked around the garden, breathing the fragrant air with delight. The scent of spring was very different to the scent of summer. She could smell the sweet grass, the Daphne, the fertile aroma of the earth, warming slowly in the milder weather. She still fed her birds, although she didn't really need to now, for there were worms in the soil and insects on the breeze. Yet she so enjoyed watching them flying about the feeder. She just so enjoyed them.

When she got to the kitchen, Nan was at the table, doing the crossword. 'Burst of bad temper, seven letters,' she said.

'Tantrum,' said Marigold.

'That was an easy one. How about, waste away, nine letters.'

'Oh, that *is* hard.'

'Droop? No, not enough letters. Wither?'

'Ah, I know . . .'

Nan looked up expectantly.

'It's on the tip of my tongue.'

'Well, what is it? Fourth letter is I, because three down is rib, for tease. I got that one.'

Marigold could *feel* the word as if it were a potato in her mouth, as if it had round bits and smooth bits and knobbly bits. As if it had texture. But she couldn't articulate it. 'Give me a minute and it'll come to me.' It was so close.

Nan sighed. 'Very well. I'll do another clue.'

The word bothered Marigold so much that she decided to leave the room and work on her jigsaw puzzle. She hadn't told anyone, but she was finding this puzzle very challenging. She had managed to do the border, but she was having trouble doing the rest. It was as if the cogs in her brain were having to work through porridge. They simply weren't as efficient as they once were. It was as if they needed oiling to get them moving smoothly again. She put on her glasses and went through the pieces, separating them into colours and patterns. She found two that went together and felt a rush of jubilation. She didn't notice the time passing. Suddenly, the sight of a pigeon outside her window distracted her and she looked at her watch. Goodness, she thought. I must get back to the shop. And I need to make Dennis his tea. She hurried into the kitchen and boiled the kettle. Just as she was leaving, the word came to her, as if someone had dropped it into her head from above. 'Dissipate,' she said to her mother.

'Of course. We should have known that, shouldn't we?'

Marigold felt better now that she had remembered the word. She went through the garden and opened Dennis's door. He looked up in surprise. 'Hi, Goldie,' he said.

'Your tea. A little late this morning. I got carried away doing the puzzle.' She put it down on the workbench and frowned at the mug already sitting there. 'I must get back to the shop,' she said, not noticing the bewildered expression on Dennis's face or the doubt in his eyes.

As she walked back through the garden she felt a little put out that he had made *himself* a cup of tea. He had never done that before.

A few days later Marigold forgot that Batty was coming for supper, so when he appeared in the kitchen at seven she was surprised to see him. But Marigold was getting good at hiding her memory loss. The little book helped (when she remembered to look at it). The red book in the shop was also a vital lifeline and no one questioned the amount of things she wrote in it, because it was her job to write things down. The list on the fridge winked at her whenever she opened the door. However, Suze had told her that Batty was coming for supper that morning while she had been feeding her birds, so by the time she went back into the kitchen she had forgotten all about it. Really, her mind was like a sieve. If she didn't write something down *immediately*, it vaporized. Gone. Like steam from the kettle. But she smiled graciously at Batty and told him to help himself to a beer. She went to lay an extra place at the table and didn't think that Batty noticed.

The family tucked into their roast chicken and Batty and Suze sat side by side, grinning at each other like loved-up teenagers. Marigold saw that Daisy was happy too. She was enjoying her new job, working up at the Sherwoods' farm, and was getting plenty of commissions. More, in fact, than she could handle. Nan said it was because she was so cheap. 'If you charged more, you wouldn't be so popular,' she had said, but Daisy had ignored her.

It wasn't until the end of the meal that Suze whispered something to Batty, who then stood up, as if he was about to make a speech. Batty wasn't very tall, but he was undoubtedly handsome with a chiselled face, curly brown hair and deep, sensitive brown eyes amplified by the Trotsky-style glasses he wore.

The table went silent. Dennis caught Marigold's eye. She recognized the smile in his eyes and smiled back hopefully.

'I have an announcement to make,' said Batty, his lips curling as the upturned faces looked at him expectantly. 'Last night I asked Suze to marry me and she said yes.'

Suze jumped to her feet and kissed him loudly on the cheek. 'Actually, what I said was, yes *please!*'

'Well, congratulations to the both of you. I think this calls for a bottle of wine,' said Dennis, pushing out his chair.

'Oooh yes, how nice,' said Nan. There was nothing negative about a glass of wine.

Marigold's eyes filled with tears. 'I'm so happy for you, dear,' she said when Suze embraced her. She put her arms around her daughter and held her close for a moment. 'I'm happy you've found someone to share your life with,' she said, thinking of Dennis and the many wonderful years they had spent together.

'Life is a long road,' said Nan. 'Made easier if you have someone to share the journey with. That's what your grandfather used to say. Of course he was right, but then he died, leaving me alone. One of you has to go first, I suppose. Only the lucky few go together.'

Dennis returned with a bottle of chilled white wine and Daisy steered the subject away from death, and from Nan. 'Is there a ring?' she asked.

'The ring!' Suze exclaimed as Batty pulled a grey suede box out of his pocket.

'We didn't want to ruin the surprise,' he said, opening it and slipping it onto Suze's outstretched finger. The surprisingly large diamond solitaire sparkled expensively.

'It belonged to Batty's grandmother. As it turned out, his grandfather had exceedingly good taste in jewellery,' said Suze happily. 'Isn't it beautiful? Like a star.'

'There's only one star,' said Batty smoothly.

'And that's me!' said Suze with a giggle.

Batty put his arm around her. 'That's you, sweetheart.'

'Once we're married we're going to rent a flat in town, but until we find the right place I'm going to live with Batty at his parents' house. They have more room.'

'We'll miss you, Suze,' said Marigold, suddenly feeling a pang of anxiety at the thought of her youngest flying the nest at last.

'But this is the beginning of the rest of your life,' said Daisy, lifting the glass of wine her father had just given her.

'A toast,' said Dennis, putting down the bottle and raising his glass. 'To Batty and Suze and many happy years together.'

They all raised their glasses.

'A summer wedding will be nice,' said Nan. 'Don't leave it too long, will you? I'm nearly ninety, you know, and the Grim Reaper is sharpening his scythe. I do want to be there.'

'A summer wedding will be lovely,' Marigold agreed, thinking of all the lists she was going to have to write in order not to let Suze down on her big day.

Daisy sipped her wine, resisting the envy that was creeping into her heart like a worm in an apple. She didn't want to resent her younger sister for getting to the altar before she did. However, she couldn't help but feel a little sad. If she hadn't wasted six years with a man who never intended to marry her, perhaps she'd be married by now. Maybe she'd even be a mother. Again she wondered whether she'd done the right thing. Should she have stayed with Luca and compromised? Was there anyone else out there for her?

Chapter 10

There was a lot to arrange for Suze's wedding and Marigold was quite overwhelmed at the thought. Firstly, the church had to be booked for the ceremony and the village hall for the reception. The food and champagne, the dress, the cake, the bridesmaids and pages' outfits and the invitations were only some of the many things that needed to be organized. When Marigold was younger she had relished arranging things. She had been so good at logistics. Nothing had fazed her. Now, she could barely see what needed to be done for the fog in her head. She wondered how she was going to manage. She knew it would be a great deal easier if she asked for help, but that would mean articulating her fears. She didn't want to do that. She didn't want her family to have to share them; she didn't want her family to know she had any.

And she didn't want to make a big deal out of something potentially small. If all old people were struggling with forgetfulness, why should hers be any worse? Why should hers be given special attention? The last thing Marigold wanted was to be self-indulgent.

The fact was that some days were fine, others much harder. Some days Marigold felt lucid and full of energy, other days she felt foggy and lethargic and bordering on despair. She decided she'd tackle all the arrangements on the days she felt well. Juggling the wedding and the shop was not going to be easy, but she was determined to make Suze's day special without giving her undue reason for concern. She was not going to let her little problem affect the first day of the rest of Suze's life.

Suze and Batty settled on the first weekend in June, which was just under three months' away, and hoped that the weather would be fine. Nan said it was good luck if it rained on one's wedding day. 'After all,' she said, 'it rained on mine and I had fifty-eight years of happiness with Grandad.' Which no one believed, because Nan was the sort of woman who tried very hard *not* to be happy.

Marigold booked the church and the village hall and crossed them both off her list.

When it came to planning the dress Suze had strong ideas of her own. She declared over breakfast one Sunday morning that she did not want to get married in white. 'I'm going to wear pink.'

Nan was appalled. 'You'll look like a marshmallow,' she said.

'Are you suggesting I'm fat, Nan?'

'No, I'm suggesting you'll look ridiculous coming down the aisle in pink. It has to be white, doesn't it, Marigold?'

Marigold was not having a good day. She wished she had stayed in bed, but she had had to get up to make everyone breakfast. She couldn't imagine not cooking Dennis his Sunday Special, and as for Nan, she hadn't made her own breakfast since she arrived. Suze and Daisy could easily look after themselves, but Marigold *enjoyed* looking after them. It's what she had always done and she did not want anything to change.

'Is pink a good idea, Suze?' Marigold asked tactfully.

'It's my wedding and I shall wear what I want,' Suze replied tartly, flicking her hair.

Dennis, who did not like confrontation, decided to agree with Suze for an easy Sunday morning. 'Whatever you want, love. It's your day.'

Marigold was inclined to agree with her husband, but Nan was scowling at her crossly. 'It's not just about being virginal, Suze, it's about showing your respect to God,' said Nan. 'Isn't it, Marigold?'

'Did you know, it was only because of Queen Victoria that wedding dresses are white,' said Daisy. 'Before her, women got married in colour. I think you should wear red, Suze.'

Nan pursed her lips. 'If you want to finish me off, you're going the right way about it,' she muttered. 'I've said I want to be at your wedding, but if you marry in red, or pink, or anything that is not white, I won't make it. I will be six feet under and turning.'

'Maybe not red, Daisy,' said Dennis, trying to keep the peace. 'A *pale* pink wouldn't offend God, I don't imagine. If it's pale, it might not offend Nan either. But I suspect Nan is harder to please than God.'

Nan did not look appeased.

'God created flowers and they come in all colours,' Suze replied. 'I'd like a dress that's as pink as a peony. He can't mind about that, after all, He created the peony, didn't He?'

'Speaking of flowers,' said Marigold, keen to change the subject. 'We need to find a good florist.'

'Well, that's easy enough,' Suze laughed. 'Gardening is Batty's profession, so I think we can leave that to him.'

'At least he'll be *Atticus* Buckley in church,' said Nan with a sniff. 'If you're lucky enough to be named after a character in one of the most famous novels ever written, you'd be a fool not to flaunt it.'

Suze laughed. 'If you're suggesting my fiancé is a fool, Nan, I'll go down the aisle in a fuchsia-pink dress just to spite you.'

Marigold brought Dennis his Sunday Special and put it in front of him. 'Thanks, Goldie,' he said, picking up his knife and fork and beaming a smile. 'You're the best.'

Marigold didn't feel like the best today. She went to the bathroom and opened her little book. It was so full of things to do that for a moment she felt quite dizzy. The sight of a full day exhausted her. Normally, such a day would have delighted her, but she seemed to function now on a lower gear, and every small thing felt like a step uphill. She knew she should go to church, but she had to cook the lunch, which was always a little hard if most of the morning was eaten up by the Reverend's long sermon. She had arranged to have tea with Beryl in the afternoon, which she was looking forward to, but she also wanted to spend time on her puzzle. Fortunately, the list of things her mother needed, like more shampoo and toothpaste, could be easily obtained from the shop. She sighed with gratitude for the shop. She didn't know how she'd cope without it.

Another problem was now brewing, she realized. She had her little book, which she kept in her pocket, her red shop book, which was kept under the counter, and the list on the fridge, of course, which was a constant reminder of kitchen things like meals and cooking, but she also had Post-it Notes around the house and a pad of paper by her bed. There were so many places to write things down that she was beginning to forget where she had written them. She knew she should keep all her reminders in *one* place, but her little book wasn't always where *she* was. She changed her clothes and forgot to take it out of the pocket, for example, and sometimes she simply forgot about it altogether. On good days she didn't think she needed it, then crash, her memory would fail the following day and she couldn't remember where she'd put it.

Everything was more of an effort nowadays. Making lunch was an exceedingly taxing operation because she didn't want to forget to switch on the oven, or some other important detail, and in so doing alert her family to the fact that she was getting more forgetful. She had to concentrate hard, and that in itself was making her nervous. Hiding how she was really feeling was making her very tired.

Against her better judgement, Marigold went to church with Nan and Dennis. Dennis dropped them off at the gate, then went to park the car. The two women walked into the church together. Normally, Nan would go and find a seat and Marigold would socialize, but today Marigold didn't feel up to socializing. She kept her head down and followed her mother into a pew. Then she opened her hymn book to see what they were going to sing today. She looked up to check if Dennis was coming and caught a woman's eye instead. The woman waved and smiled. Marigold smiled back, but she hadn't a clue who she was. She thought perhaps she had mistaken her for someone else. When the woman continued on down the aisle, Marigold tapped her mother on the arm. 'That woman's just waved at me,' she told her.

Nan looked at the woman and then at her daughter. She frowned. 'That's Mandy Bradshaw,' she said.

Marigold looked blank.

'Mandy Bradshaw! You know her, Marigold! She's new in the village, has a little terrier called Toby. Nasty dog. I hate terriers.'

'You just hate dogs, Mum,' said Marigold. She realized then that she was going to have to bluff when her mind drew a blank like that. If someone she didn't recognize recognized *her*, she would just have to go along with it. It was as simple as that. But as Dennis sat down beside her she felt as if the church floor were spinning away from her. She took Dennis's hand. He squeezed it. 'All right, love?' he asked. She nodded. But she wasn't all right; she wasn't all right at all.

After lunch she toiled away at the jigsaw puzzle. She knew that working on the puzzle was exercising her brain because she could feel it working. But it was exasperating. Marigold was not a woman who gave up easily. She was not *going* to give up and she was not going to voice her concerns either. Instead, she internalized her fear and her frustration and smiled in the gracious way she always smiled; a happy mask hiding the growing desperation inside.

Dennis noticed that Marigold was struggling with his jigsaw puzzle. Perhaps this one was just too big and the pieces too small for her to cope with. He wondered whether he should have given her the picture as a guide. But it was too late now. He hadn't photographed it. He had been so sure that she would complete it as swiftly as she had all the others that it hadn't crossed his mind to make a copy. Now he felt bad. What he had believed to be the best puzzle he had ever made had turned out to be a disappointment. The worst was that it didn't seem to be giving her pleasure. He knew she wanted to do it. He was certain of that. He watched her sitting at the table with her glasses on, trying to figure out which pieces went where, a determined frown creasing her brow, but it seemed to be a labour not of love but of pride, because she didn't want to admit her failure, even to herself.

When the telephone rang, Daisy answered it. After a brief chat she called to her mother, 'It's Beryl. She says you're meant to be having tea with her.'

Marigold blanched. Daisy watched her with concern. Her mother didn't register surprise, as one would expect, but fear. Daisy saw it in her eyes and felt a stab of fear in her own heart.

'I'm so sorry,' said Marigold, speaking into the phone in

a calm voice that betrayed nothing of her anxiety. 'I've been busy with Dennis's puzzle. Shall I pop over now?'

'I've baked some biscuits,' said Beryl. 'A new recipe out of a book I was given for Christmas. They're very good. I think you'll like them. Do come, but don't fret. There's no hurry.'

Dennis insisted on driving Marigold to Beryl's house even though it was only a short walk away. Once he returned he found Daisy in the hall, waiting for him. 'We need to talk,' she said and Dennis knew from the serious expression on her face that she wanted to talk about Marigold.

'Come to my shed,' he suggested quietly and they walked across the garden together. Daisy noticed the bird feeder, full of seed, and was consoled that at least her mother hadn't forgotten to do that.

Dennis closed the door behind them. Father and daughter stood looking at each other for a moment, not knowing how to broach such a sensitive subject. Neither wanted to admit that something was wrong, because doing that would make it real. But they also knew that they couldn't avoid the reality any longer. Finally, Daisy spoke. 'She's forgetting everything, Dad,' she said. 'And it's been going on since I moved back from Italy. I suspect it started long before that. I think she should see a doctor.'

Dennis frowned. 'It'll upset her if she thinks we've noticed. She's trying hard to hide it. She doesn't want to admit she's slowing down.' He smiled tenderly. 'You know Mum, she likes being in control. She likes looking after us all.'

'If it's nothing more than old age then at least the doctor can tell her to slow down. She takes on too much. If a doctor told her to slow down, she'd have to, wouldn't she? I'm not suggesting she has a brain tumour, but we should at least look into it, for our own peace of mind.'

Dennis was unconvinced. He knew how Marigold would

react. She'd be very upset and he didn't want to upset her. Then he remembered the second cup of tea she'd brought him and his heart sank. She'd never done that before. 'How about we all pull together and help her?' he suggested.

'Yes, I agree. We could do much more for ourselves.'

'I mean *really* help her. If she plans tea with Beryl then we can gently remind her, for example. We can prompt her without her knowing we're prompting her.'

Daisy sighed. 'I'm not sure it's that easy, Dad. We're working. We're not with her the whole time. We can't prompt her in the shop, can we?'

'Let's give it a go, eh? Let's just try.'

'I still want her to see a doctor.'

'Then *you* have to suggest it.'

Daisy smiled sympathetically. 'I will, Dad. Don't worry. I know this sort of thing makes you uncomfortable.' But Daisy was prepared to upset her mother if the end result gave them all peace of mind.

Beryl offered Marigold a biscuit. Marigold took one and bit into it. She nodded. 'Very good, Beryl.'

'Aren't they? I'll give you the name of the book. Simple recipes, but delicious.' Beryl looked at Marigold across the kitchen table and noticed she was looking unusually pale. 'Dennis made you another jigsaw puzzle, did he?'

'He makes me one every year, but this year I think he's outdone himself. He's certainly outdone *me*. I'm finding it quite a struggle. I can say that to you. But I can't tell Dennis. He worked so hard on it.'

'He's very talented, your husband.'

'Yes, he is.'

'That mole trap he made for the Commodore has got everyone talking. He's caught twenty-five moles, you know.'

'Goodness! That's a lot of moles.'

'He's setting them free in the countryside.' She grinned. 'I hope they don't find their way back and set up home in *my* garden.'

'So do I,' Marigold agreed with a chuckle. 'That would be ironic, wouldn't it, if Dennis made a trap, only for them to come back and make their home in *his* garden?' She began to feel better. It was good to be out of the house, at Beryl's table, drinking a nice cup of tea and eating her delicious biscuits.

'I see Daisy is becoming a bit of a local celebrity,' said Beryl admiringly. 'Her animal drawings are very popular.'

'Daisy's thrilled. She works well at the farm, with all that light and the lovely views.'

'I went to visit Rosie Price on Saturday at her nursing home. That's got lovely views too.'

'Rosie's in a nursing home?' said Marigold in surprise. Rosie was an old schoolfriend of both hers and Beryl's.

'I *did* tell you, Marigold, but you've forgotten. It doesn't matter. She's got Alzheimer's. Very sad. She doesn't remember anything anymore. She only just remembered me and that's because I'm a very old friend.' Marigold went cold. 'It's a perfectly adequate place, as nice as it can be, I suppose,' Beryl continued. 'Must have been a big old private house once. Not far from here, with a view of the sea. It has one of those commonplace names like Seaside Manor or Seaview House. The poor thing was just sitting there in the big sitting room when I arrived. My heart went out to her. I reminded her who I was and she *did* remember. Her face lit up. She was pleased to see me. We reminisced. She was surprisingly lucid about her childhood. She remembered all her dogs' names. Imagine that? We talked about our old schooldays and she was as sharp as a tack.'

'And her children? Does she remember them?' Marigold asked anxiously.

'I'm told she gets confused. Because she exists in her youth she thinks they're her uncles and aunts. She probably can't imagine she has children at all. She talks about her parents, who died years ago, and complains about the place she's in and asks to be taken home. Home for her is not with her husband Ian, but with her parents, and that house where she grew up no longer exists. I was told, very specifically, by her eldest son Julian, that I wasn't to contradict her or ask her any questions. It was a lot harder than you'd think. As long as I stuck to those rules she would remain calm and not get upset. Julian, who was there, was wonderful with her. When she said she wanted to go home he told her that they were going to have a nice lunch, take the dogs for a walk, and then they were going to go home. She was very happy to hear that. Of course, a few minutes later she had forgotten they'd even had the conversation. The trick is to make her present moment as contented as possible, because that's really all she has.'

'So, she won't have any recollection of you having been?' said Marigold.

'No. Julian told me, as we were leaving, that if I were to walk back in again, she'd greet me as she had done when I arrived. She wouldn't remember I'd been there only minutes before. It's extraordinary. Lots of people get it, you know.' Beryl sighed heavily.

Marigold shrugged. 'We all have to go somehow,' she said.

'I'd like to go in my sleep,' said Beryl.

'Me too,' said Marigold. 'Just drift away, like a cloud.'

Chapter 11

A few days later Daisy plucked up the courage to tell her mother that she needed to see a doctor. It was a cold, grey morning but the daffodils gave it the colour it lacked and shone brightly through the drizzle. Marigold was out feeding her birds, talking to the robin and enjoying with the wonder of a child the sight of her feathered friends gathering in her garden.

Daisy crossed the lawn. 'They know it's breakfast, don't they?' she said.

'They do. Although they don't get through it as quickly as they do in the winter months. I'll stop feeding them soon. I just want to see them through until they've had their young.'

Daisy thought how happy her mother was here in the garden. It was probably her happiest place, and now Daisy was going to disturb it.

'Mum, I wonder whether you should see a doctor.' Daisy held her breath.

'A doctor?' Marigold hung the feeder on the branch. 'Why?' But she knew and her cheeks flushed. She thought she had managed to dupe them all.

'You've just been a bit forgetful lately. I'm sure it's nothing, but I'd feel happier if you had a check-up. Everyone should have them at your age. An MOT. You know. Maintenance.'

Marigold inhaled through her nostrils, wondering how much she was going to share. 'I've already been,' she confessed, putting her hands in her coat pockets and looking at her daughter from under her wrinkled brow.

Daisy was surprised. 'Really? When?'

'Just before Christmas. I was worried too. But he said it's normal at my age to forget things. That's why I started going for walks in the morning. He told me to take exercise and to exercise my brain as well.'

Daisy nodded. 'Hence the Sudoku.'

'Hence the Sudoku,' she repeated.

'I see. So, there's nothing wrong. That's a relief.'

'Yes, it is. I thought I was getting dementia or something awful.' Just saying that word out loud made Marigold shudder. She smiled at Daisy. 'Thank you, dear, for worrying about me. But really, you don't need to. I'm fine.'

Daisy was so relieved, she put her arms around her mother and embraced her. And yet, beneath her relief lingered a shadow of anxiety that wouldn't shift, however much she and Marigold held on to the doctor's opinion. Did the doctor know *everything*? Daisy remembered her mother's strange turn in town the day they went Christmas shopping. Did the doctor know about *that*?

Yet she couldn't ask her mother to go again.

Daisy decided that she was going to help more around the house and try to be her mother's memory whenever she could. She agreed with her father not to worry Nan and Suze, especially in the run-up to Suze's wedding. Neither of them wanted to upset Suze, or for her to lose confidence in the person organizing her big day.

Dennis thought Daisy was overreacting. If the doctor had told Marigold that there was nothing to worry about, then there really was nothing to worry about. Dennis trusted the medical profession. In his experience, doctors were always right.

In the weeks that followed, Daisy prompted her mother whenever she could. She did it tactfully so that Marigold wouldn't notice. When her mother had a committee meeting for the church, Daisy simply suggested she take an umbrella because she was sure it would rain. 'I know it's a short walk to the church hall, but you don't want to get wet,' she said. Marigold, who had forgotten she had a meeting, suddenly remembered and turned up on time without realizing that Daisy had nudged her on purpose. When Daisy pre-empted her in the kitchen, she would explain that, as she was passing the freezer, she might as well take out the cottage pie for supper, or switch on the oven, or cook supper herself because she missed cooking, having cooked a lot in Italy. It was a challenge, because she wasn't at home all the time, or in the shop, but as the social things happened on weekends, she could be her mother's memory for those at least. She even went to church on Sundays, which she hadn't done in years, just so that she could accompany her mother and prompt her if she failed to recognize a face. Nan and Suze were oblivious, Dennis was in denial and it was only Daisy who realized how much her mother was forgetting, and how tired she was. But until her mother recognized that she had a problem there was little that Daisy could do besides subtly prompting her when she was able to.

Daisy said she wanted to help with the wedding preparations. 'It'll be fun doing it together,' she said and Marigold agreed, feeling relieved. Suze was too busy posting things on her Instagram site and writing articles about planning a wedding, of which Suze knew nothing, to be of any use.

'Why don't you write something with more substance?'
Daisy suggested one evening at supper, when Suze was telling
them about the blog she was writing about the tradition of
'Something old, something new, something borrowed, something blue, and a sixpence in your shoe'.

'I beg your pardon,' said Suze, glaring at her. 'Are you suggesting that what I write is superficial?'

'No, of course not, there's a place for fashion and frivolity,
but you're such a good writer. You're intelligent. You're sharp
and perceptive and clever. I think you're selling yourself short.'

Suze looked at the faces around the table with the defensive
glare of a cornered animal. 'Is that what you all think? Have
you been discussing me behind my back?'

Dennis gave her a reassuring smile. 'I don't mind what you
do, love, as long as you're happy.'

'I *am* happy,' said Suze sulkily. 'I'm getting married, how
could I possibly be anything but happy?' She rested her
gaze on her sister and added tightly, 'You might be the next
Leonardo da Vinci, but I'm very contented doing what I
do. I have over forty thousand Instagram followers now and
thousands of people read my blog. Do you think Aimee Song
and Samantha Maria think they should be writing articles
with more substance? There are enough people out there
writing polemics about politics, the failure of the NHS,
global warming and the troubles in the Middle East. I'm not
interested in adding to their number.' No one had a clue
who Aimee Song and Samantha Maria were, but they were
too nervous to ask.

'I don't mean writing about that,' said Daisy, wishing she
hadn't said anything. 'I've told you before. You should write
a novel. You always used to write stories. Why did you stop?
You could earn a lot of money being a novelist.'

'You don't need money to be happy, Daisy. You should know all about that.'

'It's not just about the money, although no one would turn their nose up at making good money. You'd be doing something really satisfying. You'd be fulfilling your potential. I think you've got a lot of potential but you're just too frightened to give it a go.'

'I'm not frightened,' Suze retorted. 'I'd give it a go if I had an idea. Anyway, I'm too busy to write a book.' She folded her arms defensively.

'Suze, I'm not criticizing you. Quite the opposite. I *believe* in you.'

'You've got a funny way of showing it, Daisy.'

Nan caught Marigold's eye and changed the subject. 'Moira Barnes has a fancy man,' she said. When they all looked at her in astonishment, she continued blithely. 'He's eighty-six and she's ninety-two and it's a proper love affair. She says she's discovering parts of her body she had forgotten were there.'

Suze nearly snorted up her food. 'Nan, that's way too much information!' She burst out laughing and the tense atmosphere immediately evaporated.

That night, after dinner, Daisy's telephone rang. When she saw Luca's name on the screen her heart stalled. She hesitated, unsure whether or not to pick it up. It was a strange feeling knowing that right now he was somewhere in Italy, thinking of her, ready to speak to her. All she had to do was press accept on her phone and she'd hear the voice she had missed so dreadfully. And yet, she was nervous. What did he want? Was he ready to compromise? And if he was, did she want him to? She was beginning to settle into her new life. She was beginning to like it. Finally, after what felt like an eternity, she put the phone down and walked away. She was not ready to compromise. She hadn't given her new life a chance.

When she later retrieved her phone there was a text. *I miss you* was all it said. She stared at those three words, certain now that she had done the right thing in ignoring his call. For the words that she longed for him to write cried out to her in their absence. *I'll give you whatever you want, Daisy. Marriage, children, a home. Because I love you.*

'It turns out that the Commodore is releasing the moles on Sir Owen's farm,' said Eileen, leaning against the counter of the shop the following morning.

'How do you know?' asked Marigold.

'Sylvia told me. She was taking their dogs for a walk and she saw him with a wooden box, looking suspiciously like it had a mole inside it.'

'Why would he do that?'

'Because it's a safe place, I suppose. And he couldn't very well release them into someone's garden.'

'Do you think Sir Owen knows?'

'I doubt it. Sylvia's a friend of Phyllida's, so she won't want to get him into trouble.'

'Well, I hope those moles don't create havoc on the farm.'

Eileen looked at her darkly. 'I'm afraid I think they create havoc wherever they are,' she said in a portentous voice. 'They can't help it. It's what moles do.'

Marigold set out on her walk along the cliffs. The mornings were getting lighter now, the air was warmer and resonating with the uplifting sound of birdsong. Nothing gave Marigold as much pleasure as listening to the dawn chorus. It was loud and joyous and full of positivity. It promised rebirth and regeneration, an end to winter and a beginning to spring. It made her think of life and the possibility of life after life. She was sure, as she allowed her spirit to soar on the elevating sound of birdsong, that Heaven was up there just beyond the clouds. Somewhere in the great blue. And that it was a place of beauty and serenity where she would eventually reunite with all those she loved who had gone before. As she strode briskly along the path, with the horizon emerging out of the night in a blaze of reds and golds, she was certain that God was behind the magic, for no earthly creature could touch her heart like He did. She basked in the splendour of the Divine.

And then she fell.

She wasn't aware of how it happened, not even *after* it had happened as she lay face down in the grass with her cheekbone throbbing and a pain shooting through her left shoulder. Never before had she had such a sense of being aground, of being utterly in her body, just at the point when her spirit was being carried off into the sky. She lay there blinking, her pride wounded as much as her body, tears stinging her eyes and merging with the blood now seeping from her face. Her euphoria had been cruelly snatched away and in its place was despair.

She remained inert on the grass, trying to turn her mind back to the fateful moment. If she had tripped, what had she tripped on? Or had her legs simply given way all on their own, unprovoked? She didn't want to move. She wanted to lie there a while and gather her thoughts. She could feel the wet soaking into her trousers. Then she began to tremble with cold.

Suddenly a furry face prodded hers and a warm, slimy

tongue licked her cheek. A moment later Mary Hanson's worried voice. 'Marigold? Is that you? Are you all right? Bernie, come away. Bernie!'

Marigold knew she had to get up or Mary's account of finding her lying inert in the grass might worry Dennis unnecessarily. She allowed Mary to take her arm and help her to her feet. She stood a little unsteadily as the blood rushed from her head, making her swoon. 'Goodness,' she mumbled, forcing a smile. 'I must have tripped. I was going at quite a pace.'

Mary's face was crinkled with concern beneath her plum-pudding hat. She looked Marigold over with a searching gaze. 'You've got an awful cut to your face, Marigold.' She put a hand in her pocket and pulled out a scrunched-up tissue. She dabbed at the blood. 'Poor old you,' she said kindly. 'It's a nasty cut. Can you walk, do you think?'

'Oh yes,' said Marigold in a hearty voice that she hoped would convince Mary that nothing was wrong. 'I'm fine, really.'

'Then Bernie and I will accompany you home. Come on, we'll go at a gentle pace.'

Marigold examined the ground for the thing that had tripped her up, but there was nothing obvious. 'That'll teach me to drag my feet,' she said.

When they reached the village, she thanked Mary. 'You're very kind to have accompanied me home. I'm fine now. I'll pop in and clean up before I open the shop.'

'Are you up to opening the shop today? Perhaps you should rest a little. You've had an awful shock. Look, you're shaking. Tasha can cope on her own, can't she?' Then Mary grinned. 'I mean, it's about time she took some responsibility, if you don't mind me saying.'

'Thanks, Mary. I'm sure I'll be all right. I'll have a cup of tea. Everything's better with a cup of tea.'

Mary laughed. 'You're so right, Marigold. You go and put the kettle on. And call me if I can do anything. I'll happily help in the shop, if Bernie can come too.'

Marigold hoped she'd be able to nip up to her bathroom to clean her face before anyone saw her. But as she went into the hall Nan was coming down the stairs. 'I had the strangest dream last night,' she said. 'Dad was alive and telling me to look after you. Isn't that strange? He did have a soft spot for you, though, didn't he? People do say that daughters are closer to their fathers and sons are closer to their mums.' She sighed as she reached the bottom. 'Though, I can't say your brother pays me much attention ...' Her eyes settled on Marigold's face. 'Good God, Marigold! What have you done to yourself?'

'I tripped on the path.'

'Well, your father was right, then, wasn't he! Come into the kitchen so I can have a look at you.'

A moment later she was sitting at the table being observed by her mother as if she were a child again. 'That's a bad cut you've got there,' she said. 'Does anything else hurt? You're trembling.'

'My shoulder,' said Marigold reluctantly, nursing it with an unsteady hand.

'I hope you haven't broken it,' said Nan, shaking her head dolefully. 'Bones don't heal very well when you're old. Do you think you should see the doctor?'

'No, I'm fine,' said Marigold for the umpteenth time that morning. 'Really, it's just a bruise. I can move it.' And she did, to prove she could.

When Dennis came in he was horrified to see his wife's face. He noticed at once how white she was, and how frightened in spite of the smile she pulled to hide it. 'What happened, love?' he asked, coming over to look at her face.

'She tripped on the path, silly girl. Must have been marching along with her head in the clouds,' said Nan, mixing a bowl of disinfectant and water at the sink.

'I'll put the kettle on,' said Dennis, knowing that nothing would restore his wife as well as a cup of tea.

'That would be lovely,' said Marigold, suddenly feeling tearful now that Dennis was here. Dennis who was so strong and capable and wonderfully reassuring. 'Mary was up there and walked me home. Very kind of her.'

'With that horrible dog?' said Nan disapprovingly. 'You're lucky he didn't eat you.'

'He licked me, actually,' said Marigold.

'That's revolting! Dogs lick their bottoms. Just think what he put all over your face. Disgusting!' Nan put a wet cotton-wool pad onto Marigold's cut. It stung. 'Are you sure you don't need a few stitches?' she asked.

'I'm sure it's not that bad,' said Marigold, hoping she wouldn't have to go to A&E.

'Have you seen it?' asked Nan. 'Go and have a look in the mirror and decide for yourself.'

Marigold went to look in the hall mirror. When she saw the gash in her skin she was horrified. Her heart sank. She probably did need to see a doctor, after all.

Dennis gave her a cup of tea, just the way she liked it, with a dash of milk. The first sip was enough to restore her a little. Daisy came in and Marigold had to explain all over again what had happened. 'Before we rush you to A&E,' she said, 'let's call the surgery. You never know, they might have an appointment.'

'But what about the shop?' asked Marigold anxiously.

'Tasha can look after it on her own. It will do her good,' said Nan. 'And if she needs help we can send Suze in. Give her something proper to do.'

A few hours later Daisy and Marigold were sitting in Dr Farah's surgery on account of a last-minute cancellation. He brought up her records on his computer, then examined her wound closely, took her blood pressure, checked that she could move her arm and asked her lots of questions, not just about her fall, but about her memory in general. All the while he wore a serious, pensive expression. Then he sat down behind his desk and knitted his fingers. 'You don't need stitches, but I'm going to put a dressing on it to keep it clean. No broken bones, but that shoulder of yours has taken quite a bruising, Marigold.' He hesitated and inhaled slowly through his nostrils. 'I'd like to run some tests. Nothing to worry about, but as you say your memory loss has got worse since I saw you before Christmas, I'd like to take a closer look.' Then he took some blood and said that the receptionist would be in touch with the results. Marigold had hoped he'd suggest a brain scan, just to check that there was nothing wrong with her brain, but he didn't. She was too shy to ask, and besides, it was presumptuous to tell a professional man like Dr Farah how to do his job. So she said nothing and decided that, if the doctor didn't think her symptoms warranted a brain scan, there was unlikely to be anything wrong with her brain. That, in itself, was something of a relief.

When Marigold and Daisy left the surgery, Marigold had a big white dressing on her cheek. Daisy wondered whether her mother might have had a small stroke up there on the cliffs and was surprised the doctor hadn't considered that. But there had been no mention of an MRI and Daisy assumed, like her mother, that if the doctor had had the slightest concern he would have sent her off to have one. Marigold was certain the blood test would reveal nothing new. She was fit – after all, she marched up that hill every morning at dawn – and she was healthy. This was the first time she had tripped like that and she was sure it would be the last. She had just been unlucky.

Marigold wasn't happy leaving Tasha to man the shop on her own and, even though she was still feeling a little fragile, her sense of duty prevailed. Nan and Daisy were adamant that she take the day off, but Marigold ignored their pleas and hurried across the cobbles.

No one was as pleased as Eileen to see her behind the counter. 'I came in at nine and you weren't here,' she said in a mildly reproachful tone. 'I hear you fell. Mary told me. She said her dog found you in the long grass like the St Bernards in the Alps find people in the snow. You're lucky to be alive.'

'I'm fine,' said Marigold, taking out her red book to see what she had to do today. 'It looks worse than it is.'

'I'm glad to hear that. Because I've come with some terrible news.'

Marigold looked up from her book. 'What news?'

Eileen shook her head. 'Terrible, terrible news.' She hesitated and took a breath. 'Sir Owen is dead.'

Marigold's mouth opened in a gasp. 'What! Dead? How?'

'This morning,' said Eileen darkly, adopting an important tone on account of being the first to relay the news. 'He saw the moles the Commodore has been letting out on his farm and *wham*, just like that, dead. A heart attack.'

'I don't believe it!'

'It's true. Sylvia called in tears. She's in shock, poor lamb.'

'Are you sure it's because of the moles?' said Marigold, knowing how Eileen enjoyed exaggerating a story.

'Of course it's the moles. What else could it possibly be? Sylvia said he was up in the fields, walking his dogs, when he keeled over and died. He was found by the gamekeeper. I'll bet he suffered a heart attack when he spotted the molehills all over his fields. I hope, for the Commodore's sake, that no one tells the police.'

'Does the Commodore know?'

'Everyone will know by now. I bumped into Cedric on my way here and told him. Between me and Cedric the news will have reached town by teatime.'

'This is terrible. Poor Lady Sherwood. Poor Taran. Sir Owen was so young.'

'He was too young to go, that's for sure. To think of poor Lady Sherwood up there in that big old house on her own. Maybe Sylvia will move in for a time, to keep her company. He was a lovely man, Sir Owen, just like his father. A lovely man.'

Marigold thought of Daisy in the middle of the drama and hoped that she was all right. It must have come as an awful shock to her too.

Eileen slowly shook her head and sighed. 'To think Sir Owen might have been done in by a mole. If it had been the Commodore, I would have called it karma.'

Chapter 12

Sir Owen's sudden and untimely death diverted Marigold's attention from her fall and her memory loss. When Daisy returned home at the end of the day, Nan, Dennis and Marigold took their tea into the sitting room to hear all about it.

'Poor Lady Sherwood is beside herself,' Daisy informed them gravely. 'She asked me to keep her company while the police were there. Obviously they needed to rule out anything sinister. Then the ambulance came to take away the body. Lady Sherwood, or Celia as she is to me now – she specifically asked me to call her Celia – telephoned Taran. He's flying home this very minute. Poor thing, hearing that his father's dead like that over the phone. Dreadful shock.'

'Do we know how he died?' Dennis asked.

'Eileen thinks he saw the Commodore's moles and had a heart attack,' Marigold told her.

Daisy looked doubtful. 'Well, they do think he died of a heart attack, but no one has said anything about moles.' Her eyes filled with tears and her shoulders slumped. 'I feel so sorry for Celia. She's in so much shock, she can't even cry.'

'I know what that's like,' said Nan. 'When Grandad died, my eyes were as dry as the Sahara Desert. The tears came later, when the body caught up with the emotions. Then they were like Niagara Falls. It was such a shock to wake up to a dead body beside me. Like a statue it was. Cold and clammy and stiff. Not like Grandad at all.'

'Oh Mum,' said Marigold, putting a hand on her heart. She hated to think of her father like that, clammy and stiff. He had been such a warm, vibrant man. Even after so many years it was hard to accept that he'd gone.

That night when Marigold went upstairs to bed she felt exhausted, as if her shoes were made of lead. She took the steps slowly, leaning on the banisters for support. She didn't notice Dennis behind her until he commented on her laborious movements. 'Are you all right, Goldie?' he asked.

She stopped and turned round. There he was, with Mac on his shoulder. 'Just getting old,' she replied with a weak chuckle.

'We're both falling apart,' said Dennis, thinking of his bad knees and his aching back. 'A hot bath will restore you.'

'I think I'll just crawl into bed,' she replied, resuming her climb up the stairs. 'Not sure I'll make it into the bath.'

When she got to the bedroom she sank onto the bed. Dennis sat beside her. Mac jumped lithely onto the quilt and made himself comfortable against the pillows. 'You've had a bad day,' he said gently. 'Let me run you a bath and bring you a shot of brandy. That'll make you feel better.'

'You don't have to do that, Dennis.'

'I don't have to do anything for you, Goldie. I do it because I want to.' Marigold's eyes filled with tears. Dennis's face furrowed with concern. 'Hey, what is it, love?'

Marigold didn't want to worry him and yet she needed to share things. They'd been married for over forty years and she had always shared things with Dennis. He put his big arm around her and drew her close. 'What is it?'

'I don't think I tripped today. I think my legs just gave way. I found myself on the grass and couldn't get up. It was as if I lost my body for a moment. It frightened me.' Her voice was a whisper, as if she was afraid to articulate her fears out loud.

'What did the doctor say?'

'Nothing, really. Just that I'm getting older. But I feel I'm finding it harder than everyone else. Do *you* struggle to see the world through a fog?'

'No,' said Dennis.

'Do *you* forget everything? People's names? People's faces? Things you would normally remember. Do they just vanish?'

Dennis thought about it a moment, because, like all ageing people, he did have the odd lapse of memory. 'No,' he replied. 'I don't forget things like that.'

'The doctor did a blood test.'

'I'm sure the results will be okay.'

'I don't even know what they're testing me for.'

'Did he suggest a brain scan? Just to see what's going on in there.'

'No, he didn't.' She frowned. 'Do you think he should have?'

'Not necessarily. If he thought there was a problem with your brain he would have sent you off for one, wouldn't he. Dr Farah knows best.' Dennis kissed her temple. 'I'm here, Goldie. You're not alone. We've done everything together and we will continue to do everything together. Now you need to stop worrying, because worrying doesn't help, it just makes you unhappy. Do you remember what your father used to say?'

She smiled tenderly. 'What's wrong with now?'

'Yes, that's right. So, Goldie, I'm going to ask you, what's wrong with now?'

She gave him a small, grateful smile. 'Nothing,' she replied.

'Exactly. We're here, together. I'm going to run a bath and

bring you up a brandy. Just a small one. Then you're going to get into bed and you're going to go to sleep. Suze is getting married. Daisy is enjoying her new job and Nan is, well, swimming in her glass, which is half empty, as it's always been. We're doing okay, you and I. And if the blood test comes back and it isn't okay, we'll tackle it together and we'll still be okay.'

Marigold leaned her head against his shoulder and sighed. 'Oh Dennis. Wasn't I the luckiest girl in the world when I married you?'

'And I the luckiest man,' he replied.

Dennis ran the bath and then went downstairs to fetch the brandy. Marigold sat at her dressing table and took off her necklace. She opened the little drawer in the exquisitely crafted jewellery box that Dennis had made her when they first met, and took a while to admire it. It was made out of ash and walnut in the shape of a miniature wardrobe. One side was a cupboard, with hooks, the other side had five drawers, all lined with velvet, the bottom drawer containing a special padded cushion with grooves for rings. She ran her fingers over it and her eyes welled with tears again. Dennis had always been thoughtful like that. He was kind and sweet and, unlike most men, he was unselfish. She thought of her brother in Australia. She hadn't seen him for about eight years. He rarely called their mother. It wasn't because he didn't care, only that he cared more about himself. Dennis wasn't like that. She knew he'd move mountains for her if he had to.

When she got into the bath she felt a little better. With the brandy inside her she felt better still. Finally in bed, when sleep overcame her, she sank into a cloud of down.

The following morning when she went for her walk over the cliffs, she took care to look where she was going. She didn't walk as fast and she lifted her feet. She stopped to focus her attention on the beauty of the dawn, on the soft golden light and the way it danced about the waves and on the pink clouds that drifted beneath the sky like candyfloss boats. She asked herself the question, *What's wrong with now?* And the answer was *nothing*; nothing was wrong with now.

When she bumped into Mary and Bernie again, she smiled as if she hadn't fallen over the day before and commented on the weather. It was a bright, sunny morning, which was rare, and the hills were a vibrant shade of green. 'I'm on Marigold patrol,' said Mary heartily, beaming a smile. She looked at the dressing on Marigold's cheek. 'You took quite a fall, didn't you?'

'I'm sure it won't happen again,' Marigold reassured her. Reassuring herself.

'Bernie and I aren't taking any chances. While you're walking up here every morning, we're keeping an eye out for you. It gives Bernie a feeling of importance, which is good for his morale. He's taken a few knocks recently.' Mary gave Marigold a look but she didn't put anything into words.

'That's very kind of you, Mary. Thank you.'

'Don't be silly. That's what friends are for.' And as Marigold walked on, she felt warm inside knowing that she wasn't alone.

Daisy cut across the countryside to the Sherwoods' house. She thought of Sir Owen as she walked along the farm tracks. It was hard to believe he had been here, in these fields, only the day before. The cornflower-blue sky and bright sunshine seemed incongruous in the wake of such a tragedy. Bluebells were beginning to open in the woods and bracken and ferns were slowly unfurling. Butterflies basked in the sunlight, spreading their wings and showing off their pretty colours. It wouldn't be long before the leaves were all out on the trees and the bluebells turned the forest floor into a sea of purply-blue. When surrounded by such beauty, it was impossible to imagine there was anything ugly in the world.

When she arrived at the house she didn't go straight to the barn, as she usually did, but went into the house to see Lady Sherwood. She found her in the kitchen, perched on a stool at the island, staring into a cup of coffee. 'Good morning, Celia. I hope I'm not intruding,' she said softly, hovering in the doorway.

Lady Sherwood raised her bloodshot eyes and gave her a thin smile. She was barefaced and her hair was uncombed, which made her look older. 'Of course you're not, Daisy. I've been waiting for you. Come and have a cup of coffee. I'm glad you're here.'

Daisy took off her jacket and went to the machine to make herself an espresso.

'You know I keep expecting to see him,' said Lady Sherwood sadly. 'I keep thinking I hear him, pottering around his dressing room, or walking along the corridor. It's such a squeaky old house. But I think it just squeaks on its own.'

'You're in shock,' said Daisy, heating up some milk at the Aga. Lady Sherwood had the most elegant kitchen, all pale greys and white with shiny marble worktops and a bleached oak floor. No clutter anywhere. Not like Marigold's kitchen. 'I imagine it will take time to accept that he's gone.'

'You know, I thought we'd grow old together. I thought we both had years ahead of us. I never imagined that a healthy, athletic man like Owen would be snatched away so soon. It seems dreadfully unfair.' She heaved a sigh. 'I only have Taran now and he lives on the other side of the world. No good at all.'

'When will he get here?'

'He'll land this morning. I imagine he'll be here in the afternoon sometime.' She hesitated a moment as she considered her son. 'He and Owen didn't see eye to eye, you know. They were very different people. Owen loved the land. His whole life was about his estate and how to preserve it and look after it and love it. Owen really loved it. But Taran is more of a city man. He doesn't appreciate nature like his father did.' She put a hand to her lips, suppressing a sob. 'God, it's so bloody awful talking about Owen in the past tense.'

Daisy brought her coffee to the island and took the stool beside Lady Sherwood. 'I know. It's just horrible. I'm so sorry.'

'Owen was a wonderful man and a good father, but he expected Taran to be like him and was disappointed when he wasn't. Even when Taran was a little boy Owen tried to mould him. He couldn't understand that a child from his loins could be so different from him.'

'Perhaps Taran was like you?' Daisy suggested.

'Yes, you're right. He's much more mine than Owen's. Poor Taran, as a boy he was given endless tennis lessons and golf lessons as Owen tried to turn him into the sporting hero that *he* was at school, but Taran just wanted to draw and build things. You know, he made the most wonderful model houses out of wood. That's what he really enjoyed doing.'

Daisy thought of her father and the model buildings he loved to make. 'Being creative is a gift,' she said.

'I agree. Owen should have been proud. Taran's talent was obvious very early on. But he had his eye on his farm and everything Taran did that foretold a different kind of future panicked him. He wanted Taran to take over after he . . .' Her eyes overflowed again with tears.

Daisy put a hand on her arm. 'I'm sure he will honour his father's wishes,' she said, although she wasn't sure at all. She barely knew him. 'I can't imagine *not* loving this place. It's so beautiful.'

Lady Sherwood smiled at her gratefully. 'I'm so glad you're here, Daisy. Isn't it lucky that we lent you the barn? Fate, I think. Because I'm not alone. Oh, I have Sylvia, of course, and she's a nice presence to have helping around the house. But you're different. You're a friend. I'm very glad you're here.'

'I'm glad I can help. If there's anything I can do . . .'

'Your company is all I require.' Lady Sherwood took a sip of coffee and grimaced because it was cold.

'Let me make you another one,' Daisy suggested and Lady Sherwood didn't dissuade her.

She sighed wearily. 'I have to arrange the funeral. A cremation is what he would want. He's got such a large family with all those sisters, it's bound to be a big affair. I'm not sure I can stomach it. Then there's the will. I'm glad Taran is coming. I can't deal with all that on my own. I don't understand anything about the estate, or the farm.'

'Don't worry about that now. Taran will take care of the business side, I'm sure. As for the funeral, I'm very happy to help. I'm an organized, efficient person when I put my mind to it. We can do it together, if you like. A problem shared is a problem halved.'

Lady Sherwood's eyes filled with gratitude. 'You are a godsend, Daisy. I would really appreciate that. If you wouldn't mind. I'm not sure where to begin.' She gave a little smile. 'I'm thoroughly spoiled, you see. Owen took care of everything.'

'We'll book the crematorium first and take it from there.' Daisy brought Lady Sherwood her coffee and sat down beside her.

'I don't want anyone besides close family at the crematorium. I don't think I want to share that moment with other people.'

'I understand.'

Lady Sherwood put a hand on Daisy's arm. 'I'm keeping you from your work.'

'Please don't worry about that. I can't draw all day and anyway Bridget Williams can wait for her bulldog.'

'I'll have to arrange a service in the church for Owen's friends, and so the local people can pay their respects. Owen was dearly loved.'

'He really was. My parents and grandmother speak very highly of him.'

'That's nice to hear.' There was a long pause. Lady Sherwood stared into her coffee and Daisy wondered whether she was going to leave this one to get cold as well. 'What do you think Owen's doing now? Do you believe there's a place for us up there once we die?'

Daisy's thoughts turned immediately to Grandad. 'My grandfather had an unwavering belief in life after death,' she said. 'There was absolutely no doubt in his mind at all that we come from a spiritual place and return there once our earthly journey is done. He used to say that *this* was the dream and Heaven was the reality. He said the ones we love and lose are always with us. I like to believe they are too.'

'I had a religious upbringing, but it's hard not to doubt. It's hard to believe in something we can't see with our eyes.'

'Well, you can't see radio waves, can you, yet you can hear the music they deliver.'

'Yes, that's true.'

'Grandad said you only have to look at nature to know that there's a higher power.' Daisy dropped her gaze, aware that she might sound a little crazy. 'He said every time you look at a sunset and feel an expansion in your chest, that's the Divine in you recognizing the Divine in nature.' She hoped she hadn't gone too far.

Lady Sherwood smiled. 'I like that,' she said. 'Your grandfather sounds like he was a very wise man.'

Daisy nodded, relieved. 'He was.'

Daisy was in the studio when Taran walked in. She was taken
by surprise. His face was sombre, the shadows dark beneath
the eyes, his mouth set in a tight line. Quite different from the
insouciant man she'd met at Christmas. She didn't imagine
he had slept much on the plane. 'Hi,' he said, closing the door
behind him.

'Hi,' she said, putting down her pastels and peering round
the easel. She hesitated a moment, searching for something
less banal to say, but settled on the usual words because she
couldn't think of more original ones. 'I'm so sorry about
your father.'

'Thank you,' he replied. The aqua-green cashmere sweater
he was wearing brought out the aqua-green of his eyes, or perhaps it was the contrast with the purple shadows beneath them
that turned them so vivid. Whichever it was, they looked quite
startling. 'Mum says you've been a real support. I just wanted
to thank you.'

'I'm thankful I was here when it happened,' she said.

He walked further into the room and put his hands in
his trouser pockets. 'They think it was a heart attack. Mum
says Dad was in great shape, but he drank too much and had
high blood pressure and high cholesterol. He didn't believe
in changing his diet. He was a true pudding and port man.
His father lived until eighty-eight. I'm sure he expected to do
better than that.'

'I know your mother hoped he would.'

'Yes. She'll be lost without him.' There was a pause. He

shuffled, took his hand out of his pocket and scratched his head. 'I'd better go in. I just wanted to say thank you.' His gaze strayed past her to the easel. 'How's it going, by the way? The animal portraits. Might I take a look? Mum says you're very good. I haven't seen the one you did of her dogs yet, but she told me it has pride of place in the hall.'

'I'm drawing Bridget Williams's bulldog, Baz, but I'm finding it hard to establish a connection with him. He's rather aloof and snooty. I've spent a lot of time trying to win him over with treats, but he's definitely playing hard to get.'

Taran wandered round to look. 'Wow. You're seriously good.' He stared at the drawing and rubbed his chin thoughtfully. 'You really are. I'm impressed. It's awesome.'

Daisy felt his mood lift at the distraction and smiled. 'Thank you.'

'No, I mean, *really* good. I can't say whether or not he looks like Baz, but he looks like a real dog, and a snooty and aloof one at that.' He moved his head from side to side. 'He stares out of the page, doesn't he? You're really talented, Daisy.' He glanced at her and grinned. 'Were you a good drawer at school, along with having the neatest pigtails in the class?'

She laughed. 'I always loved art, though I'm not sure I was very good at primary school. It was something I discovered later, one summer term when I had glandular fever. I had to stay at home, so I entertained myself drawing. I'm still learning my craft.'

'It's not a craft. It's a skill and you're very gifted. If I had a dog I'd ask you to draw him too.'

'You'd have to wait in line. I think every pet owner in the village wants me to draw their dog or cat. I don't know what I'll do when I've drawn them all. I won't have any work.'

'I'll get a dog just so you can draw it.'

'Thank you.'

They looked at each other a moment. Taran's eyes were full of warmth and Daisy wondered why she had declined his invitation to go for a drink over Christmas. It seemed rather churlish now. She didn't imagine he'd ask her again.

'Well, I'd better go and see Mum. She says you're going to help her arrange the funeral.'

'Yes, I'm very happy to do whatever is required. She can't manage on her own.'

'You're right about that. Dad always did everything for her.'

'How long will you stay?'

'I don't know. I'll work from here for a while, at least, until the funeral's over.'

She watched him leave then tried to get back to work. For some reason she couldn't concentrate. She thought of Lady Sherwood in that big house on her own and felt sorry for her. It seemed callous of Taran to head back to Toronto, but what else could he do? His life was there.

Unable to draw she decided to take Lady Sherwood's dogs for a walk. Once out in the fields, striding through the long grass in the fresh air, she felt better. She absorbed the luxuriant vibrations of spring and began to think of Luca. She hadn't returned his text. That seemed a bit mean-spirited to her now. In the light of Sir Owen's death her mind honed in on what she had had, rather than on what had been denied her, and she wondered again whether she had been rash in leaving Italy, in leaving Luca. Love was love, after all, and she had thrown it away. Was she greedy and demanding? Should she have settled for what he was prepared to give her? Maybe it wasn't her destiny to have it all.

Marigold was at the back of the shop with Tasha, unpacking boxes of stationery, when the doorbell tinkled and the Commodore walked in with Cedric Weatherby. The Commodore was looking very anxious. Cedric was looking alert, fired up by the unfolding drama, which, thankfully, had nothing to do with him.

'Have you heard the terrible news?' said the Commodore, striding in with a straight back and a raised chin, a hat squarely placed on his head, a navy double-breasted jacket done up over a pair of red trousers.

Marigold made her way to the front of the shop. 'I have,' she replied, wringing her hands. 'I'm so shocked. Sir Owen was a wonderful man.'

'Have you heard about the moles?' asked Cedric, lowering his voice.

The Commodore glanced up and down the aisles warily. 'I set the moles free on Sir Owen's land. I didn't think he'd mind,' he said. 'Harmless really, moles.'

'No one has said anything about moles,' Marigold reassured him. 'No one knows what caused the heart attack, if, indeed, it *was* a heart attack. Which we don't know, do we?'

'But if he *did* suffer a heart attack because of moles, I shall feel terribly guilty.' The Commodore inhaled through his nostrils and assumed the noble expression of a martyr. 'I shall admit to my transgressions. I do not want to meet my maker with a tainted soul.'

Marigold frowned. 'I can't imagine moles would be a big enough problem to cause a heart attack,' she said sensibly.

'Sir Owen loved his land,' Cedric cut in, wanting more than anything for moles to be the cause so he could be the one in the very centre of the drama.

'I simply thought the moles would be happy up there in

those fields,' said the Commodore. 'I did not consider the farmer. I feel very bad.' He put a hand to his breast. 'Phyllida thinks I should keep my concerns to myself.'

'I think Phyllida is right,' said Marigold.

'But I cannot die with a guilty conscience.' The Commodore looked bashful, suddenly. Not at all the naval officer who had once commanded ships. 'I must confess to Lady Sherwood.'

'Are you sure that's wise?' said Marigold. 'She has a lot on her plate right now, I should imagine.'

'No, he's right,' agreed Cedric. 'He doesn't want to meet his maker with a tainted soul.'

The Commodore took a deep breath. 'I'd like a bottle of whisky, please, Marigold.'

'Of course,' she replied, going to fetch him one off the shelf.

'I need a tipple before I go. Dutch courage, you know,' he said. 'And Cedric, you're coming with me, aren't you, dear boy?' he added.

Cedric puffed out his chest. 'Of course I'm coming with you.' He watched Marigold put the bottle on the counter. 'I think I'll have a tipple too.'

Marigold put it through the till, then made a mental note to order more. That bottle had been the last one.

As the Commodore and Cedric Weatherby left the shop, Marigold watched them go. Then she tried to remember what it was that she had made a mental note to do. But it was gone. Vanished. She sighed and shrugged. There was nothing to be done. She hoped it wasn't important.

She hoped, above all, that Sir Owen had not died on account of the moles.

Chapter 13

Daisy returned from walking the dogs just as Cedric Weatherby's vintage Volvo was parking in front of Lady Sherwood's house. The dogs rushed to the car and barked. The hackles on Mordy's back stood up but the spaniels were far less territorial and eagerly cocked their legs on the tyres.

As Daisy approached the car the front door of the house opened and Taran stepped out. He looked enquiringly at Daisy. Daisy peered into the car and recognized the Commodore and Cedric. Cedric switched off the engine and climbed out. He strode straight up to Taran.

'Hello, I'm Cedric Weatherby,' he said, extending his hand. 'We're here to see Lady Sherwood. You must be Taran.'

The Commodore then marched around the car and put out his hand. He gave Taran's a firm shake and introduced himself. 'Commodore Wilfrid Braithwaite. I'm sorry to trouble you at such a difficult time, but I need to speak to Lady Sherwood. It's of a sensitive but important nature.'

Again Taran looked at Daisy, but she had no idea why they had come.

'It might have been prudent to call in advance,' said Taran. 'My mother is struggling to come to terms with her loss.'

'Of course,' said Cedric gravely. 'That is why we are here.'

He pulled a face, which was meant to convey discretion, but instead betrayed a certain self-righteousness.

'Might I just have one minute of her time? I think it's important,' said the Commodore. 'It's regarding your father's death.'

Taran ran his eyes up and down the old officer's red trousers and gold-buttoned blazer and nodded. 'Very well,' he said. 'I'll let her know you're here.'

Daisy wasn't sure what to do with herself, but she followed the three men, and the dogs, into the house.

As Taran went to inform his mother, Daisy remained in the hall with Cedric and the Commodore. The dogs bounded, muddied, into the kitchen. 'What's going on?' Daisy asked, glancing from one man to the other.

Cedric shook his head and looked solemn. The Commodore lifted his chin and said nothing. 'We're very upset,' said Cedric and his chin wobbled. Daisy thought the whole thing very strange, but wasn't able to drag herself away. She couldn't imagine why the Commodore and Cedric Weatherby needed to see the grieving widow the day after her husband had died. What on earth could be so important?

'Come,' said Taran, emerging from the drawing room. 'But please don't stay too long. My mother is very fragile, as you can imagine.'

Cedric glanced at the Commodore and nodded. The Commodore nodded back. The two men, fortified by whisky and their own sense of duty, followed Taran into the room. A moment later Taran came out and closed the door behind him. He put his ear to the door. Daisy hesitated a moment, knowing she should leave. But Taran gesticulated for her to join him. He shook his head. 'God knows what this is all about,' he whispered.

Daisy shrugged. The two of them looked at each other as the Commodore began to speak.

'I'm terribly sorry for your loss, Lady Sherwood,' began the Commodore in the old-fashioned, formal manner typical of the armed forces.

'Thank you,' replied Lady Sherwood.

'I'm sorry too,' added Cedric. 'It's a cruel God that takes the likes of Sir Owen. He was a good man,' he added, to which Lady Sherwood nodded her agreement. It was, indeed, a cruel God that had taken Sir Owen from *her*.

'What can I do for you?' she asked, more out of habit than anything else. After all, they had clearly come because of something *they* could do for *her*.

There was a long pause. Daisy and Taran stared at each other, wondering what was coming next.

'Lady Sherwood, I'm afraid I have a terrible confession,' said the Commodore at last.

The surprise was evident in Lady Sherwood's voice. 'Oh?' she said. 'Really? Do you?'

Another lengthy pause. Cedric nodded encouragement at the Commodore. The Commodore thought of the Gates of Heaven and his tainted soul. 'Lady Sherwood,' he repeated.

'Yes?'

'I had a mole infestation in my garden . . .'

Taran's expression was so comical Daisy wanted to laugh. She put a hand on her mouth to stifle it. Taran shook his head, as if he didn't believe the day could get any stranger.

'Dennis Fane made me a trap to catch them alive. You see, my wife and children were very upset that I was trying to kill them. They love animals, especially furry ones, and to them a mole isn't very different from a rabbit, say, or a guinea pig. The thing is, Lady Sherwood, that once I'd caught them alive, and very pleased I was too that Dennis's trap had been so well crafted, just the right sort of trap for catching live moles . . .'

Daisy's horror showed on her face and Taran had to suppress his laughter.

'I decided to set them free somewhere pleasant,' he continued. 'Somewhere that might be appealing to a mole. One can't very well catch a live mole, then set it free, say, by a main road, or, God forbid, in someone else's garden. The nearest and most convenient place, and the most attractive place for a mole, or so I thought, was on Sir Owen's farm.'

'I see,' said Lady Sherwood, who didn't see at all, but was rather wishing this confession would make its point and the two men would leave her alone.

'There were quite a large number of moles,' said the Commodore, focusing on the Gates of Heaven and feeling his soul washed clean of its sin. 'I must have freed perhaps eight or ten. The trap is a very good one. Far better than I could have expected, but Dennis is a talented carpenter, and my infestation was larger than I had thought. The long and the short of it is, Lady Sherwood—'

'Yes?' by now Lady Sherwood was beginning to lose patience and there was a hard edge to her voice that alerted Taran. He stood up and put his hand on the brass doorknob.

'I believe Sir Owen's heart attack was caused by . . .' He hesitated, mentally preparing for the confession. 'Molehills.'

'Molehills?' repeated Lady Sherwood slowly.

'Molehills,' added Cedric, keen to be helpful. After all, he had, up until this moment, been silent and quite useless. 'The Commodore believes it is because of his moles that Sir Owen suffered a heart attack and died.'

Long silence.

Taran rolled his eyes at Daisy. He turned the knob and entered, leaving the door open for Daisy to witness the rest of the conversation.

'I doubt very much that Dad died because of your moles,' said Taran, walking into the room, to the relief of his mother.

'But how can you be sure?' asked the Commodore, hoping for some small ray of light to relieve him of his guilt.

'For a start there are no molehills on the farm. Certainly none that draw attention. The manager would have reported it. And secondly, if anything had given him a heart attack, it would have been slugs.'

Cedric and the Commodore stared at each other a moment. No one had said anything about slugs.

'But the fact that slugs had made their way through most of Dad's rape would not have been reason enough for him to have suffered a heart attack. Please rest assured that your moles had nothing to do with his death.'

'Well, that is a great relief,' said the Commodore brightly. 'That is to say,' he added, with a little less exuberance, 'I'm very relieved that my actions did not lead to the tragedy. I am sorry for your loss, Taran, and Lady Sherwood, and just, well, thankful that my actions did not contribute in any way. Come, Cedric. Let's leave Lady Sherwood and Taran in peace. I'm only sorry we interrupted it.'

'Thank you for coming,' said Lady Sherwood graciously.

'I'll see you out,' said Taran, a little less graciously.

Daisy hurried into the kitchen as Taran led the two men to the front door and saw them into their car. The old Volvo spluttered out through the gates. Taran closed the door and retreated into the hall.

Daisy emerged from her hiding place. 'Was that really about moles, or did I mishear?'

'It was really about moles,' said Taran, trying to keep a straight face.

Lady Sherwood appeared in the doorway to the drawing room. 'Did I dream that, or did it really happen?' she asked, looking from her son to Daisy in bewilderment.

'It really happened, Mum,' said Taran.

Lady Sherwood shook her head. 'They smelt of whisky,' she added disapprovingly.

Taran began to laugh. Daisy joined him. Finally, Lady Sherwood laughed too. 'Moles indeed!' she exclaimed. 'Now I've heard everything! I only wish Owen was alive to hear it. He'd dine out on that for weeks. Moles, really! I only wish he *had* died because of moles in his fields. At least, in that case, he would have died laughing.'

'Oh Mum,' said Taran, reaching out to embrace her.

'It's okay,' she said, blinking away tears. 'I'm so happy they came. I didn't think I'd ever laugh again. But those two sweet men have reminded me that I do, in spite of everything, still have a sense of humour.'

Daisy watched Taran wrap his arms around his mother. She looked very small there, enveloped by his strong arms. Sensing it was the right moment to leave, Daisy slipped out through the front door, shutting it softly behind her. Taran and his mother needed time alone. Daisy knew she couldn't give much, but at least she could give them that.

As she retreated into the barn, she felt the tingling sensation of inspiration and hurried to her easel. There was something about the tenderness of their embrace that made her want to draw. She put the pastel to the paper and resumed, feeling the thrilling sensation of creativity flowing through her once again and sinking into the meditation of her work. The warm, touching feeling of their shared grief remained with her while she drew and enabled her to connect, at last, with the aloof and snooty dog.

A week went by, during which Daisy started work on her portrait of Cedric's cats and helped Lady Sherwood with the arrangements for the cremation and the memorial service, which was to take place in the village church a couple of weeks before Suze's wedding. Daisy sat in Lady Sherwood's study and made her way down the long list of jobs that she had been asked to do. She placed the announcement, which Lady Sherwood had penned with Taran's help, in the *Daily Telegraph*, and telephoned Sir Owen's closest relatives to let them know when and where the funeral would take place. She arranged caterers for the tea after the service and although Lady Sherwood was yet to finalize the order of service, she arranged a proof, complete with a photograph of Sir Owen, in the fields he had loved so much, leaning on a long stick in an old tweed cap and jacket, which had made Lady Sherwood cry.

Lady Sherwood cried a lot. Taran showed little emotion besides a certain tension in his jaw and a drawn look about his eyes. Daisy listened to Lady Sherwood process her grief, hopping from one emotion to another like a confused cricket. From laughing at the good old days to being debilitated, quite suddenly, by incomprehension and disbelief that the man with whom she had spent the greater part of her life had vanished. Taran did not want to be sucked into his mother's whirlpool of emotion and discreetly left the room whenever she descended into despair. He worked in his father's study, which was at the other end of the house, and spent a lot of time pacing the garden on the telephone. He did not discuss his father with

Daisy. If he discussed him with his mother, Daisy didn't know. She was not privy to it.

Then, one afternoon, when she was returning from walking the dogs, she happened to hear his voice over the herbaceous garden wall where there was a small orchard of cherry trees and a wooden bench. She wouldn't have eavesdropped if the subject had not concerned *her*.

'... I think I'll probably sell it,' he was saying. 'I mean, Dad has left it to me, which, to be honest, is a bit of a surprise. I thought it would automatically go to Mum, and then to his nephew, perhaps. He always knew I had no interest in farming or the English countryside. We argued about that. Anyway, my life isn't here, as I tried to tell him. There's no point owning all that land and doing nothing with it.' Daisy stood, rooted to the spot, heart pounding. There was a pause and then he added, 'It's worth a fortune to a developer and the council will jump at building more houses. They're desperate. Planning permission won't be a problem. I can't think why Dad didn't develop it himself.'

Not wanting to be caught listening, Daisy hurried across the lawn, a sick feeling bubbling in the pit of her stomach. If Taran sold the farm to developers, they would build houses right next to her parents' house. The view of fields would be replaced by brick and concrete. She couldn't bear the thought of the home they had lived in for nearly forty years being ruined by something so ugly. Her mother was fragile and needed the peace of her tranquil garden. Daisy couldn't imagine how she'd cope with bulldozers and noisy lorries destroying the countryside just beyond it.

She was so upset that she stopped working early and walked home across the fields. She wondered how much of Sir Owen's land would be given over to concrete. Gazing about her at the rich and fertile landscape, she realized how much she loved it. How much she treasured her morning march up the farm tracks. How much she relished the birds and trees and flowers, just like her mother did. It broke her heart to think of it ceasing to exist. If Taran sold the farm she'd no longer be able to work in the barn. She'd have to find somewhere else; but she didn't want anywhere else. She liked it here, and she liked Lady Sherwood – Celia. She liked Celia very much.

That night at dinner it was agony sitting with her parents, knowing that they were ignorant of the possible nightmare to come. Marigold had forgotten to attend the meeting at The Old Vicarage and Julia had rung up and been short with her, which had upset everyone. Daisy had reminded her before she left the house that morning, but Marigold had still forgotten. Suze threatened to go round and shout at Julia, and Dennis suggested a quiet word with her husband, the vicar. Nan said she'd never liked Julia in the first place. 'Pompous, self-important woman with ideas above her station,' was how she had described her. 'In my day, if we didn't like someone, we'd put a piece of fish behind a piece of furniture in their house, out of sight and out of reach. The smell would gather slowly over days until it became unbearable.' She grinned raffishly. 'That worked a treat!'

As Daisy put her head on the pillow and Suze turned out the light, she shared her worry with the only person she could. 'Suze, I overheard Taran speaking on the phone today.'

'Oooh! You eavesdropper. What was he saying?'

'His father has left the estate to him.'

'That's not very fair on poor Lady Sherwood, is it? What's he going to do? Turf her out?'

'No, he wants to sell it.'

'That's a shame. Just when you've settled into the barn like a cuckoo.'

'He wants to sell the land to developers.'

There was a long silence as Suze realized how serious the situation was. Then she swore.

'I can't tell Mum and Dad. They'll be devastated,' said Daisy.

'Dad would turn in his grave!' Suze exclaimed.

'Except he's not dead, Suze.'

'Yet. Not dead *yet*. Put a bulldozer on the other side of the garden fence and he'll be six feet under, *turning*.'

'It's dreadful. I don't know what to do.'

'I can tell you what to do.'

'What?'

'You have to convince Taran not to sell.'

'Oh, that's easy! Why didn't I think of that?'

'Don't be sarky. It's the only plan you've got.'

'And it won't work. He's heading back to Toronto after the funeral.'

'Then you have to get moving!'

'I'm not going to convince him to keep the estate in two short weeks.'

'Well, you're going to have to, unless you have a better idea.'

'I don't,' said Daisy in a quiet voice. 'I have no ideas at all.'

'If he sells the land to developers he won't hurt only Mum and Dad, but the entire village. He'll hurt everyone.' Suze rolled over and closed her eyes. 'He's a horrid, greedy man. Just goes to show, looks can be deceptive.'

Daisy was going to defend him, but what did she know? She barely knew him. 'Yes,' she replied. 'He's a horrid, greedy man.' She rolled over too and stared apprehensively into the darkness.

Marigold received a letter from the doctor. It was the results of her blood test, which revealed nothing out of the ordinary. Her blood was perfect. Fit for a Queen, said Dennis. It was a relief to Marigold that nothing sinister had come up. She had to accept that her memory loss was normal, that there was nothing wrong with her. Ageing wasn't a disease, it was just the way it was.

And yet it was getting worse. She was forgetting everything: people who came into the shop – she knew they were familiar but she couldn't remember their names – suppliers she'd used for a long time and tasks which were once as natural and automatic as breathing. She failed to recognize voices on the telephone, or to keep up with what they were saying. She forgot how to use the computer. She stared at the screen as if seeing it for the first time and yet it was the same screen she'd been looking at for years. And everything took longer. Simple tasks felt like enormous challenges. She couldn't tell Dennis she was struggling to complete his jigsaw puzzle and yet, it had become an impossible and daunting project. One she feared. The puzzle had become a mirror, reflecting her forgetfulness back at her like a cruel joker. She thought she was hiding these lapses well. She hoped no one had noticed. She didn't want to worry anyone and she hoped that by keeping them to herself they'd go away. If her blood was healthy, then there was nothing to worry about, was there?

Dennis was at his workbench when there came a knock on his door. He knew it wasn't Marigold, because she never knocked, but nothing would surprise him nowadays. 'Come in,' he called, shouting over the radio. The door opened and Tasha walked in, looking sheepish. 'Hello, Tasha,' he said, reaching to turn the music down. He didn't think she'd appreciate Iron Maiden like he did. He put the block plane to one side and wiped his dusty hands on his T-shirt.

'I'm sorry to disturb you, Dennis, but I need to talk to you.'

Dennis felt the anxiety squeeze his chest. 'Oh, okay,' he mumbled. Mac sensed his uneasiness and hopped onto the workbench, where he sat, staring at Tasha with suspicious eyes.

'It's about Marigold,' she began. 'She's forgetting everything. I'm struggling to cope.' She shrugged. 'I didn't want to say anything at first, I mean, there's nothing wrong with getting old, is there? But it's more than that. It's worrying. Has she been to see a doctor?'

'Yes, she has,' Dennis replied. 'She had a blood test, which was normal.'

'Well, that's good. Did they give her an MRI?'

'No, they didn't.'

'Typical. The NHS will do everything they can to wriggle out of spending money. You should make a fuss.' But Dennis never made a fuss about anything. 'In any case, I wonder whether she should step back a bit and allow me to run things for her. She doesn't like to delegate.' Tasha smiled shyly and curled a lanky tentacle of mouse-brown hair behind her ear. A small diamond stud glimmered weakly on her ear lobe. 'You know what she's like. She thinks she can do everything herself, but she should rely on me more.'

Dennis frowned. 'I don't want to be rude, Tasha, but I didn't think she could rely on you, because you're always taking time off.'

Tasha nodded. 'I know, and I'm sorry about that. I didn't think she needed me, you see. I thought she was pleased when I left her to it. Now I realize she really can't cope on her own and it's not fair on the customers. I could give you a long list of people who have been let down by the post office, and I'm not sure she's up to the computer either . . .' She took a breath. The piece of hair had come loose so she curled it around her ear again. 'I love Marigold. I really don't want to sneak behind her back like this, but I don't know what else to do.'

Dennis sighed and shook his head. He didn't know what to do either, but he knew he had to think of something. 'I'll talk to her, Tasha. See if I can convince her to step back a bit.'

'I don't think she has a clue that anyone else has noticed, but half the village is talking about it.'

Dennis's face clouded. 'They are?'

'Yes, everyone's noticed. They think . . .' Tasha looked embarrassed.

'What do they think?' asked Dennis.

But whatever they really thought, Tasha was not willing to say; Dennis's face was too agonized for her to have the heart to worry him further. 'That she's just getting older,' she said.

Dennis watched her walk back to the house through the garden, where Nan was waiting for her in the kitchen to see her out. What did the village think? he asked himself. But he knew, and the word blackened his mind and lingered there like a wisp of toxic smoke.

Chapter 14

Daisy put down her pastel and looked out of the window onto another enchanted morning of sapphire-blue skies and bright sunshine. It was the perfect day to impress upon Taran the wonders of the English countryside. She had thought of nothing else but his threat to sell up since she had overheard his conversation in the garden. It had even eclipsed Luca, who had up until now enjoyed her almost undivided attention.

She would not normally have been so bold as to ask Taran to join her on a walk, but the threat of bulldozers over her parents' garden wall was enough to force her out of her comfort zone.

So it was with an anxious niggle in her stomach that she went into the house to find the dogs. They were always with their mistress and today was no exception. Lady Sherwood was in her study, responding to the dozens of condolence letters which had been arriving since Sir Owen's death. The three dogs were sleeping soundly at her feet. 'I need some fresh air,' Daisy said from the doorway, as the dogs pricked their ears and leapt onto their four paws in anticipation of being taken out.

'It's a lovely day,' said Lady Sherwood, pen hovering over the paper. 'Just the sort of day Owen relished. If he wasn't playing golf, or in the garden, he was in the woods, coppicing. He adored those woods.'

'I wonder whether Taran might like to come with me. He works so hard, he never gets to see how lovely it is.'

Lady Sherwood pulled a face. 'Good luck with that, Daisy. I don't think Taran has been for a proper walk here for over twenty years, and even then he was never very interested in the countryside.'

'I'll see if I can persuade him. The weather's on my side, which is a start.'

'He's in Owen's study.'

'Thanks. I'll go and find him.'

With the dogs at her heels, Daisy strode through the house to Sir Owen's study. She liked the Sherwoods' home. It was spacious with big sash windows and harmoniously proportioned rooms. Everything was decorated in soft, muted greys and greens. She liked the smell too, of age, for the house must surely be hundreds of years old, and of wood smoke from the open fires that burned throughout the winter months. When she reached Sir Owen's study she stopped. All was quiet within. She wasn't even sure that Taran was inside.

She knocked.

'Come in, Daisy,' came the reply. When she entered, Taran was sitting on the sofa with his feet up on a stool, reading a document. He looked up at her and grinned. 'I thought it unlikely to be anyone else,' he said.

'Sylvia?' Daisy suggested.

'She doesn't knock. Neither does Mother. You're too polite.'

'I'm well brought up,' she replied.

'Yes, you are. You can teach Mother and Sylvia some manners.'

'Oh, I didn't mean—' she began.

'I'm joking. What can I do for you?'

She looked at him, comfortable there on the sofa, and

wanted to back out. But she couldn't think of any other reason why she might have knocked on his door, and now she was here, she had to say something. With her courage flagging, she asked if he wanted to join her on a walk. 'It's a beautiful day and I think you work too hard,' she said. 'If you stay inside and work all the time you're going to look like an amoeba.'

He gave her a quizzical look. 'That's an interesting one. I'm not sure I've ever seen an amoeba. Have you?'

'At school, under a microscope. Transparent, whitish, ugly.'

'Well, I certainly don't want to look transparent, whitish and ugly.' He put the document down and stood up and stretched. Then he clapped his hands. 'Let's go.'

They set off through the garden at the back of the house and out into the fields via a small gate in the post-and-rail fence. 'I don't suppose you're getting much work done at the moment, Daisy,' Taran said, closing the gate behind him. The dogs bolted into the field with the zeal of released prisoners. 'You've given my mother an inch, I assume she's taken a mile!'

Daisy laughed, noticing how very green his eyes were in the sunlight. 'She's very tactful and I'm happy to help her. I feel sorry for her. If it were my father who had died, my mother wouldn't know what to do with herself. She'd be lost. I imagine your mother feels incredibly lost, and lonely, without the man she's shared her life with for so many years. I just want to make her feel better. She's been very generous to me, after all.'

'Where did you draw before?'

'In the sitting room at home.'

'You still live with your parents?'

'I know, tragic, isn't it?'

'Not at all. From what I hear, they're rather special.'

Daisy was surprised. She didn't think he even knew who

her parents were. 'They're special to the people in this village,' she replied. 'And to me, of course.'

He looked at her and narrowed his eyes thoughtfully. 'You're lucky. I had a difficult relationship with my father.'

'Were you very different?'

'Different and with different interests.'

'Town mouse and country mouse,' said Daisy. 'My father used to read that story to me when I was small.'

'Did the country mouse get eaten in the town?'

'No, the country mouse hated the noise and the town mouse thought the countryside boring.'

'I suppose that was me and Dad. But I don't find the countryside boring at all. Sometimes it's nice to be in a place where nothing happens.' Taran took a deep breath and put his hands in his pockets. 'It's restorative.'

They walked into the wood and followed a narrow path through the trees. The ground was blue and green with burgeoning bluebells and unfurling leaves. Birds twittered in the branches and a gentle breeze brought with it the luxuriant scent of spring.

'I lived in Milan for six years,' said Daisy. 'Working in a fusty old museum in the centre of the city. Whenever we could, we'd escape to the mountains, or the lakes, or simply to the countryside. The heart needs beauty and if it doesn't get it, it shrinks.'

Daisy thought she detected a slightly mocking twist to Taran's smile. But she was not deterred. The image of bulldozers destroying the fields around her parents' house propelled her on and she didn't care how ridiculous she sounded. As long as he realized what those fields meant to her family and to the people of the village. 'Who's "we"?' he asked.

'I was in a relationship. But it's over now.'

Her situation seemed to dawn on him. 'Ah, so that's why you live at home,' he said, nodding.

'The point is,' she continued resolutely, 'I need nature to survive. If I couldn't live among the fields and woodland and had to stare out onto concrete every day, I think I'd lose the will to live.'

'You were with him for six years?' he asked, passing over her elegy to the countryside.

'Yes, I was,' she replied. She pictured Luca's face with its wide-set eyes and dimpled chin and felt a pinch in her chest.

'That's like a marriage.'

'Except that it wasn't,' she stated simply.

'I'm sorry it didn't work out. Six years is a massive chunk of your life. I hope he didn't hurt you.'

She looked at him squarely. 'He did.' Then, aware of her share in the break-up, she added, 'We hurt each other.'

'He's an idiot,' he said. 'He should have fought for you.'

'It's complicated.'

'Still, it's his loss.'

She shrugged. 'Actually, it's mine too.' And she recalled Luca's text and the fact that she hadn't replied. She wondered whether he'd reach out to her again, or whether her silence would extinguish any desire for reconciliation.

They walked on through the wood until they came to a track that took them out into a field of yellow oilseed rape. 'I just love this colour,' Daisy said with a contented sigh. 'Sometimes when I walk around these fields on my way to work, the sky is purple and the two colours together are spectacular.'

'Yes, it's pretty, isn't it,' he replied and Daisy wondered whether he'd ever really noticed it before. She thought of her father being inspired by *his* father, who had also been a carpenter, and accompanying him on some of his house visits and wondered whether Taran had ever accompanied Sir Owen around the farm.

'You never felt inspired to be a farmer like your father?' she asked.

'No,' he replied.

'It's a nice life,' she said. 'Waking up to this every morning.'

'And worrying,' he added. He looked at her askance. 'The weather is never quite right for a farmer. It's either too hot or too cold, too wet or too dry. When you want rain, you get drought. When you want dry, you get floods. Slugs eat crops or the rabbits do. There's not much money in it either.'

Daisy was surprised at that. She had always assumed that Sir Owen had lots of money. 'Do you make more money being an architect?' she asked.

'Yes, and I don't worry about the weather.'

'Sir Owen had looked like he had no worries at all. He was always very jolly.'

'He was more philosophical than me. An accepter. He didn't let the weather upset him. I'm a shallower man than my father, Daisy. He loved nature, like you do. He liked helping people, hence his knighthood for his charity work. He was genial and everyone loved him. The only thing was he was controlling in his enthusiasm. He wanted me to be like him and that was stifling, because I wasn't like him at all.'

'I suppose he wanted you to take over the farm when he was too old to run it.'

'That was never going to happen. I studied in Canada and chose Canada as my home. For an accepter, he was pretty unaccepting about that.'

'I think it's important for parents to let their children be who they want to be. So many try to live vicariously through their children, or push them to succeed for their own glory. I'm lucky. My parents have never been like that. They've always given us the freedom to choose who we want to be.'

'You've made a good choice in being an artist, Daisy. How's that bulldog coming along?'

'Done.'

'So which animal is it now?'

'Julia Cobbold's terrier.'

'Isn't she the vicar's wife?' he asked.

'Yes, and the village head girl.'

He smiled. 'It's a real community, isn't it?'

'Yes,' she replied. 'It really is. You know, it's nice being a part of it.'

'That's what my father thought,' he said. 'I'm like my mother. I prefer to keep people at arm's-length.'

'Your mother hasn't kept *me* at arm's-length,' said Daisy with a grin.

'Neither have I,' Taran added, grinning back. 'I'm not sure what it is, perhaps there's just something special about you . . .' The way he looked at her made her stomach lurch. Daisy laughed off her embarrassment. Was Taran flirting with her?

Marigold was in the shop, serving a customer, when Suze called. She didn't recognize her voice and told her, politely, to hold for a minute while she finished putting the goods through the till. Once the customer had left, she picked up the phone. 'Sorry to keep you waiting. How can I help you?' she asked.

'Mum, it's me!' said Suze impatiently. She thought it very odd that her own mother hadn't recognized her voice.

'Suze! Oh, silly me. Sorry. It's noisy in here.' Which wasn't true, she just found the telephone a little confusing these days.

'It's fine. Don't worry.'

'So, what is it?'

'I've got some good news!'

Marigold smiled at the quiver in her daughter's voice. 'What is it?'

'The dress is ready for its first fitting.'

'Oh, that's very good news,' said Marigold.

'And I want *you* to be the first to see it.'

'I wouldn't miss it for the world.'

'This afternoon at five? Can you make it?'

Marigold thought of driving into town and her enthusiasm deflated. She didn't feel very confident behind the wheel anymore. 'Of course I can,' she said, knowing she had no choice. Knowing how much it meant to Suze.

Just as she put down the telephone Cedric Weatherby's shiny pink face appeared in the doorway. 'I *had* to come,' he gushed, pushing the door wide.

Marigold looked at him inquisitively.

He strode up to the counter and gave Marigold a beaming smile. 'Your daughter is a genius. Yes, she is. She's right up there with the very best portraitists of our time.'

'It's finished, is it?' she asked.

'It's finally back from the framer's and looking gorgeous! She's captured every one of my ladies. And their eyes are extraordinary. They watch you as you move about the room, just like they do in real life. Now they will be for ever immortalized in pastels. I'm so grateful to her. I gave her a small tip, because I don't think she charges enough. She could ask for double, at least.'

'That's very generous of you, Cedric.'

'You must come and view it. I'm having a little drinks tomorrow night to unveil it. I hope you can all join me.

Nothing grand, just some nice wine and nibbles. I'm going home to make the nibbles now. I'm out of flour.' He turned to Tasha, who was unpacking boxes in the aisle. 'Be a darling and get me some plain flour, will you.' Then to Marigold. 'Don't forget to write that in your book.'

He watched her take the notebook from beneath the counter and open it. 'Tomorrow at 6 p.m.,' he reminded her.

'Six,' she repeated as she wrote it down. Then, just to be sure she didn't forget, after he had gone she wrote it in the little book she kept in her pocket. There, in two places. Foolproof!

Susan Glenn came in to post a parcel just before lunch, then Dolly came in for stamps, the Commodore's wife Phyllida for bread and Julia Cobbold to tell Marigold that Daisy was now going to draw her terrier, Toby, and was due in this very afternoon to make friends with him. 'She's very good with dogs,' said Julia. 'Most people get barked at, especially men in those ghastly yellow jackets. You should see them, these big, burly men, being terrorized by Toby. But he doesn't bark at Daisy.'

A couple came in just after Julia left and greeted Marigold as if they knew her, but Marigold thought they must have made a mistake, because she'd never seen them before. However, she was very polite and friendly, just in case it was her memory playing up again. Nowadays she couldn't be sure.

Eileen appeared and leaned on the counter, in her usual place, and told Marigold that Sylvia had overheard Taran and his mother talking and it appeared that Sir Owen had left his estate to his son, rather than his wife. 'Which is strange, considering he knew that his son wasn't interested in running the farm. Poor Lady Sherwood! Sylvia says she's much too upset about his death to worry about her future. Poor dear, it probably hasn't occurred to her that he might sell it.'

'Sell it?' Marigold gasped. 'I'm sure he won't do that. I'm sure he'll wait until his mother dies to do that. And she's young and fit, she'll go on for another twenty years, at least.'

'Taran lives and works in Toronto. Lady Sherwood is Canadian so maybe she'll go back. No point them both being on separate continents now that she's a widow. She'll want to be near him, won't she? And Toronto is home for her, after all.'

'But the manager can run it for him, can't he? He's a good manager is David Pullman.'

Eileen shook her head. 'I don't know what's going to happen, Marigold. But we don't want Taran selling it. You never know who we'll get living up there. Up until now we've been fortunate with Sir Owen allowing us to walk on his land. Can you imagine if we get an undesirable? It will be out of bounds. What a sadness that would be.'

Marigold frowned. She hoped he didn't sell it to a developer. She knew how hard Sir Owen had fought off those avaricious people who had no appreciation of green fields for their beauty, only for how much money they could make building on them. 'I'm sure he won't turf his mother out of her home,' said Marigold finally. That thought cheered her up a bit. There was no way, in her view, that a son could be so callous to his mother. Toronto might have been home to her when she was a young woman, but she had lived the greater part of her life in England.

'Hmm,' murmured Eileen, screwing up her nose. 'I don't think Taran is a very nice man.'

Tasha manned the shop while Marigold went to get something to eat. Nan was having her hair done in town. She had a wash and set once a week and nothing stood in the way of it – her hairstyle hadn't changed since the 1950s. Marigold made a salad with cold ham and new potatoes in butter and went to ask Dennis if he wanted to share it with her. Dennis was delighted there was lunch on the table and eagerly followed her up the garden to the house. 'You're an angel, Goldie,' he said.

Marigold was pleased to be appreciated. She laid his place and put the food on the table. Then she sat down. 'Eileen says Taran wants to sell the farm.'

Dennis knitted his eyebrows. 'I think that's highly unlikely. He's not going to tell his mother she can't live there anymore. And Sir Owen would turn in his grave if he did.'

'That's what I think,' said Marigold. 'He left the farm to Taran, probably hoping that he'd rise to the challenge and make something of it.'

'Sir Owen was a shrewd man, Goldie. If he left it to his son, then he did so knowing he would take care of his mother. Taran isn't the sort of boy to treat his mother badly. He's a good boy.'

'Eileen would disagree with you.'

'Eileen likes a bit of drama.'

Marigold laughed. 'You're right about that.' Then she remembered Cedric's invitation. She hadn't even had to look in her book. 'Cedric's unveiling Daisy's picture tomorrow. It's drinks so it must be around six.'

Dennis chewed happily on his ham and nodded. 'That's nice.'

Marigold felt good inside. She had remembered Cedric's invitation. Usually, she only remembered things when she looked in her book.

That afternoon the shop was surprisingly busy. People came in and out and everyone liked to have a chat. Tasha was very helpful, gently reminding Marigold of things she'd forgotten, and taking care of the post office, which Marigold found the most challenging part of her job.

At quarter past five the telephone went. Marigold picked it up. 'Mum!'

She recognized the voice this time. It was Suze. 'Oh, hello, dear.'

'Mum, what are you doing in the shop?'

Marigold was confused. 'I'm working,' she replied after a pause.

'You're meant to be here!'

'Where?'

'Here, at my fitting!'

'You have a dress fitting?'

'Yes, and you're meant to be here.'

'Well, why didn't you tell me?'

'I did. I called this morning. Have you gone mad?' Suze's voice quivered with fury. Marigold felt a stab of fear in her chest.

'Did you?'

'Yes, you know I did.'

'But, I don't remember—'

'That's because you don't remember anything.'

Marigold was close to tears. 'I'm so sorry, love.'

'Well, there's no point coming now. It'll take you ages in the traffic and you'll probably forget the way!'

'I could get Tasha to drive me.'

'Don't be silly. It's too late. It's not going to be fun anymore. I'll have the fitting on my own. But I want you to know you've ruined one of the most special days of my life.' She hung up.

Marigold pressed the telephone to her ear. 'Suze? Suze?' The line was dead.

Tasha appeared. 'Are you okay?' she mouthed.

Marigold slowly put the phone down. 'Did Suze call me this morning?' she asked in a trembling voice.

Tasha nodded. 'Yes, I think she did. Just as Cedric came in.'

Marigold swallowed and put a hand on the counter to steady herself. 'I need to sit down.'

'It's okay. Come, let's get you into the kitchen.'

'No, I'm going to go out,' she said suddenly, changing her mind. She grabbed her coat from the hook behind the door. 'I'll be fine, don't worry. I just need some air.'

Tasha watched her leave. She hadn't ever seen Marigold this upset. She bit the skin around her thumbnail and wondered whether she should go and tell Dennis.

Chapter 15

Marigold could barely see for tears. They blurred her vision and streamed down her cheeks. She dropped her head and hoped she didn't bump into anyone she knew. Then she set off up the hill, the same route she took every morning in an effort to help her memory. Well, a lot of good *that* had done!

The guilt she felt for missing Suze's big moment was like a dagger in her heart, twisting and turning and causing her unbearable pain. She hated herself for failing Suze. She hated her memory for failing *her*. There was nothing wrong with her devotion; if anything, she had too much of it. But there was everything wrong with her brain. How could she explain that to Suze? Suze, who was now furious and hurt and let down.

She marched up the path and allowed her unhappiness to come out in loud, rasping sobs. The doctor might tell her there was nothing wrong; her friends might try to reassure her that she was simply getting older; Beryl might say it was happening to all of them, that they were all getting forgetful. The truth was there *was* something wrong, she *wasn't* just getting older and it *wasn't* happening to all of them. It was happening to *her* and her alone. And now she had let her daughter down on one of the most important days of her life. It should have been

a special day for mother and daughter. A moment to treasure
for ever. The first sight of her little girl all grown-up and in
her wedding dress. The thought of having missed it made her
cry all the more. How could she have forgotten? How *could*
she? She had remembered Cedric's party!

Marigold walked along the clifftop with her hands in her
coat pockets and watched the gulls wheeling in the early
evening sky. The sun was a ball of fire, sinking towards the
sea, catching the tips of the waves and scattering them with
sparks. Touching the tips of the gulls' wings and turning them
to gold. It was so beautiful that she put a hand to her chest,
above the place where it hurt the most, and allowed the glory
of nature to move her further. *Oh God, what is happening to
me?* she asked. And the gulls cried mournfully for the answer
that didn't come.

The sea was a long way down. Marigold stood on the
clifftop and watched it foam around the rocks, rising and falling, ebbing and flowing, just as it always did. The sight was
mesmerizing. It reminded her of her childhood when she and
her brother had stood together on these very cliffs and wondered what it would be like to jump. She had worried that her
brother might actually try. He'd been like that, had Patrick;
daring, mischievous and brave, and hungry for attention.
Marigold had never considered jumping, but she wondered
now what it would be like landing on those rocks. Whether
it would hurt. Whether she'd die on impact, or whether she'd
lie broken on the rocks for the waves to gradually take her.
She knew she was being morbid and self-indulgent. After all,
she hadn't killed anyone, she'd just hurt one of the people she
loved the most. That didn't warrant throwing herself off the
cliff. It wasn't something one died for. But right now she *did*
want to die. She continued to stare down at the foaming sea

as a sense of helplessness descended upon her like a shroud, separating her from the light.

Suze returned home in a fury. She had spoken to Batty on the phone and he had dropped everything and fetched her from the dressmaker. She had considered breaking all the rules and showing the dress to him instead, just to punish her mother, but she'd seen sense at the last minute and met him at the door in her jeans and shirt. Batty had driven her home in his green van with *Atticus Buckley Garden Design* written on the side in purple writing, listening to her ranting all the way. 'I hate my mother,' she had grumbled. 'How could she forget? Aren't I important to her? Doesn't she care? How can she put her shop above me? I suppose now Daisy's home, Mum's not interested in me anymore.' Then she had cried hot tears and Batty had had to stop the van to comfort her.

He had embraced her, kissed her head and told her, wisely, to be patient. 'Old people forget things all the time. It's not her fault. Be kind. She's not going to be around for ever.'

'She's not old enough for age to be an excuse.'

'Then you can't punish her because she forgot,' he'd smiled, trying to ease her out of her tantrum. 'It's human to forget – and divine to forgive.'

'It's my wedding. I'm her *first* wedding. This year is about *me!*'

'It *is* about you, sweetheart. *All* about you. I bet she feels terrible.'

'She'd better. Trust me,' she'd said, looking at him with a face as tight as a fist. 'If she doesn't, I'll make her feel terrible!'

'This isn't like you, Suze, to be so hard-hearted.

You're overreacting and blowing it out of all proportion. Come on,' he'd cajoled, serious now and disapproving. 'Enough of this.'

'I'm just hurt.'

'Don't be hurt, be forgiving.' He'd smiled then, but Suze had simply folded her arms and stared out of the window, her jaw set in a determined scowl.

Batty dropped her off at her front door, but didn't come in. He had no desire to witness an unpleasant scene. He knew what Suze was capable of, especially when she was hurt. They had split up once and she had thrown all his clothes out of the window into the street. He had since learned how to avoid such a scene.

Suze stomped into the kitchen to find Nan at the table. 'Oh dear, has someone died?' she asked, looking at her grand-daughter over the rim of her spectacles.

'I'm absolutely furious!' Suze exclaimed.

'With whom?' asked Nan.

'Mum.'

'What's she done?'

Suze's face twisted into an ugly scowl as she began to cry again. 'She forgot to come to my dress fitting. I was waiting there for half an hour and she didn't come. She just left me. Then, when I called her, she couldn't even remember that we'd arranged it. She couldn't even remember me having called her. Can you believe it? I'm so cross, I could hit someone.'

'Well, don't hit *me*,' said Nan. 'You might send me to an early grave.'

Suze growled and went to boil the kettle. 'If I go into the shop, I might destroy it,' she said.

'That would be unfortunate. Why don't you just go and talk to her, without destroying anything? You're not a child, you're a grown-up. Grown-ups don't destroy things when they're angry. They talk things through in a sensible way. Once, when I was angry with your grandfather I—'

Suze couldn't bear listening to a long-winded story about a fight her grandparents once had. 'Okay, I'll go and talk to her,' she said, leaving her grandmother mid-sentence, which is exactly what Nan had hoped she'd do.

Suze crossed the courtyard at a march, jaw jutting with intention, face grey with rage. When she entered the shop, Tasha was behind the counter talking to Eileen. 'Where's Mum?' she demanded, looking from one woman to the other with impatience.

'She's gone out,' said Tasha.

Suze clicked her tongue and heaved a loud, irritable sigh. 'Where?'

Tasha glanced at Eileen. Eileen said nothing. 'She was very upset,' Tasha told her. 'She's gone for a walk.'

'She forgot my dress fitting,' said Suze. 'She's ruined the most important day of my life!'

'I think your wedding is going to be the most important day of your life,' said Eileen.

'Be patient, Suze. She's really upset. I've never seen her so upset,' said Tasha gently.

Eileen put a hand on Suze's arm. 'I think she's unwell, dear. You must be kind.'

Suze frowned. 'Unwell? With what?'

Eileen looked at Suze with compassion. 'I think she might have dementia, dear,' she said. 'She's not the first. I've got a friend who's in a nursing home and she started just like Marigold. Forgetting things, feeling tired and unwell for no reason. Falling over. Not recognizing people. It's a different sort of forgetting.'

Suze's anger evaporated. 'Are you sure?' she asked anxiously. 'Do you really think she's got dementia?'

'I wasn't going to say anything,' said Eileen. 'But I can't stand by and let you get cross with her for something that really isn't her fault.'

'What should I do?'

'She needs to see a doctor,' said Tasha. 'I spoke to your father about it, but I don't think he wants to face it. You and Daisy need to take her in hand. If it is dementia there are lots of things you can do to help. At the very least it will make you more understanding and less quick to anger.'

'Well, I wouldn't be angry if she was unwell, would I?' said Suze defensively, crossing her arms. 'I need to speak to her.'

'I think she's gone for a walk along the clifftops,' said Tasha. 'That's where she goes every morning. When she had that fall, it was there that Mary found her.'

'Okay, I'll try there,' said Suze, making for the door.

'She was very upset,' said Tasha.

'*Very* upset,' Eileen agreed, not having seen her but wanting to add her bit to the drama.

Suze felt guilty. She knew she had said something mean; she always turned mean when she was angry. If only she could control it, but when the feeling came over her, she was unable to shrug it off. It just consumed her. She had said something horrid and now her mother was upset and feeling terrible for having let her down. It wasn't really the most important day of her life; it was just a dress fitting. There would be others. She wished she hadn't made such a drama out of it.

As she strode up the hill, she thought about what Eileen had said. Suze didn't know much about dementia, except that those with the disease forgot things all the time. There had been a lot about it in the press, but as it hadn't concerned her she had never read any of the articles. She'd also heard people discussing it on Radio 4, which Nan liked to listen to in the kitchen, but again, she had dismissed the subject as irrelevant and tuned out. Of course, Eileen could be wrong, she considered. Eileen loved a situation. It would be typical of her to think the worst and to spread her theory around the village. But her mother *had* become very forgetful recently, and what was it with all those Post-it Notes and lists on the fridge door? It was like she had to be reminded of the smallest things. Things most people remembered by default. She decided she would google dementia when she got home and find out more about it. Right now, she had to find her mother.

Suze hurried up the hill. The wind had picked up and was blowing inland off the ocean with a cold and bitter edge. The sun had gone behind a thick cloud, the sort of cloud that might bring a shower. It had an angry grey belly and was charging across the sky like a bull. She couldn't bear for her mother to be upset, and worried that she might take another fall. Suze would never forgive herself if her mother got injured on account of *her*.

She almost ran along the path, eyes scanning the horizon for the diminutive figure of her mother. The bull in the sky now lingered overhead, snorting angrily. Drops of rain began to fall from its grey underbelly. They were cold and sharp. Suze wished she had brought an umbrella, but it hadn't looked like rain when she'd set off. This morning had been beautiful.

As she had expected, the rain began to fall fast and heavy. Suze started to worry. She hoped her mother had brought a coat and hat. Perhaps she'd gone home by another route. She thought of her in the kitchen, making a cup of tea, and imagined herself returning all wet and her mother telling her to change out of her sodden clothes at once before she caught a chill. She visualized embracing her and saying sorry. Tears stung, making it hard to see through the rain.

At last she spotted her mother's unmistakable figure standing on the edge of the cliff, staring down. She looked as if she was about to jump. Suze was gripped with panic. It clamped her heart like a vice. 'Mum!' she shouted.

Her mother looked round.

Marigold was not wearing a hat and her coat did not have a hood. Her hair was drenched and her face was white and pinched and strangely vacant.

'Mum! Come away from the edge!'

Marigold was confused. She didn't know why she was here. In fact, she didn't know where she was. She knew she was staring into the sea and she remembered that she and her brother used to gaze into the sea like this when they were children and wonder what it would be like to jump. But she didn't know how she had got here. When she realized that the woman shouting at her was her daughter, she was overcome with relief. Suze was like a lighthouse, shining her light from a familiar shore. Marigold took a step towards her, but her legs felt very heavy and she swayed. She swayed dangerously close to the edge of the cliff.

Suze reached her and grabbed her by the arm. 'Mum, what are you doing?' she shouted.

'I don't know, love,' said Marigold in a voice that sounded strange to both of them.

Suze stared at her, horrified. 'You don't know?'

Marigold's eyes were full of fear, which made the vice on Suze's heart squeeze tighter. 'I'm not sure how I got here . . .'

'Mum, you walked here.'

'Did I?'

'Yes. We had a fight. I said some horrid things to you on the phone. I'm so sorry.'

Marigold searched her mind for a memory of those horrid things, but her brain was full of porridge, she couldn't find anything. She shook her head. She couldn't find the words to explain the porridge feeling. She gazed at her daughter blankly. Suze gathered her into her arms and held her tightly. 'Oh Mum, I'm so sorry,' she repeated.

Marigold didn't know why she was sorry, but she forgave her anyway, because that's what one did when someone apologized.

'Come, let's get you home,' said Suze gently, linking her arm and leading her away from the cliff and back to the path. 'You're soaking. We don't want you to get a chill.'

Marigold smiled feebly. 'That's what I used to say to you when you were a little girl. "Get out of those clothes at once or you'll catch a chill." You're wet too, love.'

Suze began to cry. 'You frightened me, Mum.'

'Did I?'

'I thought you were going to jump.'

'Now why would I do a silly thing like that?'

'Because I was horrid to you.'

Marigold shrugged. 'I can't remember.'

'Well, that's one good thing about forgetting things,' said Suze and Marigold was pleased that Suze had found a silver lining where she had failed to.

The porridge in her mind began to subside and snippets of memory began to peep through like sunshine through cloud. Marigold looked around her and recognized the path and the rocks and the landscape. Her breathing began to slow and her heart rate returned to normal.

'I forgot your fitting, didn't I?' she said, wondering why she should remember that now.

'It's okay, Mum. There'll be another one.'

'I really want to see you in your dress, Suze.'

'You will. I'll make another appointment and take you there myself.'

Marigold patted her hand. 'Oh, would you? That would be wonderful.'

'But you have to do something for me first.'

'Of course. What do you need?'

'I need you to see a doctor.'

'But I've already seen a doctor.'

'You need to see him again.'

Marigold sighed. 'I doubt he'll say anything different.'

'I'm going to come with you.'

'You don't have to do that.'

'I want to.'

And as it turned out, Daisy and Dennis wanted to as well.

The four of them sat in the doctor's surgery a week later. Dr Farah brought up Marigold's notes on the computer and looked at them closely. 'Have you had another fall?' he asked, peering at her over his glasses.

'No, but she forgot where she was recently,' said Suze. 'I found her on the clifftop, bewildered and confused, and if I hadn't found her I dread to think what would have happened.'

Dr Farah nodded at Suze and then looked at Marigold. 'And this has happened before, hasn't it?' He scanned his notes.

Daisy answered for her. 'At Christmas. She forgot where the car park in town was, didn't you, Mum?'

Marigold nodded. 'It's as if a mist comes in and hides

everything. If I wait and breathe, the mist eventually lifts and it all comes back.'

'And how do you feel in yourself?' the doctor asked.

'Some days are fine, others are difficult. Some days I just want to stay in bed because I feel so tired and my brain is slow.' She turned to Dennis. 'I'm sorry, love. I'm finding your puzzle a bit of a challenge.'

Dennis put his hand on hers and smiled. 'That's all right. It's meant to be fun. Perhaps Daisy and Suze can help you with it.'

'Of course we will,' said Daisy.

The doctor continued to ask questions. He took her blood pressure and then another blood sample. Finally, he took off his glasses and sat back in his chair. 'I'm going to send you off for a brain scan and refer you to a clinical psychologist,' he said. 'She'll be able to test your memory.'

'Do I have dementia?' Marigold asked suddenly. She hadn't wanted to. She'd been too frightened to open that up as a possibility, but now, sitting in front of the doctor, she decided she'd be brave.

Dr Farah shook his head and frowned. 'I don't like to speculate without having all the facts in front of me. For certain your memory is impaired, but to give you a diagnosis without being in possession of all the facts and test results would be unprofessional.'

'Of course you haven't got dementia!' said Dennis.

'You're going to be fine, Mum,' said Daisy.

Suze knew from Daisy's forced smile that she didn't believe it.

When they got home, Marigold and Dennis sat at the kitchen table with Nan. 'They're sending Marigold off for an MRI and referring her to a clinical psychologist,' he told her.

'I know what an MRI is, but what's a clinical psychologist?'

'I don't know,' said Dennis. 'But they'll do some memory tests and hopefully find out what's wrong.'

'You're just getting older, Marigold,' said Nan in a tone that suggested she thought the whole idea utterly absurd.

Marigold was tired of being told that. She poured hot water into the teapot and brought it over to the table. 'I just want to find out what's wrong with me and to be given the correct medication to get better.' She smiled wearily. 'I want to feel like myself again.'

Nan pulled a face. 'You're making it worse by being anxious,' she said. 'If you didn't make such a thing out of it, you'd probably find it went away by itself.'

'You mean, if I forgot about it?' said Marigold with a smile. Dennis smiled back at her. Then they both laughed. 'Sadly, the only thing I'm *unable* to forget about is that,' she said and sat down. 'Now, let's have a nice cup of tea and talk about something else.'

'Good idea, Goldie,' said Dennis.

Marigold poured the tea. 'What's wrong with now?'

Nan's face softened and she smiled tenderly at the thought of her husband. 'Nothing's wrong with now,' she replied and Marigold nodded with satisfaction.

'Nothing's wrong with now,' she repeated and put down the teapot.

That evening, while Nan nodded off in front of the television and Dennis made miniature pews for his church in the kitchen, Marigold, Daisy and Suze sat at the table in the sitting room and worked on the jigsaw puzzle. With their heads down and their bodies almost touching, they pieced together the picture that Dennis had so lovingly crafted. Instinctively, Daisy and Suze conspired. They collected clusters of pieces that went together and casually placed them in front of their mother. Oblivious to what her daughters were doing, Marigold studied the pieces, compared them for colour and form and, with a rush of pleasure, fitted them together. To her surprise and delight, she was able to complete a small section of the picture on her own. 'It's a cat slipping on the ice,' she gasped, staring down at the black-and-white cat. 'He looks just like Mac. Do you think that's why Dennis chose the picture?'

Daisy caught Suze's eye and they both smiled. 'I think Mac would be just as useless on the ice,' she said.

Marigold laughed. 'If Mac's in the picture, Dennis can't be far away. I'm going to look for him now.'

'They're inseparable, aren't they?' Daisy mused with a chuckle.

'Where there's one, there's always the other,' Marigold added.

'This is fun, isn't it, Mum?' said Suze, sliding the pieces that made up a couple in front of her mother.

'Thank you for helping me,' Marigold said. 'I couldn't do this without you.'

'We're a good team,' said Daisy.

'Ah! Look what I've found!' Marigold seized upon the pieces in front of her and snapped them into place with growing confidence. 'A couple!'

'You and Dad,' said Suze.

'Could be, couldn't it?' Marigold agreed.

'They're holding hands, just like you and Dad,' said Daisy.

Marigold's smile wavered a little. 'Trust Dennis to find such a beautiful picture.' She traced it with her fingers. 'He's good like that, isn't he?'

'He is,' Daisy agreed. 'He's the best.'

'Now we have to find me and Daisy,' said Suze.

'And Nan,' Daisy added with a giggle.

They glanced over to where Nan was asleep on the sofa.

'She'll be on her back in the snow, having slipped,' whispered Suze.

'Complaining,' Daisy added.

The three of them laughed and Marigold felt normal again. Perhaps Nan was right, after all. If she stopped being anxious, it might just go away.

Chapter 16

Daisy spent the next few days playing with Julia Cobbold's terrier in preparation for his portrait, and helping Lady Sherwood with the funeral arrangements. She did the seating plan for the church and printed labels for those who required reserved seats. She kept up with the growing list of those wanting to come and proofread the order of service. On top of that she walked Lady Sherwood's dogs and managed to entice Taran to join her, even in the rain. Taran was not interested in talking about the farm, the woods or the beauty of the countryside, so Daisy gave up trying to steer him in that direction and hoped that, by being exposed to it, he might grow to love it as she had. After all, it belonged to him now. However, he never discussed his inheritance, or what he intended to do with it. They chatted about many things and enjoyed a light banter, but Daisy soon realized that, in spite of the time they spent together, she knew Taran little better than when she had first met him. He just wasn't someone who enjoyed talking about himself and his feelings. He didn't talk much about his father, either. He deftly skirted around the subject with what appeared to Daisy to be a well-practised art of avoidance, and she wondered whether he had developed that skill over years of eschewing emotions. The British stiff upper lip wasn't something she had encountered until now. Taran was funny, charming, witty and kind, but he could also be remote and cold.

Daisy compared him to Luca, who was fiery and emotional, with a penchant for drama and exaggeration. Taran was phlegmatic and dry-humoured, and she doubted he exaggerated anything. Both men were creative and intelligent, however, with a strong sense of who they were and who they wanted to be. She had always liked that about Luca. He wasn't a crowd-follower and he wasn't concerned about what other people thought. He was unashamedly himself. She sensed Taran was like that too.

She was gazing out of the studio window, thinking of Taran and how unfathomable he was, when her phone rang. She had recently chosen a dog-bark ringtone and it gave her a sudden shock. For a split second, she thought there was a dog in the room. She was surprised to see Luca's name on the screen. After a moment's hesitation she picked up. She had nothing to lose; after all, she'd already lost everything.

'*Ciao*, Luca,' she said and sat down.

'*Ciao*, Margherita,' he replied, using the name he'd given her when they'd first met, which was a direct translation of daisy. 'Thank you for taking my call. I thought you'd never speak to me again.'

'I'm not angry anymore,' she replied, savouring the sense of her old self as she slipped into speaking Italian again. It brought Italy and Luca back to her more acutely.

'It's good to hear your voice, my love.'

'How are you?' she asked.

'In my life or in my heart?'

She smiled in spite of herself. She could just picture him

standing there looking at her with sheep's eyes, a fist banging his chest for emphasis. How like Luca to be dramatic.

'Let's start with your life,' she suggested.

He sighed. 'Good, I suppose. Work is busy, as always. You remember Carlo Bassani?'

'Yes.'

'He still wants me to do the photography for his book.'

'The one about interiors?'

'Yes, I'm not sure . . .'

'But you were quite into the idea.'

'I was, but now you are gone, I've lost enthusiasm for my life. Which brings me on to my heart.'

'I suppose you're going to tell me that it's hurting as much as mine.'

'*You* broke *my* heart, Margherita. I never wanted you to leave. Don't forget that. And it has always been in your power to mend it. You only have to come home.'

'Not entirely true, Luca, if you remember rightly.'

'We could have each other and together conquer the world.'

'I don't want the world. I want a family.'

There was a long pause.

'I would give everything to have you back in my life, but that is too high a price to pay. I thought you might have missed me.'

'I *have* missed you. I miss you still, a lot.'

'A lot, a lot! What does that mean?'

'The same as you, Luca. I've missed you but not enough to compromise on what I want. I'm sorry.'

'We are the two biggest fools, you know,' he said with a sigh. 'Two big fools who can't see how good they are together.'

'I can see it, Luca. I was with you for six years because I knew how good we were together, but I feel incomplete. Running back to you will not make me whole.'

There was another long pause. The silence was so heavy Daisy wondered whether he had cut off.

'Then there is nothing more to say,' he said at last, and his voice had lost its vigour.

'Perhaps not.'

He chuckled bitterly. 'You have become English again.'

'I've always been English.'

'No, you became Italian, but now you're English.' She sensed that was not a compliment. 'You don't sound like my Margherita anymore.'

'That's because I'm not, Luca. I'm my Daisy.'

He didn't ask what that meant. 'So, it is goodbye then.'

'I suppose it is,' she answered.

There was another heavy pause. Daisy waited for him to speak. She sensed his annoyance. He always liked to be in control. Now he wasn't.

When he finally spoke his voice was soft and full of feeling. 'Just because I don't want to marry and have children does not mean I don't want to be with you or that I don't love you. Do you understand?'

'As I said, Luca, we both want different things.'

'No, you are wrong. We both want each other.'

'I have to go, Luca.' Daisy was weary of the argument.

'Think about it, Margherita.'

'Goodbye, Luca.'

When she hung up, she realized he hadn't asked her about herself at all. She wondered whether he had always been so self-absorbed. *I'm my Daisy*, she repeated to herself. It was true. She didn't need anyone to complete her.

Yet, as she turned her gaze to the big studio window, the view was blurred by a film of tears.

Suze made sure that the arrangements for her wedding were all in hand. She double-checked everything that her mother had ticked off on her list, just to be sure. Daisy had been helping her, but now she was busy with Sir Owen's funeral she didn't have time to oversee the wedding as well. Much to Suze's delight, she had gained many more followers on her Instagram site due to all the posts she was putting up about her wedding. She had curated some beautiful photographs of flowers, invitations, underwear and jewellery, none of which were her own, but taken in wedding shops and at the fairs she'd gone to for inspiration. The companies had been so delighted with her posts that they had offered her discounts.

Marigold agreed to give Tasha more responsibility in the shop, and to take on a school-leaver part-time to help. This was a challenge for Marigold. It was difficult relinquishing control and putting her trust in someone who had, historically, been fantastically unreliable. But Tasha assured her that she would not let her down. Marigold had no choice but to give her a chance.

The morning of Sir Owen's funeral dawned with a luminous beauty that would have pleased him. It was the end of spring and she was giving her very best before she stood aside and allowed summer to take her place. The horse chestnut trees that sheltered the church from the sea winds were now in full flower. The leaves were an almost phosphorescent green, the candles thick with white blossom, the birds that nested among them vociferous in their farewells to the departing season. The heavens were as blue as lapis and the sun flooded the village in a warm golden radiance, promising a long and hot summer; the day could not have been lovelier.

Nan complained of hay fever and kept wiping her nose with a tissue and sneezing loudly. 'I really shouldn't go out,' she said at breakfast. 'But Sir Owen is only going to be buried once and I don't want to miss it.'

'You need to take an antihistamine,' said Suze.

'Oh no, they make me sleepy and I don't want to nod off during the service. When your grandfather was buried his aunt Mabel nodded off and snored like a warthog during the prayers. I'll never forget it. I don't want to be like Aunt Mabel, remembered only for snoring like a warthog during the prayers.'

'I'm sure that wouldn't happen,' said Dennis. 'You'll be remembered for your wonderful sense of humour, Nan.' He had a twinkle in his eye and Marigold smiled into her teacup.

Nan nodded. 'I'm able to take a joke,' she agreed humourlessly. 'Occasionally, I make one.'

Suze couldn't think of a single joke her grandmother had made, at least, not intentionally.

'Have you ever heard a warthog snore?' she asked.

'Warthogs snore,' said Nan emphatically.

'Daisy left early,' Suze said, changing the subject. 'Lady Sherwood keeps her busy, doesn't she.? Considering she doesn't pay her.'

'But she gives her the use of the barn, rent-free,' Dennis reminded her.

'She's such a comfort to Lady Sherwood,' said Marigold proudly.

'That's right, Goldie. Sylvia popped into the shop yesterday and told you.'

'Yes, she did,' Marigold replied. But she didn't remember Sylvia at all.

They walked to the church in the sunshine. Nan complained all the way about her hay fever. 'The horse chestnuts are the worst,' she whinged. 'The pollen gets into my eyes and throat and makes me want to scratch them. But if I scratch my eyes I'll smudge the mascara and then I'll look as if someone's hit me. I wouldn't want to have to explain to everyone who asked that it was just hay fever and not domestic violence.'

'They'd all be so disappointed,' said Suze. 'They love a drama in this village.'

Marigold had slipped her hand round Dennis's arm and they walked slowly, side by side. Marigold was not having a good day. Her head was fuzzy, as if it were full of wool. It took her longer to focus, longer to respond, longer to recognize the world around her. But Dennis was patient and didn't rush her. Even Suze, who could be irritable, was being kind. Nan seemed not to notice.

Daisy was at the church doors when they arrived, greeting people, handing out orders of service and showing family and close friends to their reserved seats. She'd been at the church all morning, putting the names in the pews and overseeing the florist, assisted by Sylvia who was little help snivelling into a wet handkerchief. Marigold's breath caught in her chest when she saw the flowers. The smell was heady, like a bouquet of lilies and gardenia pressed up against her nose. She blinked in wonder at the candles. There were hundreds of them, their little flames dancing on every surface, each one radiating a bright aura of gold. Dennis took her hand and led her into a pew at the back where David Pullman, the farm manager, was sitting with his wife and two daughters. They shuffled up so that Suze and Nan could join them, and saved a space for Daisy at the end.

But Daisy didn't need a space. Lady Sherwood had insisted that she be seated with the family, and had placed her at the end of the second pew against the wall, right behind the front row, which was reserved for herself, Taran and Sir Owen's sisters. Daisy didn't feel comfortable sitting there, when her family was at the back, but she was too grateful to Lady Sherwood to move.

Eileen began to play the organ. Her fingers skipped lightly over the keys and moved the congregation to silence. It was then that Lady Sherwood made her way slowly down the aisle, leaning on her son, who walked tall with his shoulders back and his chin up and his face set in a solemn, impassive mask. Daisy watched him in fascination. In his dark suit and tie, Taran looked dashing. He betrayed no emotion, however, unlike his mother who was struggling to hold back her tears. He didn't catch anyone's eye, but walked on at a stately pace. He took his seat in front of Daisy and she noticed the stiffness in his jaw and guessed he was controlling his feelings *there*, blocking them in like a dam. Her heart went out to him.

Daisy opened the order of service and looked at the photograph of Sir Owen in his tweed cap and wondered where he was now; where his consciousness was. Was he in the church, watching them all mourning him as her grandfather had believed? 'I won't have any of you wearing black at my funeral,' Grandad had said. 'The heavy black vibrations will just make it harder for me to reach you and I want to be there to hear what you all have to say about me.' He had laughed. Daisy remembered his laugh, deep and infectious, and she marvelled at how certain he had been that death was no more than a waking up from a long dream. She wondered whether Sir Owen had awakened from *his* long dream and whether he was here, waiting to hear what his family had to say about *him*.

She realized then that the entire congregation was wearing black. Perhaps those heavy vibrations would make it impossible for him to come. Everyone had worn colour at Grandad's funeral and at the end of the eulogy the candle in front of his photograph had gone out, supposedly all on its own.

No candles went out at Sir Owen's funeral, but there were lots of tears, shed by the women in his family who perhaps wanted to make up for the lack of tears in the eyes of the men. Lady Sherwood's shoulders shook and Taran put an arm around her to comfort her. The sight of them together stirred something in Daisy and a lump lodged itself in her throat and her vision misted. She had only met Sir Owen half a dozen times, but it wasn't for him that she cried, it was for Taran and Lady Sherwood. One didn't cry so much for the deceased as for those who would have to continue living without them. If her grandfather were to be believed, mourning the dead was pointless. One should really only grieve for those left behind, he had said.

After the service there were drinks and tea in the village hall. It was an ugly room with no redeeming features and Daisy had had a hard time filling it with flowers and bay trees to conceal the plain white walls and distract from the cold white strip lights. No expense had been spared and Lady Sherwood was pleased at how beautifully it had turned out. 'You've done a marvellous job,' she said to Daisy when they had a moment alone together. 'I hardly recognize this place with all the flowers.'

'I really had nothing to do with it,' Daisy replied. 'The florist should take all the credit.'

After that it was impossible to get near her, for everyone wanted to pay their respects and tell Lady Sherwood how much Sir Owen had touched their lives. Nan and Marigold had taken advantage of the seats and small tables set up around the edge of the room and sat down, just the two of them. Nan did not want to talk to anyone and Marigold was afraid to, in case she failed to recognize them. They both watched the slow movement of people as they mingled. Dennis mingled more than anyone. He was an arch-mingler, and because he was so genial and kind everyone felt better for having spoken to him.

Daisy found herself searching the faces for Taran's. She wanted to check that he was all right. She imagined how much of a trial an occasion like this was for someone who preferred to keep people at arm's-length. She weaved through the crowd, smiling graciously at Sir Owen and Lady Sherwood's friends as they stepped aside to let her pass. She saw Eileen and swiftly changed direction; she did not want to engage in a long conversation; Eileen did like to talk. At length she realized that the only place Taran could be was outside. She left the hall and found him smoking a cigarette in the car park.

'I didn't know you smoked,' she said, approaching him.

He grinned. 'I don't. I bummed one to keep me going. I'll be very happy when everyone goes home.'

'It was a lovely service, though.'

'Uncomfortable,' said Taran, inhaling deeply before letting out a stream of smoke. 'I hate funerals at the best of times.'

'Well, they're not the most fun, I agree. How was the cremation?' she asked.

He shook his head. 'Unspeakably awful. There's something chilling about the industrial nature of a crematorium. One after the other, into the oven—'

'Don't,' she stopped him.

'He should have been put in the ground. Less shocking somehow.'

'Both are unappealing, if you ask me.'

'It's hard to think of him like that. In a coffin. Hard to picture it.'

'I wouldn't try, if I were you.'

'I can't help it. Morbid fascination. The mind keeps going back to it.' Taran took another drag and blew out the smoke. 'Dad was a force of nature. Strong, capable, ebullient and charming. It was terrible thinking of that life force lying extinguished in a wooden box. I just can't imagine him like that.'

'You have to remember him at his best.'

'I know. Of course I do. But like I said, the mind keeps going back to it. Do you want to go for a drink?' he asked suddenly.

'Now?'

He shrugged. 'Well, perhaps not *right* now. Later? We could go to the pub. I'll be leaving for Toronto tomorrow.' He looked at her steadily, waiting for her to decline, as she had declined at Christmas.

'Sure,' she replied, surprising him. 'This evening is good.'

'Great. I'll meet you there at six.'

Daisy laughed. 'Have you been to the pub before, Taran?'

'Well, not *this* pub.'

'I didn't think so.'

'Do they bite in there?'

'No, it's a friendly crowd. A little dull perhaps for someone who lives in Toronto.'

'I'm not going for the crowd.'

His green eyes twinkled. Daisy's laugh was a defence mechanism. She knew she shouldn't read too much into his flirting. 'I'll see you there at six,' she said. 'I'd better check on your mother. She'll be needing a whisky, I suspect.'

He put his hand in the small of her back and escorted her into the hall. 'Make that three,' he said. 'We all need one.'

Daisy was relieved when the funeral was over and everything had gone smoothly. Lady Sherwood thanked her profusely, embracing her with a warmth of which Daisy had not thought her capable. 'I don't know what I would have done without you,' she said, eyes filling again with tears. 'If Owen were here I'd tell him how wonderful you've been, but he's not, so I've got no one to tell.' Daisy thought of Taran and Lady Sherwood added, as if she'd read her mind, 'Taran already knows how wonderful you are.'

That remark stayed with Daisy as she made her way home. Her parents, Nan and Suze had left the tea a long while before and she was alone with her thoughts. *Taran already knows how wonderful you are.* Was that simply a throwaway line? She couldn't believe he really thought that. She imagined he flirted with girls all the time. It meant nothing. He was just feeling vulnerable because his father had died.

When she got home her mother had returned to the shop. Suze was sitting at the kitchen table with Nan, discussing the funeral. 'There's nothing pleasant about a funeral,' Nan was saying. 'They just remind you of where you're going to end up. That's the only certainty in life, isn't it? Death. It's the great equalizer. It will come to us all, no matter who we are.'

'I love your positivity, Nan,' said Suze, hugging a mug of coffee. 'Really, you are a beacon of light in these dark times.'

'There's no point in hiding the truth, Suze. We're all waiting in line to drop off the end of the world.'

'You could possibly sugar-coat it a little.'

'I am what I am, Suze. I've been a sourpuss for eighty-six years, I'm not going to change now.'

Suze looked up at Daisy and registered her glowing face. 'What's going on with you?' she asked.

'Nothing,' Daisy replied quickly.

Suze narrowed her eyes. 'I know you well enough to know when "nothing" means "something".'

'Taran's asked me for a drink.'

Nan sucked the air through her lips. 'Where's he taking you?'

'Like a date?' Suze asked.

'It's only at the pub. Nothing special and no, it's not a date.'

Suze grinned mischievously. 'Just two friends going for an innocent drink. Sure it's a date, silly!'

'A date!' repeated Nan, looking uncharacteristically positive. 'About time you got back into the game, Daisy. After a break-up like yours the trick is to only look forward, never to look back.'

'And you know about that, do you, Nan?' said Suze, arching an eyebrow.

'You could say I'm something of a dark horse, Suze. If I had looked back, I'd never have married your grandfather. I'd have married little Barry Bryce – he was always called "little" even though he was over six feet tall.' She screwed up her nose and shook her head. 'Barry went off to live in Bodrum and got eaten by a shark, I think. Never look back, Daisy. I'd have been a widow at twenty-six and Grandad would never have known my charm and wit.'

Daisy laughed and went off to change out of her funeral clothes.

'Where's she going then?' asked Nan.

'Forward,' said Suze. 'She's going to show Taran her charm and wit.'

Chapter 17

Daisy arrived a little late at the pub. She hadn't intended to, only Marigold had lost something and they had all had to help her search for it. The trouble was, she couldn't remember what it was that she had lost, just that it was important. This had made the search almost impossible. It wasn't her phone, or her keys, or her handbag. They couldn't imagine what it could be.

Daisy had gone through her mother's pockets and found a little notebook in one of her cardigans. When she had shown it to her, Marigold had held it in her hands as if it were a wounded bird. 'That's it,' she had said, the worry expelled in a breath. 'I won't lose it again.' But even she had known that wasn't likely.

When Daisy appeared in the pub, Taran was perched on a stool at the bar with what looked like a glass of whisky in front of him. He had changed into a dark grey T-shirt and jacket. He smiled, the same dashing smile he had given her before his father's death had diminished it. 'You came,' he said, looking surprised.

'Of course I came,' she replied. She took the stool beside him.

'What'll you have?' he asked.

She would normally have gone for a glass of wine, but

there was something about Taran that made her want to drink something less conservative. 'A G&T, please,' she replied.

Taran called the barman over. The barman, who Daisy knew from growing up in the village and attending the same secondary school, greeted her enthusiastically and with some surprise. It was the first time she'd been into the pub since she'd come back from Italy. 'Are you here to stay?' he asked, looking at her appreciatively.

'I'm not sure,' Daisy replied, recalling her conversation with Luca. 'Perhaps.'

'Well, it's nice to see you back,' he said and went to make her drink.

'I think you've unintentionally become Mother's personal assistant,' said Taran with a grin. 'And I don't imagine she's paying you for your services.'

'I just helped out for the funeral. She won't need me now.'

'Oh, I expect she will. She thinks you're marvellous.' The barman put the G&T in front of her. 'You'll be even more indispensable now, as she's going to be lonely without Dad.'

Daisy frowned at him. 'Why don't *you* move back so you can be close to her?'

He shrugged. 'I've made my life in Canada.'

'You can always change your life.'

'I can, but I don't want to.'

'You have one of the most beautiful estates in England. I know, I walk there every day, and your mother won't be around for ever.'

'I know that.' He made a face which alluded to things he wasn't prepared to discuss. 'It's difficult,' he said.

She took a sip of her drink. 'Look, it's none of my business. I'm just very pleased I came back from Italy at a time when my parents needed me.'

He arched an eyebrow. 'Are they okay?'

'Mum's not great. She's becoming very forgetful and diso-rientated. I fear it's the start of something serious.'

Taran nodded, guessing what she feared but not wanting to articulate it. 'Life gets more serious the older we get, doesn't it?' he said softly. 'I mean, when we were young we only had to think about ourselves, but now we have our parents to worry about. It's a total role reversal and one I'm not very comfortable with, to be honest.'

'You're an only son, which is tough. Responsibility rests on your shoulders alone. At least I have Suze, although my sister's not really very capable. She only thinks of herself.'

'You're going to end up looking after all the oldies,' he told her with a mischievous smile. 'My mother included.'

'No, I'm not,' she replied. '*You're* going to look after your mother, Taran.'

'I'll always be there for her. It'll just take me about nine hours to reach her.'

They remained in the pub until it closed. They had ordered more drinks and some food and chatted with the ease of old friends. The fact that they had grown up in the same village and been in the same class at school gave their growing friend-ship roots and the illusion of familiarity. Daisy forgot all about her conversation with Luca as she laughed with Taran. When the bill came, Taran insisted on paying.

By the time they left the pub, Daisy had lost count of the amount of drinks she had had. Taran had drunk a lot too and was a little unsteady on his feet. A pregnant moon hung low and heavy in the sky, drenching the landscape in a luminous silver light. Daisy didn't think she'd ever seen it so big or the stars so bright. They were mesmerizing. 'Let's go for a walk,' she suggested impulsively.

'What? Now?' Taran asked. 'You do realize it's night-time, don't you?'

'It's beautiful. Come on, let's walk around the fields. It's too lovely to sleep through it.' She tugged his sleeve. 'It'll be over in a few hours.'

'I suppose I should sober up,' he conceded. 'I don't want to wake Mum by crashing through the house.'

'The fresh air will do us both good.' *And I want to show you just why your father loved it so much,* she thought to herself a little drunkenly, setting off the way she went every morning with a purposeful stride.

They left the village and headed up the farm track towards the woods. Daisy's heart expanded at the sight of the trees silhouetted against the deep indigo sky and the fields of wheat and oilseed rape, which lay silent and still beneath it. It was as if they were stepping into a parallel world. A more beautiful world. A serene and secret world, full of the gentle rustling of small animals and the eerie hooting of owls. 'Have you ever seen it look lovelier?' she asked in delight, inhaling the earthy smells that rose up from the ground and lingered in the cool night air.

'I remember once, when I was a teenager, having a party and taking a girl for a walk just as the sun was beginning to peep over the horizon. It was lovely then too.'

'Do you remember who she was?'

'Haven't a clue.' Taran laughed, putting his hands in his trouser pockets. 'But I remember where we kissed.'

'And where was that?'

He looked at her and grinned roguishly. 'Well, seeing as we're up here, I'll show you.'

'I wonder whether *she* remembers *you*.'

'I doubt it. I was a pretty uninspiring youth!'

'I somehow doubt that.'

He laughed. 'You're just being nice, Daisy Fane.'

They wandered slowly around the edge of the wood for it was too dark to venture through the trees. After a while they came to a bench set back from the track and sat down. From there they had a magnificent view of undulating hills of farmland as far as the eye could see. It glowed magically in the watery light of the moon. 'When Dad inherited the estate he put this bench here because of the view. It was his favourite place on the farm. He used to stop and sit here every time he passed it, just to savour the sight.' Taran sighed deeply, pausing a moment as if seeing it differently now. 'It's beautiful, isn't it?' he added wistfully.

'You're so lucky, Taran,' said Daisy with feeling. 'All this is yours. All this beauty. You can walk for miles and miles and not meet a soul. It's for you and you alone. And it's here whenever you want it. Do you know how lucky you are?'

Taran leaned his elbows on his knees and rubbed his chin. 'I've never thought of it like that. I suppose I've always taken it for granted.'

'That's natural. We don't often realize what we have until we lose it.'

At that Taran put his head in his hands. Daisy let her gaze rest on the view, captivated by the curving contours of the hills, stacked one behind the other in diminishing shades of night, and embellished with inky blue trees and tidy hedges. Taran remained with his head in his hands for a long while. At first Daisy thought nothing of it, she guessed he was perhaps trying to sober up, but after a while she noticed his shoulders were shuddering. She realized then that he was crying. She put a hand on his back and leaned forward to see his face, horrified that she had been blithely enjoying the view while he was quietly sobbing his heart out on his own. 'Oh Taran. I've been chattering away here without any consideration for your loss. I'm so sorry. I should have been more tactful.'

He collected himself, wiping his eyes with the back of his hand and sitting up. He heaved a sigh. 'I never appreciated Dad and now he's gone . . .' Daisy didn't know how to reply to that. There were no words that would bring Sir Owen back. She tried to remember what her grandfather would have said, but she didn't think it was the moment to tell him that his father would always be with him in spirit. That seemed such a cliché, a con, and she wasn't entirely sure she believed it. 'We had our differences, he and I, but I loved him,' Taran continued. 'Now it's too late to tell him.' He stared over the hills and the tears that came again were left to fall in rivulets down his cheeks. 'I wish I hadn't been so proud.'

'I'm sure he knew you loved him,' said Daisy, wanting so badly to comfort him but not knowing how. She was appalled that she had written him off as being cold and unfeeling. 'From what I understand, your father was a deeply generous man.'

'Everyone loved him. He gave people his time and made them feel important. He was a legend, a big man in every way.'

'You're right,' Daisy agreed. 'He was noble in the true sense of the word.'

'He was a better man than I am, Daisy.' Taran's mouth twisted as he struggled to control his bitterness.

'That's not true. Just because you're different doesn't mean you're less.'

'His farm meant everything to him. Everything. He bought land to expand it and spent all his time in the woods, coppicing, and walking the dogs around the fields. I get it, you know, I do. He loved the land. He loved his home. He wanted me to take it on after he died, but I didn't expect him to die so soon. I'm not ready.'

'He wanted you to love what he loved because he wanted to share it with you. You were his only child. It was a life that suited him and made him happy. I'm sure he probably thought it would make you happy too. Ultimately, I suspect he only wanted you to be happy.'

'But I'm not a farmer, Daisy. I never wanted to be and I don't want to be now. I don't know the first thing about running an estate. I'm sure I'd be useless.'

'Your estate manager would tell you what to do. I can't imagine it's that difficult, with the right help. You're capable of more than you realize. We all are.'

They sat in silence for a long while as he thought about what she had said. Until they began to grow cold waiting for the dawn that was yet to come. 'You know, this is where I kissed that girl,' Taran said at last, a small smile creeping across his face.

Daisy laughed. 'It's a very romantic place. I can see why you chose it.'

He turned and looked at her, his green eyes damp and shiny and gazing at her with gratitude. 'You're very kind,' he said softly.

Daisy felt the air around her still. He had a tender look on his face. His smile was no longer dashing but vulnerable. 'Thank you for listening.'

'I'm glad you felt you could talk to me.'

'I *can* talk to you.' He frowned and studied her face, as if seeing it anew. 'I didn't realize I could until tonight.'

Daisy realized then that he was going to kiss her. She'd seen that look before. She'd felt the air still around her like this and the change in energy that occurs when two people suddenly connect. She knew *she* had sobered up, but she wasn't sure Taran had. Of course she found him attractive. She wasn't sure, however, that he really found *her* so. She couldn't be sure she wasn't just a sympathetic friend on a bench where he had once kissed someone.

She stood up and put out her hand. 'Come on, Taran. Let's get you home.'

He looked up in puzzlement, unable to conceal the disappointment in his eyes. The whiskies had certainly melted his inhibitions. He grinned at her, as if sizing her up and trying to work out what game she was playing. As if he couldn't believe that she had rebuffed him. Daisy sensed he was about to say something. But he must have thought better of it for he resignedly put his hand in hers and got to his feet. But when Daisy tried to take back her hand, he didn't let her. They headed off in the direction of the village. Daisy tried to convince herself that it didn't feel unnatural to walk hand in hand with someone she barely knew.

'I'm not drunk,' he said after a while, attempting to hide the unsteadiness in his gait.

'I know that.'

'A little light-headed, perhaps. But in a good way.'

'Me too,' she replied.

'Do you mind me holding your hand?'

'Of course not.'

'Good.'

'Are you in a relationship, Taran?' she asked suddenly, aware that such a question might ruin the moment, but conscious that an attractive man like him was likely to have a girlfriend.

He hesitated, slowing his pace. 'Kind of,' he replied uncertainly.

Daisy was surprised by how much his answer stung. 'What does "kind of"' mean?'

'It means I'm in a relationship I'm not entirely committed to.'

'Ah.'

'It sounds callous, but it's isn't. We've been together, on and off, for about two years. We don't live together or anything. She's more like a friend with benefits, if you know what I mean. I'm fond of her, she's a fun-time girl, but it's not going to go anywhere.'

His explanation did not make her feel any better. It made him sound cold-hearted and she didn't want to think of him like that. 'Does *she* know it's not going to go anywhere?'

He shrugged. 'I don't know. We haven't talked about it. We just kind of get together every now and then.'

Daisy let go of his hand. 'You should tell her. It's not fair to keep a girl hanging on, hoping for a future when there isn't one.' She hadn't meant to sound so defensive.

'Is that what your Italian did to you?'

She nodded. 'Kind of.'

Taran put his hands in his pockets. They walked on in silence.

When they reached Daisy's house, they lingered outside the front door awkwardly, not sure how to say goodbye, and not wanting to. 'I leave tomorrow,' he said, a little sadly.

'I'll take care of your mother, don't worry.'

'I know you will.' He gave her a long look, as if he didn't want the night to end. As if he feared that dawn would steal the brief magic they had enjoyed up there on the bench. 'You're a special girl, Daisy Fane.'

She shrugged. 'I can't turn my back on a person in need.'

'I realize that.' He grinned provocatively. 'Is that what I am to you, too? A person in need?'

'You're a friend,' she replied carefully. 'An unlikely friend.'

'Unlikely? I'm not sure I agree with that.' He bent towards her and kissed her on the cheek, lingering there a little longer than was necessary. 'Goodbye, unlikely friend.'

She smiled. 'Have a safe flight.'

He straightened up and stretched. 'I think I'll sleep the whole way.'

'Better if you do.' She frowned. 'Are you sober enough to drive?'

'No, I'll leave the car at the pub and walk. The exercise will clear my head. Though I'd rather walk with you.'

She went to the front door and unlocked it, turning to bid him farewell. 'Night, Taran.' Then the dejected look on his face prompted her to add, 'I had a good time tonight.'

'Me too,' he agreed. 'Night, Daisy.'

And he watched her disappear inside.

When Daisy's head touched the pillow, Suze raised hers. 'Hey, you've been out all night! What have you been up to?'

'We went for a walk.'

'In the middle of the night?'

'It was so beautiful. I couldn't resist.'

'You were drunk!'

'Tipsy.'

'And Taran?'

'Tipsy too.'

'Did he kiss you?'

'Of course not.'

'What? He didn't even try?'

'We didn't kiss.'

'You wanted to, though. I can tell.'

'Suze, it's four in the morning. You should be asleep.'

'You woke me up, so now you have to give me something.'

Daisy sighed. 'Give you what?'

'I don't know. *You* tell *me*.'

Daisy sighed again. 'You're impossible. It's like you're still twelve.'

'I'm getting married, don't forget.'

'In two weeks' time.'

'So give me something.'

'Then you'll let me sleep?'

'Yes.'

'Okay, so I like him.'

'You *like* him.'

'Yes, I didn't realize how much I liked him until tonight.'

'Thought so.'

'But . . . there's Luca.'

'There is no Luca. He's an idiot. Move on.' Suze rolled over. 'Night, Daisy.'

Daisy smiled and closed her eyes. 'Night, Suze.'

A few days before Suze's wedding Daisy accompanied Marigold to her appointment with the clinical psychologist. They sat on the sofa in the waiting room of a white stucco building, which must once have been a sumptuous private house, on the smart side of town. The walls were a pale green, the carpet a restful geometric pattern in muted hues, the low table in the centre neatly laid out with glossy magazines. Marigold was nervous, picking at the cuff of her jacket where a piece of thread had come loose. Daisy was nervous, too. She had sensed for some time that her mother wasn't herself, but she'd been too afraid to face it. Today she would find out if her fears were well-founded.

After what seemed like a very long time a young woman in an elegant trouser suit appeared in the doorway. 'You must be Marigold,' she said, smiling warmly. Marigold and Daisy stood up.

'Yes, I'm Marigold and this is my daughter, Daisy,' said Marigold, smiling in the way she did to cover her anxiety, sweetly but without it reaching her eyes.

'I'm Caroline Lewis. Come, let's go into my office and have a chat.'

Caroline led them into an office decorated in the same soothing colours as the waiting room. She offered them a couple of chairs, then sat the other side of a large antique desk. 'Now, I'm going to give you four words to remember, Marigold,' she said. 'I'll ask you to tell me what they are at the end of our session, okay?'

Marigold nodded. 'Okay.'

'Jogger. Pony. Island. House.'

Marigold repeated the words, committing them to memory. 'Jogger. Pony. Island. House.'

It seemed easy enough.

Caroline asked Marigold about herself and Daisy watched her mother gradually relax. They talked about the shop and her daily routine as well as going back over her history to the time when she met Dennis. While Marigold talked, Caroline wrote things down in a notebook. Daisy sat back in her chair and listened. Her mother was eloquent and articulate and, as her nervousness left her, she even made a few jokes. Daisy wondered whether Caroline would think them mad to have come because there really didn't seem to be anything wrong with her mother at all.

At length, Caroline looked at Marigold and asked, in a gentle, compassionate tone, what her memory was like. As

Marigold told her about the little book she carried around all the time (and occasionally lost or forgot to consult), the red book she kept beneath the counter in the shop, the Post-it Notes by her bedside for things that came to her in the night that she knew she'd forget in the morning and the list on the fridge door, Daisy began to see that Caroline didn't think them mad at all. On the contrary. As she scribbled, Daisy sensed that her mother's symptoms were nothing new to Caroline. She was nodding and mumbling 'I see' and looking at Marigold with an enquiring, searching expression in her eyes. The more Marigold told her about her falls, her disorientation, the fogginess in her head, the forgetting of names, people, places and things, the more Caroline's interest grew. This was her field. The field she knew better than any other, and the very fact that her interest was aroused caused the dread in Daisy's heart to deepen.

When at last Marigold had listed all the many occasions of forgetfulness, Caroline asked her if she remembered the four words she had given her at the beginning of the session. Marigold narrowed her eyes. She searched through the fog in her mind, but saw nothing besides the void into which those four elusive words had vanished. She shook her head. 'I'm sorry, I can't remember them,' she said in disappointment. Daisy's heart went out to her. She looked crestfallen.

Caroline smiled sympathetically. 'Oh, don't worry. We've talked about so many things today. They'll probably come back to you on the way home in the car.'

Daisy put a hand on her mother's arm. She was going to tell her that *she* had forgotten them too. But it would have been a lie. She hadn't: Jogger. Pony. Island. House.

Caroline stood up. 'You're a busy woman with many responsibilities, Marigold,' she said. 'Running the shop, your family and all the committees you sit on in the village. I think, perhaps, you do too much. I'd recommend you slow down. Give up some of the responsibilities you don't need. Concentrate on the things that give you the most pleasure. When you feel foggy, don't worry. Let it happen. Breathe and it will pass. And rely on your family for support. You clearly have a loving family. I'm sure they will be happy to help you when you need it. Most importantly, don't hide it. You need support, so let them support you. I'd like to see you again in six months' time so I can assess you again. In the meantime, I'll pop a report in the post to you and send a copy to Dr Farah. I gather he's sending you for an MRI.' She glanced at her notes. 'Next week, isn't it, your appointment?' Marigold nodded. 'Good. So, until December.' She stood up and shook Marigold's hand.

'How did you think that went?' Marigold asked as they made their way to the car.

'You did very well, Mum.'

'I didn't remember those words.'

'Don't worry about that. Caroline wasn't worried, was she?'

'I don't suppose she was. Not that she let on, anyway.' Marigold sighed. 'She didn't say what she thought was wrong, did she?'

'No, she didn't. I imagine she'll give her opinion in a letter.'

'More waiting,' said Marigold despondently.

'I'm afraid so.'

Marigold searched for the silver lining. 'Well, Suze is getting married,' she said, her spirits lifting.

'Yes, let's look forward to that.'

'And a cup of tea,' said Marigold, cheering up. 'I'm looking forward to a cup of tea.'

'Me too,' Daisy agreed. 'There's nothing quite like a cup of tea, is there!'

Chapter 18

On the morning of Suze's wedding, Daisy's phone buzzed with a text. She found herself hoping it would be from Taran. It was from Luca. Her spirits deflated. *I'm still missing you, Margherita.* The truth was that she wasn't missing him. Since her midnight walk with Taran she had thought of no one else.

It had been two weeks since Taran had left and she hadn't heard a word. She wondered why she expected to. He hadn't said he'd text her. They had met in the pub as friends, and although it had looked like he was going to kiss her on the bench, he *hadn't* kissed her. She might have imagined it. After all, she'd been tipsy; so had he. If he had wanted to kiss her it had probably been nothing more than a momentary urge, fuelled by alcohol and grief. It would have meant nothing. Well, at least, not to *him*.

Daisy had spent most days in the barn drawing, sitting in Lady Sherwood's kitchen talking over cups of coffee and taking the dogs out around the fields. She had grown to relish those walks in the woods. The bluebells had been spectacular. A sea of blue. Now it was June they were over, but the rhododendrons were still blooming, their giant pink and red flowers waxy in the sunlight. The leaves on the trees and bushes were out too and darkening as they thickened. She loved early summer when everything was so fresh and new. Now when she walked the dogs she took time to sit on the bench where she and Taran had sat. Where Sir Owen used to sit and enjoy the view. Daisy enjoyed it too. To her it was now more than a bench with a view; it was where she had nearly been kissed by Taran.

She wondered whether her sudden change of heart was a rebound thing. After six years with Luca, it was difficult to believe that she could fall for another man so soon. And Taran was not a good bet. He lived in Canada, he had not shown any ability or desire to commit – he was, after all, leading his on–off girlfriend a merry dance. He was just the kind of man she should be running *from*. Yet, she couldn't stop thinking about him.

She ignored Luca's text and switched off her phone. Until he called to say that he was ready to give her what she wanted, she did not want to hear from him.

Suze was standing at her bedroom window in her dressing gown, gazing out at the rain and photographing it. Why did it have to rain today, on the most important day of her life? She was furious. Nan appeared in the doorway with a little blue embroidered flower. 'This is for something blue,' she said. 'You hadn't forgotten, had you, Suze?' she asked.

Suze had definitely not forgotten. She had written a whole article about the tradition for *Woman and Home* magazine. Beneath her dressing gown she wore a blue garter she had bought especially and posted on her Instagram site (which had received a lot of likes), but she didn't tell Nan.

'Thank you, Nan. I'll pin it to the inside of my dress. But the rain is making my mood blue, so I'll wear that too!'

'Don't worry about the rain. It's good luck. It rained on the day your grandfather and I got married and we had fifty-eight happy years together.'

Suze sighed. Nan must have told her that a dozen times. 'I know, but luck won't stop my hair frizzing.'

'No, it won't. I'm sure Atticus likes you for you and not your straight hair.'

'*I* like myself for my straight hair, Nan. That's the point. This is *my* day and I want it to be perfect.'

'Then you'll be disappointed,' said Nan briskly. 'Nothing is ever perfect.'

Suze turned back to the window. 'You're right, nothing is ever perfect.' She sighed heavily and put her hands on her hips. 'But I don't think it's asking too much to have a sunny day.'

Marigold had awoken feeling positive. She was going to have a good day. She didn't feel tired, her head felt clear and she was full of energy. Today was Suze's big day and Marigold was going to enjoy every minute of it. She had been a little disappointed when she saw the weather, but then she had cheered up because it looked brighter on the horizon so there was a chance that the sun would come out in time for the wedding.

She picked up the Post-it Notes she had written in the night to remind her of the things she needed to do. Then she looked in her little book. There was a long list of things, but she didn't think she needed prompting today. How strange, she thought as she slipped into her dressing gown, that some days were bad, but other days, like now, she felt almost back to her old self. Since the brain scan the week before she had begun to feel a little better. Perhaps it was all in her mind, as Nan said. Perhaps she was making a right old mountain out of a molehill!

The post arrived after breakfast, when everyone except Marigold was upstairs getting ready. She wandered into the hall and picked up the pile of letters from the mat and brought them into the kitchen. There were a couple of bills, but those were Dennis's department, and the usual junk mail of unsolicited catalogues. Then she noticed a letter addressed to her. She turned over the envelope and lifted the gummy flap. When she saw the letterhead, from Caroline Lewis's office, she sat down, a little nauseous suddenly. Her eyes scanned the sentences about how articulate and intelligent she was, and how impressed Caroline was that she managed to do so much etc . . . Then her eyes homed in on the only important word on the page. *Dementia.* In Caroline Lewis's professional opinion Marigold was possibly *in the early stages of the dementing process.* But she would know more in six months when they met again.

Dementia. A cold, hard grip squeezed Marigold's heart and held it tightly. She had worried she might have dementia, but Beryl had insisted she was just like everyone else, growing older and forgetting things, which was normal. But Marigold had known she was *not* normal. She had known her level of forgetfulness was higher than other people's. She had feared that word and because she had feared it, she had buried it deep. But now it had unearthed itself and lay right in front of her eyes, in black letters on the page, and the truth was undeniable and unavoidable, and devastating. She put the letter back in the envelope and resealed it. She didn't want Dennis to know that she'd read it. He would only worry about her, which would ruin his enjoyment of Suze's big day.

Marigold had closed the shop for the day because of the wedding. Now she switched on the lights and the computer and googled dementia. If she had it, she might as well know what it meant. Without the worry of being disturbed, she pulled up the stool, put on her spectacles and looked into the screen.

Dementia *is not a specific disease. It's an overall term that describes a group of symptoms associated with a decline in memory or other thinking skills severe enough to reduce a person's ability to perform everyday activities. Alzheimer's disease accounts for 60 to 80 per cent of cases.*

There are no treatments to stop the diseases that cause dementia . . .

Investment in dementia research is still low . . .

Dementia has a bigger impact on women . . .

There was nothing positive to be found. Nothing at all.

As Marigold made her way back across the courtyard to the house, she considered the word 'dementia'. Why did they have to choose a derivative of 'demented'? She was good with words. She knew what 'demented' meant. It meant insane, deranged, lunatic, crazy, mad, disturbed. *As mad as a March hare, eight letters.*

She could hear Nan calling her name. 'Marigold!'

But she wasn't calling for the answer to a crossword clue. She was calling because she'd just spoken to Patrick.

Marigold hurried into the house. Nan was in the kitchen, still in her dressing gown. 'Patrick is coming to the wedding,' she told her excitedly. 'He's here, with Lucille, staying at The Gables down the road. Isn't that good of him to come all the way from Australia for Suze's wedding? He said he wouldn't miss it for the world. He wanted to surprise us. Well, he's certainly done that!' Nan smiled proudly. 'He's a good boy, is Patrick!'

Marigold hadn't seen her brother in about eight years and, as much as she was pleased he was going to be at her daughter's wedding, she couldn't help but feel the old resentment bubbling to the surface. Patrick had always been careless with other people's feelings, thinking only about himself and how to get the maximum amount of attention. It was typical of her brother to make Suze's day all about *him*. 'Goodness! That is a surprise. How lovely,' said Marigold, struggling to muster some enthusiasm. Years of being sidelined by Patrick's dominant personality and infectious charm had rather tempered her affection for him. 'Though I do wish he'd just replied to the invitation like everyone else,' she added. 'We're going to have to redo the seating in the church. I'll have to tell Daisy.'

'He's so busy and Australia is the other side of the world. But family is family and I knew he wouldn't miss his niece's big day. He might be cavalier when it comes to phoning his mother, but he's got a good heart.' Nan smiled. A wide smile that made her face look unfamiliar to Marigold. 'He's always had a good heart.'

Marigold went to find Daisy. In her panic about the seating plan, she forgot about Caroline Lewis's letter. It lay on top of the pile of post on the kitchen table, which is where Dennis found it.

He read the name Caroline Lewis. Then, when he read the woman's opinion at the bottom of the letter, he froze. Marigold couldn't have dementia. She just couldn't! Not his Marigold.

He sat down slowly and scratched his beard. She was just forgetful, that was all. It wasn't dementia. Dementia was what old people got. Marigold wasn't old, she was sixty-six. He recalled hearing somewhere that dementia eventually killed the brain entirely, so that it ceased to work at all. The body would forget how to breathe and die. A nasty end. That couldn't be Marigold's future. It just couldn't. Not his Marigold's.

Dennis heard the scuffle of feet and hastily folded the letter and put it in his pocket. He decided he wouldn't tell Marigold until after the wedding. He would try to forget about it for today. He didn't want anything to spoil Suze's big day. He didn't want anything to spoil Marigold's, either.

Marigold appeared. 'Guess who's turned up? Patrick!' she told him. 'He wanted to surprise Suze.'

'He's surprised us all,' said Dennis.

'So typical of him. I've had to ask Daisy to find him a place in the church. Of course she's thrilled he's here and isn't at all anxious about the seating plan.'

'I suppose living in Australia for twenty years has made him rather laid-back,' said Dennis, searching Marigold's face for evidence that she'd read the letter. There was no sign of anything other than concern about places in the church. He realized, with some relief, that she hadn't seen it.

'It's got nothing to do with being laid-back,' said Marigold. 'And everything to do with having to be the big star. But Suze will be thrilled. She loves Patrick and she'll be touched that he's travelled halfway across the world to see her married. And it's going to be a lovely day.' She glanced out of the window. 'Look, it's already brightening up.'

'I won't have rain on my little girl's big day.'

'Our little girl, all grown-up.'

'And moving out,' Dennis added wistfully.

'We'll only have Daisy then, and Nan, of course.' Marigold frowned. 'It's going to be quiet without Suze. I might even miss her tantrums.'

'There's bound to be one today.'

Marigold chuckled. 'One last tantrum. Very like Suze. Still, it's the way it should be. It's time she started the rest of her life with Batty. Do you think we'll have to call him Atticus after they're married?'

'No, I have a feeling that nickname's going to stick.'

'He's a nice boy, though. We couldn't ask for a nicer one.'

'No, we couldn't.'

'I hope Daisy finds someone as decent as Batty.'

'Let's marry Suze off first and then we'll concentrate on Daisy,' he said.

'Good idea,' said Marigold. 'One at a time.'

Dennis glanced at his watch. 'I think you should go and change, Goldie.'

Marigold looked down at her dressing gown. 'Goodness, you're right. I thought I had!' She got up. 'Lucky you noticed, Dennis. I wouldn't want to have gone to the church like this!' She smiled at him. 'You look handsome. All dressed up.'

Dennis smiled back. 'I don't want to let Suze down.'

'Neither do I,' Marigold agreed and left the room hurriedly.

As she climbed the stairs she remembered the letter. It just popped back into her head. Her mood deflated a little. Dementia. She remembered now: she had dementia.

She dressed in the skirt and jacket she had bought especially in town with Daisy. It was pale blue and she had found a pale blue handbag and hat to match. She felt very together, as Daisy had assured her she would. Marigold didn't wear much make-up, just a dash of powder and some mascara. She had never been a beauty, well, not in the eyes of anyone but Dennis. She stared at her reflection and knew that Dennis would like the way she looked today. *That* was a silver lining. A silver lining that was always there. She was lucky to have married Dennis.

Daisy had helped Suze into her dress. Her beautiful, princess-style, pink dress. The pink of a delicate sugared almond. Marigold stood in the doorway and looked at her with tears in her eyes. 'You look beautiful, Suze,' she said huskily, for her emotion had made her throat tight. 'Really beautiful. The most beautiful bride ever.'

Suze's eyes shone and she fanned herself with her hand. 'If you make me cry, Mum, I'm going to be furious. You can't imagine how long it took me to do my make-up.'

'And it's perfect,' said Daisy.

Suze went to the window and looked at the sky. 'I think the sun's going to come out.'

'Of course it is,' said Marigold. 'It's your big day. It's not going to stay in and miss it.'

'You look perfect too,' said Daisy to her mother. 'It was a good choice, that blue.'

'I suggest you go and get ready, Daisy. It's not long before you and I should head to the church with Nan.'

'It's okay. We've got plenty of time before Cedric comes to pick us up.'

'Good old Cedric,' said Suze. 'And good old Commodore for lending us his Bentley. It's an old one too. Gorgeous.'

Nan appeared behind Marigold and pushed her way through. 'Goodness, you look lovely, Suze,' she exclaimed. 'I wouldn't have chosen pink myself, but I don't doubt that Atticus is going to be dazzled by his bride.'

'Batty,' corrected Suze.

'I think you'll find he'll change it to Atticus after he's married. No child wants a father with such a silly name. He'll get bullied at school.'

'He can't change it now. It's tattooed on my shoulder,' said Suze with a wicked grin.

Nan's mouth fell open. Marigold gasped. Daisy screwed up her nose. 'Seriously? A tattoo?'

'He's got *Suze* on his. Romantic, isn't it?' Suze enjoyed the horror on the faces of her mother and grandmother. It was just the reaction she had hoped for. 'It was a pre-wedding present we gave to each other. I'm going to Insta it on our honeymoon. My fans will love it.'

'Fans?' repeated Daisy.

'Fans,' said Suze, admiring herself in the mirror. 'I'm becoming a bit of a celebrity, you know. Someone recognized me in the mall the other day. Imagine that?'

'Nothing good comes of fame, Suze,' said Nan, recovering slightly. 'Nor tattoos. I hope you don't divorce. You'll never find another man called Batty.'

When Daisy, Marigold and Nan reached the church all the guests had arrived and were already seated, except for Patrick, who was walking down the road with his wife Lucille. Daisy climbed out of the car and hurried to greet them. Nan didn't wait for Cedric to open her door and followed hurriedly after her, throwing her arms around her son with more enthusiasm than she had mustered in years. Patrick bent down and embraced her back.

'You've grown!' she exclaimed.

'I think you'll find *you've* shrunk, Mum,' he replied with a chuckle.

'And you sound like an Australian.' She pulled away and scrutinized his face. 'But you're still my boy, Australian or not.'

Marigold waited for a pause before she stepped forward. 'Hello, Patrick,' she said.

'It's my golden girl!' said Patrick, flashing her his big, dazzling smile. 'You look great, Marigold.' He kissed her powdered cheek. 'And you smell nice, too.'

Patrick never changed. He'd aged in the greying of his hair around his temples and in the lines around his eyes and mouth, but he was tall and slim and athletic, which made him look younger, and his expression was still full of humour, as it always had been. 'You look good, too,' she said truthfully. Patrick had always been handsome. 'I've aged more than you have. If I'm not careful, everyone will think you're *my* son!'

She turned to the woman he was with. She was smiling at her as if she knew her, but Marigold was sure she had never seen her before. Panic gripped her stomach but she smiled back and allowed the woman to kiss her with the familiarity of someone who had known her a long time. 'Lovely to see you, Marigold,' said the woman, in an Australian accent.

'You too,' Marigold replied. But she knew she was looking vacant. She could tell by the puzzled expression on the woman's face.

Nan embraced her and Marigold was mystified. She watched Daisy link arms with her and the two of them walk off towards the church. 'I've put you at the front with us,' Daisy said. 'But really, Patrick could have let us know.'

The woman laughed, the light, tinkling laugh of a woman at ease with the people around her. 'You know Patrick,' she replied. 'He's so laid-back, he's horizontal.'

Patrick walked between his mother and sister. Marigold longed to ask who the woman was, but everyone seemed to know her. They must have been dating then for some time, she deduced. She needed to ask subtly, so as not to give away the fact that she hadn't recognized her. She cursed her forgetfulness. As they reached the door to the church, she turned to her brother. 'Patrick, is that the woman you're going to marry?'

Patrick looked at her and frowned. 'Sorry? What did you say?'

'Is that the woman you're going to marry? She seems very

nice.' Marigold smiled up at him, expecting him to be pleased that she had complimented his girlfriend.

'That's my wife, Marigold. Lucille. You know, Lucille?' He stared at her, confused.

Marigold froze. She manged to hold her smile even though it felt as if her stomach had hit the floor. 'Lucille, yes, of course it is. Must be wedding nerves. Really, I'm as nervous as the bride.'

Patrick smiled, but it didn't reach his eyes, which were gazing down at his sister with concern. 'That's all right, Marigold. You're the mother of the bride. It's a big day for you, too.' They walked down the aisle and Marigold tried to recall that Patrick was married. But she couldn't. She had no memory of his wife. No memory at all. Did he have children? She wasn't sure. She certainly couldn't remember any. And now she was too embarrassed to ask. She couldn't bear that baffled, apprehensive look he had given her. It made her feel like an alien. She never wanted to see it again.

As she passed her friends, who sat on the right side of the church, Marigold realized that many of the faces were unfamiliar to her. She knew she should know them. They were all here *because* she knew them. Yet, they might just have well have been strangers, gatecrashing her daughter's wedding. Then she remembered the letter. The word 'dementia' appeared again, in her mind's eye, and clung on with sharp claws. Was this what it was going to be like? Forgetting that her brother was married? Forgetting faces she had known for years? Just forgetting, over and over again?

Now she knew why they had chosen to name it after 'demented', because one went mad with frustration, worry and embarrassment. One went crazy with fear – if one let oneself. She sat down in the pew and put her hand in the empty place beside her that was reserved for Dennis. She wouldn't let herself go crazy with fear, she told herself, because Dennis was here to look after her. As long as Dennis was here, she'd be okay.

Until she no longer remembered *him*.

Suddenly, the doors opened wide for the bride. The congregation stood. Marigold had to strain her neck to see her. But there she was, her daughter, resplendent in her princess-cut wedding dress, with flowers in her hair and pearls sewn into her veil, and Marigold began to cry quietly. Dennis was beside Suze, in the suit he had bought especially, looking so handsome and happy. Marigold wasn't sure whether her heart felt as if it was going to burst on account of her pride, or her pain.

How long until she forgot who Suze was?

Or Daisy?

How long until she forgot the people she loved?

How long had she got?

Marigold didn't see them walk down the aisle because of the tears in her eyes. But suddenly Dennis was beside her and Suze was standing next to Batty, who was grinning across at her, his eyes brimming with affection.

Dennis took Marigold's hand.

Marigold looked at him. In her eyes he saw her pain, raw and fearful, and he knew then that she had seen the letter. He squeezed her hand and turned away. He couldn't witness that fear, knowing there was nothing he could do to help her. He just couldn't do it. He focused on his daughter, taking her vows, and tried to suppress the ache in his heart.

Dementia. The word hung between them like a demon, refusing to move. But Dennis held on to her hand. He held on to it all the way through the service and he held on to it when they walked out into the sunshine when the service was over. He wanted to hold on to it for ever and never let it go.

Would there come a time when she would no longer hold his hand?

Because she wouldn't know it was *his*?

Chapter 19

Marigold was pleased that the wedding had been everything that Suze had hoped it would be. Suze had embraced her, kissing her on the cheek and whispering, 'Thank you, Mum. You're the best,' and Marigold's eyes had filled with tears again. Dennis had put his arm around her and drawn her close. He hoped she'd always remember this day. But hope had no power against dementia. Hope was futile, like a feather in a hurricane.

Nan had agreed that the wedding had been beautiful. 'I'm so pleased Patrick was there,' she sighed when they had returned home. 'We were all together again, just like old times.' Then she had pursed her lips and added sourly, 'He looked rather tired, though. I hope Lucille isn't making too many demands. He needs his sleep. He always has. I might have a quiet word with her later when they come for supper.'

It wasn't until the next morning, when Dennis and Marigold were alone in their bedroom, that Dennis broached the subject of the letter. He perched on the edge of the bed while Marigold sat at her dressing table, looking for a suitable pair of earrings in the jewellery box he had made her. 'Goldie, we need to talk.'

Marigold's eyes dimmed at the sight of the letter he held in his hand. Her fingers trembled a little as she closed the door of the jewellery box. She got up and went to sit beside him. She sighed and laid her hands in her lap. 'That doctor person, whatever she's called, thinks I have dementia.'

Dennis's jaw tensed. He knew he had to be strong for both of them. 'Yes, she does,' he replied. 'The early stages.'

There was a long silence as they stared at the letter. They knew what it said and yet they gazed at the word as if hoping it might change and become something else. Something less frightening. Something that didn't sound like 'demented'. Eventually, Dennis put the letter aside and took her hand instead. He brought it onto his lap where he sandwiched it between the two of his. Marigold looked at it there, small and fragile between his big, rough ones. Like a bird it was, and she felt encouraged.

'I looked it up on the internet,' she told him. 'There wasn't much that was positive. Apparently, it's like a bookshelf full of books. The books on the top shelf are new memories, those below are older. The ones right at the bottom are the oldest memories, from childhood. If you shake the bookshelf with dementia, the books on the top shelf fall off. Perhaps some on the shelves below fall off too. But the ones at the bottom remain. Well, they remain until they fall off as well. I suppose they *will* fall off, in the end, won't they? They'll all fall off in the end.'

'Maybe not for a long time,' said Dennis.

'Maybe not for a long time,' Marigold agreed.

There was another lengthy pause. They heard Nan in the corridor asking Daisy whether she'd finished in the bathroom. Dennis squeezed Marigold's hand. 'You're not alone, Goldie. I'm here for you. I always will be.'

'I know that, Dennis,' she replied and leaned her head on his shoulder. 'I'm so lucky to have *you*.'

'What shall we tell the girls, and Nan?' he asked.

'I suppose we'll have to tell them, won't we? I don't want to upset them. But I think they had better know. If I get worse, I won't be able to keep it from them, will I?'

'I think it would be for the best. That way we can support you together, as a family.'

Marigold lifted her head off his shoulder and looked at him with large, frightened eyes. 'What will happen when I no longer remember who the girls are, Dennis?'

Dennis looked appalled. 'Of course you'll remember who *they* are, Goldie. They're your children. You won't forget them.'

Marigold was reassured. 'No, of course I won't forget them. I gave birth to them and brought them up. They're part of me, aren't they? I can't forget parts of myself, can I?'

'Of course you can't, love.'

'But, Dennis,' she said, the fear dimming her eyes again. 'What will happen if I forget that I love you? What will happen then?'

Dennis's throat tightened with the effort of having to hold himself together. He clenched his jaw and pulled her against him to hide the tears now stinging his eyeballs. He pressed his cheek to hers and smelt the familiar scent of her face cream. He closed his eyes. 'It doesn't matter if you forget that you love me, Goldie, because I have enough love for the two of us.'

Marigold cried then. She wrapped her arms around his big shoulders and let him envelop her with a strength that *she* didn't have. She felt the warmth of his body, the muscles in his arms and chest, his beard against her temple, and she felt secure and cherished.

At length she pulled away from him, took his face in her hands and looked into his eyes. 'Dennis, if I forget I love you, it doesn't mean I don't. Do you understand? I will *always* love you. You mean everything to me. Everything.'

Dennis felt the tears running down his face and her thumbs wiping them away. She kissed him tenderly on the mouth. He couldn't find the words to reply, but he didn't need to. She rested her forehead against his and smiled. 'But I won't forget, because love isn't in my brain, is it? It's in my heart and there's nothing wrong with that. Nothing wrong at all.'

He laughed in spite of his deepening sorrow. 'No, Goldie, there's nothing wrong with your heart.'

At breakfast, Marigold casually told Daisy and Nan about the letter. She didn't wait for Dennis to come down. She didn't want to make too much of it and alarm them. Daisy stared at her mother in horror. Nan shook her head. 'Caroline Lewis says it *might* be dementia,' she said tightly. 'She can't be sure until she sees you again in six months' time. That's December. I don't think it's necessary to make a drama out of it until we know for sure that it *is* dementia. And by the way, doctors get things wrong all the time.'

'I'm afraid I think the psychologist is right,' said Marigold calmly, concentrating on not alarming her daughter. 'I imagine the brain scan will confirm it. But life goes on. I'm determined that my life is not going to change. With your help and understanding, I don't think dementia will make a difference. I'm just more forgetful than most people.'

'We're all forgetful,' said Nan sharply. 'Being forgetful does *not* mean your brain is dying.'

'Nicely put, Nan,' said Daisy sarcastically.

'Marigold's got a better brain than I have,' she argued. 'She's brilliant at crosswords and puzzles. She always has been.'

'I can't do Dennis's puzzle,' Marigold admitted. 'I could have done it a year ago, without any trouble. But I can't do it now, not on my own.' Her smile faltered then. 'But you've been such a help, Daisy,' she added. 'I can do it if you do it with me.'

Nan folded her arms. 'That woman has a lot to answer for, putting ideas into your head to frighten you. If you don't have dementia now you will have it soon enough, because she's led you to believe you've got it. Belief is a dangerous thing. The brain is very suggestible. Do you know, once when we were on a cruise, your father said he hoped I didn't get seasick. Well, if he hadn't mentioned it, I wouldn't have got seasick. But he put the idea in my head and I threw up for the entire ten days. It was very unfortunate. That cruise had cost him an arm and a leg, and he had to go and mention seasickness!'

'We'll support you, Mum. Don't worry,' said Daisy, reaching out to touch her arm.

'I'll tell Suze when she's home from honeymoon. I hope she's having a lovely time.'

'I'm sure she is,' said Daisy.

'The food is terrible in Spain,' grumbled Nan. 'It's all pork. I've never liked pork. It's too pink.'

Dennis came into the kitchen in his best suit, ready for church. It being a Sunday, Marigold got up to make his favourite breakfast. 'Morning, love,' she said brightly, boiling the kettle and taking a mug down from the cupboard.

Dennis gave her a kiss, holding her close a little longer than he normally did. 'Morning, Goldie.'

'Marigold tells us she *might* have dementia,' said Nan.

Dennis looked at his wife enquiringly.

Marigold shrugged. 'It's fine. Let's not make a big song and dance about it,' she said.

'We won't,' said Daisy, anxious to cut her grandmother off before she said something else that was tactless. 'It *will* be fine, because we're all going to rally round and help.'

'That Caroline Lewis woman is very irresponsible if you ask me,' said Nan tartly. 'If it *might* be dementia it doesn't need to be said. No point upsetting a patient unless you're sure of your diagnosis.'

Dennis squeezed Marigold's shoulder in a silent show of support. 'That'll do, Nan,' he said firmly and Nan looked at him in surprise because it was rare for Dennis to use that tone.

Marigold went to the fridge to get the milk. Her eyes homed in on the list on the door: *Lunch Patrick and Lucille here* was written in red. She hesitated a moment, confused by the sudden sense of apprehension that cramped her stomach. What was she going to cook everyone? Would she cope? And who was Lucille? Patrick's girlfriend? She searched through the fog to find Lucille's face, or any small detail, but nothing emerged.

Daisy noticed her mother staring at the list in bewilderment. 'Mum, I'm cooking lunch today,' she said brightly. 'You don't have to do anything.'

'Whatever you're going to cook, you'd better cook double,' said Nan. 'Patrick has a large appetite. He always has.'

'We're having an Italian lunch,' Daisy told her. 'I'm good at Italian food.'

'After six years in Italy, I'd be surprised if you weren't,' said Dennis.

'It's a miracle you're not the size of a house,' said Nan. 'Italian women are all enormous.'

Daisy laughed. 'That's not true, Nan. When were you last in Italy?'

Nan ignored the question, because it was so long ago. 'Why

do men always pinch women's bottoms in Italy? Because they're always big.'

'That's ridiculous, Nan.'

She lifted her chin. 'Ridiculous but true.'

Dennis chuckled. 'If a man tries to pinch a woman's behind these days he gets a thick ear and quite right too. Times have changed since you were there, Nan.'

Marigold stood by the stove, stirring the baked beans and watching the eggs frying in the pan. She knew she should be grateful to Daisy for helping her, and she was, *very* grateful, it was just that she was accustomed to cooking all the meals and looking after everyone. She loathed the thought of becoming redundant. Of not being useful, of relying on others and becoming a burden.

When Dennis's breakfast was ready, she brought it to the table and placed it in front of him. 'That looks delicious, Goldie,' he said, beaming up at her. She made an effort to smile, showing him the face he knew, not the pinched, anxious one he didn't, and wondered how long it would be before she could no longer make him breakfast. Before Daisy had to do it in her place. Marigold looked down at her hands and felt a sinking feeling in her heart. When she was incapable of doing the simplest household tasks, what would she do with her time? She glanced out of the window, at the birds diving in and out of the hedges and playing on the grass, and knew that as long as she had her garden and her birds, she'd be content.

On the Monday morning Daisy went for a walk. She felt sick in her heart. Nan might be in denial about Marigold's dementia, but Daisy wasn't. It made perfect sense. As if the pieces of the puzzle that were Marigold's forgetfulness, disorientation, bewilderment and tiredness had at once fitted together to make a clear and logical picture. Of course, Nan didn't see it, because Nan didn't *want* to see it. She liked to have everyone looking after *her*.

Daisy had tried to smile and laugh through breakfast as if nothing had changed and was exhausted from the effort. But everything was so uncertain now. What was Marigold's prognosis? How long did she have before she had to retire from the shop, step down from her committees and remain at home? How long before they had to care for her? Daisy thought about the fields around the house that Marigold loved so much and felt more strongly than ever about Taran wanting to sell the estate to developers. How often had she heard her mother sigh with pleasure at the changing seasons so beautifully represented in the landscape beyond their garden. Yellow oilseed rape in spring, golden wheat in summer, richly ploughed earth in autumn and green shoots in the frosted ground in winter. Every day dawned with the same sun, but a different quality of light transformed the land and made every moment unique. If Marigold's view became concrete and brick she'd no longer witness the seasons from her bedroom window. Daisy couldn't bear to think of her being denied that pleasure, when so many of her pleasures were going to be taken from her.

The following morning she arrived at the Sherwoods' farm to find Lady Sherwood in the hall with a couple of men, one old and bespectacled, one young and fresh-faced, holding clipboards and looking officious. 'Daisy, may I introduce you to Simon Wentworth and Julian Bing from the auction house. They're here to value everything for probate. Such a bore.' She sighed and watched Daisy shake the men's hands. 'It's going to take weeks to go through the house and all of Owen's things.'

'Can I help?' Daisy asked.

'Sadly not,' Lady Sherwood replied. 'Only I know what belonged to him. And he was a hoarder, unfortunately. Before you die, Daisy, make sure you don't leave any clutter. It's a pain in the neck for those poor souls left behind who have to deal with it. When this is over, I'm going to go through all my cupboards and have a good clear-out.'

'That's a good idea,' said Daisy. 'I'll go to the barn, but don't hesitate to disturb me if you need any help.'

'Thank you, Daisy. I'll leave you to get some drawing done. I've taken up rather a lot of your time recently.'

'Dogs can wait,' said Daisy.

'Yes, but can their owners?' Lady Sherwood added with a smile. 'Some of them are awfully demanding, I know.'

Daisy left them to it and walked across to the barn. She was working on a springer spaniel who belonged to a woman in town. Cedric had recommended her and it was her first commission outside the village. A big step. Daisy hoped it would lead to more commissions further afield.

At two, Lady Sherwood entered the barn in a fluster. She was holding out the telephone. 'Daisy,' she called. When Daisy stepped out from behind the easel Lady Sherwood dropped her shoulders with relief. 'I've got Taran on the phone. He needs a whole lot of stuff from Owen's study. I don't know where to look. Really, it's beyond me. I wonder if you could help.'

Daisy's heart gave a leap. The last time she'd seen Taran was outside her front door in the middle of the night, not long after he had possibly tried to kiss her. Her belly was seized by a pang of nervous excitement. She strode across the room and took the phone. 'Hello, Taran,' she said, determined to sound nonchalant.

Lady Sherwood left the barn, closing the door softly behind her.

'Hi, Daisy, how are you?' Taran's deep voice was so familiar it instantly brought him back to her.

'Fine. All good. You?'

'Busy, you know. Got back and hit the ground running.'

'Your mother's busy here too, showing a couple of men around from the auction house.'

'So I gather. Bloody tax man. Forty per cent is downright robbery.'

Daisy wondered, with a sinking feeling, whether such a large tax bill would mean he would *have* to sell the farm. That he'd have no choice.

'Have you been doing any work, or has my mother been using you as cheap labour?'

Daisy laughed. 'She's lovely, your mother. I'm getting enough work done to keep the wolf from the door.'

'What are you drawing?'

'A spaniel called Rupert.'

Taran chuckled. 'Funny name for a dog.'

'His owner is called Mrs Percival Blythe. I don't know what her first name is. She's Mrs Blythe to me.'

'Old?'

'Sort of. One of those formal types.'

'Not like my mother, then!'

'Your mother asked me to call her Celia.'

'She must love you a lot.'

'Well, the feeling is mutual. She's got a lot on her plate right now, and grieving on top of it. I feel sorry for her.' Daisy hoped she'd shame him into coming home.

'Listen, I'm reluctant to use you as cheap labour, Daisy, but Dad's study is a mystery to her. No, it's worse than that, it's a migraine. There's a list of things the executors need for probate. I'm coming over in a few weeks, but in the meantime, can I ask you to go in there and dig out a few things for me?'

Daisy's spirits lifted at the thought of him coming back. 'Of course,' she replied. 'Anything you need, just ask. I'm here. And your mother really shouldn't have to deal with that sort of thing. I worked in an office at the museum in Milan and had to deal with admin all the time, so I'm used to it. Fire away.'

'All right. Do you have a minute right now?'

'Yes.'

'Good. Go to his study and I'll call you back in a few minutes. It's easier if we do this over the phone than texts and emails. I can talk you through it. Dad's filing made sense only to him, but I'm sure together we'll find everything.'

Daisy went into Sir Owen's study. The only time she had seen it was when Taran was using it for work. She remembered him lounging on the sofa with his feet up on the stool, reading a document. She could see him now, lifting his eyes off the page, a note of irritation in his voice as he'd told her to come in, but a twinkle in his eye that belied it. That was the moment they had become friends. The room was quiet now, and empty. It smelt of smoke from the open fire and of Sir Owen; a slightly musty smell of old tweed, walking boots, worn leather and dog. Although Daisy hadn't known Sir Owen well, she recognized him in the smell and felt the resonance of his presence, as if he had only just been in there, sorting through the papers on his sturdy antique desk.

The telephone rang. She answered it. 'Hi,' she said.

'Hi,' said Taran. 'Right. You're in Dad's study.'

'I am,' she replied.

There was a pause as if he was picturing her there. 'It's as he left it,' he said and Daisy detected the wistfulness in his voice.

'As *you* left it,' she replied, hoping to raise his spirits a little. 'It's a bit chaotic.'

'Organized chaos. Don't be fooled.'

'There's a shelf of what look like old ledgers.'

'Yes, Dad was a bit Dickensian. He liked to write everything down by hand. If he'd had a feather and quill he'd have used them.'

'There's a shelf of silver trophies,' said Daisy, wandering over to take a closer look at them. 'Farming trophies.'

'He was very proud of those.'

'They need a good polish.'

'Tell Sylvia.'

'No, *you* tell Sylvia. It's not my place. She'll think I'm muscling in.'

'I'm not sure that woman does much more than a little dusting here and there.'

'And gossiping,' Daisy added wryly. 'She keeps the village informed of what's going on up at the big house.'

He chuckled. 'That's good to know. I can have some fun with that when I come back.'

Daisy laughed and wondered what he meant.

'Shall we go out again?' he asked suddenly.

Daisy hadn't expected that. 'Sure,' she replied, recalling their drunken midnight walk. 'I might not drink quite as much, though.'

'On the contrary, I insist that you do.' Taran laughed and she laughed with him. 'We can go for another midnight walk and sit on Dad's bench.'

'I'd like that,' she said, envisaging the bench and the view. Envisaging the kiss that didn't quite happen. 'Shall we get to work?'

'I suppose we must. I'd rather just talk to you.'

'You can talk to me as we work.'

He sighed. 'All right. Go to his desk . . .'

'I'm here.'

'Move the papers so you can see my name scratched into the wood.' She did as she was told. *Taran* was carved in childish scrawl on the beautiful desk.

'You little vandal!'

'I did that when I was about seven and Dad went crazy . . .' Daisy sat down in the big leather chair and smiled. This was going to be a long call. She wondered whether he needed her help after all, or whether he just needed to talk.

Marigold sat at Beryl's kitchen table with a cup of tea. Beryl was now walking without her stick and was in high spirits, having just baked fifty chocolate brownies for the summer fair. Marigold had totally forgotten about the summer fair and had made nothing. She wondered why no one had asked her.

'Enough about me,' said Beryl. 'How are *you*?' She narrowed her eyes and scrutinized her friend. 'You've been a little distracted lately.'

Marigold swallowed a mouthful of tea and summoned her courage. 'I have dementia, Beryl,' she said.

Beryl's eyes widened and she looked cross. 'Rubbish,' she exclaimed. 'Of course you don't.'

'Why do you say that, Beryl?'

'Because you can't have it. It would just be so unfair.'

'Life isn't fair, is it?'

'Who says you have it? Your doctor? Not that useless GP, what's he called? You see, I forget things too! That GP has misdiagnosed me more than once. I wouldn't listen to a word he says.'

'I've been tested.'

'By whom?'

'A clinical psychologist.'

'Well, you can't be that bad if you remembered "clinical psychologist".'

'I can't remember her name, though.'

'That doesn't mean anything.'

Marigold looked her friend in the eye. 'Beryl, I also had a brain scan which showed my brain deteriorating. I think it looks like a piece of cheese. Anyway, I've looked up the symptoms.' She tried not to show her fear. She smiled. 'It's not the end of the world, is it? I'm still here, at least. Many aren't that lucky, are they?'

'If you have it, Marigold, I'll do anything to make your life easier.'

'There is one thing I would like you to do for me.'

'What's that? Make your excuses at the meeting tonight?' Marigold wasn't aware there *was* a meeting tonight. 'Julia is very annoying,' Beryl continued. 'I'd like to make my excuses too, but my sense of duty to the community won't allow it. I'm stuck, but I can make excuses for you, Marigold.'

'No, it's not that. I remember you saying you had a friend with dementia in a nursing home not far from here.'

'Yes, I did. Well remembered. You see, you can't have dementia if you remember things like that. Rosie Price. Poor thing.'

'Yes, Rosie. I'd like to visit her.'

Beryl was horrified. 'Why would you want to do that? Won't it be very depressing?'

'I want to see where I might end up.'

'Dennis won't let you end up in there.'

'He'll have to if he can no longer look after me himself.'

'He'll always be able to look after you, Marigold. Your Dennis is not like other men—'

Marigold interrupted her. 'He is just a man, Beryl, and in spite of his greatest efforts, he might find it gets too much.'

Beryl sighed helplessly. 'Oh Marigold!'

'I *know*, I've googled.'

'You shouldn't google, you should ask an expert. Google is very unreliable.' She sighed again. 'All right. If you must, I'll take you. When do you want to go?'

'Today?'

'Who's manning the shop?'

'Tasha. I've taken a back seat now. It's beyond me these days.'

'Eileen will be sad if you're not there to talk to.'

Marigold smiled. 'Don't worry. Eileen will find me in my kitchen instead.'

Beryl stood up. 'All right. I'll arrange a visit this afternoon.' She gave her friend a searching look. 'If you're absolutely sure you want to go.'

Marigold nodded firmly. 'I am, Beryl,' she said. 'I *need* to go.'

Chapter 20

Beryl and Marigold stood in front of the big oak door of Seaview House and rang the bell. Marigold had felt sick from the moment she had got into the car, but she felt sicker now. The sight of the austere Gothic mansion gave her chills. If she was going to end up here, in this cold, formidable place, she might as well throw herself off the cliff and end it all now.

'It's nicer inside,' said Beryl.

'It's got a pretty view,' Marigold conceded.

'Oh yes, that's why they bought it, I suspect. The view is very comforting.'

The door opened and a middle-aged woman appeared in a pair of navy trousers and cardigan, comfortable shoes and a short, practical haircut. She smiled and Marigold imagined she spent her life trying to make people feel better about the building by smiling. 'We've come to visit Rosie,' said Beryl.

'Of course you have. Welcome to Seaview House. Please come in.' She stepped aside and Beryl and Marigold made their way through a porch into a large hall where the ghost of a fireplace, flagstone floor and elegant sweeping staircase remained from when the house was once a private home. A display of flowers on a round table in the middle of the hall – lilies, roses and cow parsley – made Marigold feel much better about the building, or perhaps she was just clutching at anything that lifted her flagging spirits. Trying, as she always did, to find the silver lining around a black cloud.

They were led into a cosy drawing room. The first thing that struck Marigold was how homely it was. A big flat-screen television was on, one or two women were on the sofa watching it, others were sitting in armchairs and on sofas arranged in clusters around the room. There were large sash windows looking out onto a lawn, trees, borders of shrubs and flowers, and the navy-blue sea beyond. It felt more like a club than a nursing home. This was encouraging. This was definitely a silver lining. Marigold felt better about that.

Until she realized that no one was talking to anyone else. They were all alone, lost in thought, or perhaps just lost. People further down the line than Marigold, *much* further, she hoped, existing in the moment because that was all they had.

Beryl went straight for a tidy, well-dressed lady who was sitting on her own by the window, gazing out onto the garden, her hands neatly folded in her lap. She didn't look unhappy or distressed. She had a vacant look, to be sure, but it wasn't tortured or depressed. It reminded Marigold of Winnie-the-Pooh. Her father had read those stories to her when she was a little girl. *Sometimes I sits and thinks, and sometimes I just sits.* Remembering Pooh made Marigold feel a great deal better. Rosie was just sitting. There was something rather peaceful about that.

'Hello, Rosie,' said Beryl, smiling. 'I'm Beryl, your old friend.'

Rosie smiled back, a flicker of recognition lighting up in her eyes. It was the same gracious smile that Marigold gave people when she didn't remember who they were. A smile that concealed the fear and panic she felt inside. But Rosie didn't appear to be hiding anything other than her lack of memory. 'Hello, Beryl,' she replied.

'This is Marigold. The three of us were at school together a very long time ago!'

Rosie did not recognise her. 'Hello, Marigold,' she said, still smiling serenely. She turned to Beryl and lowered her voice. 'I don't know who all these people are and why they're in my house.' She slid her eyes around the room suspiciously. 'I wish they'd all go home.'

'They'll be leaving soon,' said Beryl, taking a chair and sitting down. This seemed to be welcome news to Rosie.

Her shoulders relaxed and her smile became more natural. 'Oh, I *am* relieved to hear that. You see, Mum and Dad will be back later and Aunt Ethel is coming for tea. They won't want all these strange people here.'

'They'll be gone by then,' said Beryl, and Marigold knew that Rosie's parents were both dead, as was Aunt Ethel. Beryl was just humouring her. And why not? She wouldn't remember the conversation and if it made her happy anticipating seeing her parents and aunt, then what was the harm in pretending?

'Shall I make a cup of tea?' Marigold asked, looking around hopefully. 'There must be somewhere I can get us all a cup of tea.'

'There's tea and coffee in the kitchen next door,' said Beryl, pointing to the end of the room.

'I'll go and make it, then.' Marigold fled to the kitchen. She searched for comfort in the taking down of mugs and the boiling of the kettle. A routine that had served her well over the years. But her heart was racing and the palms of her hands had grown damp. Was this her future? Not knowing where she was? Thinking she was home when she wasn't? Believing her parents were alive when they were dead? Was this what she had to look forward to?

She didn't want to be put in a nursing home, not ever. She couldn't imagine living anywhere else but where she lived now, with Dennis and Nan and Daisy. She liked her things around her. She liked the familiar feel of her own home. Her throat grew tight and her movements shaky as panic took possession of her.

When she appeared with the tray of mugs, Rosie looked at her and smiled, the same gracious smile she had given before. 'Hello,' she said and it was clear from her tone of voice that she was seeing Marigold for the first time.

Beryl didn't flinch. 'This is my friend Marigold,' she repeated, as if Marigold had only just arrived.

'Hello, Marigold.'

Marigold tried to smile, but she couldn't. 'Hello, Rosie,' she said, trying to keep the sadness out of her voice. 'I've brought you a nice cup of tea.'

'Oh, that's lovely,' said Rosie, looking pleased. 'I like tea.'

'You like it with sugar,' Beryl added.

'Do I?' Rosie frowned, trying to remember. 'Yes, I think I do.'

Marigold handed out the mugs, then she sat down and took a gulp. She had never needed a cup of tea more than she needed it now.

As soon as Beryl had dropped her back at home, Marigold went for a walk. She didn't go into the shop, so great was her despair. She didn't go into her kitchen, either, because she didn't want to see Nan, who thought there was nothing wrong with her. And she didn't go and find Dennis, because she didn't want to upset him; she needed to be alone.

Up there on the cliffs she cried into the wind. Big sobs that hijacked her body and left her gasping for breath. She found a bench and sat down facing the horizon, now flushing pink as the sun turned its attention westward and descended towards the sea.

She felt utterly helpless. So completely lost. As if she were a little boat with a rudder that was fixed towards a dark and frightening horizon, and there was no way to change it. That whatever happened, she'd eventually reach that dark and frightening place and be consumed by it. The inevitability of such an end was terrifying. It snatched her courage. It made her want to run away. But how could she run away from herself?

A movement to her left caught her attention. At first she thought somebody had come and sat down on the bench beside her. But then, as she focused, she realized that it wasn't just somebody: it was her father.

'Dad?' she gasped in surprise. 'Is that you?'

Her father turned and smiled at her tenderly. 'Yes, Goldie. It's me.'

And it really was.

'Oh Dad, I'm so frightened,' she choked.

He put a hand on hers. It felt reassuring, just as it had done when she was a child in need of comfort. 'You mustn't be frightened, Goldie. You're not alone, you know.'

'But I feel so alone.' She began to cry again. 'I feel like I'm slipping down a slope and no one can stop me.'

'No, no one can stop you if you're meant to be slipping down a slope.'

'Am I *meant* to be slipping, Dad?'

'Of course you are. This is part of what you're here to experience. No one can interfere with that. It's all part of the

Big Plan. But you're not slipping on your own. I'm always with you, Goldie. I'll never leave you. You won't see me, not every time, but like I always used to tell you, no one really dies. They just shed their bodies, which are really very heavy when you've spent time without one, and go home.'

'You're here now.' She blinked at him gratefully and managed a wobbly smile.

'I'm here *always*,' he said firmly, and the knowing in his smile took away some of Marigold's fear.

He looked well. Not the frail old man who had died of cancer, but a vibrant, healthy man with glossy brown hair and bright hazel eyes, more alive than ever.

'I'm losing my memories, Dad,' Marigold told him. 'I think I'm losing my mind as well.' She looked at him in desperation. 'What am I without my memories?'

'But don't you see, Goldie,' he said calmly. 'You'll always be *you*. No disease can take that away. You're eternal. Nothing can ever destroy *you*.' He looked at her with such confidence, as if he was telling her something that was so obvious he was surprised she didn't already know it. 'Imagine you're driving a car. The car is your body and the engine is your brain, but you, you're separate. You're only driving the car while you're on your journey. Once you finish your journey, you'll no longer need it. Right now, the car is losing the odd wheel and the engine's breaking down, but you're as perfect and whole as you always have been. As you always will be.' His smile was now beaming. 'You don't need the car where you're going, Goldie. All you need is love, and you've got enough love to get there and back.'

Marigold's eyes shone. 'There and back,' she repeated, as if hearing those words for the first time.

'Like me, Goldie. That's why I'm back, because of love.' He

put a hand on his heart and patted it. 'This is the only thing that matters. Simple really and strange that so many people don't realize it. They waste their lives, missing the whole point of it.'

Marigold rallied. 'If you're with me, Dad, I think I can manage the journey.'

'That's my girl! Your journey was planned before you came into the world. And I'll tell you a secret.' He grinned mischievously.

'What's that then?' she asked, finding the twinkle in his eyes irresistible and smiling too.

'You're making a very good job of it.'

She brightened. 'Am I?'

'Oh, yes. You're getting full marks.'

Marigold's eyes filled with fresh tears. 'I never got full marks in anything at school.'

'Life's the most important school. The one that really counts.'

'How long have you got before you have to return ... *there*?'

He shrugged. 'A little while longer, I suspect.'

'But you'll come back?'

'Oh, I will, Goldie. You can be sure of that. I'll come back whenever you need me to.'

And Marigold knew he would.

A few days later a small gathering of people met in Beryl's sitting room. There was Eileen Utley, Dolly Nesbit, Cedric Weatherby, the Commodore and his wife Phyllida. The atmosphere was sombre and a little tense. They all waited. Eileen was good at talking about nothing. She used to talk about nothing to Marigold, but now Marigold wasn't in the shop every morning she had to talk nothing to Tasha, which was difficult because Tasha wasn't very interested in nothing, nor did she have time for it. She was always racing around unpacking things, or behind the counter tapping away on the keyboard. Everyone seemed very grateful for Eileen now, though, as they waited. She alleviated the heavy atmosphere and distracted them from the purpose of their meeting.

Beryl had given them wine. Phyllida didn't like wine, she was more of a vodka girl, but she didn't want to be rude, so she gingerly sipped the Chardonnay, which was slowly warming in the glass because of her hot, nervous hands. She noticed that she'd left a red-lipstick smear on the glass and wiped it off with her thumb. Cedric, flamboyant in a pink shirt and yellow corduroy trousers, sat on the sofa beside Dolly, who smelt of violets. Dolly had a shaky hand. It wasn't anything sinister, she'd had it checked out by the doctor. But it meant she had to hold her glass in her more steady one. Sometimes she forgot and spilled her drink. Beryl's sofas were dark green and patterned, and the wine was white, so it wouldn't matter. Eileen chattered on. She was quite safe talking about the weather – everyone loved talking about the weather – and about food. Animals, however, were a sensitive subject, considering Dolly's cat, and the Commodore's moles. Eileen was careful not to upset anyone by mentioning animals. But she was beginning to run out of steam. She hoped Tasha would arrive soon before she dried up altogether.

At last the doorbell rang and Beryl showed Tasha into the room. Dolly moved closer to Cedric to allow her to sit down. Tasha greeted everyone a little nervously, before sinking in beside Dolly. Beryl poured her a glass of wine. Tasha took a sip and gulped loudly. 'Excuse me,' she said, clutching her throat. Everyone smiled at her reassuringly. Smiles that said it didn't matter because they were *all* nervous.

'Right,' said Beryl in an officious tone of voice. 'You know why you're here, so let's get started.'

They nodded solemnly. Eileen shook her head and drew her lips into a thin line. Out of all those present, she very much believed that *she* was Marigold's closest friend. 'I can't believe it,' she said. 'It just doesn't seem fair, does it?'

'Life isn't fair,' said Cedric. They all nodded their agreement. No one could disagree with *that*.

'Why do bad things happen to good people?' asked Phyllida.

'If we knew the answer to that,' said her husband, 'we'd know all the great mysteries of the world.'

Beryl inhaled through her nostrils. 'I called a meeting this evening because we need a plan. We need to form a united front. Now, I have a friend in a nursing home who has dementia, so I know better than most how to manage the situation. And it *is* management, I can assure you. There are rules, and if we abide by them, then Marigold's life is going to be a lot more pleasant.'

'What kind of rules?' asked Eileen. She didn't really want anyone telling her what to do about Marigold. Being her closest friend, she figured she knew how to deal with her illness.

'Marigold's memory will slowly deteriorate,' said Beryl.

'I wouldn't use the word "slowly",' interrupted Cedric. 'I've noticed a certain quickening over the last few months. She didn't recognize her own sister-in-law at Suze's wedding. Most of the time she covers it up, because she's clever. But she's a lot more forgetful than she lets on.'

'Soon she won't be able to retain new information,' Beryl continued, ignoring Cedric's contribution. 'She'll recall the distant past and that will confusingly merge with the present. For example, yesterday she told me she had had a long chat with her father. Well, Arthur died, what, fifteen years ago?

You see, her brain plays tricks on her. She thinks he's still alive. So we have to go with her and not try to put her right.'

'What did you say when she told you she had seen her father?' asked Dolly, secretly wondering whether Marigold had seen his ghost, for *she* had once seen the ghost of her grandfather.

'I said, "How lovely." I didn't ask her what he had said, because she probably wouldn't remember. Do you see? I went along with her and I suggest you do as well. We need to form a united front,' she repeated, pleased with the metaphor.

'Such a shame,' sighed Phyllida.

'Always happens to the nicest people,' added the Commodore gravely.

'You're suggesting, Beryl, that we *lie* to her?' asked Eileen suspiciously. Eileen prided herself in calling a spade a spade.

'It's not really lying,' Beryl replied. 'It's joining her in her world. It's making her present moment happy. If I had said, "But your father is dead, Marigold," would I have made her happy? No, I would have made her very sad and confused. Let's try to avoid that.'

'But Marigold isn't that bad yet,' said Eileen. 'She knows very well that her father is dead.'

Beryl put her glass down on the little table beside her armchair and knitted her fingers in her lap. 'Of course she does, *most* of the time. Some days are good, some days are bad. I assume that when she told me she had seen her father, she was having a bad day. But soon she'll forget that he's dead and it won't be because she's having a bad day. It will be because her brain is being devoured, like a piece of cheese being eaten by mice. If we all stick to the same song sheet, we can protect her from unpleasantness.' Beryl turned to Tasha, who had only opened her mouth once since she arrived. 'What do *you* think, Tasha? You see more of her than any of us.'

Tasha's cheeks flushed as all eyes settled upon her. 'She gets very embarrassed when she forgets things,' she said. 'When she was running the shop she was forgetting things every day and it was becoming serious. It's difficult to run a business if the owner is forgetting everything. Of course, she thought no one noticed, but we all did, didn't we? I think she's more relaxed not having to worry about the business now.'

'It can't have been easy stepping down,' said the Commodore. 'When I retired I felt bereft.'

'Yes, you did,' agreed his wife, nodding gravely.

'But I found things to do to keep me busy, and I can't say now that I miss the old days.'

'Marigold won't miss them either,' said Tasha.

'Well, she won't remember them, will she,' said Eileen.

'So, what are the rules?' asked Cedric. 'I like to know where I am. I like to have boundaries. I don't want to put my foot in it.'

'Don't contradict her,' said Beryl firmly. 'That's the main one. Go with her, whatever she says. Don't expect her to remember things. Be patient when she forgets. Don't ask questions or put her under pressure to remember something. We don't want to send her into a panic. We need to be there for her.'

'How long until she forgets who *we* are?' asked Dolly anxiously.

'I don't know,' Beryl replied. 'Everyone is different.'

'I remember when she forgot to cook the Christmas puddings for Lady Sherwood,' said Cedric. 'That was last Christmas. I didn't think anything of it then.'

'None of us did,' said Beryl.

'I just thought she was getting older and a little dotty,' added Dolly.

'We all are.' The Commodore chuckled cheerlessly.

'But her forgetfulness was different,' said Phyllida quietly. 'It wasn't normal. I think we all noticed that.'

'I thought it might be dementia, but I didn't want to say,' confessed Eileen. She dropped her gaze into her wrinkly old hands that fidgeted anxiously in her lap. 'I hoped it wasn't. I don't want to lose a friend. I don't want to lose Marigold.'

'We're not going to lose her,' said Beryl determinedly. 'If we work together, as a united front, we'll hold on to her.'

'And we mustn't let on that we know,' said Cedric, looking at the sombre faces in turn. 'Marigold is very sensitive.'

'I agree,' said the Commodore. 'We must keep it hush–hush.'

'Such a shame,' repeated Phyllida with a sigh. 'Why does it always happen to the nicest people?'

The Commodore shook his head again. They all went quiet. Tasha drained her glass. Beryl noticed. 'Let's have some more wine,' she suggested, forcing a smile and pushing herself up from her chair. 'I think we need it.'

Suze returned from her honeymoon as glossy brown as polished teak. She wore her hair in tiny plaits secured by colourful beads, and clothes more suited to a 1970s hippy. 'I smoked so much weed,' she confided to Daisy as they sat in the kitchen. 'I've been floating for the last ten days.'

'Well, it's just as well you're coming down to earth. I've got some bad news for you.'

Suze's face fell. 'What? Is it Nan?'

'No, it's Mum.' Suze stared at Daisy but said nothing. 'She's got dementia.'

Suze went white. 'Are you sure?'

'The test results came while you were away. The diagnosis

is almost certainly dementia. She also had a brain scan, which confirms it.'

'Is there a cure?' Suze demanded.

Daisy shook her head. 'I'm afraid not.'

'What? No cure! We can fly rockets into space and land on the moon and yet we can't find a cure for dementia.'

'There aren't cures for lots of diseases.'

'There should be a cure for *this!*' Suze swore, spitting out the word with frustration and anger. 'Is she going to die?'

Daisy looked into her sister's stricken face and felt her own face drain of blood. The thought of their mother dying was inconceivable. But the thought of losing her little by little was somehow worse. She didn't want to contemplate a future where all that remained of her was a shell. 'Of course she's not going to die!' she exclaimed.

Suze smiled bitterly. 'You're such a bad liar, Daisy.'

'Well, we're all going to go eventually.'

'Is she getting worse?'

'Yes.'

'Do we talk about it? Is it a secret? How do I behave around her?'

'As normal, but we have to be patient.'

Suze stared into her tea. It was just as well that she had moved out and gone to live with Batty, because she didn't think she had much patience for sickness. She was frightened that she wouldn't have much patience for her mother. 'Everything is going to change, isn't it?' she said apprehensively. 'I mean, *we're* going to have to look after *her*. It's always been the other way round.'

'I'm glad I came home,' said Daisy suddenly. 'I'm glad I'm here when Mum needs us most.'

'I'm glad you came home too. You're good at this sort of

thing,' Suze agreed. 'I couldn't cope on my own. I'm not very good at responsibility.'

'You'll learn,' said Daisy. 'We'll both learn to be good at it.'

Suze turned her eyes to the window and sighed. 'Do you think she'll forget to feed her birds?' she said with a smile, remembering how irritated she used to get with her mother claiming they belonged to her.

Daisy looked into the garden, at the apple tree where the feeder remained empty during the summer months. 'When she does, that's when we really need to worry,' she said.

Chapter 21

Marigold had been very down. She hadn't gone into the shop in days, preferring to hide away in the house, trying to do the Sudoku, or staring passively at the television. Dennis decided to take her away for the weekend. The present that Daisy and Suze had given them for Christmas had been on his mind for a while now. He had hoped to go in the spring, but Suze's wedding had got in the way and Marigold had been much too busy in the shop. But now that Tasha was managing it, Dennis felt it was the right time to go. It was the beginning of August and they both needed a rest. They needed time to be alone together. And Marigold needed something to distract her and lift her spirits. Daisy had assured them she'd look after Nan. Nan had assured them that she didn't need looking after. Suze was busy settling into married life. She'd barely poked her head round the door since she'd got back from honeymoon.

Dennis drove while Marigold sat in the passenger seat. The hotel was a two-hour drive down the coast. The girls had shown them photos of it. It looked lovely, just the kind of place where they could rest and put aside their worries. They listened to the radio, to old songs that appealed to both of them. Marigold didn't like rock. She never had. She liked country music and Abba. So Dennis played Magic Radio and they watched the lush green countryside whizz by.

After a while Marigold slipped into a doze. With her eyes closed and her face relaxed, Dennis thought how young she looked. Her brow smooth, her lips parted slightly and, if he wasn't mistaken, a very small smile curling the corners of her mouth with contentment. Gone was the anxiety that seemed to plague her much of the time nowadays, and in its place was serenity. It gave him pleasure to see her like this and he found himself humming along to the radio.

They arrived at the hotel just before lunch. Dennis parked the car and a porter came to take their suitcase, although they only had one and it wasn't very big. Marigold was impressed with the building. She liked pretty houses. This one was white with turquoise shutters and a sloping grey-tiled roof, and had a view of the sea. 'This is nice, isn't it, Dennis?' she said, taking his hand. She needed to hold his hand these days. She needed the sense of security that only Dennis could provide.

'It's going to be just the thing,' Dennis replied. 'It reminds me of the place we once went to near Land's End. Do you remember?'

Marigold didn't have a problem with old memories. It was new ones she struggled with. 'It had blue shutters, didn't it. I like shutters. They remind me of France.'

'Would you like me to make you shutters for our house, Goldie?'

Marigold was thrilled. 'What a lovely idea,' she said. 'I'd like that very much. Then I can sit in the garden with my birds and imagine I'm in Provence.'

'Then I'll make some and paint them blue, just for you.'

'I think green would be nicer,' she said. 'To go with the

garden. Blue is nice by the sea, but we're surrounded by fields, aren't we. So green would probably look better.'

'Then green they'll be.'

'Thank you, Dennis,' she said, smiling up at him.

Her smile made him feel good. It was full of admiration and gratitude, and a childlike wonder, which was a recent happening; she hadn't smiled like that before. 'Anything for you, Goldie,' he said and pulled her close to plant a kiss on her temple.

As soon as they stepped into the hotel they realized what a special present the girls had given them. Everything was decorated in a bright blue and white. From the white walls and blue sofas in the reception area to the blue-and-white-striped bedcover and matching pillows in the bedroom. It was chic and understated and in very good taste. Marigold went out onto the balcony and saw that the flowers on the terrace below were blue as well, as were the parasols shading guests from the sun while they ate their lunch. Her eyes strayed to the fishing boats bobbing about on the water, and beyond, on the far side of the bay, to the smooth green hills that descended all the way down to the sea.

Marigold loved the sea. It drew her out of herself, detaching her from angst and fear and anchoring her in the moment. *What is wrong with now?* she asked herself and smiled, because everything was perfect.

Dennis came and stood beside her.

'Isn't this lovely,' she said, sighing happily.

'It really is,' he agreed.

'Clever of you to think of it.'

'Well, it wasn't my idea.'

'Wasn't it? Whose idea was it then?'

Dennis frowned. 'Daisy and Suze's. It was their Christmas present, remember?'

'Was it? How nice.'

Dennis knew better than to cause her embarrassment by drawing attention to her fading memory. 'Are you hungry?' he asked.

'I suppose I am,' she replied.

'Let's have lunch outside, under one of those umbrellas. They're smart, aren't they?'

'I like that blue. It's a happy colour.'

'On a day like this, it's the same colour as the sea.'

'Yes it is.'

'We'll go for a walk after lunch. We can go up the beach. You can put your feet in the water.'

Marigold laughed. 'I used to do that as a child, put my toes in the water. It was very cold. I don't like being cold. I think I'll keep my shoes on.'

As they walked downstairs, Marigold slipped her hand into his. 'How clever of you to bring me here,' she said and this time Dennis did not correct her.

After lunch they strolled up the beach. Gulls wheeled in the skies above them and gannets and terns hopped about, searching the sand for small creatures left behind by the tide. The afternoon sun was warm on their faces, the wind fresh and blustery in their hair. Marigold pointed out things that interested her, like small crabs racing for cover, shells peeping out of the sand and the odd piece of bottle-green sea glass, which she bent down to collect, imagining precious treasure from a pirate ship shattered on the rocks many centuries ago. As they enjoyed these small pleasures Dennis realized that Daisy and Suze's gift was, in fact, more than a couple of nights in a chic hotel, it was the Present. The Now. It was where Marigold was most comfortable. It was where they could co-exist without doubt. The Present was the very best present they could have given.

That evening they had dinner in a restaurant in the harbour. The twinkling lights of the houses stacked up the hillside were mesmerizing, shining like the stars in the night sky above them. It was warm enough to sit outside so they took the table at the edge of the terrace, close to the water, and Dennis ordered a bottle of wine.

'What are we celebrating, Dennis?' Marigold asked when the waiter poured a little Pinot Grigio into Dennis's glass for him to taste.

'We're celebrating *us*,' said Dennis, sipping it.

Marigold smiled. 'That's nice.'

Dennis raised his eyebrows. 'Good,' he said approvingly. 'Very good.' The waiter filled their glasses then left them alone. Dennis reached across the table and took Marigold's hand. His eyes were shiny, his face boyish in its desolation. Knowing he was going to lose her made his desire to hold on to her urgent. 'You've always been my sweetheart, Goldie,' he said. Marigold's face flushed with pleasure. 'Ever since we first met. Do you remember, Goldie, when we first met?'

'You were wearing a red carnation in your buttonhole.'

'I was. You're so right. You were wearing a yellow dress with blue flowers, and a blue flower in your hair.'

'And you asked me to dance.'

'I did. You were the best-looking girl in the hall.'

'Only to you, Dennis.'

'You smiled at me and I was yours.' She laughed with pleasure and felt his hand tighten its grip. 'And every smile you've given me since has won me all over again.'

'Oh Dennis, you're such a romantic.'

'Only to you, Goldie.' He hoped she didn't notice the tear he wiped away with his free hand. 'I do love you, you know.'

'And I love *you*.' She frowned, trying to harness a memory

that came suddenly and was now slipping away. 'Love is all that matters,' she said. She didn't remember who had told her that, but she remembered the warm, secure feeling that person had given her. 'Most people don't realize it, but life is just about love. They go through life missing the whole point of it.'

'You sound just like your father,' said Dennis.

'Do I?' she replied.

'Yes, that's the kind of thing he would have said.'

'Well, he'll laugh when I tell him then, won't he?' Marigold picked up her wine glass and took a sip. Dennis frowned and looked at her sadly. 'Very nice wine, Dennis,' she said, oblivious of the sorrow in his eyes. 'To us.' She raised her glass.

'To us, Goldie,' echoed Dennis.

Dennis was awoken by the screaming of the telephone. It was dark. The middle of the night. He reached across to the bedside table and felt about for the phone. When he found it, he pulled it to his ear. 'Hello?' he said sleepily.

'Mr Fane, I'm sorry to disturb you at this hour, but your wife is in reception. I think you should come down and get her.'

Dennis sat up with a start. He looked across at the empty space which should have been occupied by Marigold: it was empty. His head was thick with sleep. He tried to make sense of the thoughts now crashing through it. He wasn't sure he wasn't having a nightmare. He switched on the light and replaced the receiver, got up swiftly and grabbed the dressing gown off the back of the bathroom door. He then hurried out into the corridor. A sick feeling was building in his belly. What was Marigold doing in reception at this time of night? he asked himself. Was she unwell? Why hadn't she woken him up? He waited impatiently for the lift. It seemed to take an eternity. All the while his heart was thumping in his chest. Marigold was in trouble.

The reception was empty when he stepped out of the lift. He looked around frantically until his gaze found Marigold's white face. She was sitting on one of the blue sofas in her nightdress, wringing her hands and crying. The receptionist was sitting with her, trying without success to comfort her.

When Marigold saw Dennis she stood up and ran to him like a child. 'Oh Dennis!' she cried with relief. 'There you are!'

'What are you doing down here, Marigold?' he asked, wrapping his arms around her. He could feel her trembling against him, which sent him into further panic because he had never seen her like this before.

The receptionist walked over, clearly grateful to have been relieved of the responsibility of having to look after a crazy woman. 'She appeared in here, asking to go home. I don't think she knew where she was.'

'Thank you,' said Dennis. 'She was probably sleepwalking. I'll lock the door tomorrow night.' He led her back to their room and settled her into bed. 'You all right now, Goldie?'

She looked up at him in bewilderment. 'I didn't know where I was,' she said.

'That's okay. Next time, wake me up.'

She nodded. 'But I didn't know where you were.'

'I was right next to you.'

'Were you?'

'Yes.'

She sighed and closed her eyes. 'I'll be fine in the morning.'

'Of course you will. We'll go and explore and find a pub for lunch.'

'That'll be nice,' said Marigold. Dennis watched her a moment. She was sleeping now.

Peaceful, all the worry gone from her face.

But Dennis was unable to shake off his own worry as easily. He went to the mini bar and found a small bottle of whisky. He poured it into a glass and took it outside onto the balcony. The moon was high. Big, round and luminous, like a fortune teller's crystal ball. It cast a trail of silver over the ocean, a magical pathway to Heaven. He leaned on the railing and took a swig. The whisky warmed his gullet and settled the nerves in his belly. Marigold was getting worse. There was no denying it. Her decline had started to gather momentum. It wasn't just the forgetfulness, it was a general slowing down, of her movements, of her speech, of her ability to focus. She was distracted and dreamy. She had always been good with words, but now the simplest words eluded her. He remembered the way she used to finish his puzzles. He'd really thought he'd made the best jigsaw puzzle for her ever, but it had turned out to be the worst. It remained on the table in the sitting room, incomplete. A metaphor for her brain. But in her case, the lost pieces would never find their correct place.

He sighed heavily and surveyed the silvery beauty of the night. He looked at it through Marigold's eyes and smiled with tenderness, because he could hear her voice commenting on the tips of the waves that sparkled, the deep indigo sky that shone with stars and the large, swollen moon, so close one could almost reach out and touch it. Marigold found enchantment in everything. That was one of the things he loved about her the most. Her ability to see the best in everything. He wondered where she'd find a silver lining to *this*. He took another swig. Because, with all the will in the world, *he* couldn't find one anywhere.

The following morning Marigold had forgotten all about her midnight wander. She awoke with enthusiasm and went straight to the window. 'Another beautiful day, Dennis,' she said. 'What shall we do?'

'We'll go and explore. I think there's a ruined castle near here.'

'I love ruins,' she said.

'So do I.'

Dennis put the drama of the night behind him and concentrated on making the day special, for both of them. They didn't go away much and he wondered whether they'd ever go away again. He was determined to make this holiday one he would never forget.

Taran called Daisy almost every day. He claimed he was calling to find out how his mother was, or for small pieces of information that could only be found in his father's study, but Daisy recognized very quickly that those were merely excuses. The truth was, he wanted to talk to her. Mostly about nothing, but increasingly about his father. Slowly those occasions became more frequent and the conversations about his loss grew longer. He began to open up and Daisy was flattered. She realized that she had misjudged him. He was just a typical product of his class and education. The emotions were there, he just didn't know how to express them.

She guessed he didn't talk to his on–off girlfriend about his father. Otherwise he wouldn't need to talk to *her*.

'That boy calls you a lot, doesn't he,' said Nan, who was watching the television in the sitting room, while Daisy sketched by the window. It was too hot to sit outside and Nan enjoyed watching quiz shows. She liked to get the answers right before the contestants did.

'Taran? He's calling because I'm helping him sort out his father's estate as well as looking after his mother.'

'I would have thought Lady Sherwood had an army of helpers. A house of that size requires a lot of maintenance.'

'She just has Sylvia.'

'Ah, Sylvia, a paragon of discretion.'

'She's not very discreet, is she?' Daisy agreed.

'Sir Owen has left the entire estate to Taran. He was hoping to live seven years so that he wouldn't have to pay tax on it. But sadly, the Commodore's moles scuppered his plans. Poor Taran will probably have to sell the place. The inheritance tax on it will be horrendous.'

Daisy put down her charcoal. 'Did Sylvia tell you that?'

'No, she told Eileen, who told me.'

'The village grapevine is very efficient.'

Nan chuckled. 'You have no idea.'

'Did she tell you anything else?'

'He's going to sell it to developers. Apparently, he's already got interest there. It wouldn't be hard to get planning permission because the council are desperate for more houses. The logical place to build them would be right outside our back gate.'

Daisy bit her lip. 'We can't tell Mum and Dad. Not until it happens.'

'Well, they'd have to move house, of course.'

'Nan!'

'We couldn't stay here with all that noise going on! It would drive me mad. I'm old and frail and need peace and quiet.'

'And Mum can't move. I've been doing my research and people with dementia have to stay in the same house where everything is familiar. The worst thing for them is to be moved to an unfamiliar place.'

'Your mother doesn't have dementia,' said Nan, tweezer-lipped.

'Why are you so sure?'

Nan folded her arms and lifted her chin. 'Doctors get things wrong all the time and that scan was not decisive. Dementia is hard to diagnose. As for the clinical psychologist, well, I wouldn't trust her opinion if my life depended on it.'

'Caroline Lewis is an expert in her field,' Daisy argued.

'What is a clinical psychologist anyway?'

'To be honest, Nan, I don't think a diagnosis is really going to make a difference. There's nothing they can do for her anyway.'

'She's pushing seventy, Daisy. It's natural to become forgetful.'

Daisy didn't want to argue about this again. Nan was determined not to accept that her daughter was declining.

'Everyone has to label everything these days. The slightest deviation from the norm and there's a label for it, a diagnosis, a therapy – and a therapist. It's all come from America. And everyone has something. Dyslexia, autism, Asperger's, Alzheimer's, dementia – people are just people and not everyone is the same. Marigold is just doddery, as simple as that. In my day it was called "getting old". But if you all feel better putting a label on her, then go ahead.'

'I hope they're having a nice time,' said Daisy, changing the subject.

'Well, it's England, isn't it,' said Nan. 'You can never be too sure about the weather. Your grandad and I went to Spain once and every day was beautiful. Sunshine, warm, perfect. They've been lucky with the weather, I suspect, but there's nothing like going abroad.'

Daisy went back to her sketching and switched off as Nan launched into a long tale about a holiday in Cyprus with Grandad. She turned her thoughts to Taran and the developers to whom he was supposedly going to sell his estate. Surely there was a way to stop him. Perhaps if she told him that her mother had dementia he'd reconsider. It wasn't much of a plan. But she couldn't think of a better one.

Her phone buzzed with a text. *Still missing you, Margherita*, it read.

This time Luca had attached a photograph to his message. It was of the two of them, arms around each other, smiles on their faces. A happy, carefree moment. Before Daisy had realized she couldn't change him. Before she had realized how much she wanted to.

Nan's voice grew distant as Daisy stared into the photograph. *Two fools*, she thought sadly. *Two stubborn fools.*

Chapter 22

Dennis and Marigold returned home in high spirits. Daisy put the kettle on and the four of them sat round the kitchen table while Dennis told them how the weekend had gone. He shared all the stories, except the one about Marigold's midnight wander. He decided he wouldn't tell anyone about that. Marigold would not want him to, even though she had forgotten about it.

They were aware of Suze's absence. The house felt imbalanced without her. They had got used to Daisy being at home, but her presence did not make up for the lack of Suze's. They missed her wit and her laughter. They even missed her sulks. They never thought they'd miss *those*.

'Have you heard from Suze?' Marigold asked.

'No, I think she's busy being married,' Daisy replied wryly.

'Hasn't she even popped in?' Dennis remarked in surprise. 'Surely there's something she must want.'

'Well, she has Batty's mother to do her washing and ironing. I'll give her a call. See how she is.'

'I'm not very good on the telephone these days,' said Marigold. 'Perhaps she can pop over for a cup of tea. I'd like to hear how she's getting on and I'm sure she'll want to know how our weekend went. So clever of Dennis to think of it.'

Dennis caught Daisy's eye. From the subtle look he gave her, she knew not to correct her.

But Nan didn't. 'It was Daisy and Suze's idea,' she said firmly.

'Was it?' Marigold flushed. 'Of course it was,' she said quickly. 'That's what I meant. How clever of Daisy and Suze to think of it. We had a wonderful time, didn't we, Dennis?'

'We did, my love,' said Dennis, giving her a broad smile, hiding his irritation at Nan's tactlessness.

'It was their Christmas present to you,' Nan continued. 'Very generous of you, Daisy. I don't imagine Suze contributed much.'

'Oh, she did,' Daisy lied. 'She paid her share.'

'How she makes any money is beyond me,' said Nan. 'She should get a proper job.' And Daisy thought that if her mother was losing her memory, Nan was becoming very repetitive. She wondered whether Suze was avoiding coming home in order to keep clear of them both.

Suze did not want to go home. She knew she should. She knew her parents would be missing her, but she didn't know how to behave around her mother. The truth was, Marigold's decline frightened her. She'd rather avoid her altogether than witness her deterioration.

Suze was aware that she was being selfish, but she couldn't help the way she was. After all, hadn't her parents made her this way by doing everything for her? It really wasn't her fault. The trouble was she had grown accustomed to her mother taking care of *her*. She wasn't ready for this new shifting of roles, of suddenly having to take care of her mother. She wasn't ready to be the adult in the relationship. Even though she was married and living with her in-laws, she wanted her dynamic with her mother to stay the same. She wanted the foundations of her home to remain reliably solid. She wanted her mother's support when things weren't going well, her ear when she needed to offload, her strength when she was feeling unsure. Suze just wanted Marigold to be the mother she had always been; but from now on she wasn't going to get what she wanted.

Then there was Daisy. Daisy who was good at everything. Daisy who was even-tempered and genial. Everyone heaped praise on Daisy. No one heaped praise on Suze, they just rolled their eyes. Daisy knew how to look after their mother. She had patience, compassion and a strong sense of responsibility and duty. Suze had none of those things. She'd never had to acquire them. She'd been able to stand back and let Daisy do everything for her.

Dementia meant an end to Suze's childhood. She was going to have to grow up.

Batty was now looking to rent a flat locally so they could have a space of their own. Suze was a little anxious about this because she knew she'd have to be responsible. She wasn't used to tidying up after herself, or washing and ironing her own clothes, and she hated cooking. It wasn't that she couldn't do all those things, rather that she didn't like to.

What if they decided to have a baby? Who would help if Marigold wasn't capable? Suze liked her mother-in-law, but she wasn't cosy like Marigold. She wasn't as maternal as Marigold either, or as generous, and she was very busy with her job as a teacher. The mountain of homework she had to mark was horrendous. Suze realized, with a sinking feeling, that Marigold was irreplaceable.

Suze hadn't telephoned her mother, because Daisy had told her that she found the telephone confusing. Suze couldn't really understand why, but for some reason Marigold was unable to recognize her voice or follow the conversation without seeing her. So, a few weeks had gone by without contact. And because Suze felt guilty, she had ignored her sister's calls. She had shut them out and justified her actions by telling herself that she was very busy with her blog and the articles she was writing and being a wife (which, in reality, wasn't at all different from being a girlfriend). Therefore, it didn't really come as a surprise when Daisy turned up at the house without prior warning. 'Let's go and get a coffee,' she suggested, and Suze couldn't very well decline, seeing as she had been caught in a pair of slippers, holding a copy of *Vogue* magazine.

They took a table in the local café by the window. A pair of enormous seagulls squabbled over an ice-cream cone discarded on the pavement. 'They're the size of dogs,' said Suze with a smile. She hoped that humour would crack her sister's scowl. But it didn't. Suze asked the waitress for a caffè latte then began to pick at the scarlet polish which was peeling off her thumbnail.

Daisy ordered an espresso. 'Why haven't you been to see Mum?' she asked, looking at her sister steadily.

Suze flinched at her hard tone and reproachful stare. 'I've been busy,' she answered curtly, looking at Daisy with the same steady gaze, hoping to stare her down.

'You've been ignoring my calls as well. No one's too busy to take a call or to reply to a text. Certainly not you, Suze. You spend your life on the phone. What's going on?'

'Nothing,' came the swift reply. But Suze knew her body language told a different story.

'Mum and Dad are longing to tell you about their stay at the hotel. They loved it. It was the best present ever. Aren't you even curious?'

Suze averted her gaze as the waitress returned with the coffees. She took the opportunity to gather her thoughts as the waitress placed the mugs in front of them. Turning her eyes to the window she noticed that the seagulls had flown away, leaving a large piece of cone. There was no such thing as a hungry seagull in this town.

Suze decided it was futile hiding her fears from Daisy. She'd prise them out of her in the end, one way or another. 'I just can't deal with this, Daisy,' she said with a sigh.

'With Mum's illness?'

'Apparently it's not an illness.'

'You're splitting hairs, Suze.'

She sighed again and sipped her coffee, then looked at her sister with big, anxious eyes, now shining with tears. 'I'm sorry. I just can't cope with Mum's decline.'

'What do you mean, *you* can't cope? This isn't about *you*, Suze! Mum needs you. She needs all of us. You can't just walk away because things get tough. Family look out for each other. Mum's looked out for you all your life. Now it's your turn to look out for *her*.'

'I know. I hate myself for being scared. I'm such a loser.'

Daisy bit her tongue. It was so typical of Suze to play the self-pity card at this point in the argument. 'You're not a loser, Suze,' she said with forced patience. 'But you're going to have to step up.'

'You're suggesting I'm selfish!'

And typical to put words into her mouth which Daisy hadn't said.

'Listen, can we just stop bringing this back to you. I'm scared too. We're all scared. None of us wants to see Mum lose her memory, but we can't desert her at the moment she needs us the most. What sort of people would we be if we abandoned the one person who has been there for us our whole lives, at the very time she needs *us* to be there for *her*?'

A tear trickled down Suze's cheek. She brushed it away. 'But dementia is awful. One day she won't know who we are. She won't remember. She'll even forget how to breathe and then she'll die.' Suze clutched her throat. 'I can't bear to watch her suffer.'

Daisy's chest grew tight and she fought tears of her own. 'That's a long way down the road, Suze,' she said quietly. 'Don't think of that. Remember what Grandad used to say?'

'He said many things. Which one in particular are you thinking of?'

'*What's wrong with now?*'

Suze bit her lip. '*Everything's* wrong with now, Daisy. Our mother has dementia.'

'You're missing the point. Right now you and I are sitting in a nice café having coffee. The point is to live in the moment and not project into a future that hasn't happened yet. Right now, Mum knows who you are. She's perfectly normal, most of the time. Dad is home and missing you, and so is Nan, who is saltier than ever, so *I* need you too. Why don't you pop in for tea? Say you've been busy looking after Batty. Nan will approve of that.'

Suze managed a small grin. 'I think it's more the other way round.'

'I know that,' said Daisy, grinning back. 'In fact, we all know that, even Nan. But it sounds good.'

Suze sighed and Daisy knew she had got through to her. 'All right,' she conceded. 'I'll come over this afternoon.'

'Good. Mum will be really pleased.'

'Can we talk about something else now?'

'Sure. Whatever you want.'

'Have you made any progress with Taran?'

'About the land?'

'Yes, about that. And, have you kissed him yet?' Suze's grin grew wider.

'He's still in Toronto and I haven't made any progress in either area, but I'm only working on one.'

'The kissing one,' said Suze.

'No, the *land* one,' Daisy replied with emphasis.

'If I were you, I'd kill them both with one stone.'

That afternoon, as Marigold was sitting in the garden with Dennis and Nan, listening to the birdsong and watching the shadows lengthen across the lawn, Suze stepped through the back door with Daisy. Dennis smiled in delight. 'Ah, Suze. We haven't seen you in a while!'

Marigold, who couldn't remember the last time she'd seen her daughter, smiled too. 'How lovely,' she said.

'I've been so busy looking after my husband,' Suze declared.

Nan nodded her approval, just as Daisy said she would. 'Husbands are a full-time job,' said Nan. 'The trouble is their mothers spoil them, so when they get married their girl-friends turn into their mothers and they sit back and expect everything to be done for them.'

'I think that's a little harsh,' said Daisy, pulling up a garden chair.

'Oh, it's all very well modern women claiming that men share the housework, but the truth is, they don't. They're not made for the vacuum cleaner and the washing machine. It's just not in their DNA and you can't change thousands of years of habit. Your grandfather never learned how to put his plate in a dishwasher and I'm not wrong in saying that

Dennis hasn't either. If Atticus loads the dishwasher, I'll eat my hat.'

'I'd be careful making promises you can't keep,' said Dennis. 'I think Batty is the sort of man who knows how to make himself useful around the house.'

Suze sat next to her mother. 'How are you, Mum?' she asked, trying not to notice the small changes in Marigold's appearance. There wasn't anything major. Certainly nothing that anyone who didn't know her would notice. But to Suze, the slightly dreamy look on her mother's face was new and alarming.

'Very well, dear,' Marigold replied, smiling vaguely.

'How was the hotel?'

There was a long pause while Marigold tried to work out what Suze had asked her. Something about a hotel, but which hotel?

Dennis intervened. He had become used to compensating for Marigold's lapses in memory now and his interruptions were fast becoming habit. 'We went to that lovely hotel by the sea, didn't we, Goldie? The one with the blue-and-white decoration that you loved so much.' Marigold narrowed her eyes a little, which betrayed the fact that their weekend away had been swallowed into the fog, but her smile tried to fool them all that she remembered. 'We went for walks up and down the beach, and out for supper. The wine was very good and the service was excellent. Really, you two,' he said to Daisy and Suze, 'it was the best present ever. It really was.'

'Yes, it was very sweet of you,' Marigold agreed. She was getting good at dissembling when she didn't remember something.

Dennis turned to Suze. 'So tell us, Suze. How is married life? How is Batty—'

'Atticus,' Nan cut in firmly. 'You can't call a respectable married man a silly nickname like that, even if Suze has tattooed it onto her shoulder!'

Marigold sat up with a start. 'You have a tattoo, Suze?' she gasped.

Suze glanced at Daisy in panic. Hadn't they already had this conversation?

'Yes, Mum, she got it done before the wedding,' said Daisy.

'I told her she can't divorce him now his name is tattooed onto her shoulder,' Nan added. 'You might regret that, Suze. You'll never find another man called Batty.'

Daisy caught Suze's eye and grinned. Really, with their grandmother repeating everything and their mother forgetting everything, they were turning into a right old comedy act. Perhaps the only way to deal with the situation was to see the funny side of it.

Daisy shook her head and laughed. Suze was only too ready to release her angst in the same way and laughed with her. Dennis looked at them both and chuckled. 'What's so funny, girls?'

'Nan's repeating everything,' said Daisy, glancing at Nan and hoping not to offend her.

'Am I?' she asked incredulously. 'I'm sure I'm not.'

Daisy nodded. 'I'm afraid you are. And Mum's forgetting everything,' she added bravely, taking her mother's hand and smiling at her lovingly.

Marigold smiled back, reassured by the gentle look in her daughter's eyes. 'I suppose it *is* funny, isn't it,' she said quietly.

Nan lifted her chin. 'Well, we are getting older, aren't we? So you shouldn't be surprised.'

They all began to laugh, even Nan, albeit a little grudgingly.

'What was it Grandad used to say?' said Suze.

'What's wrong with now,' said Marigold promptly, and everyone turned to look at her in surprise. 'I don't think I'll ever forget *that*,' she added. Then she swept her eyes over them with gratitude. 'There's nothing wrong with now, is there?'

Chapter 23

Daisy sat on the bench at the edge of the wood and looked out over the fields. It was a warm afternoon in late August. Feathery clouds lingered unmoving in the sky and a glider wheeled silently beneath them, like a graceful bird on the wing. Mordy the Labrador lay at her feet panting while the two spaniels darted about the wheat in pursuit of the pheasants and rabbits that took refuge there.

Her mind turned to Luca. His texts were becoming more frequent and more needy. He was missing her and wondering whether they couldn't reach some sort of compromise that suited them both. *How about we get a dog?* he had written. A dog? Daisy had laughed at that, because it was too ridiculous to take seriously. But every time she thought of Luca, Taran interrupted her thoughts, striding into her mind with his long legs and big personality, stealing her attention.

Yet Taran was not a good bet. He lived in Toronto. He was clearly a man who avoided commitment. The fact that he was planning to sell the farm to developers and build houses in the field right next door to her parents' home made a romantic relationship between the two of them impossible. She would not want to be with a man who allowed that to happen, a man who put money before people's welfare. She didn't imagine

Sir Owen had left his beloved farm to his son just so that he could sell it off to the highest bidder. And what about Lady Sherwood? Where would she go once he'd sold it? Didn't Taran have any consideration for her?

Even Daisy could see that she was repeating a pattern. Why couldn't she fall in love with a man who lived close by and loved the countryside like she did? Yet, the heart didn't allow for choice. It went where it went and it didn't listen to reason. Her brain could override it, of course, and right now that's what it was trying desperately to do. She could never leave her home now that her mother was unwell. Her mother was her priority; *her* need was greater than Daisy's. She'd been away for six years and as a result there was no doubt in her mind where her home was; she wasn't going to live anywhere else but *here*.

Mordy lifted his head off his paws and pricked his ears. Daisy imagined he had seen a rabbit and looked in the direction of his gaze. To her surprise she saw a man approaching up the farm track. She recognized his gait at once. It was Taran.

Her spirits lifted with a jolt of excitement. She stood up as Mordy raced down the track to meet him, followed by Archie and Bendico who shot out of the wheat like bullets. The three dogs circled him, tails wagging fiercely, and he bent down to pat them. He was smiling when he reached her, looking casual in a navy shirt with the sleeves rolled up and a pair of jeans. He was unshaven and his hair was curling at the collar. His eyes were very green against his tanned skin. Daisy felt awkward suddenly and lost for words. It was hard to imagine that he had ever attempted to kiss her. Hard to imagine that she had ever been in a position to rebuff him.

'Hi, Daisy,' he said, bending down to plant a bristly kiss on her cheek. He looked at her intensely. 'You look well.'

'Have you just got here?' she asked, wishing she had applied some make-up and washed her hair. Instead, she wore her hair in a ponytail and her face was as God had intended it.

Hands on hips he took a deep breath through his nostrils and swept his eyes over the fields. 'Just got here. It's good to be home.' He turned back to her and grinned. 'I hope I didn't disturb you.'

'Not at all.'

'This isn't a bench for one,' he added, sitting down beside her.

'Your father wouldn't have agreed with that,' she said.

'It's not his bench now.' He rested his arm along the back, behind Daisy. 'It's mine and I prefer to have company.'

'Your dogs are happy to see you.'

'They know who's the boss now. They never noticed me much when Dad was alive.'

'I've grown very fond of them, especially Mordy. He lies on the sofa in the barn and watches me draw.'

'How's that going? Did you finish Rupert?'

She laughed. 'Rupert is finished and I've started drawing Basil.'

He shook his head. 'Basil! What's that? A terrier?'

'You got it,' she replied.

'Typical.' He leaned forward with his elbows on his knees and turned his head to look at her seriously. 'Thanks again for being there for Mum. You're a godsend.'

'I'm glad I've been helpful. I can't imagine what it must be like to lose someone you've lived with for so long. The hole your father has left must be enormous. I just want to make her feel less alone.'

'You do that very well. She says she wouldn't have got through these past months without you. She says you're very wise. Deep and wise were her words, if I remember rightly.'

'You should spend more time here, Taran,' she suggested boldly. 'You're her only child. I can't replace *you*.'

He sat back and swept his fingers through his hair. 'You're making me feel guilty.'

'Good,' she replied. 'Someone has to.'

He chuckled. 'You're the voice of my conscience, Daisy Fane.'

'There's nothing like family when things go pear-shaped.'

'Speaking of family,' he said, changing the subject. 'How's yours?'

Daisy wasn't intending to share her heartbreak with him, but it just slipped out. 'Mum's got dementia,' she said.

Taran looked at her with surprise and compassion. 'God, I'm sorry, Daisy,' he said, putting a hand on her shoulder. 'That's really tough.'

'It is,' she agreed, fighting the now familiar feeling of impending loss.

'When did you find out?'

'It's been gradual. Ever since I came back from Italy she's been getting increasingly forgetful and vague.'

'Has there been a diagnosis?'

'Sort of, but there's nothing anyone can do. We just have to support her as much as we can, until . . .' Her throat tightened.

'Until?' he asked gently.

'Until we can't support her anymore.'

He nodded, understanding. 'Does she know?'

'Yes, she's aware, for the moment. I suppose there will come a time when she ceases to be aware. That will go too, along with everything else. It's a cruel disease. Except that it's not a disease apparently.' She shrugged. 'I don't know what it is.' She noticed the tenderness in the way he was looking at her, and she found herself looking back at him in puzzlement, surprised that the man she condemned as arrogant and materialistic could feel such empathy and show it. 'You know what she loves more than anything else?' she said, hoping that she was going to discover that he had a generous spirit as well. 'Her garden. Her greatest joy is feeding the birds and looking out over your fields.'

He smiled reflectively. 'I'm glad they give her pleasure,' he said.

'As her world gets smaller, those things will be the only things that give her pleasure. She won't go into the shop now. Tasha has come good and proved that she can be reliable after all. Perhaps because Mum wasn't very good at sharing the responsibility, Tasha didn't feel she had any. Now she's needed, she's committed.' Daisy smiled wryly. 'Mum's like that, or she was. Doing everything for everyone so that no one could do anything for themselves.' She was thinking of Suze and Nan, of course, but as she spoke she realized that her father was used to being waited on as well. They'd all have to learn to look after themselves.

Daisy wanted Taran's reassurance that those fields her mother loved would always be there for her, but she didn't know how to bring the conversation around to that. She didn't want to admit that she had eavesdropped on his telephone conversation. Taran had never discussed his inheritance with her. Neither had Lady Sherwood. She'd only heard bits of gossip from Eileen. As far as he was concerned, she had no idea what his plans were. The only thing she could do was emphasize how much she loved the farm and hope that she could infect him with her enthusiasm. 'Do you miss home when you're in Canada?' she asked.

'Funny you should say that. I didn't, but since Dad died, I look back in a way I never did before.'

'Does the place mean more to you now because it's a part of your father that lives on?'

He frowned at her. 'Perhaps that's what it is.' He shifted his gaze and contemplated the land his father had loved so much. 'It is the part of Dad that lives on, besides me, of course.' He paused as if considering it for the first time. 'He used to take me round the farm when I was a boy. I'd sit on the roof of the jeep with the dogs running behind us and he'd call it a safari. I'd spot deer and hares, rabbits and pheasants, and the dogs would give chase across the fields. We'd sit on the bonnet and eat sandwiches at harvest time and watch the combines chomping through the wheat and barley. I remember the dust and the way it glittered in the sunlight like gold. Funny, I haven't thought about that in years.'

'It sounds idyllic.'

'And all the while, *you* were in the village and I didn't know you.' He looked across at her and smiled. 'With your pigtails.'

'I'm sure I didn't have pigtails.'

'I think you did.'

'No, I really didn't. Bunches.'

'Pigtails!'

She smacked him playfully. 'What else did you do with your father?'

'He showed me the land and tried to infect me with enthusiasm for farming, but every time I saw land I just wanted to build on it.'

'You couldn't build on this!' she exclaimed. 'This is beautiful. Just beautiful.'

'I don't mean literally build on it. I was already an architect as a boy, building houses in my imagination, seeing structures, *beautiful* structures, in the landscape.' Daisy wondered whether that was an assurance that he had decided not to sell the land. She couldn't be certain. She didn't want to press him.

'Do you have to build structures in Toronto? Couldn't you do it here so you could be close to your mother?'

'I could, but ...'

'I mean, she won't be around for ever. You need to spend time with her while she's around.'

She noticed the rising passion in her voice and checked herself. She could tell from the way he was looking at her that he knew she was thinking about her own mother.

'You're right to have come home, Daisy,' he said. 'You're right to be spending time with your mother.'

'I don't know what I'll do when she goes,' she said quietly. 'She's been the centre of our world. The gravitational pull. Without her we'll all lose our footing. God, it'll be dreadful. I can't imagine it. I'm sorry I'm making this all about me. I just watch my mother decline, and watch your mother coping on her own, and I know how important love is. When they're gone, they're gone. That's it.'

'Dementia certainly thrusts one into the present, doesn't it.'

'That's all she's going to have.'

'But the present isn't bad, Daisy.'

'What's wrong with now,' she muttered. 'That's what my grandfather used to ask when we worried about the future or regretted things we'd done in the past. He'd say, "What's wrong with now, Daisy?" and there never was anything wrong. It's just hard to stay in the present moment. The mind wanders back and jumps forward and worries about things that aren't happening in the now. They're just in the memory or the imagination and yet, they're so powerful, pulling us this way and that. Grandad never worried about anything. He always seemed to be in the now.'

'Your grandfather sounds like he knew a thing or two about how to live. Don't think about the future until you have to. Don't lose the present moment, which is real, to the future which is just in your imagination. There's a lot to be said for that. We'd all be happier if we could live in the moment.'

'I try. I really do. But I fear the future, because it's going to be heartbreaking.'

'Do you look back at the past?'

She sensed he was referring to Luca. She shrugged. There was no reason why she shouldn't tell him about Luca. It wasn't as if they were in a relationship. Taran was her friend, after all. Her *unlikely* friend. 'If you're referring to my past heartbreak, I can tell you he's been in touch. He wants to make another go of it. He says we're fools to let something good slip away from us.'

Taran shook his head. 'You don't want to do that.'

'Why?'

'If it's broken, it's broken for a reason. You'd only be going back because it's familiar and because you're afraid of the future.'

'I'm not afraid of the future. At least, not *my* future.' Daisy knew that wasn't true. She *was* afraid of being alone. 'I'm afraid of Mum's future. Anyway, I'll never go back to Italy. I'm here now and I'm staying. Mum needs me and Dad needs my support. I could even go as far as saying it's lucky that I came back just as Mum got unwell. It's as if Fate designed the break-up especially.'

Taran nodded slowly, as if working something out in his head.

'How's your on–off girlfriend?' she asked, deciding that Luca was not a comfortable subject of conversation.

'Off,' he said with a grin. 'I did the right thing. You've made me a better man. Will you have a drink with me tonight?' he asked. 'We could go for another drunken midnight walk.'

'I don't know about the drunken midnight walk, but I'll have a drink with you.'

He stood up. 'If you were a character from fiction, you'd be Elizabeth Bennet.'

'Are you suggesting I'm buttoned-up and sensible?' she replied.

He grinned down at her. 'Clever and quick-witted, with the undercurrent of something far more interesting, given a little alcohol.'

'Oh really!' Daisy exclaimed, getting to her feet. They whistled for the dogs and began to walk in the direction of Taran's home. 'I'm glad to say, you're nothing like Mr Darcy,' she said. 'He has no sense of humour.'

'I disagree. I think he'd be very amusing once you got to know him.'

'With a little alcohol,' she added wryly.

'It helps loosen the seams.'

'Do I need my seams loosened?'

'We all do. We all need to get out of our heads. We all think too much.'

'What do *you* think about, Taran?' she asked.

He looked down at her and smiled. 'That's my secret,' he said.

'You're not going to share it?'

'Maybe later.'

'With a little alcohol.'

His green eyes twinkled with the humour that Mr Darcy lacked. 'Like I said, it loosens the seams!'

When they reached the house Lady Sherwood was in the kitchen reading the papers at the island. She raised her eyes over her glasses and smiled. 'Ah, you found her,' she said. The dogs trotted in, panting, and flopped into their baskets. 'Would you like a cup of coffee, Daisy?'

'Well, I should really get back to my easel,' she replied.

'Basil can wait,' said Taran. 'I make very good coffee. How do you like it?'

'Strong,' Daisy replied, taking the stool beside Lady Sherwood. 'I've lived in Italy, the home of the best coffee in the world, so no pressure.'

'Italians are no match for me,' said Taran, taking a cup out of the cupboard. 'Just you wait and see. We make a mean coffee in Toronto, I can tell you.'

Daisy laughed.

A little while later Taran brought over two cups and placed one in front of Daisy. 'Go on, tell me it's the best coffee you've ever had.'

She grinned at him and lifted the cup to her lips.

He raised his eyebrows.

She nodded. 'Not bad,' she said. 'For a Canadian.'

Lady Sherwood feigned horror. 'Taran's not all Canadian, you know. He's half English. He just doesn't want to acknowledge it.'

'I'm beginning to,' he said, taking a sip of his, and as he said it Lady Sherwood noticed he was looking directly at Daisy.

Dennis had finished the church for his model village and was at the kitchen table, painting the village hall, when Daisy came home. 'Where's Mum?' she asked, putting her bag on a chair.

'Having tea with Beryl.'

'Oh good. That's nice,' she said, pleased to hear her mother was getting about.

'Nan's at bridge. She was grumbling about not wanting to go anymore because apparently one of the ladies is a cheat. I can't remember which one. She says the others turn a blind eye, but as Nan's a woman of integrity, she can't sit back and let it happen. I fear there's going to be a fight. Just preparing you.'

'Nothing would surprise me,' said Daisy.

'I'm glad I've got you on my own, though. I've been thinking,' Dennis began, putting down his paintbrush.

Daisy took the chair opposite her father. 'I like it when you're thinking, Dad. It means something creative is afoot.'

'You're not wrong, Daisy.' He paused and two small red stains flourished on the apples of his cheeks. 'I want to make Marigold a puzzle,' he said.

'She still hasn't managed to finish the last one you made her,' said Daisy sadly.

'No, I mean a different kind of puzzle, Daisy. A puzzle of her memories.'

Daisy felt a stab of pain in her chest. She put a hand there and rubbed it, but rubbing it didn't make it better. 'Oh Dad, that's such a lovely idea,' she managed. 'It really is.'

'You see, what worries her is who she'll be without her memories. But I've reassured her that she doesn't need them, because we've got them, and we'll keep them safe for her. You see, we know her, don't we? She'll always be Goldie to me and Mum to you and Suze, and Marigold to Nan. She might not remember things about her life, but we will. I thought you and I could do a memory board, but make it into a puzzle. We could all do it together,' he said softly. 'We could choose the memories, as a family, and you could paint them.'

'I'd love to!' Daisy exclaimed.

'It would be a big puzzle in scale, with large pieces, but not too many of them. You know, something she could cope with. Something to remind her of the good things in her life.'

'So she doesn't forget,' Daisy added quietly.

'So she knows she's loved.' Dennis looked down at his hands

and Daisy thought how forlorn he looked suddenly. Like a boy; like a *lost* boy. 'She's not going to get better, Daisy,' he croaked.

'I know.'

'We have to keep her with us for as long as possible.'

She nodded.

'I thought the puzzle would be a good way to get her back whenever we feel we're losing her,' he added.

'And once she's completed it, she can do it again and again. It will exercise her mind as well as jog her memory and remind her of who she is,' said Daisy. 'She can do it as many times as she likes.'

'I thought we could write the memories on the back of the pieces, to go with the pictures. I want her to know that what we've had, as a family, is very special.'

'I love that idea, Dad,' said Daisy, gazing lovingly at her father through the mist that had blurred her vision. 'It's the best idea you've ever had.'

'I think it is,' he agreed bashfully.

She reached across the table and took his hand. It was big and rough and somehow terribly vulnerable. 'She'll love it,' she said.

'I know she will,' he replied, picking up his paintbrush. His old eyes shone with emotion as he looked at her. 'I think, the picture in the middle of the puzzle—'

'Should be a cup of tea,' Daisy interrupted with a smile.

Dennis's face lit up. 'Just what I was thinking,' he said. 'All of us at the table with a pot of tea.'

Daisy wiped away the tears with her fingers. 'When shall we start, Dad?'

'Right away,' he replied. 'We've got no time to lose.'

And that was the saddest part of all: they had no time to lose. No time.

Daisy was feeling emotional when she walked up the lane to the pub. The sun was sinking in the western sky, catching the wisps of cloud and turning them pink. They looked like pretty feathers, floating slowly across the heavens. Marigold had come home in good spirits. She'd had a nice afternoon with Beryl, looking through Beryl's photograph albums of when they were girls. Marigold had no problem remembering the past. She loved reminiscing. It was a phase of her life she could be sure of. Then Beryl had invited Cedric and Dolly, the Commodore and his wife Phyllida and Eileen for tea. They'd sat in her sitting room, discussing the way things were back in the day, when Reg ran the petrol station and the village hall held tea dances and Brownies. It had warmed Daisy's heart to see her mother so happy.

Then Nan had come back full of complaints. She had sacked the bridge cheat, apparently, in spite of her protestations of innocence. Nan was having none of it. Now she needed to find another player to complete the four. Dennis had given her a glass of sherry and switched on the television, then he had sat with Marigold and helped her with the puzzle. When Daisy had left they were making real progress. *What's wrong with now?* Daisy asked herself as she reached the pub. Nothing. Nothing at all. She couldn't deny that, right now, everything was positive.

Taran was at the bar. He was wearing a white shirt and jeans and a wide smile. Something in Daisy's stomach fluttered when she saw him. He was handsome, but there was a deeper connection between them now that rendered his looks superfluous: they were friends.

This time Daisy asked for a glass of wine and she resolved

to have only a couple. They moved to a table tucked away in a corner and ordered something to eat. They didn't notice the coming and going of people, or the passing of time; they had eyes only for each other and neither wanted the evening to end. Taran made Daisy feel good. The way he looked at her made her feel feminine. The tenderness in his gaze made her feel special. Above all, his humour dispelled her anxiety. It was so good to laugh when there was too much to cry about. When they left the pub it was dark and the moon was indeed big and round and shining brazenly upon the fields and woods as they wandered slowly up the farm track. When he took her hand it no longer felt strange.

They sat on the bench and he put his arm around her. 'You asked what I was thinking,' he said.

'I did,' she replied. 'Are you going to tell me now?'

'Yes.'

She turned to look at him.

'I was thinking of this bench and how I'd like to sit beside you again, in the middle of the night, just like this, sober.' She frowned and he hooked her hair behind her ear. 'I know you thought I was drunk last time. I wasn't. I wanted to kiss you then and I want to kiss you now. One drink or six won't change that. I just want to kiss you, period.'

Daisy caught her breath.

He didn't say anything else. He wound his hand around her neck, beneath her hair, and touched her nose with his. She didn't pull away. Then his lips found hers and he kissed her. She closed her eyes. *What's wrong with now?*

Chapter 24

Dennis was in his shed, working on the window shutters for Marigold, when there came a knock on the door. Mac lifted his head off his paws and watched suspiciously from his warm place on the windowsill. It was Eileen.

'Hello, Eileen,' said Dennis, looking up from his workbench.

Eileen slipped in and closed the door behind her. 'I'm glad I've found you, Dennis,' she said, clutching her handbag to her chest and looking decidedly guilty.

'What can I do for you?' he asked. He wasn't used to people coming into his shed.

'It's about Marigold.'

He raised his eyebrows.

'I hear you're making a puzzle for her. A puzzle of her memories.'

Dennis was astonished. 'Who told you that?' he asked. He had only discussed the puzzle with Daisy.

'Sylvia.'

'Sylvia!' Dennis was even more astonished. 'How does *she* know?'

'I suspect Daisy told Taran and Taran told his mother and his mother told Sylvia and Sylvia told me. But I won't breathe a word, I promise.' She pressed a finger to her lips.

Dennis suppressed a smile because it was well known that Eileen was incapable of keeping a secret. 'You know Daisy and Taran are dating,' she added, cocking her head and hoping she was the first to know.

Dennis raised his eyebrows again. 'No, I didn't.'

'They were at the pub last night. I think they make a lovely couple. He's so tall and handsome and she's so pretty. I predicted it, you see. I knew from the first time he walked into the shop and they saw each other. They hadn't seen each other since school and that was decades ago. She barely gave him a second glance. That's what did it. Men like Taran Sherwood are used to women fawning over them. The fact that Daisy didn't, did it. I could tell.'

'It's always been hard to keep one's business to oneself in this village,' said Dennis, scratching his head.

'The point is. I would like to add a memory to the puzzle, Dennis. I have a nice little story that you could symbolize with a music score.'

'A music score?' he repeated.

'Yes. Do you remember when Marigold joined my little church choir? It was a long time ago, but she did enjoy it. She has a lovely voice, doesn't she?'

'Yes,' said Dennis. 'She loved to sing.'

'We had such a laugh. Do you remember how Beryl warbled? She warbled so loudly that none of us could keep a straight face. Well, perhaps you could get Daisy to draw the choir, or Beryl warbling, or me at the organ. I'm ninety-three, you know, and I still play like a young girl.'

'I think that's a great idea, Eileen,' he said. 'It would be nice to add some memories from her friends. Why don't you have a word with Daisy? She's making a list.'

Eileen was thrilled. 'Oh, I will!' she exclaimed happily. Then she put a finger to her lips. 'I won't breathe a word!'

Dennis realized he would have to tell Suze and Nan quickly before the whole village was talking about it.

Now that Marigold had no reason to go into the shop, she began to feel redundant. No one needed her anymore. Daisy cooked, Dennis helped wash up and somehow things got done without her. She began to feel low and the silver linings to the black clouds seemed harder to find these days. She knew they were there, she just couldn't see them. Everything began to look dark and hopeless and Marigold felt more alienated from herself than ever.

Then Dennis asked her to do some work in the garden. 'I wish I had the time, but I'm so busy,' he claimed, looking desperate. 'It's getting so overgrown and if we don't do something now it will become a real mess. It's full of ground elder and bindweed. More weed than flower.' Marigold was pleased she was able to help. She was also pleased to be needed. She wondered why she hadn't thought of spending more time in the garden herself. With the little robin as her constant companion, she got onto her knees and began to pull out the ground elder, leaving it in little piles on the lawn for Dennis to collect later with the wheelbarrow. Whenever she felt tired she went inside to make herself some tea. Then she brought it outside and sat on one of the garden chairs and looked out over the fields. Sometimes she spent so long there, mesmerized by the oscillating leaves and the combine churning through the wheat, sending glittering clouds of gold dust into the air, that the hours went by and she forgot about her weeding. She forgot what she was meant to be doing and just sat there, gazing, as content as a cat in sunshine.

After Eileen, there came more knocks on Dennis's shed

door. Nan let the visitors into the house with a scowl and rolled her eyes. Dennis had told her about the puzzle, but she thought it unnecessary. In her opinion he was making a mountain out of a molehill. The fact that, one by one, the locals were traipsing in with their memories, wanting to be part of this gift, irritated her. No one had rallied around Arthur when he had done his back in with a shovel or got cancer and no one had rallied around *her* when she had had a hysterectomy. Why was everyone rallying around Marigold? The whole thing was absurd. She was getting older – granted, she was more forgetful than most, but she was in fine health notwithstanding. And this game they all played of agreeing with her was just silly. When Marigold claimed to have had a chat with her father, Dennis didn't raise an eyebrow. He simply said, 'How nice, and how is he?' But Nan was having none of it. How was Marigold ever going to improve if everyone told her she was right all the time? If she didn't realize she was getting muddled? Arthur died fifteen years ago and Nan was the only one prepared to say it. It wasn't like Marigold to get cross, but she did with her, especially about her father. 'Dad isn't dead!' Marigold exclaimed and her eyes shone with frustration. Dennis tried talking to his mother-in-law and Daisy appealed to her good nature, but she didn't budge. She hadn't brought Marigold up to go doolally on her now. If anyone was going to go doolally it was *her* as she was the oldest by a long way! It was only a matter of time before *she* lost her marbles. Would Dennis make a puzzle for *her*?

After Eileen, the first to knock on the door had been the Commodore. He wanted to be represented by a mole. Then came Dolly, who asked whether Daisy might like to paint her with Precious. Cedric thought a Christmas pudding surrounded by his feline ladies would work exceedingly well. Mary

suggested painting her on the path with Bernie, in her favourite red coat, which Marigold always admired, and Beryl came
with a black-and-white photograph of herself with Marigold as
schoolgirls. When the vicar heard what Dennis was doing he
was full of admiration and strode into Dennis's shed, armed with
quotes from the Bible about selflessness and love and told Dennis
that he was sure to have a very special place reserved for him
in Heaven, when his time came. Dennis wondered what Daisy
could paint to represent the vicar and came up with a soapbox.
He and Mac had a good laugh about that once the vicar had
gone. The vicar's wife, Julia, suggested her china tea set, which
was made in Hungary by Herend. Marigold loved her tea, as
they all knew, and Julia's set was very expensive. Phyllida, the
Commodore's wife, had had a disagreement with her husband
about the mole and thought it more appropriate, not to mention
more dignified, to be represented by a battleship. They had
come to a compromise and agreed that the two of them on the
deck of a ship with a mole perched on the Commodore's shoulder (like Mac on Dennis's) would represent them well enough.
When Sylvia took Dennis aside at church to ask to be included,
Dennis struggled to hold his patience. Was this project getting
too big? Could he and Daisy cope with all the requests?

At the beginning of September Dennis put up the shutters
on the main windows of their house. He spent three days at
the top of a ladder, while Marigold worked in the garden
beneath him. When he was finished, he stood back to admire
his work. Marigold came to stand beside him. 'They look
nice,' she said, taking off her gardening gloves.

'They're for you,' he told her proudly.

'For me?'

'Yes, you said you wanted shutters, so you could imagine
you're in Provence.'

'Have I been to Provence?' she asked.

'Yes, we went once, when we were young.'

She looked at them sadly now. 'Is that another memory I've lost?'

'It doesn't matter, Goldie,' he said, pulling her close. 'It's not an important one.'

'They're very pretty.'

'I'm glad you like them.'

'I do. I'll admire them while I'm weeding.'

'That's the spirit. It's not the past that's important, but the present.'

'You sound like Dad. That's what he says.' Marigold laughed.

'I probably got it from him,' said Dennis.

'He's very wise. Really, if it wasn't for you and Dad, I don't think I'd have got through the last six months.' She put her gloves on again. 'Better get back to work. Thank you for the shutters, Dennis. They're lovely.'

Daisy struggled to work with Taran hijacking her attention. Every time she managed to get behind her easel, he came to drag her away. And she went willingly, leaving her half-finished dog on the paper. Weary of the missed calls and texts from Luca, she changed her phone number.

Taran only planned to be in the UK for two weeks and he wanted to spend all of it with Daisy. They went for long walks with the dogs. They kissed on the bench. They made love in the woods and they picnicked on Sir Owen's bench, looking out over the harvested fields that shimmered like gold in the early autumn light. On bright nights they lay side by side on the lawn outside Taran's house and gazed up at the stars. They held hands, they talked about nothing and they laughed, a lot. Whenever Daisy felt the creeping insinuation of fear she asked herself: *What's wrong with now?* And there was nothing wrong with now because she was with Taran and love made her feel careless and filled her with optimism; love made her feel invincible.

'Come to Toronto,' he said on their last evening together.

They lay entwined in the barn, in the bed that was intended for Taran's holidays and weekends, but which had never been slept in, until now. Taran was tracing his fingers down Daisy's naked spine.

'I can't,' she replied. 'Mum needs me here and I've got the puzzle to paint with Dad.'

'Those things can wait. Come and spend some time with me. You might find that you like it.'

'I know I'd like it. But I don't want to like it. I'm needed here.'

He sighed and thought for a moment. Then he curled a tendril of hair behind her ear and looked at her seriously. 'I'm falling in love with you, Daisy,' he said candidly. 'I haven't said that to anyone, ever. This is a big deal for me. I just want to be with you. I don't want to be on another continent. One of us will have to give.'

'I've just given the last six years of my life and it's taught me a valuable lesson.'

'What's that?'

'I don't want to be the one to give any more.'

He pulled a face, intended to appeal to her heart. 'What about me? Don't you want to give to me?'

She shook her head. 'I don't want to compromise, Taran. I know what I want and I won't accept anything less. Not for anybody.'

'You want to be near your mother. I understand that.'

'And I want to be here.'

'Here?'

'Home.'

He nodded. 'Okay. So come for a week. Let me show you my city. Even if you like it, which you will, I won't ask you to stay.'

'I'll think about it,' she replied. 'Maybe.'

He smiled, then took her wrists in his hands and rolled her onto her back. He lay on top of her and kissed her. 'Maybe is nearly a yes.'

'Maybe is maybe,' she laughed.

'It's a yes,' he said, kissing her again.

'Perhaps.'

'That's a yes, too.'

After Taran left, Daisy was grateful to have something with which to occupy her time. Otherwise, she knew she'd just spend it mooning over him. It was hard working in the barn, because everything in it reminded her of him, and she missed him. But she managed to finish the portrait of Basil, then turned her mind to the puzzle. And in the late evening, just before she went to bed, Taran FaceTimed her and they spoke long into the night.

The jigsaw puzzle had got the whole village talking. Even those who didn't really want to talk, like John Porter and Pete Dickens who were feuding over the overgrown magnolia tree in Pete's garden. Much to their wives' surprise, after they had met with Daisy and discussed Marigold's puzzle, the two men agreed to meet over a beer in the pub and talk about the tree like the sensible adults they were. They left the pub two hours later, after a game of darts, the best of friends, and Pete wondered why he hadn't agreed to trim the tree in the first place. 'Life is short,' he explained to his wife. 'And uncertain. I don't want to waste the time I have left on this planet fighting over a bloody tree.' Daisy knew that her mother would be thrilled that her condition had prompted a reconciliation between the two neighbours, but she couldn't tell her because, on the one hand, the puzzle was meant to be a surprise and, on the other, Daisy wasn't sure her mother would remember who John Porter and Pete Dickens were. People were slowly falling out of the top of her memory and John and Pete were most likely to have been among the first to go.

Eileen took it upon herself to help Daisy collect people's stories, even though Daisy had assured her that she was perfectly capable of doing it herself. The truth was that Eileen missed her mornings with Marigold, chatting in the shop, watching the locals wandering in and out and gossiping about them. It wasn't the same now that Marigold wasn't there. Eileen visited Marigold at home instead and shared the local news, but Marigold was growing increasingly vague and seemed less interested now in what everyone was up to. Sometimes Eileen wondered whether she even knew who the people were that she talked about. Bored with little to do and lonely on her own, Eileen needed a project. Marigold's puzzle was just the thing.

Dennis set about making the board for the puzzle. He cut the sheet of plywood down to size. It was six millimetres thick and a better choice than wood because, unlike wood, it didn't warp or crack. He stuck some backing on the reverse side to prevent it from curling and paper to the top side, which Daisy was going to paint. This posed more of a challenge than any other, because Daisy was going to write who each picture represented on the back, so that Marigold would remember who her friends were. So that she didn't forget the people she had known for years; so that she didn't forget she was loved.

Eileen went about the village collecting everyone's stories. She went from house to house with a skip in her step, drinking cups of tea in every kitchen and sharing the village gossip. Marigold and Dennis's neighbours, John and Susan Glenn, had an amusing tale about Marigold and a lost key; Mary's husband, Brian, remembered her teaching their daughter how to bake cupcakes that looked like bumble bees. At the end of the day Eileen popped in to see Jean Miller, who was recently widowed and lived on her own in a small white cottage with a view of the bay. Jean was a good decade younger than Eileen, but looked older on account of her grief and her loneliness. Eileen always greeted her in church and if they happened to be in the shop together, but she didn't seek her out. Jean was quiet and a little shy and was always quick to hurry on her way like a timid mouse anxious to get back to her hole. Eileen took her notebook, ready to write down Jean's story, and followed her onto the patio where they sat at a table with cups of tea and looked out over the water. 'I'm very sorry about Marigold,' said Jean in her small voice. 'It's a very sad thing, dementia. So many people have it.'

'Marigold is doing very well, though,' said Eileen, knowing that her friend would not like her to be pessimistic. 'She enjoys her garden, her family and friends. The trick is to live in the moment. Philosophers have told us to live in the moment for thousands of years. Marigold doesn't even have to try.'

'Marigold is a good person,' said Jean gravely. 'She's kind and thoughtful and has always looked out for other people. It's nice that we're all doing something for her for a change.'

'She's becoming a catalyst for good,' Eileen told her. 'You know, Pete has agreed to trim his magnolia.'

Jean's eyes widened. 'No, really?'

'Oh yes, he and John went off to the pub together, having called a truce. It was a very silly argument, I can't imagine why they let it go on for so long.'

'Was that because of Marigold?'

Eileen nodded. 'When someone's in trouble it makes everyone else appreciate their own good fortune.'

'I suppose it does,' said Jean thoughtfully. 'You know, I struggled after Robert died, but Marigold popped in every now and then and listened to me. That's all I wanted really, someone to listen to me. I needed to talk about him. Marigold is a good listener. She has a compassionate face. Anyway, she gave me some wonderful advice.' Now Jean's face livened unexpectedly and her grey eyes shone. 'She told me to find a project. It didn't matter what it was, but it had to be something I was passionate about.'

'What is it, your project?'

Jean looked bashful. 'It's a bit embarrassing, but I don't suppose it matters.'

'You can tell me. I won't tell a soul, I promise.'

'I love watching old romantic films. Like *Gone with the Wind* and *An Affair to Remember.*'

Eileen's mouth opened in a gasp. 'I like those films too. How do you watch them?'

'On DVDs. I collect them. Shall I show you?'

'Yes please!' Eileen followed her into the sitting room. Jean opened a cupboard. Eileen nearly fell over. The entire cupboard was a neat library of films. Row upon row of them. She began to read the spines. 'Oh, I loved *Doctor Zhivago*. That's a classic.'

'Wasn't Omar Sharif wonderful!' gushed Jean excitedly.

'*Roman Holiday!* What a smasher!' Eileen couldn't contain her pleasure. 'I'd love to watch some of these.'

'I'll lend them to you, if you like. Do you have a DVD player?'

Eileen was bitterly disappointed. 'No, I don't. What a shame!' She gazed longingly at all the films and bit her lip.

'You can watch them here, with me, if you like. I mean, you don't have to. It's just a suggestion.' Jean smiled tentatively.

'That would be lovely. If you wouldn't mind.'

'Actually, I'd like the company.'

Eileen sighed. 'I would too,' she agreed, accepting at last that she was tired of being alone. 'It's lonely on your own, isn't it?' she said.

'Yes, it is,' said Jean.

'We could start our own club,' said Eileen enthusiastically. 'A film club.'

'What a good idea!' Jean exclaimed. 'A film club for two.'

'Oh yes. Just for two. A very exclusive club. We'd better not tell anyone else or they'll all want to join.' The two women laughed. 'Now, what would you like Daisy to paint so that Marigold remembers *you*?'

'The cover of *Gone with the Wind*. We both agreed that that was our favourite film of all time. I'm sure she won't ever forget *that*.'

A couple of weeks later Dennis and Daisy had completed the list and Daisy was making the preliminary sketches. Suze came round to see how the idea was progressing, then she sat with her mother and Nan in the kitchen and told them that she and Batty were moving out of his parents' house because they had found a small flat in town. 'It's very nice,' she said, looking a little apprehensive. 'It's a few yards from Starbucks, so I'll never have to make my own coffee.'

'You will when you realize how expensive coffee is,' said Nan. 'Much better to buy yourself a coffee machine and make it at home.'

'There's no fun in that, Nan. The whole point is to go in and people-watch. How do you think I get my ideas for the articles I write? I need to be with people, to see what they're wearing and what they're doing and to eavesdrop on their conversations.'

While Nan and Suze chatted Marigold sat quietly, trying to keep up. She watched them with a serene but vague look on her face. She picked up the name Batty and knew she should know who he was. It sounded so familiar. However, she knew better than to ask. She was certain that if she met him, she'd recognize his face. But the name on its own had no face attached to it at all.

'Dad says you're doing wonderful things in the garden,' said Suze, wanting to include her mother in the conversation.

'It's full of weeds,' Marigold replied slowly. 'I must take them all out so they don't . . .' She searched for the word. 'You know . . .' She fumbled around in the fog. To her surprise, she found it. '*Stifle* the plants.'

Nan laughed. 'There's not a single weed left, Marigold. You've taken them all out, as well as a few good plants besides.'

'I'm sure you'll find one or two more, Mum. You've got a good eye,' said Suze, upset by her grandmother's impatient tone. 'And you're still feeding the birds, I see, even though it's early autumn.'

Marigold smiled happily. 'I like to watch them come into the garden,' she said.

'You used to have a friendly robin, didn't you, Mum? Is he still here?'

Marigold nodded. 'He's still here,' she said. 'I feed him, even though it's autumn.'

'She's getting very repetitive,' said Nan to Suze, as if Marigold wasn't there.

Suze was incensed. 'If I remember rightly, Nan, you're quite repetitive yourself.'

'We're all getting older. It'll happen to you one day, you know. Nothing good about getting old!' said Nan.

'Old age is not for sissies,' said Marigold with a grin.

'That's my line,' said Nan.

Suze laughed. 'I'd better be going. I've got a party tonight and I need to get ready. I need to straighten my hair.'

'You should let it dry naturally. It's much softer when it's wavy,' said Nan.

'We could buy you some straightening tongs for your birthday,' said Marigold.

'That would be lovely,' said Suze.

Nan clicked her tongue. 'You bought her a pair the Christmas before last, remember?'

'That's okay. Why should Mum remember that?'

'It's only with you that I forget things,' said Marigold to her mother, affronted. 'With everyone else, I have no trouble at all.'

Suze didn't want to tell her that that was because Nan was the only person who corrected her when her memory failed.

'Where are you going, Suze?' Marigold asked.

'The party's in town. A thirtieth birthday party at a restaurant in the harbour. It'll be very glamorous.'

'Then you'd better go upstairs and have a bath.'

'She doesn't live here anymore, Marigold,' said Nan brusquely.

'I've found a flat, Mum,' Suze told her, as if for the first time. 'I'm moving in with Batty. We're going to live together.'

Marigold leaned towards Suze, smiling like a child with a

secret. 'Don't tell Nan,' she whispered. 'She doesn't approve of people living in sin.'

'Good Lord!' said Nan, standing up. 'I'm going to watch the telly.'

'You see,' said Marigold, as her mother left the room. 'She's doesn't approve of you living in sin.'

Suze's smile faltered, but she remembered what Daisy had told her, that she shouldn't try to correct her when she got things wrong. She took her hand. 'But you approve, don't you, Mum?'

'I just want you to be happy,' said Marigold, her eyes full of love.

'And I just want *you* to be happy too,' said Suze, and she turned away so that her mother did not see her tears.

Chapter 25

By the end of September Daisy had finished drawing the jigsaw puzzle. All that was required now was for her to paint it. She had almost three months in which to do it, if they wanted to give it to Marigold at Christmas, which was plenty of time.

As well as including the funny and more often eccentric anecdotes from the village, Daisy had incorporated items from Marigold's family life, bordering the entire picture with the birds and flowers she loved so much. She had drawn in Dennis's shed, Suze's mobile phone, Nan's crosswords and her own box of paints. Dennis had given her things from their marriage that were important, like a photograph of the church where they got married, the name of the hotel where they went on honeymoon and the cuckoo clock he had given her after a holiday in the Swiss mountains. Daisy included Mac, of course, and the cats that had lived before. The result was going to be a wonderful kaleidoscope of shape and colour, designed especially for her.

Daisy was in the barn preparing her paints when Nan came in. Daisy was surprised to see her, as she'd never been up to the Sherwoods' house before. 'Hi, Nan,' she said. 'Is everything all right?' She glanced at her phone to check that it was switched on. If there had been a problem with her mother, they would surely have called her.

'Everything's fine, Daisy.' Nan ran her eyes around the room. 'Well, this is grand,' she said. 'No wonder you get so much done. It's a sanctuary.'

'I know. I'm lucky,' Daisy agreed. She noticed Nan was carrying a book. 'Did you walk up here?'

'No, Dennis brought me in the car.'

'Oh.' She couldn't imagine what she'd come up for.

Nan wandered across the room. She looked at the puzzle laid out on the table. 'It's going to be very special,' she said and Daisy noticed her face tighten.

'Everyone's taken part. It's fantastic,' said Daisy. *Everyone's taken part except for you.*

Nan offered her the book. 'This is an album of your mother growing up. It's been gathering dust for years. No one looks at albums anymore. Everything's on their computers. Such a shame. We went to great trouble putting these books together and now no one bothers to look at them. I thought you might like to cast your eye over the pictures. You might find something relevant, for your puzzle.'

'That's a great idea, Nan,' said Daisy excitedly. 'Let's sit down together and you can show them to me. I may not know who everyone is.'

'Well, you'll know Patrick. He might be older but he still looks the same. And Grandad, of course.' They went to the sofa and sat down. Nan opened the album across their knees and put on her glasses. 'Now, here she is, as a baby,' said Nan. 'She wasn't a very pretty baby, was she!'

'She was adorable,' Daisy argued.

'She liked that bear. It had bells in its ears. It was called Honey. Why don't you put Honey in somewhere. She wouldn't go anywhere without Honey in those days.' She turned the page. 'Now, you can see how besotted Grandad was with Marigold. She was his little girl. Always was. He was harder on Patrick. Men are always harder on their sons, I think. Patrick was my boy.' She sighed. 'Until he went to live in Australia. You can't get further away than that. They don't even share the same time, being always a day ahead.'

'He went off to make his own way in the world,' said Daisy pensively.

'He could have done that in England.'

'He wanted adventure, I suspect.'

'No, he just wanted Lucille.'

Daisy laughed. 'I agree that Australia is quite a dramatic distance from home. It would have been nicer for you if he'd stayed closer. Europe wouldn't have been too bad.'

'No, he had to choose the furthest point. When Grandad died, I was left with just Marigold.'

'Who has looked after you very well. I doubt Patrick would have done anything. He's much too into himself.'

Nan considered that a moment. Then she turned the page. 'Yes, I think you're right. Marigold has been a saint putting up with me all these years.'

'She's a good person,' Daisy agreed.

'A better person that me,' said Nan.

Daisy settled her eyes onto a photograph of Marigold aged about ten. 'She had a sweet face, didn't she?' she murmured.

'She still has,' said Nan, running a crooked finger down the photograph. 'She gets that from her father. He had the same hazel eyes, like you, Daisy, and the same sweetness in his smile.' She pointed at a photograph of her husband. 'There, you see. How very alike they are. Patrick takes after me. We're both selfish and neither of us is sweet.'

'Don't be hard on yourself, Nan.'

Nan stiffened and lifted her chin. 'I'm not coping very well with Marigold's condition,' she confessed suddenly, putting her hand on the page and spreading her fingers. 'It's hard, you know, as a mother. Hard to watch. I'm not a good person. I don't have the patience. Your grandfather would have said all the right things. He'd have made her feel better. He'd have made *me* feel bad for not being more understanding.'

'We all cope in our own way,' said Daisy, trying to console her.

Nan said nothing. She turned the pages until she found a photograph of the four of them together. Nan and Grandad, Patrick and Marigold. 'Grandad always said the greatest life lessons are learned within the family. That's why there are families. You can't choose who you come into the world with. You just have to work it out and get along, but you can choose your friends. I'd say I've done well with my family.'

'You haven't done too badly with your friends, either,' said Daisy.

'Elsie's a cheat,' Nan retorted. She gave a sniff. 'I always suspected she was a cheat and now I know.'

'What are you going to do about your bridge four?'

She shrugged. 'I don't have to play bridge, you know. I can find something else to do.' But she didn't know what.

At that moment the door opened and Lady Sherwood walked in. 'Oh sorry, Daisy, I didn't realize you had company.'

'Come in, it's just my grandmother.'

Lady Sherwood smiled. 'Oh hello, I didn't realize it was you.'

'We're looking at an old album of Mum as a girl,' Daisy told her.

'Oh, albums are such fun, aren't they?' said Lady Sherwood, wandering over to have a look.

'We're finding things to include in the puzzle,' said Nan proudly.

'That's what I've come about.' Lady Sherwood looked at Daisy. 'Would it be all right if I gave you something? I'm not too late, am I?' She glanced at the board on the table. 'It looks like you're ready to paint it.'

Nan closed the album. Daisy stood up. 'Of course you can. I'd love to include something from you.'

'It's just something small. You see, whenever I went into the shop, your mother was always so friendly and smiley. I'd like you to paint the sun. You might have a sun in there already.'

'Actually I don't,' said Daisy.

'Then perhaps you can fit a sun in and say it's from me. It's the way I always see her. The sun shining indiscriminately on everyone in the village. And the village can't do without sunshine, can it? I don't think we can do without Marigold. I want her to know that. She's very special.'

Daisy was touched. 'Thank you, Celia,' she said quietly.

Nan was so starstruck by Lady Sherwood that she found she had nothing sour to say. 'Marigold is sunshine, you're right,' she agreed. 'I can't think of a better way to describe her.'

Daisy looked at her grandmother in surprise. It was unlike Nan to be so nice.

'How are you getting on, Lady Sherwood?' Nan asked gently. 'It's hard being widowed, especially when you were married to such a good man.'

A shadow of pain dimmed the light in Lady Sherwood's eyes. 'It is hard,' she agreed. 'And Owen was a very good man. I miss him all the time.'

'I still miss Arthur,' said Nan. 'I don't think the pain ever goes away. It deepens somehow, like a voice at the bottom of a well. It's far away and less acute, but it's always there. Always.'

'How lucky you are to have your family around you,

though,' said Lady Sherwood enviously. 'Taran's in Toronto and he's all I have.'

'Yes, I am very lucky,' Nan agreed, giving Daisy a small smile. 'Even Suze, who lives in town, pops in every now and then. But my son Patrick went to live in Australia and I rarely see him. You must rattle around in this big house.'

'It's not too big for one,' Daisy said quickly. It was just like Nan to be tactless.

'Well, it is, actually,' said Lady Sherwood. 'I should really fill it with people, shouldn't I? I haven't been very good at getting out since Owen died, or inviting friends over.'

'It's still early days,' said Daisy.

'Do you play bridge?' Nan asked. Daisy blushed. She couldn't imagine Lady Sherwood joining Nan's bridge nights.

'Yes, I do,' Lady Sherwood replied. 'Owen and I played a lot of bridge. He was very good at it. I'm not so good, but I enjoy playing. Especially with a large glass of wine.'

'Me too,' said Nan. 'I like a little brandy, myself.'

'Oh, brandy. Now that would be even better.'

'I had a bridge four, but one player has just left. Would you like to join us? We play often.'

'Would I learn the village gossip?' asked Lady Sherwood with a smile.

'You'd learn more than you'd want to learn,' replied Nan.

'Well then, I'd love to give it a try. You might want to sack me after the first game, however. I'm not very good.'

'We're not very good either. We get together for the fun of it.'

'Would you like to come here? I've got lots of brandy. Owen loved brandy.'

Nan's face lit up. 'That sounds lovely. You do have the space, after all.'

Lady Sherwood clapped her hands. 'Then that's settled.' She glanced at Daisy who was looking back at her in astonishment. 'When shall we begin?'

Marigold sat in the garden and looked out over the fields. Her father sat beside her, as he often did, in his favourite heather-coloured V-neck sweater and brown corduroy trousers. He looked across at her and his hazel eyes sparkled with affection. 'How's it going, Goldie?'

'Mum says you're dead.' She smiled because she knew that he wasn't.

'There is no dead. You and I know that, don't we?'

'I suspect she thinks my brain is playing tricks on me.'

'Your brain might play tricks on you, Goldie. But I'm not one of them.'

'I'm glad you're here, Dad. I don't feel so frightened when you're with me.'

'You don't need to be frightened. Just let life take you. Be a leaf on the water. Let it carry you downstream.'

'Will it carry me to a nursing home, Dad? I'm not sure I'd be very good at living in a nursing home.'

'It might. You never know where it's going to take you. But everything in life is an adventure. Even a nursing home can be an adventure.'

'I like being here.'

'I like being here too. That's why I come back. It's a nice place, looking out over the fields.'

'I suppose if I had fields to look at, I would feel at home. Or the sea. I love the sea.'

'You grew up by the sea, Goldie.'

'And birds. If I had birds to watch, I'd feel at home as well.'

'You've always loved birds.'

'And you'll be with me, won't you?'

Her father smiled. 'You're my girl, Goldie. I'm never going to leave you. Like I always tell you. I never have. I'm always here.'

'Don't you have better things to do?'

'What can be better than being with the people I love?'

'I don't know. You like gardening. Don't you have some gardening to do?'

He shrugged. 'I have all the time in the world to do that.' He smiled, a big and radiant smile. 'Oh, the flowers, Goldie. You won't believe the flowers!'

'Do you remember when Dennis brought me all those pale pink roses?'

'That was just after you'd met.'

She smiled tenderly at the recollection. 'They were the palest pink and they had the most delicious smell. A soft and delicate smell. The smell of love.' She turned to her father, panicked suddenly. 'What will happen when I forget those memories?'

'You can still enjoy roses without your memories, Goldie. Roses will smell just as soft and delicate now as they did back then. They'll still smell of love.'

Marigold thought about this for a moment. 'Yes, you're right. I don't need the memory to know that Dennis loves me.'

'He does, Goldie. He loves you very much.'

'I need to tell him that it's okay if one day he has to put me into a nursing home.'

'That would be a wise thing to do.'

'I'd hate him to feel that he was letting me down.'

'And it would be just like Dennis to feel that way.'

'He mustn't suffer.'

'You've always been a kind girl, thinking about other people,' said her father.

'I must tell him before I forget. You know, I forget everything these days.' She looked anxiously at her father. 'How will I remember to tell him?'

'I'll remind you,' said her father.

'Can you do that?'

'You'd be surprised what I can do.'

'You're magic,' said Marigold.

'We're all magic.' He patted her hand. 'Why don't you go and tell him now. He's in his shed.'

'That's a good idea.'

Marigold stood up. *I mustn't forget to tell Dennis,* she thought as she walked down the garden. *I mustn't forget to tell Dennis.*

Dennis put down his saw when Marigold opened the door to his shed. 'Hello, Goldie,' he said. 'You all right?'

Marigold nodded. She was concentrating hard. 'I mustn't forget to tell you . . .' she began. Then whoomph, it was gone. Just like that. One minute there, the next minute vanished. How was that possible?

'What were you going to tell me, love?' he asked.

Suddenly a gust of wind blew in through the open door and the newspaper on Dennis's table fluttered and opened onto an inside page. Marigold looked at it. There was a big photograph of a nurse. With a jolt, the memory returned. 'I need to tell you that if you have to put me in a nursing home one day I'm all right with that. I'll understand.'

Dennis looked horrified. He strode over and took her in his arms. 'I'll never do that to you,' he said.

Marigold wrapped her arms around his big frame. 'Don't

say that, Dennis. Life is full of adventure and a nursing home just might be another adventure for me. I don't want you to suffer.'

He held her tightly. 'The only thing that will make me suffer is your suffering.'

'Do you remember those roses you gave me, just after we'd met?' she asked.

'They were pale pink. I'm not sure how I found them. They were lovely.'

'They had the most beautiful smell.'

'Yes, they did.'

'If I'm in a nursing home it's because I won't remember anything anymore. But if you bring me pale pink roses, I'll remember the feeling they evoked. I'll know that you love me.'

'Oh Goldie,' he groaned, burying his face in her hair. He couldn't speak anymore. He didn't know what to say. There weren't words big enough for his love.

And Marigold said nothing either. She was becoming adroit at living in the moment, and she wanted to live in the very centre of this moment for as long as she could.

Mary Hanson stood outside Dolly Nesbit's house with a small box. She was nervous. So nervous, in fact, that her bones were trembling. She hoped she'd find Dolly on her own. Not with Cedric. Dolly was always less friendly when Cedric was around. She figured Cedric gave her courage, and inspired her to be mean. Not that Mary didn't deserve it. She knew she did. She was aware that her dog had done something unforgivable. But with all the will in the world she couldn't bring Precious back. What she would give to be able to rewind the clock. But no one could do that. She'd have to live with the regret, while Bernie her dog lived in the moment. There was no regret there.

Her finger hesitated over the bell. Was this unwise, turning up unannounced on Dolly's doorstep with a gift? Was she foolish? Would Dolly just slam the door in her face? Mary knew that, if she did, she might very well have to move to another village. Brian wouldn't like that, of course, but she'd have to persuade him. She couldn't go on living in a place where there was such hatred. Wasn't Jesus's greatest lesson about forgiveness? Didn't Dolly go to church every Sunday? Surely, she could find it in her heart to forgive.

She pressed the bell and waited. Her heart thumped against her bones. Her already trembling bones. She tried to remember to breathe, but every time she got distracted, she held her breath. It wasn't good to hold your breath. They'd done it as children at school and the teacher had caught them and told them that they could die that way. No, she must remember to breathe.

At length, and it did seem like a very long time, the door opened and Dolly's face appeared in the crack. When she saw Mary, her eyes widened and she looked panicked, like a startled rabbit. 'Please don't shut the door,' said Mary bravely. 'I have a present for you.'

'I don't want a present,' said Dolly sharply.

'I know you don't. I can't bring Precious back but I can give you someone else to love, and this little kitten really needs a home.'

The door opened a little wider and more of Dolly's face could be seen through the crack. Her eyes narrowed. 'A kitten, you say?'

'Yes. She's very small.' Mary held up the box.

'But I don't want another cat. Nothing can replace Precious.'

'Of course not. There was only one. But here is another one, a different one. You never know, you may grow to love her almost as much as you loved Precious.'

Dolly was about to close the door when a thin meow floated out of the box. The door stopped midway. Dolly remained behind the crack, as still as a stone. Mary seized her chance and opened the box. She delved inside and lifted out a tiny white kitten. Dolly's mouth opened and with it, the door. Her eyes settled on the helpless creature and her heart flooded with love.

'She's beautiful!' she gushed. 'Where did you find her?'

'I looked everywhere. I didn't want to get you the same breed as Precious, because Precious is irreplaceable, but I wanted to find something special.'

'Oh, she is special. May I?' Dolly put out her hands.

Mary passed the kitten into them, her own heart flooding with relief. 'She's very young.'

'She needs a mother.'

'I thought you'd be perfect.'

'Yes, I think I would.' Dolly pressed her face into the kitten's fur. Then she looked at Mary and her eyes were no longer hard and hostile. 'Would you like to come in?'

'Really? I'd love to,' said Mary.

'I've just boiled the kettle.'

'How lovely.'

'Does she have a name?'

Mary followed her into the kitchen. 'No, I thought you might like to name her.'

'Then she shall be called Jewel. I always thought, if I ever had another cat, that I'd call her Jewel. What do you think?'

'I think Jewel really suits her. She's like a diamond. Like a lovely white diamond.'

Dolly smiled. 'I like Diamond as well. If I ever have another cat, I'll call that one Diamond.'

When Daisy got home at the end of the day she found an email from Taran. It was an electronic ticket to Toronto. She realized that 'maybe' had indeed meant yes.

Chapter 26

October in Toronto was unseasonally warm. Daisy stood for a long time at Immigration, fanning her face with a magazine, watching the queue lessen at an agonizingly slow pace. She couldn't wait to see Taran who had promised to come and pick her up. She pictured his face and smiled to herself. His longish hair, swept off his forehead but always falling over it, the short beard her grandmother disapproved of and those penetrating green eyes which were often lit up by a humorous twinkle, or occasionally dimmed with sorrow when he remembered his father. That she could have thought him heartless and unfeeling was unbelievable now.

She collected her suitcase at Baggage Claim, then pushed her trolley hastily through Customs, impatient to see him. When she emerged into the Arrivals Hall she spotted him immediately. He was a head taller than everyone else. She smiled broadly and quickened her pace. Taran threaded swiftly through the crowd and gathered her into his arms.

He kissed her ardently. 'God, I missed you!' he murmured.

'I missed you too,' she replied, inhaling the familiar scent of him with delight.

He put an arm around her shoulders and pushed the trolley with his free hand. 'Let's hurry back so I can show you just how much I've missed you!' He pulled her against him and kissed her on the head. 'Mmm,' he sighed, drawing in the scent of her hair. 'You smell of home.'

Daisy had not expected Taran's condo to be so luxurious. It was a modern loft conversion in an old factory in Trinity Bellwoods, which was downtown Toronto and, according to Taran, the hippest neighbourhood in the city. It was within walking distance of the park, he assured her, so she'd get her fix of green. Outside, the sky was dark. Toronto glittered with thousands of lights against the rumble of traffic and the wailing of sirens. The air was cool now and vibrated with the restlessness of a city forever in the grip of insomnia.

As soon as they arrived, Taran kissed her passionately. Daisy felt the vigour of his body as he pressed it against her and the strength in his hands as he touched her. The thrill of being in Toronto with this dynamic man was revitalizing and she felt as if a great weight was being lifted from her shoulders. The weight of responsibility, of a potentially traumatic future. The constant weight of dread. As Taran took her to his bed she felt liberated.

They went out for dinner in a French restaurant on the Ossington Strip nearby. The lights were dim, the atmosphere Parisian, the Mojito strong. 'I want to show you how I live,' he told her, taking her hand across the table and looking at her steadily.

'I already like the way you live,' she replied, sighing with pleasure.

'You've seen nothing yet. We have a whole week.'

'Don't you have to work?'

He grinned. 'Sure, but I'm the boss. I can pretty much choose when I work.'

Daisy frowned. For some reason she hadn't expected him to own his own business. 'Really?'

'It's a small company, but we're quite successful,' he added. 'I might surprise you.'

'You've never told me about it.'

'You've never asked.' He grinned. 'You're much more concerned with trees and flowers to care much for buildings.'

'Oh, I can see the beauty in buildings. You don't get more magnificent buildings than in Italy.'

'Most people only see beauty in old architecture, but I'm going to show you that modern architecture can be beautiful too.'

'I'd love to see what you've designed.'

He nodded, withdrawing his hand as the waiter brought their food. 'You shall. I'll take you to my office tomorrow. I'll show you what I do. It's not so very different to what you do.'

The following morning they breakfasted at a café round the corner from Taran's apartment. Taran introduced Daisy to the old man who owned it. He had a full head of curly grey hair, vivacious blue eyes the colour of forget-me-nots, which belied his bristly face that seemed to be set in a permanent scowl. 'This is Mr Schulz,' said Taran.

'Nothing to do with Snoopy,' said Mr Schulz in a weary tone. Until he mentioned it Daisy hadn't made the connection.

'He makes the best coffee in Toronto,' Taran continued. 'It'll put your Italian coffee in the shade.'

'And *your* coffee, I presume,' Daisy teased.

'I'm afraid so,' Taran agreed. 'Mr Schulz is in a class of his own.'

Mr Schulz nodded. 'I've made coffee in this town for fifty years. I haven't changed my methods, in spite of all those fancy machines they keep bringing out. If you want to make good coffee, it's got to be real coffee, the old-fashioned way.'

'We'll have a couple of espressos, the old-fashioned way,' said Taran.

'Coming up,' said Mr Schulz, and Daisy thought he was probably happiest making his coffee for he turned with a little bounce before disappearing behind the counter.

Taran led Daisy outside and took a table on the pavement in the shade. Sitting at one of the other tables was an elderly woman in a bright pink-and-yellow sweater with a pair of large dogs sleeping beside her chair. A couple of young men in jackets and ties sat at another table, reading newspapers. Taran greeted them all and asked the woman about her dog, who was recovering from a minor operation. He ordered coffee and smoked salmon bagels, insisting Daisy eat a proper Toronto breakfast. People came and went and Taran seemed to know most of them. 'It's a real neighbourhood,' he told her. Then he ducked his head and grimaced. 'Here comes pushy Milly Hesketh. Don't catch her eye or you'll turn to stone. She's been trying to set me up with her daughter for months and she won't be at all happy to see me with *you*!'

Daisy reached across the table and took his hand. She laughed. 'Just putting a stop to her plans once and for all, darling.'

Taran's office was in the historic core of Toronto, near the St Lawrence Market where red brick Victorian houses rubbed shoulders uneasily with modern glass and steel structures, like disapproving grandparents unsure of the new, faster generations growing up around them. Situated on the fourth floor of a converted brewery Taran's studio was one giant open-plan room with white walls, big glass windows and shiny oak floorboards. Daisy wandered around while Taran talked to one of his colleagues, gazing at the large framed photographs of the buildings he had designed which hung on the walls. There were apartment refurbishments in Toronto, wooden beach houses by the sea and modern, geometric-shaped homes in the hills. They were impressive. Beautiful, just as Taran had said, and Daisy realized that he was right: there wasn't a great deal of difference between what *she* did and what *he* did. They were both artists.

She also realized, with a pang of anxiety, that he couldn't leave all this to go and live in the middle of the English countryside. She had been a dreamer to think that he could.

'You're so gifted,' she told him when he came up behind her and wrapped his arms around her waist.

'Thank you.'

'There are some really stunning properties here.'

'I love what I do,' he said.

'Did you ever show your father?'

He nuzzled her neck. 'He wasn't very interested in what I did.'

'Why? Why wouldn't he be interested in this?'

'Because to him architecture had to be over a hundred years old to be beautiful. To him these were unforgivable assaults on the landscape.'

She gazed at a photograph of a glass-fronted, flat-roofed poolside house. It was clean, harmonious and light. 'He can't have thought that. Not if he'd seen them.'

'Darling Daisy, you see the best in everyone. My father was a good man. Everyone said so. But he was also a narrow-minded one. He thought proper writers were people who sat in leaking attics, scratching on parchment with quills. He hated computers, the internet, mobile phones. He should have been born in Victorian times. He was not made for the modern world. He only bought a combine because he had

to. If he'd had his way he'd have hired workers to stook the
sheaves by hand.'

'I don't even know what that means.'

'Because you're a modern girl.' He turned her round.
'You shouldn't be living in a quiet village full of old people,
Daisy. Not yet anyway. You should be drawing here in
Toronto with me.'

She looked into his eyes and knew he really meant it. 'You
promised you wouldn't ask me. That was the deal.'

'I never intended to keep my promise.'

'Taran!'

'I want you to come and live with me. What can I
say? I lied!'

'Look, I have nothing against a city. You know that. I lived
in Milan for six years and I loved it, at the time. It's Mum. I
can't desert her now when she needs me.'

Taran nodded slowly and she wondered whether he was
thinking about his own mother and feeling guilty. 'Toronto
isn't that far away, you know.'

'I know. I just can't leave Mum, or Dad for that matter.
I just can't.' She moved away and went to the window. It
looked out over a quiet, leafy street with a coffee shop, an
Italian restaurant and a few boutiques in the line of low-rise
buildings opposite.

Taran stood next to her. 'You need to live for you too,
Daisy,' he said.

'You mean selfishly?'

'No, it doesn't mean you're selfish to live a little for yourself. You're young, you're beautiful, you're talented and
you're smart.'

She smiled sadly. 'And those are qualities that don't belong
in a little provincial village full of old people?'

'Oh, they belong, all right. They belong anywhere. The thing is, I want them to belong here, with me.'

She looked at him and sighed. 'And I want them to belong with you, too.'

'Think about it,' he said. 'There's no rush. But I'm here, you're in England and there's a great big ocean between us. We can't live like this for ever.'

The word 'for ever' hung between them and Daisy wondered whether he realized what he had said. In all the years she had been with Luca he had never uttered that word. Not in English or in Italian. Did Taran really see them in the for ever?

Taran seemed to read her mind. He put his hand on her shoulder and drew her against him, pressing his chin to her head. 'At our age there's no point playing games,' he said softly. 'I know what I want.'

In the days that followed, Taran took the time off to show her the sights of Toronto, which he must have seen a thousand times. They went jogging in the park, dined in the most fashionable restaurants and wandered around the city's famous Royal Ontario Museum. They went to the top of the CN Tower and visited Ripley's Aquarium, which boasted sixteen thousand aquatic animals. Taran insisted they buy tickets for a boat tour, which Daisy thought hilarious. That was one thing Taran had never done either and the two of them sat on the deck while tourists took photographs and a woman with a microphone pointed out all the sights in a twangy, nasal voice which Taran spent the rest of the day imitating.

Daisy imagined living there, in Taran's apartment. There was certainly enough space for her to draw, for the condo was big with high ceilings and lots of light, not unlike the Sherwoods' barn back at home. She could picture her easel and see herself drawing there, pausing every now and then to look out over the Victorian building with the fire escape that stood on the opposite side of the street. Perhaps she'd try and draw people as well as animals, she mused, expand her range. She no longer doubted she could.

It was easy to envisage herself making a home in his. Her clothes in the cupboards, her toiletries in the bathroom. She could see herself pottering about the kitchen, chopping vegetables on the island, boiling pasta on the hob. She would add a feminine touch to the apartment: long-stemmed roses by the sink, scented candles in the bathroom, geraniums on the windowsill, perhaps some brightly coloured cushions on the sofa. It wasn't hard to imagine herself in Taran's condo. It wasn't hard at all.

One morning, while Taran was busy on the telephone, sorting out a sudden problem that had arisen in the office, Daisy went out on her own to explore the neighbourhood. She wandered up the streets, browsing in shop windows, venturing into the deli, which was her favourite type of shop, and pausing to enjoy the flowers in the flower shop. Eventually, she sat on a bench and watched this foreign world saunter by. It was vibrant and colourful with everything one could possibly need, and it had charm, lots of charm. She had made a home for herself in a foreign city once already, she knew she could do it again. Besides, she realized that there was something envigorating about starting over in a new city. She thought of her parents who had lived in the same village all their lives and considered herself lucky to have the opportunity to experience different cultures, to gain a wider perspective of the world. She had learned Italian in Milan, at least here in Toronto she wouldn't have to learn a new language.

Daisy was curious to meet Taran's friends and cousins, and was pleasantly surprised at how welcome they made her feel

when they met for dinner one night towards the end of her
stay. But the moments she treasured most were the ones when
it was just the two of them, in his sumptuous and airy apartment, lying entwined on the bed and talking about nothing,
or making love long into the night, to the distant roar of the
city that Taran called home. Being together was the most
precious thing of all.

On the last morning, Daisy awoke to the murmur of Taran's
voice in the room next door, talking on the phone. She got up
and stretched, then went to brush her teeth and have a quick
shower. She put on his dressing gown and padded into the
kitchen to help herself to some orange juice from the fridge.
The room was open-plan with tall windows letting in the
light. The rumble of a truck in the street below drowned out
his voice for a moment. Daisy poured herself a glass of juice.
Besides orange juice and cheese there was little in the fridge.
Daisy wanted to fill it with salad and vegetables and fresh
meat and cook a delicious dinner. She longed to make herself
at home. But that wouldn't be possible. As long as her mother
was unwell and her father needed her help, for ever was not
going to happen.

Taran was pacing the room in nothing but a pair of stripy
pyjama bottoms, one hand on his head, the other holding
the telephone to his ear. When Daisy heard the words 'land'
and 'sell', her ears pricked up. She stood behind the marble-
topped island and listened. 'How far do you think we are
from getting planning permission?' There was a long pause
while the person on the other end of the line replied. It was
clearly not a simple thing to answer. 'I'm going to take on
the project myself,' he continued. 'It's what I do. I'll relish
the challenge.' Again, another pause. Taran's face darkened.
'Those bloody highway people!' he snapped. 'They're going

to hold everything up. English councils are so slow. You'd have thought they'd be desperate for houses. The last time *I* heard, there was a housing crisis in the UK!' He noticed Daisy and his face softened. He smiled at her. How could he smile, she thought, knowing how much that land meant to her family? She stood frozen to the spot as he discussed selling and developing the land he had inherited from his father, the land that bordered her parents' garden; the land her mother loved so much.

At last he hung up. 'Aren't you a sight for sore eyes,' he said, and approached her.

She looked at him in confusion. 'What's this about developing land?'

He didn't seem to notice how upset she was. 'Oh, boring stuff.' He put his arms around her. 'Let's go back to bed.'

'No, wait. You said you weren't going to sell your land.'

Taran frowned. A shadow of irritation swept across his face as he registered her fury and was confused by it. 'What are you talking about?'

'The farm.' Her eyes filled with tears. Taran had lied to her. In her heart she had believed him when he had said 'for ever'.

'I'm not selling the farm.'

'But you said—'

'You've picked up a fag-end, and you know what happens to people who pick up fag-ends?'

'Taran, this is not a joke.'

He looked down at her and put his hands on his hips. 'I *am* selling a farm, but not the farm you think.'

'Is there another one?'

'Dad also had a farm in the Midlands. It never made much, in fact, most of the time it made a loss. He had already started the process of developing it before he died. Anyhow, it's mine now and I'm going to develop it myself. I don't want to live up there and neither does Mum.' He grinned at her. 'But of course, if *you* want to live there . . .'

She couldn't help but smile. 'I'm sorry. It's none of my business.'

'It *would* be your business if I was considering selling the land that your parents' house looks out onto. But I would never do that.'

'You really wouldn't? Do you promise?'

'My darling Daisy, my father loved that land more than anything in the world. He probably loved it more than he loved people. It was his life and his passion and it's my home. I don't want to live there now, but one day I will.' He took her face in his hands and gazed down at her with affection. 'And *you* love it too.'

'Yes, I do,' she said, holding on to his casual allusion to eventually moving back and hoping that he meant it.

'Game, set and match, then. I'll guard it with my life.'

She laughed as he swept her off her feet and carried her into the bedroom. 'Now, what was I saying? Ah yes, do you know what happens to people who eavesdrop?'

Daisy left for England with a heavy heart. She felt she was leaving sunshine and going back to fog. The images of cooking pasta in Taran's apartment, placing flowers by the sink, nipping into the deli to buy supper evaporated like dreams eclipsed by the reality of her mother's failing health and her unwavering sense of duty. On the plane, her worries returned to her in flurries and her heart pined for Taran. She was in an impossible situation. Why was it that the only two men she had lost her heart to in her life lived abroad? Why couldn't she find a man who lived close to home, like Suze? She was in her mid-thirties and living at home. Having spent a week with Taran, she longed for her independence again. She yearned to have her own house – her own fridge, her own oven, her own space, so that she could make a home with the man she loved. Yet, she was tied to her parents. Dennis needed her support. Marigold was fading fast. Suze was little help. Daisy felt that she was indispensable. Indispensable to them all and their need suffocated her.

Having thought she could never abide living in a city again, she began to wonder whether Taran was right. That she needed to live for herself. That she was too young to settle down in a sleepy village full of old people. Had she forgotten so quickly the fun she had had in Milan?

She arrived home in time for dinner, exhausted. Her family were pleased to have her home. Marigold had roasted a chicken and invited Suze and Batty to join them. They sat around the kitchen table, eager to hear how her trip had gone. Daisy noticed the notes all over the kitchen, reminding Marigold how to cook the chicken, from the simplest tasks like switching on the oven to taking the potatoes out of the larder. She felt sad, because as time went by her mother relied more and more on these little notes, and her notebook, of course, which she always kept in her pocket, but often forgot to consult. Taran had shown her another life in a glittering city and her heart suddenly ached for it.

She settled back into her routine. She walked across the fields every morning to Lady Sherwood's barn to paint the jigsaw puzzle. She had turned down numerous requests to draw people's pets, putting them off until after Christmas. Right now her priority had to be the puzzle. There was no way she'd get it finished otherwise.

She joined Lady Sherwood for coffee in the kitchen on the first morning back to tell her about her son. 'I had no idea what an accomplished and successful architect he is,' she said.

Lady Sherwood picked up her espresso cup and smiled wistfully. 'Oh, he is very talented. But Owen wanted him to learn the ropes here so that one day he could take over the farm. He didn't realize it would be so soon.'

'Having seen his life in Toronto, I would say it suits him perfectly. He's very happy there. Everything's perfect, right down to his morning coffee.'

'That's nice to hear. You know, as a parent, one just wants one's children to be happy. I'm fortunate that Taran has found his calling. It might not be what his father wanted, but parents have to let their children be themselves. Owen wasn't very good at that. I miss Taran, of course I do, but I would hate him to feel he has to be here for me. I like to think I'm more generous-spirited than my husband was. And I do have my own life.'

Daisy arched her eyebrows. 'How's bridge going with Nan?'

Lady Sherwood laughed and her green eyes came alive. 'You know, it's really fun!'

Daisy was surprised. 'Is it?'

'Yes, your grandmother is a hoot.'

'A hoot.' That didn't sound like Nan.

'Oh, yes, she's extremely funny. I don't think she means to be funny. She's a terrible old grumbler, but we all laugh and pull her leg and she rather enjoys it. Her friends are nice. She did lie to me though.'

'She did?' said Daisy in alarm.

'They're *very* good.'

Daisy's shoulders relaxed. 'Oh, yes, I could have told you that. Nan has played for years.'

While Daisy painted in the barn and Dennis worked in his shed, and Nan watched television and did the crossword, Marigold received visitors. Some popped in for a quick cup of tea, others for longer. Some, like Cedric, brought cakes, others, like Eileen, brought news. Marigold enjoyed the cakes but she never remembered the news. Eileen realized very quickly that she could tell her anything because Marigold always forgot the moment she left. Dolly came to show off her new kitten, Jewel. Mary to tell Marigold that she and Dolly had made up – and Marigold had to pretend that she remembered that they had fallen out.

Whenever Daisy saw any of the locals they asked after the puzzle. They couldn't wait to see their contributions, but more than that, they couldn't wait to see Marigold's face when she laid eyes on it for the first time. They all voiced their desire to be there for that moment. Daisy talked to her father about it and they decided to give her a tea party in the village hall to present her with it, so everyone who had been involved could be present. 'You don't think she'll be offended?' asked Daisy, worried suddenly that she wouldn't like everyone discussing her failing memory.

'I don't think she'll be offended at all,' said Dennis with certainty. 'I know my Goldie. She'll appreciate the thought. I'm sure of it.'

Daisy hadn't thought about Luca in months. Until he turned up at her door a couple of weeks before Christmas.

Daisy stared at him in astonishment. In a heavy coat, felt hat and olive-green scarf, he looked ruggedly handsome. His face was unshaven and his greying hair curled about his ears. He smiled and his chestnut-brown eyes took her in with the intensity of a man who suddenly appreciates the errors of his ways and the value of the woman now standing before him. 'Luca? What are you doing here?' she gasped.

'Getting cold,' he replied. 'Can I come in?'

Daisy opened the door and watched him walk past her into the kitchen. Nan was sitting at the table, playing solitaire. When she saw Luca her jaw dropped. 'Good God,' she said. 'It's Lazarus, risen from the dead!'

'Hello, Nan,' he said, and bent down to kiss her as if he being there, in that kitchen, was the most natural thing in the world.

Marigold, who had been in the sitting room, watching old episodes of *Frasier*, hurried into the kitchen. 'Luca?' she gasped. She hadn't forgotten who *he* was.

'Marigold!' Luca embraced her, nearly lifting her off the ground. 'It's so good to see you!'

Marigold was confused. Were he and Daisy married? She couldn't remember. She decided to say nothing until she was sure.

Daisy walked slowly into the room. She folded her arms. 'Why didn't you call?' she demanded.

'Because you changed your number,' he replied, giving her a hard stare.

Marigold sensed the tension and went straight for the kettle. 'Let's have a cup of tea,' she said cheerfully.

'No,' Daisy replied. 'Luca and I are going to go to the pub, aren't we, Luca? We've got lots to talk about and we don't want to disturb you.'

'Oh, you're not disturbing *me*,' said Nan quickly. 'You can say anything in front of us. Marigold won't remember what you say anyway, and I'm really not interested. Put the kettle on, Marigold. I might lace mine with a little brandy.' When Daisy looked at her in bewilderment, she added with a grin, 'Celia does it, so why shouldn't I?'

Chapter 27

Daisy and Luca sat opposite each other at a table in the corner of the pub. Daisy ordered a glass of wine, Luca a Peroni. How strange, she thought, watching him watching her with those brown eyes into which she had gazed more times than she could count, that, after a year apart, it was as if they had seen each other only yesterday. It was as if the last twelve months had never happened. As if it had all been a dream.

'What do you want, Luca?' she asked in Italian, taking a fortifying gulp of wine.

'I haven't come all this way to just say hello. I want you back,' he said resolutely. When she tried to protest, he interrupted her. 'I know I hurt you, Margherita. I'm sorry for that. I didn't realize how much you meant to me.' He sighed and his mouth twisted with emotion. 'I didn't realize that I loved you quite so much. We'd been together for such a long time, I suppose I took you for granted. But now I've had almost a year to think about it and to try other relationships. And I've discovered that no one comes close to you. There is no one else out there for me but you. You can have whatever you want. You don't have to compromise. You can have it all. I shouldn't have denied you a child. That was selfish.' He smiled bashfully. 'I've got over myself, Margherita.'

Daisy felt a surge of fury rise up from the pit of her chest. 'It took you a *year* to realize how much I meant to you? And *now* you're willing to give me what I want? Don't you think you're a little late, Luca? Do you think I've been doing nothing but waiting for you all these months?'

'I hoped you'd feel the same as I do,' he said quietly, looking genuinely shocked by her angry response.

'Why do you think I changed my number?'

He shrugged in the way Italians do. 'I just wanted to talk.'

'I just wanted to get on with my life,' she retorted.

'I suppose you did get on with your life.'

Daisy didn't want to hurt him, but she wanted to tell him the truth. 'I'm seeing someone else,' she told him.

He gazed at her and the wounded look in his eyes jabbed her conscience. 'Six years, Margherita. That's what we gave to each other. Six years. And you want to throw all that history away?' He swigged from the bottle. 'Who is he anyway?'

'You don't know him.'

'Is he English?'

'Yes.'

'Terrible lovers, the English.'

'You've slept with them all, have you?'

'I'll come and live here,' he offered. 'If that's what you want.'

Daisy was stunned. 'You'd do that for me?'

'Look, I'm ready to commit.' He delved into his pocket and pulled out a little red box. 'You've taught me a valuable lesson, Margherita. No person is an island. Love is about giving and compromise, it's about making the other person happy. I want you to be happy, with me.'

'Are you seriously trying to tell me that you've changed this much? The man who didn't want marriage and children because it would make him "less, not more" is now willing to move to England and become a husband and father?'

'It is only the very stupid who stubbornly stick to a path and rigidly refuse to try another. I'm a photographer. I can take my work anywhere. If you want to live here, I'll move. I'm kind of done with Milan anyway. I'm in my mid-forties, perhaps it's time to settle down and experience a different way of living.' He slid the box across the table. 'I want to marry you, Margherita,' he said, his brown eyes full of hope. 'You loved me once. I don't think that kind of love just goes away. I know that *I* still love *you*. The truth is that I love you more now than I did before and that has surprised me, and wounded me more deeply.' His gaze intensified. 'Come on, Margherita. You know this is what you want. It's what you've always wanted. Don't punish me for discovering too late that it's what *I* want as well.'

She opened the box. 'Oh Luca,' she sighed. The sight of the sapphire surrounded by small diamonds induced tears. 'It's beautiful.'

'I knew you'd like it. I know how you like simplicity. You see, I know you better than anyone else. Better than this Englishman you've just met. You barely know him. Think of the history you and I have. The years we've lived together. It was like a marriage, only without the ring and the cere-mony. Now it will be a proper marriage.' He took her hand. 'Come home,' he said. 'Or just say the word and we'll make a home *here*.'

Daisy withdrew her hand. She closed the lid of the box and pushed it back across the table. 'I don't know, Luca. You've thrown me. I wasn't expecting this. I thought I knew what I wanted, but now I'm not sure.'

'Think about it. No pressure. This Englishman, do you

really know him? Of course you don't. You know *me*. You know me better than I know myself, I suspect. You can rely on me, Margherita. Can you rely on him?'

There ensued a long pause as she considered his words.

'What are you going to do now?' she asked him finally. 'Are you going to fly back to Milan?'

'I'm going to spend Christmas with my family in Venice, but all the while I'm going to be thinking of you and hoping that you'll allow me to put this ring on your finger and start our life together.' He tapped the box on the table. 'Tonight I'm staying in the Bear Hotel in town. I'll be on my phone if you want to reach me. If you want to talk.'

So much had happened in the last year, she wouldn't even know where to start. Taran knew about her mother's dementia and her new job as an artist. He knew about the present, but she and Luca had put down some very deep roots and he knew her past. 'I'd better go,' she said, getting up.

'I'll walk you home,' said Luca. And they wandered down the lane together.

'I'd invite you in,' she said. 'But I think it's for the best if—'

He cut her off. 'It's okay. I understand.' Then he put his hand in the small of her back and pulled her against him, kissing her on her cheek. The familiarity of him tugged momentarily at her heart. 'Think about it,' he whispered into her ear. '*I'll* be doing little else.'

Daisy decided not to tell Taran about Luca, at least not on the telephone. She knew how awkward the phone could be and she wasn't sure he'd be too happy about their meeting. She didn't want to incite his jealousy, or make him angry, and she felt guilty that she was feeling torn. It was better to avoid his calls altogether and text him instead, telling him she was busy. Just until she had sorted out her head. She needed time to think. The only reason she had broken up with Luca was because he hadn't been prepared to give her what she wanted. Now he had turned up out of the blue and offered her *everything* she wanted. Where did that leave her and Taran? Taran, whom she loved. Did she still love Luca? She wasn't sure. Did she just love the familiarity of him? The sense of security? The sense of the *known*?

Did she love them both?

Was it possible to love two men at the same time?

A few days later Daisy finished painting the puzzle. Dennis drove up to the barn to collect it in his car and, without Marigold seeing it, they carried it into his shed so that he could cut it into pieces large enough for Marigold to manage, but small enough to still pose a challenge. He knew Marigold still liked a challenge, even though she wasn't up to much these days. He set to work with a bandsaw, switching to a fretsaw for the fiddly bits. He worked long into the night, eager to finish it. The result was a puzzle more exquisite than any he had crafted before. With Daisy's help he had truly created something special.

Dennis unveiled it to Daisy the following morning. 'It's a work of art,' she said, catching her breath with excitement.

He nodded. 'I think she'll like it.'

'Oh, I know she will, Dad,' said Daisy. 'She'll love it.'

Dennis put his arm around her. 'You're a good daughter,' he said. 'I know your mother appreciates you, but I want you to know that I do too. Your support is invaluable. We're lucky to have you living at home.'

A lump lodged itself in Daisy's throat. She turned to embrace him. 'I'm happy I'm here to support you,' she said and rested her head against his big chest. She could hear his heart beating beneath his shirt. His heart that carried within it his unswerving love for Marigold. She thought of her own heart and wondered how, if she chose Taran, they were going to resolve the complicated geography of their situation. He was there and she was needed here. Between them was the vast Atlantic. There was nowhere to meet in the middle. Either he had to come here, or she had to go there. Or they simply wouldn't meet at all.

Or she could choose Luca and live here, close to her parents. But was Luca really intending to move, or did he just want her back so badly that he was willing to make promises now that he wouldn't be able to keep later? Was Luca's proposal attractive simply because he had offered to move here?

Daisy was in such a state of turmoil that she didn't telephone Luca either. She needed to clear her head. She needed to work out what she wanted. More specifically, she needed to work out *who* she wanted.

However, Luca continued to text her. *I can't think of anything else but you,* he wrote. *You're in my heart and in my head and I'm pining for you.*

Suze offered to help decorate the village hall for Marigold's party. She believed she had a good eye for that sort of thing. Daisy was happy to relinquish control. She and Dennis had created the puzzle, it was only fair that Suze contributed something. With an enthusiasm that surprised her sister, Suze and Batty recruited a small group of friends and together they worked tirelessly transforming the cold, functional hall into a winter fairyland. Suze knew how much her mother loved snow, so she covered the fir trees and holly that Batty had arranged around the room with fake snow purchased in town. The snow sparkled with millions of diamonds in the fairy lights that they draped over all the surfaces and along the spider's web of string they had put up just beneath the ceiling. Along those strings they threaded thick gold and silver tinsel and hung bright red baubles. The effect was mesmerizing. The final touch was the three hundred battery-powered tea lights that they arranged in a path from the street to the door, and in clusters along the edge of the hall floor. They turned off the ugly strip lights and the whole place sparkled like a magical ballroom in a fairy tale.

Satisfied with her work, Suze photographed it for Instagram. Her fans would be impressed, she thought happily. She'd get loads of likes for *this*. And she'd rally Daisy and her friends to help her take it all down in the morning.

It was a miracle that Marigold's party had been kept secret. Nan had claimed that even if someone had let the cat out of the bag, she'd have soon forgotten all about it anyway. But Daisy wasn't so sure. She was certain that Marigold would not forget such an exciting event as a party in her honour.

Dennis had invited people by word of mouth in case someone left the invitation on a mantelpiece where Marigold might spot it. Eager to help with the party the Commodore had insisted on paying for the wine. Not to be outdone, Cedric had said he would bake cupcakes. Dolly promised to bring mini sausages in honey-and-mustard sauce. Mary was quick to suggest that she supply the paper plates and cups. Jean wanted to contribute too and said she'd supply the cutlery. Bridget offered to make a big salad and Beryl brought an enormous ham. Eileen baked potatoes wrapped in foil. Pete and John suggested they bring beer for those, like them, who preferred it to wine, and Tasha said she'd arrange the soft drinks. Batty appointed himself DJ because he said he wouldn't survive the afternoon if any of the oldies chose the music. Suze made him promise he'd play songs that Marigold liked.

Daisy had invited Lady Sherwood, certain that she would decline. But to Daisy's surprise she was eager to join in and keen to help in any way that she could. 'Is there anything I can bring?' she asked when Daisy was in the barn, putting away her paints.

'I think we've got more than we need,' Daisy replied. 'But you're sweet to want to contribute.'

Lady Sherwood was disappointed. 'Oh, I so wanted to help.' She narrowed her eyes. 'I'll have to think,' she said. 'I'm sure there's something you haven't thought of.'

The guests turned up in good time and laid out their contributions on the long trestle tables Suze had put up at the back of the room. They sighed in wonder at the beauty of the decorations, oohing and aahing over the pretty lights and pretend snow. Suze was quick to tell them that it was *her* vision. 'Oh, you're an artist, just like your sister!' gushed Eileen. 'What a talented family you are! Marigold is going to love this!'

Dennis told Marigold to put on a pretty dress. 'Are we going out?' she asked excitedly. 'I do love dressing up.'

'Yes,' said Dennis. 'We're going to a party.'

'I love a party!' she exclaimed, hurrying into her bedroom to find something suitable to wear. 'Which dress do you think, Dennis?' she asked. The truth was she couldn't remember what dresses she had and this was a good way of hiding it.

'Let me see,' said Dennis, opening her wardrobe. He flicked

through the hanging clothes until he settled on a red dress with white polka dots. 'I like this one. Red suits you.' He lifted the hanger off the rail and showed it to her.

'Oh yes, that's a lovely dress,' she said, but she couldn't ever remember wearing it.

Marigold had a bath then sat at her dressing table to do her hair and make-up. She looked old, she thought a little sadly. Fortunately, she was plump so that her skin didn't sag like her mother's. But there was something different about her eyes. They were still a pretty hazel colour, but there was a vague look about them now that was foreign to her. She shrugged off her anxiety because she was going to a party. She couldn't remember the last party she'd gone to. She did remember a party long ago where she had worn a yellow dress with blue flowers. Dennis had been there. Then he'd bought her roses. The prettiest shade of pale pink, they were, and they'd smelled divine. She smiled with pleasure as she remembered the roses, and Dennis. Somehow she couldn't think of roses without thinking of Dennis.

Dennis put on a suit. He stood in front of the long mirror in the bedroom and admired it. He'd bought it especially for Suze's wedding. It had cost a small fortune but it had been worth it. Look, he was wearing it now! Marigold came and stood beside him. The two of them gazed into their reflection. Marigold took his hand.

'You look beautiful, Goldie,' he said.

'And you look handsome, Dennis,' said Marigold.

'We still cut a dash, don't we?' he said with a grin.

'Only to you,' she laughed.

He turned and kissed her forehead. 'You're still my Goldie.'

She felt his lips linger on her skin. 'I'll always be your Goldie,' she replied.

'Are you ready for the party?'

'I don't know.'

He looked at her and frowned. 'You don't know?'

'Do I like parties?'

'You love parties.'

'Okay. Then I'm ready.'

'Your chariot awaits,' he said, leading her out of the room.

When Dennis pulled up outside the village hall, Daisy, Suze and Nan were waiting for them at the door. Marigold saw the candle-lined path first and gasped. 'Oh, it's beautiful!' she sighed, gazing at the dancing lights with the wide eyes of a child. Then she saw her family. 'Ah, that's nice,' she added, watching them smiling at her through the car window.

Dennis parked and walked round to open her door. He gave her his hand and she stepped out. 'You look lovely, Mum,' said Daisy, walking towards her.

'Yes, you really do,' agreed Suze.

'You'd better come inside before you catch your death of cold,' said Nan and Marigold was too overwhelmed by the beauty of the candles to argue.

They entered the hall and everyone turned to look at them. Marigold smiled shyly. She recognized some of the faces, although she couldn't put names to them all. Dennis held her hand tightly. This time he was not going to let her go. They walked through the crowd of happy people and Marigold took in the lights, the tinsel, the fir and holly and snow. 'Oh, it's snowed!' she exclaimed. 'I love snow.'

'*I* decorated the room,' said Suze proudly.

'You are clever,' said Marigold. 'Is it your birthday?'

'Not today, Mum,' Suze replied.

Dennis showed her to a chair where Beryl and Eileen were waiting for her, seated around a table. Marigold recognized *them*. 'Hello,' she said. 'Isn't it a lovely party!'

'It really is,' said Eileen. 'You know, Suze did all the decoration.'

'Did she?' said Marigold. 'Isn't she clever.'

She sat down.

Jean offered her a glass of wine. Dolly brought her a sausage. Marigold looked at Dolly and remembered something about a cat. But the memory had left an unpleasant residue so she did not mention it.

Daisy and Suze watched their mother talking to her friends from the side of the room. 'It's nice to see her happy, isn't it?' said Daisy.

'I'll always remember her like this,' said Suze. Her smile faltered. 'It's been hard, hasn't it? But we're strong together.'

Daisy lifted her chin. If she looked at Suze now she'd cry. 'You've really done a great job with the decoration,' she said, changing the subject. 'It's amazing. I didn't realize you were so talented.'

'I hide my light under a bushel,' Suze replied.

'I don't think you should hide it anymore.'

'Are you suggesting I decorate halls for a living?'

'No, but you're wasted doing a blog.'

'Well, I've been thinking about writing a book.' Suze smiled shyly as Daisy's eyes widened with surprise. 'But don't tell anyone. I don't want anyone to know if I fail.'

'That's great news. What's your idea?'

She hesistated, unsure whether to share it. 'I want to write about Mum,' she confided.

Daisy looked at her steadily. 'A book about Mum and dementia?'

'Yes.' Suze turned away. Her eyes had suddenly filled with tears and she didn't want her sister to see.

Daisy was moved. 'Wow, I didn't see that coming.'

'You're not pleased?'

'On the contrary. I don't think you could have come up with a better idea, Suze, I really don't.'

'Thank you.' Suze basked in the warmth of her sister's admiration. 'I'm going to call it something like: *Living with Dementia, Loving with Dementia.* I've been mulling over the idea for some time.'

'You'll write a beautiful book.'

'I hope so.' Then she smiled again and it was full of nervous excitement. 'I've never been more inspired in my life.'

Daisy embraced her. Suze was caught off guard. They weren't the kind of sisters who hugged each other. At first she stiffened, but as Daisy held her tightly she slowly allowed her body to yield. It felt good.

'And I have some advice for *you*,' said Suze. 'While we're on the subject of advice.'

Daisy let her go. 'What's that then?'

'Go and live in Toronto with Taran.'

'What?'

'Don't look so bewildered. I know that Luca came to the house and I know you spent two and a half hours with him in the pub. Don't ask me where I gleaned that juicy bit of gossip. All I will say is that the village grapevine is still alive and kicking.'

'God, Suze, is there no discretion in this place?'

'None at all. Thank goodness, because otherwise I wouldn't be able to give you my two and a half pence. Go to Toronto and start a new life with Taran. You love him and he's right for you. If Luca had been right, you would have fought harder for him. You would have compromised. I don't know much, but I know you well enough to know that you left Luca because you *wanted* to leave him.' Daisy tried to protest. 'Don't argue with me, Daisy. Deep down you wanted to leave him or you wouldn't have done it. As Grandad used to say, don't look back.'

Daisy smiled. 'Grandad sure made a lasting impression on us all, didn't he?'

'When you were with Luca, could you honestly say "There's nothing wrong with now"? No, you couldn't. But with Taran, I bet you can. I bet you can say it every moment you're with him. Because he makes you happy.' Suze grinned at her sister. 'Go to Toronto, silly, and live!'

Daisy folded her arms. 'I can't. I'm needed here.'

'Of course you are, but you also have your own life to live and they'll understand that. If you hide *your* light under a bushel you'll lose the one man who really deserves to see it.'

'But what about Mum and Dad?' Daisy watched her mother, so vulnerable now, and bit her lip. 'I can't leave them.'

Suze pulled a face. 'They have *me*, silly!'

'You?'

'Let me rise to the challenge. We survived without you for six years, I'm sure we can manage again.'

'But Mum wasn't sick then.'

'And she's not sick now. It's not a disease, apparently.' Then, 'Daisy, don't be a fool. Live your life. You only get one.'

At that moment Daisy felt a hand on her shoulder. She turned. There, standing in front of her, grim-faced and distant, was Taran.

She blanched.

'Excuse us, Suze,' he said gravely. 'I think Daisy and I need to talk.'

Daisy felt the blood drain into her feet. He wasn't the warm, dry-humoured man she had last seen in Toronto, but cold and remote and clearly furious. 'Let's go outside,' she said and followed him.

Once in the dark street he turned to her and shook his head with fury and disappointment. 'I should have known something was wrong when you stopped taking my calls,' he said. 'Then Mother told me your ex-boyfriend had been here. Were you going to tell me or were you just going to drop me like a stone?'

Daisy was horrified. He looked so hurt. 'I just needed time to clear my head.' She reached out her hand, but he rejected it by thrusting his in his pockets.

'I know you've been having a hard time with your mother, but we all have to deal with stuff like that. It doesn't excuse your behaviour. It doesn't justify you ignoring my calls. I deserve respect at the very least.'

'I'm sorry,' she said quietly.

'As far as I was concerned we were in a relationship.'

The use of the past tense injected her with panic. 'I didn't tell you about Luca because I didn't want to worry you,' she explained. 'It meant nothing.'

'If it had meant nothing, you would have called me and told me about it.' His jaw hardened. 'You would have just called me, Daisy.'

'Luca asked me to marry him,' she told him, hoping that if she told him the truth he would forgive her.

'I know he did. The whole village knows he did!'

Bloody grapevine, Daisy thought crossly. 'But I didn't accept. It's not Luca I want, it's you.'

He sighed wearily. 'Look, Daisy. I don't want games. I thought I'd found someone who didn't want games either.'

'I'm sorry. I should have called. I should have told you. He said he'd come and live here, so I could be near my parents, and for a brief moment I thought I wanted that.' It sounded pathetic when said out loud.

'So, this is about geography, is it?

'I was just thinking of Dad ...' She felt her eyes sting with tears.

'Have you asked your father how he'd feel if you went to live abroad again?' She looked at him in surprise. It was true, she had never consulted him. 'If he's the man I believe him to be, he'll say go, live your life, be free. I think you're insulting him by making him responsible for your life in this way. If there's one thing your parents are not, it's selfish.'

'I want to be with you, Taran,' she said firmly.

'Do you?' He looked at her steadily.

'Yes, I do.'

'Then don't make it about geography.' He began to walk away.

'Where are you going?'

'Home.'

'Toronto?'

'No, here. Let's speak in the morning. You need to get back to the party. You also need to talk to your father – and I need time alone to think.'

She watched him disappear into the darkness, leaving her alone with her regret. She remained in the street, wiping away tears, hoping her face wasn't red and blotchy. Hoping no one would know she had been crying. Then she returned to the party, determined to put on a brave face for her mother. Inside, she felt broken.

Dennis took the microphone and slowly the voices in the room hushed. Marigold was surprised to see him on the little stage. She wondered what he was doing there. She wondered what they were *all* doing there. She tried to recall. Perhaps Dennis had told her and she had forgotten. She thought it was just a party, but she was obviously mistaken. She decided to smile to cover up her forgetfulness. Really, it wasn't getting any better. The fog was definitely getting thicker. But it didn't matter. She was having a lovely time.

'Welcome, everyone,' said Dennis. He settled his gaze on Marigold. She felt a little conspicuous and blushed. 'Today is a very special day because we have all come together to celebrate someone in our community who is very special.' Marigold thought it was a sweet idea and she wondered who it was they were celebrating. She saw Suze and Daisy moving through the crowd in her direction and looked around for spare chairs. There weren't any.

'This special person is someone who has looked after those around her all her life. She's unselfish and kind and we just want to give something back.' He was still looking at her. But now they were *all* looking at her. Marigold felt uneasy. Was it her birthday? Had she forgotten?

Daisy and Suze were beside her now and Daisy had taken her hand. She noticed Daisy's eyes were moist and wondered why she was crying. Then she felt Suze's hand on her shoulder. They were reassuring, the two of them, like guardian angels, taking their places beside her to protect her. She remembered them as little girls. It had been *her* duty to protect *them* then. She wondered when that had changed. She couldn't recall.

'Marigold,' said Dennis, and Marigold nearly jumped out of her skin. 'We're all here tonight to celebrate *you*.'

Marigold panicked. A cold, prickly sensation spread across

her skin and she was seized by the sudden urge to flee. She looked at Dennis in alarm. He held her gaze. He held it firmly and he barely blinked, and in it she sensed security, familiarity and strength. There, in the warmth of his eyes, she felt reassured and she didn't turn away. She didn't look at anyone else. She just looked at Dennis, *her* Dennis, and his words sunk in.

He was celebrating *her*.

She was the member of the community who was special.

'Every Christmas I make you a jigsaw puzzle, Goldie,' he was saying. 'But this year everyone wanted to help me. First it was just one or two, but the trickle of people turned into a river and I was swept away by the kindness and thoughtfulness of our small village.' Marigold's vision blurred. She clung to Dennis's gaze, but he was becoming increasingly fuzzy. She blinked to clear it and tried to focus. 'Everyone came with their memories of you, Goldie. Daisy painted them and I cut the pieces, and Suze and Nan added our family's memories to the many already collected. It's a celebration of you. We hope you like it.'

Nan appeared then, carrying the box. She handed it to Suze and Daisy who placed it on the table in front of Marigold. Nan pulled a handkerchief out of her sleeve and handed it to her daughter. Marigold dabbed her eyes. Daisy passed her her glasses and she put them on with shaking hands. Then she looked at the picture on the lid of the box. There were so many lovely things to look at, she couldn't take them all in. There were animals, birds, people, a large sun, cupcakes, a Christmas pudding – really, it was a gorgeous medley of delights. Then Daisy lifted the lid and showed her the underside. The back of the puzzle was drawn onto the cardboard and there was lots of writing. 'On the reverse of each picture is the explanation, Mum,' she told her. 'Every memory represented by a picture is explained on the other side.'

Marigold's eyes overflowed with tears. 'It's beautiful,' she whispered. She lifted her gaze to look at the faces of those she realized she knew. 'And you did all this?' she asked softly. She saw one or two of them nod. She heard some of them say they did. But really, everything was just a blur and a rumble of voices.

'Thank you,' she managed, and these people, her friends, began to clap.

Dennis took her hand. 'Fancy a dance, Goldie?' he asked.

Marigold didn't have the words, but Dennis didn't mind. He could tell she did from her beaming smile. Batty played 'The Lady In Red' and Marigold allowed Dennis to hold her as they slowly swayed to the music in the area in the middle of the room that Suze had arranged for dancing. 'You once asked me, what would happen when you forgot all your memories,' he said.

'Did I?' she asked, frowning up at him.

'Yes, you did.'

'How did you reply?'

'I said that you didn't need to remember because *I* would remember for you. But I was wrong.' He pressed his face to hers and felt her tremble. 'All these people here tonight will remember them too.'

Chapter 28

That night Daisy couldn't sleep. She lay on her back, staring at the ceiling, thinking about Taran and Luca, her mother and father, and in those dark and silent hours she felt helpless, as if she were drowning. Had she destroyed her relationship with Taran simply because Luca had marched back into her life and offered to give her everything she wanted? How easy it would be to slip back into the past. To continue on from where she had left off. But was that what she really wanted? It was familiar and comfortable, but was it enough? She remembered Toronto and there was something wonderfully vivid and alive about those memories. They were shiny and new and full of possibility. There was something tarnished about her memories of Luca. They lacked brilliance. Perhaps they had been tainted by the arguments and disagreements they'd had in the last months of their relationship. Or perhaps Suze was right, that she had left Luca because she had wanted to. Maybe their story had reached its end and the fact that they wanted different things had just given her an excuse to leave. Perhaps it had run its course.

By morning she knew whom she wanted to be with, simply because Taran was the only man occupying her mind and her heart, along with a burning sense of regret. She picked up her phone and called Luca. '*Ciao,* Margherita!' His voice was up, as if he was expecting good news.

'I don't know how to say this, Luca—' she began.

'You're going to break my heart all over again,' he interrupted in a dull voice.

She sighed and put a hand on her chest. She hadn't expected this to hurt so much. 'I don't want to break your heart, Luca. But I'm calling to tell you that it's over. It's over, now, for good.'

'Then we have nothing more to say to each other. Six years have all gone in a puff of smoke.'

'I'm sorry.'

'Me too. I hope you don't live to regret your decision. Unfortunately, I will regret it for the rest of my life.'

Daisy did not know how to respond to that.

'*Addio,* beautiful Margherita.'

'*Addio,* Luca.'

When she came down to breakfast she found her father and Nan at the kitchen table, discussing the party. Marigold wasn't down yet. She took longer getting up these days.

'You did well last night,' said Nan over the rim of her teacup. 'You all did. I'm proud of you.' Daisy waited for her to add a typically caustic remark, but she didn't.

'Marigold had a lovely time,' said Dennis, reaching up to stroke Mac, who was settled on his shoulder and purring into his ear.

Daisy made herself a cup of coffee, then went to join them at the table.

'*You* look like you've wrestled with an entire army,' said Nan, noticing the purple shadows beneath Daisy's eyes. 'What's going on, Daisy?'

Daisy cupped her mug and looked at her father with apprehension. 'Dad, can I ask you something?'

Her father frowned, taking in his daughter's distraught face with confusion. 'Of course you can, love. What is it?'

Daisy took a deep breath. 'Taran asked me to move to Toronto. I told him I need to be here, with you and Mum. That I can't leave you to look after Mum on your own. That you need my support. But ...' Her voice trailed off. Saying those words out loud gave her pain. She put her hands in her lap and stared into her coffee cup. She couldn't look at her father in case she saw hurt in his eyes. That would be too much to bear. She didn't want him to think she was deserting him during his hour of need. 'I want to be here to help you look after Mum, but I love Taran ...'

Nan clicked her tongue and looked at Daisy sharply. 'And you'd be a fool to let *him* go,' she said.

'I know, only ... ' Daisy wished her father would say something.

'No *only*,' Nan snapped. 'You're not getting any younger and I'd say Taran is the Last Chance Saloon. We'll cope without you.' She chuckled and glanced at Dennis. 'We have the entire village helping out now, so really, one more would be a nuisance.'

Dennis put his hand on Daisy's. It was big and warm and achingly tender. 'Daisy, love. You've been a good daughter. You *are* a good daughter,' he said. 'But it's time you gave Suze a chance to shine.'

'If you do everything for people, they never learn to do anything for themselves,' Nan said, and Daisy noticed that she, too, had got good at making her own breakfast these days.

'I'm not sure he wants me now. You see, Luca—'

'Yes, we know Luca proposed,' Nan interrupted. 'I don't

think there's anyone in the village who *doesn't* know that. But if you wanted to marry him, you'd have said yes straight away. When there's hesitation, there's doubt, that's what your grandfather used to say.'

Daisy smiled through her tears. 'What else did Grandad say?'

Nan returned her smile and it was gentle and affectionate. 'Your grandad would have said everything happens for a reason. That there's no such thing as coincidence. The people who come into your life, however briefly or permanently, do so for a reason. He believed we are all here to learn and grow in love. That this is the Big School of Life. I imagine he would tell you that you learned some very important lessons during those years with Luca, but now it's time to close that chapter and start the next. You and Taran have a lot to learn from each other, that's why you've met. It's karma. It's you attracting things into your life that are important for your spiritual growth and development. You see, I might have pretended not to listen, but I remember everything he said.' She pulled a face. 'Your grandfather loved talking about those deep and meaningful things. But do you want to know what *I* think?'

Daisy nodded.

'I never liked Luca. I wouldn't trust him as far as I could throw him. Taran's got substance, and . . .' She grinned. 'I like his mother, and an apple doesn't fall very far from the tree, does it? He's a good sort. Take it from me. I've known a few sorts in my time to be a good judge of them.'

'Taran's furious with me for not telling him about Luca coming over.' Daisy sighed and put a hand on her chest. 'I don't know what to do now. I've said I'm sorry.'

'That's all you can do, love,' said Dennis.

'No, it isn't,' said Nan. 'If you want him you have to fight for him. You're not a damsel in distress waiting for your knight in shining armour to rescue you. Dear God, women have come a long way in my lifetime and thank goodness for that. I wouldn't leave it a moment longer. Go up there and tell him how you feel. And a few tears will make all the difference, believe me.'

Daisy laughed. 'Nan, you've just undermined your argument.'

'It's a wily woman who knows how to use her powers. It's not an even playing field and never will be. Men may be stronger, but women will always be more cunning. It's just the way it is.'

'So, if I went and lived in Toronto, you'd be okay without me,' said Daisy, pushing out her chair and standing up.

'Good God, Daisy, it's the twenty-first century. Toronto is a hop across the Atlantic,' said Nan. 'Not a three-week voyage in a ship!'

'Nan survived the *Titanic*, you know,' joked Dennis.

'I'm not *that* old,' Nan protested. Then she looked at Daisy, who was hovering by the door, ready to leave. 'You do make heavy weather of everything, Daisy,' she said. 'Take a deep breath now and go!'

Daisy put on her coat and hat and hurried out into the wintry morning. Frost lay thick upon the ground, melting slowly in the places where the sun shone, revealing patches of green. She trudged up the path that cut across the farmland, as she had done pretty much every morning for almost a year. The sky was a weak blue, the clouds that gently floated across it fine and feathery. Every day was beautiful, she thought to herself as she ran her eyes over the brown fields and distant woods. She soaked in the splendour of nature and, as her heart expanded, she began to feel more positive. She was filled with a buoyance and a brightness and quickened her pace. She'd tell Taran how she felt, she resolved, because she was sure now of how she felt. Surer than she had ever been.

As she walked along the side of the wood, she saw someone sitting on the bench up ahead. At first, she thought it might be David Pullman, the farm manager, but as she got closer she realized it was Taran. He too was wearing a big coat, hat and scarf and sat with his elbows on his knees, staring out over the hills.

He sensed her presence and turned away from the view.

He didn't get up but leaned back against the bench, his expression impassive. It was impossible for Daisy to read him.

She stopped, uncertain suddenly of how to begin.

'You haven't been here all night, have you?' she asked with a smile, hovering in front of him, trying not to be deterred by the invisible wall that had suddenly grown up between them.

But Taran didn't smile back. 'If I had, I'd be a block of ice by now,' he replied solemnly. *How formidable he is*, she thought, suddenly wondering whether it had been wise of her to take Nan's advice and come. There was no give on his part, just a hard, unfriendly expression that sapped her resolve.

She could hear Nan telling her that now would be a good time to release a few tears.

She lifted her chin and went to sit beside him. She felt more comfortable there, facing the immense view that stretched all the way to the farthest horizon. Roused by the magnificence of it, she felt her confidence return.

She looked at him and sensed, behind the hard, unfriendly expression, suffering. 'I'm sorry I hurt you,' she said quietly. 'I panicked. And I only thought of myself. There's no excuse. I should have called you and trusted you to understand.'

Taran leaned his elbows on his knees again and knitted his fingers. Their gazes met on that distant horizon. 'I'm sorry too,' he said wearily. 'I overreacted. I was jealous.'

'You have no reason to be jealous. I don't want to lose you, Taran. I don't want to be with Luca, either in Milan or here. I want to be with you, wherever you are.'

He sat back and looked at her intensely. 'Why the sudden change of heart?'

'I talked to Dad, just like you told me to. You were right. He's not going to make me feel I'm letting him down by going to live abroad again. Or that I'm letting Mum down. I think I'm probably letting myself down by not following my heart. Nan said I make very heavy weather of everything. I think she's right.'

His face softened and the tenderness returned to his eyes. 'That's only because you care,' he said.

The change in his expression brought real tears to her eyes, not the ones Nan was talking about. 'I *do* care,' she emphasized, relieved that he was perhaps giving her a reprieve. 'I carry the weight of my family's struggle on my shoulders, because I care. But I have to learn that I don't have to care alone. There's Suze and Nan, who, as it turns out, *can* look after herself after all.' She gave a small, hesitant smile. 'And Toronto is only a hop across the ocean.'

He smiled back, a smile that broke the stranger and brought the friend back to her, with all his warmth and wit and love. 'So you'll come?' he asked, reaching out and touching her cheek with the back of his hand.

'I'll come,' she replied.

He pulled her into his arms and pressed his face into her neck. 'You frightened me, Daisy.' He squeezed her tightly. 'Please don't frighten me like that again.'

Daisy hurried home, anxious to share her news. She needed to tell her mother first. It was important not to overwhelm her and to break it to her gently that she was going to live abroad again. She didn't look forward to telling her that bit.

Dennis and Nan were still at the kitchen table. Marigold was yet to join them.

'Someone's happy!' commented Nan when she saw Daisy's flushed face. 'Was it the crocodile tears that did it?'

Dennis raised his eyebrows. 'All's well, I see,' he said.

'I'm going to live with Taran in Toronto!' she exclaimed.

Nan looked surprised. 'In my day people got married before they moved in together.'

'This isn't your day,' said Dennis, getting up to embrace his daughter. 'This is *your* day, love,' he said to Daisy, and planted a kiss on her forehead. 'It's wonderful news.'

Nan shook her head at the disappointing lowering of standards these days, but put out her hand to beckon Daisy to her. 'I'm happy for you both,' she said, shrugging off her disapproval and cheering up at the thought of the possibility of Lady Sherwood eventually joining her family. A Sherwood tying the knot with a Fane, she mused with something close to excitement. *That* wouldn't have happened in *her* day. 'When you finally do get married, you'll do it in white, won't you, pet? I'm sure Taran is a young man who likes to do things correctly. He'll come and ask for your hand, won't he, in a suit and tie?'

'I'm moving in with him, Nan. One step at a time,' said Daisy, but she couldn't see Taran in a suit and tie.

When Marigold came downstairs at last, Dennis got up to make her a cup of tea. He kissed her cheek. 'Morning, Goldie,' he said. 'Daisy's got some good news.'

Marigold looked at Daisy and smiled. She wondered whether Luca had asked her to marry him at last.

'I'm moving in with Taran,' said Daisy. She braced herself for her mother's response.

There was a long pause while Marigold tried to remember who Taran was. She was certain he was called Luca. 'How lovely, dear,' she said and went to sit down.

'They're going to live in Toronto,' said Nan.

'But we're going to come and go,' added Daisy quickly, desperate to avoid upsetting her mother, who was looking puzzled. 'It's only an eight-hour flight so we'll come back every few months at least. Taran will want to see his mother too.'

Marigold's smile did not falter, although she was sure Daisy's boyfriend lived in Italy. 'Toronto is a lovely city,' she said evenly, taking the chair at the head of the table, next to Nan.

'And he told me he'll move back here one day, so it's not for ever,' Daisy reassured her.

'Toronto's a dreadful city!' Nan exclaimed. 'Noisy, dirty, too many people and the buildings are too high.'

Daisy frowned. 'Have you ever been to Toronto, Nan?'

'I don't need to go to Toronto to know what a dreadful city it is.'

Daisy gazed at her mother searchingly. She wasn't sure Marigold had understood what she'd said. 'You see, Mum, Taran works in Toronto. He's an architect. A good architect. He has his own business and designs the most beautiful buildings. When I went out there, I realized that he couldn't leave his business to come and live here. At least not yet.'

'You don't have to explain, Daisy,' said Dennis gently, putting Marigold's cup of tea in front of her. 'You'll have fun in

Toronto. You're young. It'll be good for you to have fun in an exciting city like Toronto.' He sat down on Marigold's right.

Marigold understood that Daisy would be leaving her, but she focused on the part where she said she'd be coming back. As long as she came back, Marigold didn't mind her going.

'Maybe Suze will step into the breach,' said Dennis hopefully. 'She's grown up a lot in the last year and she's a respectable married woman now.'

'It'll be nice to see more of her,' said Nan. 'Suze is the sort of girl who'll jump only as high as she has to. Let's raise the bar and see what happens.'

Marigold sipped her tea, settling into the familiar routine with the relish of a nesting hen. 'Dad says that our children are not our children, they're sons and daughters of Life's longing for itself,' she said.

Nan noticed Marigold's use of the present tense and bit her tongue. She knew now not to correct her these days, even though the urge to do so was almost irresistible. 'Your father said many wise things,' she said instead.

'That's Khalil Gibran,' said Dennis. 'How clever of you to remember, Goldie.'

'They come through us but are not from us, and although they are with us, they don't belong to us,' Marigold continued, soaking up Dennis's praise. 'Dad has always encouraged me to take my own path, whatever that may be.'

Dennis smiled broadly. 'He's right, of course. And I have always encouraged our girls to do the same. You go to Toronto, Daisy, without any regret. You'll make a home of it with Taran.'

Marigold was confused. She was certain Daisy's boyfriend was called Luca.

'Dreadful city,' repeated Nan.

'Yes, I'll make a home of it with Taran,' Daisy said, her anxiety lifting at the sight of her mother's gentle smile.

'Home is where love is, dear,' said Marigold. Then she turned and looked at Dennis.

Taran liked to leave the city on weekends and head to Muskoka, a large region of lakes, islands and mountains north of Toronto. He enjoyed hiking and canoeing, hanging out on the dock in the summer and snowshoeing and cross-country skiing in winter. He'd rented a small cottage from a client who owned a large estate in the hills and it was there that he took Daisy. Thirsty for the serenity of nature she drank in the big blue skies, the crystal water, the forests of ever-changing colour and the wild flowers that grew among the long grasses. She didn't hanker for her English home because she'd made a home there with Taran and was perfectly content.

One weekend at the beginning of March Taran declared that he wanted to show her something special. He drove further into the hills, up a long dirt track, to a secluded place among the trees where a barn stood derelict and forlorn, staring out over the uninterrupted view of a lake. He took Daisy's hand. 'Do you think this would be a good place to build a house?' he asked.

'I think it would be amazing. Is it for a client?'

'No.' He turned to her and smiled. 'It's for you.'

Daisy was so taken aback that she laughed. 'Ha ha, funny joke.'

'I'm not joking. I want to build a house here with you. A house for us.'

Daisy stopped laughing. 'You're really not joking, are you?'

Without letting go of her hand he went down on one knee.

Daisy felt a surge of emotion and pressed her palm to her chest to steady the sudden rush of fitful beating. He looked up at her, his eyes shiny and his cheeks suddenly flushed in the amber glow of sunset. 'Daisy Fane, love of my life, will you marry me?'

Daisy knelt and took his face in her hands. She blinked away tears. 'I would love to, Taran Sherwood, love of *my* life.' She rested her forehead against his, then gently kissed his lips.

He wrapped his arms around her and held her tightly. 'I bought this land a long time ago. I was just waiting for the right girl to share it with,' he said. 'Now I've found her.'

Daisy closed her eyes and allowed him to envelop her. *Mum was right,* she thought, cherishing the familiar feel of him. Here was where she belonged. Here with Taran.

Home is where love is.

Daisy and Taran were married in the village church in June. Lady Sherwood helped Daisy with the arrangements. She couldn't help but draw parallels between their marriage and her own. While *she* had left Toronto and moved to England to marry Owen, Daisy was leaving England to move to Toronto to be with Taran. She'd secretly hoped that Daisy would entice her son back, but she understood that his business was there, as were so many of his childhood memories. But Taran had assured her that they'd move back eventually and she believed him.

Suze and Batty decorated the tent which had been put up in her garden for the reception and dinner dance. Nan was very impressed. It was much more glamorous than Suze's reception had been. Taran's friends and cousins flew in from Toronto and Patrick and Lucille came all the way from Sydney. There were two hundred and fifty guests, all seated at elegant round tables, beneath a ceiling studded with little lights, like stars. Dennis had to hire a morning coat especially. Suze and Daisy took Nan and Marigold into town to buy new dresses and hats. Suze made sure that Marigold didn't miss any of Daisy's fittings. Nan insisted on coming too and had nothing sour to say about the dress, which was white, but she did tell Daisy to eat more. 'No man wants to lie with a bony woman,' she said with a sniff. 'I'll bet Taran's a man who likes something to hold on to.'

Marigold watched Dennis take Daisy down the aisle with tears in her eyes. She hoped she'd remember this moment for ever, but she had already forgotten Suze's wedding. She would inevitably forget Daisy's. However, she was learning to live in the moment. To savour the present. Not to regret what was lost or anticipate what would vanish. Her father told her to enjoy the simple things which can only be found in the Now. 'The Now is the only thing that is real, anyway,' he told her during one of their chats in the garden. 'Dementia throws you into the Now, Goldie. Enjoy the birdsong, the breeze, the changing seasons. Enjoy it all in the Now. It is only by being alert to the present moment that you can connect with the real you, which is eternal.'

'The me who is driving the car,' she said proudly, pleased that she remembered.

'The you who is driving the car,' her father repeated. 'Your eternal soul.'

'I'm going to be okay, aren't I, Dad?'

'Yes, you are, Goldie.' He smiled so that the crow's feet at the corners of his eyes deepened. He took her hand. 'You're going to be okay, because you're loved. That's all anybody needs.'

In the months that followed, the fog in Marigold's mind closed in. Little by little, inch by inch, her world shrank. Daisy FaceTimed regularly, telling her mother about her new life in Toronto, that she was becoming quite a successful artist, even though she realized that her mother found it hard to follow what she was saying. Suze stepped into the breach and jumped way beyond the bar that had been raised for her, surprising even Nan with her dedication and attentiveness to her mother. Without Daisy there to do everything for her, Suze relished the sense of responsibility that looking after Marigold gave her. She felt needed and full of purpose, and the admiration she received from her grandmother and father, and from Batty too, made her feel good about herself in a way she hadn't before. It felt good to shine.

And she started to write. After she wrote the first line the words became a torrent and she could barely type fast enough to keep up with it. That was inspiration, creativity flowing through her from a higher place. She realized then that she had never been inspired before.

In early summer Suze and Batty's first child was born. Suze came over often so that Marigold could enjoy being with her granddaughter. While Marigold gazed tenderly into the baby's face and held her tiny hand, Suze made her cups of tea and helped with the household chores, until Dennis realized that it was too much for Suze and paid Sylvia's eager young niece Karen to do the cleaning and laundry instead. Nan enjoyed talking to Karen. It was a little dull in the house now that Marigold's health had declined and the girls had moved out, and Karen was full of gossip like her aunt. Marigold spent a lot of time in the garden watching the birds, or in the sitting room doing her new puzzle. Even though it was becoming too great a challenge for her she enjoyed looking at the pictures and reading the explanations on the back. They made her feel warm inside.

In November it snowed again. Nan complained, as she always did. Marigold gazed onto the white garden with wonder and Dennis commented cheerfully that it looked like Narnia. Yet, this year Marigold forgot to feed the birds. Nan reminded her. 'If you don't feed them, Marigold, they won't make it to spring.' She handed her her coat. 'You don't want to catch a chill,' she said, helping her into it. Mother and daughter went out together to fill the feeder and talk to the robin who waited for them on the roof of Dennis's shed.

Determined to do his best for Marigold, Dennis devised systems so that she could look after herself. He knew her independence was important to her. In the bathroom he put a basket of her toiletries and medicine by the sink to help her remember what she had done, to avoid doing things twice. After brushing her teeth, she put the brush and paste to one side. After washing her face, she added the soap to the brush and paste. After moisturizing, she added the cream, and so on until the basket was empty. That way she knew everything had been done as it should. She then put all the items back in the basket for next time. He refashioned the kitchen cabinets, giving them glass doors so Marigold could see what was in them. He labelled the bathroom door and the drawers and cupboards in the kitchen and sitting room. He added more lights, so Marigold could see more clearly, and made sure the floors were smooth so she wouldn't trip over. He kept the house clutter-free so as not to confuse her, and ensured that important things like keys and her mobile telephone were always put in the same place. Most crucially he agreed with her, all the time. However crazy she sounded, and she did sometimes sound a little crazy, he simply smiled at her with encouragement and understanding. He hoped she would never know how far her brain had deteriorated.

It never occurred to Dennis that the day would come when he would be incapable of looking after her anymore. He had made his vows in church before God, to look after her in sickness and in health, and he wasn't about to break them. He didn't think her condition would deteriorate to such an extent that he could no longer care for her himself. Yet, it did.

As the books on the metaphorical bookshelf in Marigold's brain began to show empty top shelves, Marigold began to exist on the bottom shelves – in the memories that were still there, from long ago. She tried to run away various times, claiming that she wanted to go home. 'But home is here,' Dennis explained patiently when he found her in the lane in her nightdress and bare feet, shivering with cold.

'No,' she replied, shaking her head in panic. 'I want to go home to Mum and Dad and Patrick. They're missing me, you see. They're worried. I need to go home so they don't worry.'

Dennis struggled against the fear that threatened to over-whelm him and tearfully gathered her into his arms and carried her home. How could he be a good husband to her if she no longer recognized their house as home?

Then one night, she refused to get into bed because she didn't recognize Dennis.

'I'm your husband,' he said in desperation. 'You're married to me. We've been married for over forty years, Goldie.' But she remained pinned to the wall in her dressing gown, trembling with fright, until Dennis was forced to ask Nan to come in and talk to her.

Nan found the whole situation unbearable. She couldn't

understand how Marigold could forget Dennis. Dennis, the light of her life. How could she? 'He *is* your husband, Marigold,' she said, lips white and quivering. 'You *love* him.' And there was something about the word 'love' that brought him back to her. But if it happened again, would love be enough?

After that, Nan knew that Dennis wouldn't be able to cope for much longer. Dennis knew too, deep down, and yet he couldn't bring himself to face up to it. He couldn't bear the thought of being without Marigold. He'd do everything possible to avoid that happening. And besides, where would she go? Into a hospital? He shuddered. He'd heard terrible things about dementia patients being neglected in hospitals. But he couldn't afford a nursing home. There was only one thing to do. With a heavy heart he wound down his work and declined new commissions. The miniature village he was making remained abandoned in his shed, gathering dust. He helped Marigold bathe and dress. He made her meals. He brewed her tea. He dedicated every moment of his life to her with patience and compassion, and for a while he felt he was swimming with his head above the water. Yet as Christmas came and went again, he felt the force of the undercurrent gradually pulling him down until he could barely breathe. Marigold was getting worse and the devices he'd created to help her were now defeating her. Worst of all, *she* was defeating *him*.

Dennis wasn't a man who cried easily, but the moment he realized he had failed her he cried like a boy. A helpless boy. A boy who could see no way out.

Nan telephoned Patrick. She rarely telephoned him because it was very expensive calling the other side of the world and Patrick was very busy. But she needed him. She needed his advice. In the old days she would have asked her husband, he

would have known exactly what to do. But since he was no
longer here, she had no choice but to call her son. 'Is everyone
all right?' he asked when he heard his mother's voice.

'No, it's Marigold,' she replied and she was much too aware
of the cost to embark on a lengthy story.

'Has she got worse?' he asked.

'Much worse, Patrick.'

'I thought as much,' he replied, then sighed heavily because
there was very little he could do to help from where he was.

'Dennis is trying to look after her himself, but she's breaking him. I've never seen him so strained. I need to know
whether Marigold should go into a nursing home, Patrick. I
know Dennis won't hear of it. But *I* think we have no choice.
What do *you* think we should do?' Patrick thought about it a
moment. Nan's mouth twitched with impatience. 'I'm not sure
I can take much more of this,' she added with a sigh. 'She's
going to break me too.'

'Then you have to do what's best for all of you, including
Marigold, and you mustn't feel bad,' said Patrick. 'You, Daisy
and Suze need to persuade Dennis that it's not only for your
good, but for Marigold's too. Professional carers know how
to look after people like her. She'll be safe. Of course Dennis
can't look after her on his own.' He chuckled. 'I commend
him for doing it, but I can tell you, I'd last five minutes before
I cried out for help.' Nan hoped Lucille never needed him to.

Nan telephoned Daisy and asked her to fly back. Suze left
her baby at home with Batty and drove over. The three of
them confronted Dennis together around the kitchen table,
while Marigold was sleeping upstairs.

Daisy was shocked to see her father looking so tired and
grey. He had aged a great deal since she had last seen him
at Christmas. If she had had reservations about putting her

mother into a nursing home, Dennis's decline convinced her that it was the right thing to do, for both of them.

Dennis hugged his mug of tea and gazed forlornly at his daughters and mother-in-law with glassy eyes. 'I know what you're all here for,' he told them sadly.

'We're not going to sit back and let you deteriorate too,' said Nan, and she smiled and added with typically dry humour, 'I have to live with you and it's not fair on me.'

Dennis managed a wan smile in return, but the truth was made no easier to bear cushioned with jest.

'It's not fair on *you*,' said Daisy kindly, looking at her father with tenderness. 'You need to live your life, Dad.'

He stared at her in bewilderment. 'But Marigold *is* my life, Daisy.'

'I know, Dad. But if you don't get help, she'll take you down with her and none of us will be able to bear that.' Daisy's eyes stung. She couldn't imagine Dennis without Marigold. The two of them went together like a pot and its lid. Like bread and butter. Like laughter and love.

'We don't want Mum to leave home any more than you do,' said Suze. 'But, she wouldn't want you to suffer, would she?'

Dennis remembered the conversation they'd had in his shed, when Marigold had told him that she would understand if he put her into a nursing home. He had been appalled. The idea had seemed inconceivable then. Now it was just unbearable.

'I can't afford a nursing home,' he admitted and the words cut him deeply, because when he had said his vows in church he had really meant them. *In sickness and in health . . . till death us do part.* Call him old-fashioned, but looking after Marigold was not only his desire but his duty. Now he was ashamed that he was failing in that duty. He lowered his eyes.

'I still have the money I got from selling my house,' said Nan. 'I put it away for a rainy day. Well, I'd say it's pretty much a downpour now, wouldn't you?'

Dennis nodded. 'A downpour is exactly what it is.'

Daisy cleared her throat. She didn't want to undermine her grandmother's generous offer, but she had done her research and knew how much a good nursing home would cost. Her grandmother's money would soon run out. 'Taran and I would like to pay,' she said, glancing anxiously at Nan. 'I mean, we'd like to share the cost with Nan.'

Nan smiled at Daisy and then put her hand on Dennis's arm. 'That's what family is for,' she said. 'You can't rely on the government. But you can rely on us.'

Dennis looked from Nan to Daisy and his eyes shone. He couldn't find the words to express his gratitude. He couldn't find any words at all.

'I'll contribute too,' said Suze, not wanting to be left out, although she and Batty had little to give. 'It won't be much but it'll help.'

'It's the thought that counts,' said Nan. 'The point is, it can be done and must be done. For you, Dennis, but also for Marigold. She needs professional care now.'

He took a sip of tea and sighed. 'I don't know what I'll do without her,' he muttered. His hollow eyes glistened. 'She's my Goldie, isn't she? She's always been my Goldie.'

'You can visit her every day, if you like,' said Daisy.

'We'll choose a place that's close by,' said Suze.

'Beryl told me that she took her to visit Seaview House a few years ago,' Nan told them. 'It's about a twenty-minute drive. On the coast, so she'd be able to see the sea. You know how much she loves the sea. I believe it's a nice place.'

'Will you look at it with us?' Suze asked Dennis.

'You don't have to make any decisions now,' said Daisy gently. 'Just come and have a look around. If you don't like it, we can find somewhere else.'

There was a long pause as Dennis considered their proposal. No one spoke. Daisy looked at Suze and frowned. Suze gave a little shrug. They drank their tea and waited. Finally, Dennis spoke. 'I don't know how Marigold will manage without me,' he said quietly. 'She's always had me to lean on.'

'She doesn't recognize you half the time,' said Nan. 'It's only going to get worse.'

'I wish I could cope,' he said. 'I'm afraid I'm letting her down.'

'Oh Dad,' Daisy cried. 'You're not letting her down. You've been her knight in shining armour.'

'You couldn't have done more,' added Suze tearfully.

Nan nodded. 'No, you couldn't have done more. No one could have. You're a good man, Dennis, like Arthur. Good men. Marigold and I have been very lucky. We both know that.' She put out her hand and patted his across the table. 'Marigold might be losing her mind but she's still got a heart. She knows you love her and she'll know that any decision you make will be done with love.'

'And we know too,' added Daisy.

'All right,' Dennis said, nodding his agreement. 'Let's go and take a look at this Seaview House. Let's see if it's good enough for our Goldie.'

Chapter 29

The seasons came and went, one after the other in regular succession, and Marigold watched them all from the armchair by the big sash window that looked out onto the lawn of Seaview House. Although they were labelled with the words summer, autumn, winter and spring, none of them was ever the same. The reds and yellows of autumn were sometimes a deeper crimson and a brighter gold. Sometimes it snowed, but most often it didn't. Occasionally frost drew pictures on the window panes and it was fun to try and work out what they were. Marigold found fairies, goblins and leprechauns in the ice, but they'd melt away in the sunshine and then, just as she lamented their departing, the birds would draw her attention, flapping about the feeders in the garden, because no matter what season it was, there were always birds. Marigold loved birds. Their light-hearted song touched her somewhere deep and timeless, in the place where all the love she had received in her life was stored, even though she couldn't remember those who had given it.

Little by little Marigold's memories faded away, like wisps of smoke from a dying fire. But she didn't notice their passing. She gave them up without a fight. There was no struggle, no anxiety, no pain, just a gentle relinquishing of pictures that were no longer vital to her sense of self. As her father had told her, the car was gradually deteriorating and the engine was flagging, but Marigold was still in the driving seat and she was as perfect and whole as she always had been, as she always would be. She took pleasure in the moment. There was lots to enjoy there. She watched the sea, the undulating waves, the light dancing on the water, the foam about the rocks and the seabirds flocking to feast on the shoals of fish just beneath the surface. If one remained in the moment one was never bored or unhappy. *What's wrong with now?* she asked herself; nothing was ever wrong with now.

Sometimes Marigold sat and thought, other times she just sat. Occasionally, she would emerge out of the mist and the engine would unexpectedly fire up and the car would cough and splutter and Marigold would come back to life with a little of the enthusiasm that had characterized her former existence. But those days were rare.

It was Christmas Day. Two cars pulled up outside Seaview House and six adults stepped out into the snow with various small children. There was a wreath on the front door and, when they entered the hall, a large Christmas tree decorated with silver tinsel and snowflakes was in the place of the round table that was usually positioned in front of the fireplace which was never lit. The building smelt of cinnamon and baked apples.

Dennis led the way through the hall, armed with a basket of gifts and a bunch of pale pink roses. Behind him Nan followed, holding Suze's young daughter, Trudie, by the hand. After them came Daisy, carrying her ten-month-old son Owen, and Suze, who was pregnant again. Behind them Batty carried their fifteen-month-old boy and the nappy bag. Taran brought a box of mince pies from his mother, which Sylvia had made.

They entered the sitting room and saw Marigold at once. She was settled into her usual armchair by the window, gazing out onto the white garden. She looked neat and tidy in a skirt and cardigan. The collar of her floral shirt had been ironed with care. Her hair had recently been washed. She wore a little make-up, not too much, just enough to look her best. On the table beside her was the puzzle they had given her. She couldn't put the pieces together these days, but the nurses said she liked to look at the pictures and read the inscriptions on the back. She was often seen smiling at them, they said, with a tender look on her face.

The party made their way across the room. It was very quiet. The television was on and a group of white-haired ladies were sitting on the sofa, watching a carol service. On the coffee table in front of them, among the magazines, was a recently published book by Suze Fane, entitled *Loving with Dementia*. It had been a bestseller.

As the family approached, Marigold turned away from the window.

She swept her eyes over the approaching group, not realizing at first that they had come for *her*. Her expression was curious, the face of a passive observer. Of someone who wasn't expecting to be part of the action but was quite content to watch it happen around her. Then Dennis smiled at her and she looked a little startled. 'Hello, love,' he said gently. He knew better than to bend down and kiss her. That's what he used to do but things were different now. He took one of the chairs and sat down. 'Happy Christmas, Goldie. We've brought you some presents.' He hadn't brought her a puzzle. She didn't remember their tradition anymore.

When Marigold saw Nan, her face lit up and she smiled with recognition. She remembered her mother. 'Hello, Marigold,' Nan said and took the chair beside her. Suze's daughter climbed onto her great-grandmother's knee and watched Marigold warily. Batty and Taran pulled up some more chairs and the four of them sat down. There was a lot of bustle as Batty put the nappy bag on the carpet and Taran found a table for the mince pies. Daisy sat close to her mother, her baby in her arms, while Suze sat beside Nan. A moment later Trudie put out her arms and Suze gathered her onto her knee. The little girl continued to watch Marigold with suspicion.

'Well, isn't this nice,' said Dennis, heartily patting his knees, trying to act as if everything was normal. 'Isn't the snow lovely. Like Narnia,' he added.

'You like snow, don't you, Marigold?' said Nan. 'You've always liked snow.'

Marigold turned her eyes to the snow and remained there a while, enjoying the way the sunlight caught the crystals and made them glitter.

'I love Christmas,' said Suze. 'I've always loved presents.'

Marigold turned her attention back to the group. She smiled at Daisy, the gracious smile of a stranger. 'How very kind of you,' she said.

'And I've brought mince pies from my mother,' said Taran.

Marigold didn't know who *he* was, let alone his mother, but she didn't want to let on. 'That's very sweet of her. Thank you.' Again the gracious smile of someone wanting to be polite, of someone not wanting to say the wrong thing.

'How about we make some tea,' suggested Daisy, hoping to diffuse the tension that was slowly building around them.

Marigold's face grew animated suddenly. 'That's a good idea. Let's have a nice cup of tea,' she said. 'There's nothing nicer than a cup of tea when it's cold outside.'

Daisy stood up and handed the baby to Taran. 'I'll pop to the kitchen and boil the kettle.'

Suze stood up too. 'I'll help you,' she declared. 'We're a big party and I imagine we all want one.'

Marigold looked at the two pretty girls, then at the men. What a handsome group, she thought. Then she turned to Nan. 'Whatever happened to that lovely man, Dennis? Did he ever marry?' she asked. 'He was handsome, wasn't he?'

Daisy and Suze froze. They looked at their father in panic. Dennis stared at Marigold. She did not notice the pain she had inflicted.

Nan opened her mouth to say something. Daisy felt an urgent need to pre-empt her, but couldn't find the words. Then Nan patted her daughter's hand and nodded, realizing at last what was required of her. 'He was indeed very handsome,' she said softly. 'He married a lovely girl. A beautiful, kind and unselfish girl. The two of them have been very happy. In fact, I'd say, they've been happier than anyone else I've ever met.'

'How nice,' said Marigold.

And Dennis realized then that the book entitled *Dennis* had finally fallen off the shelf. He wondered what the point was in coming here, week after week, year after year. What was the point of it all? He looked at the pale pink roses on the carpet at his feet and wondered why he bothered. They had long ceased to bring her back to him. He lifted his gaze to her guileless face, to the sweet smile that hovered uncertainly upon it, and something snagged inside his heart.

And then he knew. He knew with a certainty that rose in him like a powerful wave, an indestructible wave of unconditional love, and he understood. It didn't matter that she didn't know who he was, because *he* knew who *she* was. She was his Goldie, his beloved, beautiful, irreplaceable Goldie, and she always would be.

Acknowledgements:

My heart goes out to all those living with dementia and to the friends and family members who love and support them. During my research I met some truly inspiring people, both patients and carers, and was struck by the strength of their devotion. *Here and Now* is the story of Marigold's decline, but above all it is about love, enduring love, the kind of love that survives whatever obstacles are put in its way.

I could not have brought Marigold and Dennis to life without the wisdom and advice of my dear friend Simon Jacobs. It was the time I spent with him that inspired the core message in the book, which is a spiritual one: as the memory fades and the personality retreats, the soul – the true self – is still perfect and whole and eternal. I'm so grateful for our many years of friendship and for the magical things he has taught me.

Dennis is inspired by my friend Jeff Menear, who is an extremely talented carpenter. He's made many wonderful things for me over the years, converting my wild ideas into masterpieces with the skilful craftsmanship of a truly gifted artist. I can't thank him enough for his time and for all the details he gave me about the profession which helped me develop my character. I also want to acknowledge his wife Siobhan and his late mother Jean, because the little, seemingly irrelevant things they chipped into the conversation were pearls.

When I saw Sam Sopwith's beautiful drawings of animals I decided that Daisy had to be an artist like her. Sam's animals are extraordinary. They gaze out of the paper with a depth of emotion one doesn't find in photographs. I wanted my heroine to have that talent and sensitivity. So, thank you, Sam, for being my muse and inspiration. It's only a matter of time before I ask you to draw *my* dog!

I would also like to thank my Argentine friend, Pablo Jendretzki, who is an architect living in New York. Handsome, charismatic, charming and gifted, he was the perfect man to inspire Taran. Thank you, Pablo.

I am grateful to my parents, Charlie and Patty Palmer-Tomkinson, for giving me the most loving, free and stable childhood, and for being my best friends and wise advisors during my adult years. I thank my aunt Naomi Dawson, James and Sarah Palmer-Tomkinson and their four children, Honor, India, Wilf and Sam, because as I get older I understand more fully the value of family. I thank my late sister, Tara, for teaching me about loss and love. I miss her.

I am deeply grateful to my brilliant agent, Sheila Crowley, and my film agent, Luke Speed, and to all those at Curtis Brown who work on my behalf: Alice Lutyens, Katie McGowan, Callum Mollison, Anna Weguelin, Emily Harris and Sabhbh Curran. A huge thank you to my editor Suzanne Baboneau, who works so diligently and sensitively on my manuscripts, my boss Ian Chapman, and their excellent team at Simon & Schuster: Gill Richardson, Polly Osborn, Rich Vlietstra, Dominic Brendon, Sian Wilson, Rebecca Farrell and Sara-Jade Virtue.

I had many a happy hour working in the peace of Fountains

Coffee Shop and the Bel & Dragon in Odiham, listening to Hans Zimmerman's *Pearl Harbour* soundtrack and drinking caffé lattes sprinkled with chocolate. I'm so grateful I'm able to write books because they give me such pleasure. However, it would have remained a hobby had it not been for the booksellers and my readers, I thank you all.

Finally, and most importantly, I thank my husband Sebag and our children Lily and Sasha, for the laughter and the love.

booksandthecity.co.uk
the home of female fiction

| NEWS & EVENTS | BOOKS | FEATURES | COMPETITIONS |

Follow us online to be the first to hear from
your favourite authors

booksandthecity.co.uk

@TeamBATC

Join our mailing list for the latest news, events and
exclusive competitions

Sign up at
booksandthecity.co.uk